THE HASTINGS CONSPIRACY

The Hastings

Conspiracy

ALFRED COPPEL

HOLT, RINEHART and WINSTON   New York

Library of Congress Cataloging in Publication Data

Coppel, Alfred.
    The Hastings conspiracy.

    I. Title.
PZ4.C785 Has   [PS3553.064]   813'.54   80-10366
ISBN: 0-03-056058-6

Designer: A. Christopher Simon

Printed in the United States of America

10 9 8 7 6 5 4 3 2

Once again, for Liz

ONE

The honorable thing, that which makes the real
general, is to have clean hands.

—ARISTIDES TO THEMISTOCLES, PLUTARCH,
The Lives of the Noble Grecians and Romans

The war had been under way for three hours.

In the heavily guarded command center under the rock and ice of Severnaya Zemlya island the atmosphere crackled with tension. The moving symbols on the situation map in the amphitheater below the visitors' gallery indicated early successes. Warsaw Pact armor, led by crack troops of the First Soviet Shock Army, had overrun NATO's forward defense: already they were more than a hundred kilometers inside the German Federal Republic.

The steeply pitched gallery had been designed to accommodate a hundred people: the Minister of Defense; the commanders of the Soviet Army, Navy, and Air Force and their battle staffs; key members of the Politburo, and a heavy protective force from the Committee for State Security. But as the wall clocks came up on the fourth hour of the invasion, the only three occupants of the gallery were Colonel Yevgeny Denisovich Santorin, the War Plans chief; Yuri Pavlovich Koniev of the KGB; and General Piotr Ivanovich Galitzin, Commander of the GRU, the Military Intelligence Directorate of the Soviet General Staff.

The air was icy. The computer required an ambient temperature of ten degrees Celsius and no concessions had been made to human comfort in the hastily constructed shelter. The three men in the gallery and the soldier-technicians on the floor below wore heavy clothing. The hardened chamber smelled of ozone and stale tobacco despite the frigid wind that blew from the air-conditioning ducts.

Koniev, the KGB man, said, "Can we find out what is happening in Moscow?"

"Easily done, Comrade Koniev," Colonel Santorin said, and addressed himself to the computer terminal next to his seat. On a display screen across the narrow cavern, a series of symbols appeared.

"What's that gibberish?" Koniev asked.

"Fortran, Comrade. Computer language. It says that the city has been evacuated except for essential personnel, all of whom are in shelters. The SAM batteries ringing the city are manned and the defensive air patrols are airborne. President Nikitin and his staff are in the hardened command post at Krasnogorsk. Everything is as it should be."

"Washington?"

"On the hot line." Santorin allowed himself the ghost of a smile. "They are encountering technical problems in establishing the link."

Koniev, a thick and ruddy Ukrainian with deep-set, bright blue eyes, studied the map on the electronic table below. It extended from the Baltic to the Persian Gulf, from the Urals to the western approaches to the British Isles. The red arrows marking the rapid advance of the Warsaw Pact armies were penetrating ever deeper into West Germany. One had reached the outskirts of Onasbrück. Elements of the First Shock Army were circling north toward Kiel.

The southern advance, begun thirty minutes after the attack in the north, was even swifter. Pact forces, led by the Second Soviet Guards Army, were racing south toward Abadan at the head of the Persian Gulf. The Guards' airmobile units, helicopter borne, spearheaded an army group composed mainly of Bulgarians and Romanians. It was a fist of doubtful real strength, but fortified by a cestus of the best troops in the Soviet Union. The bulk of the Soviet Army and Air Force was being held in reserve in European Russia and along the Sino-Soviet border to defend the motherland against any treachery by the neo-imperialist Maoists.

Thus far there was no sign of the difficulties Santorin seemed to expect. The plan seemed flawless. Koniev sat back in his cushioned steel chair, stubby hands folded on his stomach, and waited. His hooded gaze left the electronic displays, which did not really interest him, and rested on Santorin, who did. Koniev was very interested in ambitious men.

Yevgeny Santorin was young for his rank and responsibilities. He was the son of a hero of Stalingrad and the grandson of a general of the Civil War. He had graduated from the military academy at Frunze, of course, but he had also graduated from Moscow University and, under an identity contrived by the GRU, had studied for two years in the United States at the California Institute of Technology. He had never soldiered with troops; his brilliance would have been wasted in the field. But he had served as a member of the Military Intelligence units attached to the Soviet embassies in Havana, Hanoi, and Managua, and he had come to his present post directly from an assignment as chief *rezident* of the GRU in the military attaché's office in the London embassy. He was a favorite of General Galitzin's. The GRU had funded the construction of this computer center under the ice of Severnaya Zemlya specifically for Santorin's work. His single task for the last three and a half years had been to develop the strategy for the inevitable Soviet drive to the Rhine. To Koniev, the youthful colonel seemed as cold and single-minded as his computer. But it had to be said that he was good at his job. Galitzin believed in him enough to risk his own position as head of Military Intelligence. That, Koniev told himself, had to count for something.

The third man in the gallery, General Piotr Ivanovich Galitzin, had spent thirty years within the complex structure of the Glavoyne Razvedyvatelnoye Upravleniye, the Intelligence Directorate of the Soviet General Staff. A protégé of Pavel Nikitin's, he had assumed command of the directorate when Nikitin reached the apex of the hierarchy in the Kremlin. Galitzin was still new to his exalted post and he felt a strong need to present his patron with a dazzling and unexpected success.

Nikitin made no secret of his concern for the troubles facing the USSR. The ethnic minorities were poisoned with a swelling nationalism. Though it was not generally known, the Afghans were still giving trouble despite savage repressions. Soviet Muslims seethed with religious anger. The Soviet-backed Tudeh party had not yet been able to quell the uproar in Iran that had begun with the death of the Ayatollah Khomeini. Even inside Russia, dissidents and *refuseniks* continued to agitate for freedoms and rights intolerable to the regime. And the Soviet masses, seduced by visions of consumer goods and the good life they saw in the West, chafed under the necessary discipline of Socialist Leninism.

To solve these problems at a stroke, the motherland needed the industrial base of Western Europe. It was Galitzin's hope that Santorin's strategy could secure it, quickly and with a minimum of risk.

On another display on the far wall, a readout of the now-flowing hot-line traffic between Moscow and Washington was appearing. Santorin, deferring to his guests' ignorance of the language of the computer, ordered the messages to be run through the general translator, and they flashed onto the screen in Russian.

The Americans seemed to be demanding explanations and clarifications. Their intelligence services, long constrained by domestic political considerations, appeared to be incapable of understanding what was taking place in Europe. The Americans had long since concentrated on "national technical means"—on satellites and recce aircraft. But these devices were now being selectively blinded by the new particle-beam armed Voshkods. They could see the inactivity of the Soviet Strategic Rocket Forces, but they could get nothing but electronic garbage from the satellites looking at Western Europe and the Persian Gulf area.

General Galitzin leaned toward Yuri Koniev and said, "The computer indicates that our tactical air strikes have caught the West German and American air superiority fighters on the ground." It was extremely important that Koniev understand the meaning of the swiftly changing readouts. Santorin's lesson had to be hammered home with ultimate force.

"How far can we go before the Americans go nuclear?" Koniev asked. He was not a specialist in military matters. He was, essentially, a policeman. He commanded the greatest espionage organization in the world, but he understood his limitations.

"When we last gamed this problem, Comrade Koniev," Santorin said, "the conflict went nuclear when we crossed the Weser River." He tapped out a coded query on his terminal and studied the miniature screen above the keyboard. "There is nothing definite yet from the Intentions of the Enemy program, Comrade. It is still too early to make a judgment."

Koniev felt a chill run down his backbone. A *civilian* reaction, he thought dryly. The soldiers seemed untroubled—yet. He grunted and looked down at the floor of the amphitheater.

The arrows were moving steadily across the map of the German plain. On the southern front, the pace was even swifter. The misbegotten Islamic Republic of Iran, shattered from within by Marxist radicals and betrayed by the communist Tudeh government, offered little resistance. The only opposition was coming from irregular forces armed with ancient American weapons. The Guards Army, according to the computer, would complete the conquest of Iran in hours.

Colonel Santorin said, "No difficulty is expected in Iran, Comrade Koniev. It is the northern operations that set the level of risk."

"Is something happening now?"

Santorin tapped out another instruction on his terminal and data appeared on another screen across from the gallery. He said, "The Americans are waking up at last. They are beginning an airlift. Moving troops from U.S. bases to England."

General Galitzin read the display and his lips drew into a thin line. England again, he thought bitterly. There was no escaping the problem. He said, "Are you making the change here, Yevgeny Denisovich?"

Santorin shook his head. "With respect, General. I think Comrade Koniev should see for himself."

Koniev looked from one to the other, not understanding the exchange. What Koniev did not understand made him suspicious.

"Now," Santorin said, watching the swiftly changing displays closely.

"What?" Koniev snapped. "What do you mean 'now'?"

"We have the ultimatum from NATO command," Santorin said. " 'All Soviet and associated forces to stop in place and prepare to withdraw.' "

Koniev watched, frowning. The readouts were flashing across the screens so swiftly that they were difficult for the untrained eye to follow.

Galitzin indicated a screen near the end of the concrete room. "There is an offer of negotiation from the British Prime Minister." He glanced at Santorin. "That was expected?"

"Yes, Comrade General. He is the most pro-Soviet Prime Minister since the Great Patriotic War."

"But he is demanding our withdrawal?" Koniev asked.

"It is to be expected, Comrade Koniev," the colonel said.

A new message appeared and Galitzin nodded with satisfaction. "The offer is rejected. Comrade Nikitin accuses the NATO forces of acts of aggression and demands a meeting of the United Nations Security Council." The general glanced approvingly at Colonel Santorin. "That was a good touch, Yevgeny Denisovich."

Santorin spoke quietly. "Simultaneously, our Strategic Forces are being ordered to a first-stage alert and the missile submarines in port are being ordered to sea."

"I thought that was not supposed to happen," Koniev said anxiously.

Santorin ignored the protest and translated still another line of symbols. "The Americans have done the same." He pressed a key and all the screens momentarily went dark. General Galitzin seemed to take this as a cue. He turned to the KGB man and said, "Well, Yuri Pavlovich? What should we do?"

Koniev exploded, "Do? How should I know? These things are not my business!"

Colonel Santorin said smoothly, "Of course, Comrade Koniev. The question was rhetorical." He lifted his finger from the key and the screens came to life once more. He spoke calmly, "The Comrade President has told the Americans that we will stop at the Rhine—that it is impossible to bring matters to a halt sooner." On the table below, the red arrows continued their inexorable advance. "The Americans, of course, are objecting."

Along the upper level of displays, a series of yellow lights began to flash. Koniev did not need to be told that they were signaling: *Danger of Nuclear Attack*.

A large display across from the gallery printed a map of the Soviet Union. On it, more yellow lights appeared.

"Interesting," Santorin said. "The computer indicates that this base has been targeted for the first time. Some of their satellites are functioning remarkably well. We should have programmed a more extensive particle-beam attack."

Koniev had a vision of the island above them: the rock and ice washed by the blue-black water of the Kara Sea on the south, the Arctic Ocean on the north. It was early summer and the broken floes were grinding against the dark basalt shore in the tides. He imagined the flash, brighter than sunlight, and the rock and ice vaporizing, rushing skyward to form that hateful mushroom cloud. . . . He closed his eyes. Santorin found that "interesting," did he? What sort of beings were these new people with their cold blood and their computers and their terrible technology?

General Galitzin spoke. "A second warning from the Americans. They have abandoned the hot line now and are broadcasting in the clear. A personal message from President Demarest to President Nikitin." He shook his head. "It is going like all the rest, Yevgeny Denisovich."

Santorin said, "We must play it through to the end and be certain, Comrade General." He read a message from his terminal's screen. "Here it comes. The IRBM force in Britain is on full alert."

"Would it be possible to hold where we are now?" Koniev asked.

"A second offer to negotiate is coming from Prime Minister Evans," Galitzin said. "We are informed that the demand for withdrawal is not negotiable. British strategic forces are now being readied."

The three men watched the computer-generated displays in silence for a tense moment. Then Santorin said, "Here it comes now. The sequence is the same as before, Comrade General. The Americans are announcing that they will withhold their strategic forces if our SS-18s stand down."

"Can we do that?" Koniev demanded.

"Of course," Santorin said. "But it will not change anything.

The British-based forces are not considered strategic weapons by the Americans. They regard them as Theater-based weapons. You'll remember NATO grew stubborn about Theater weapons when there was that trouble about SALT II."

A harsh klaxon sounded in the center. Santorin shrugged and said to Galitzin, "They have launched."

Galitzin shook his head and muttered a curse under his breath. "Well, we expected it," he said.

Koniev felt ill. He covered his dismay by lighting a cigarette, taking a long time about it.

"I will ask for targets and casualty predictions," Santorin said.

Koniev said to Galitzin, "Can we not reply with our own battlefield nuclear arms?"

"Of course, but if we did it would destroy the very things we are seeking to gain."

Santorin said, "Here we are now." He read the new symbols on his terminal display screen. "The warheads are two kilotons. They have sent only six of them. Targets are the support areas for the northern group of armies: Magdeburg, Halle, and Karl-Marx-Stadt in the Democratic Republic. Bialystok in Poland. And Vitebsk and Smolensk in the Soviet Union." He smiled grimly. "Apparently we are not a Priority One target here. But it is, nevertheless, an interesting selection of targets. They have been chosen as much for psychological effect as for military value I should say. The northern army group is composed mainly of Germans and Poles."

Koniev listened, only half believing the coolness with which Santorin regarded this disaster.

"Casualties are projected at under two million," Santorin said. "The warheads are not going to impact directly on population centers. The imperialists cling to their sentimentality even under these conditions."

Galitzin read another display and translated for Koniev. "Another ultimatum, but directed at the troops of the northern armies. They are warned that parts of their homelands are being destroyed because of 'Soviet adventurism.' " He looked across at Santorin and asked, "Have you run a projection on the probability of mutiny among the Pact troops?"

Santorin consulted his terminal and replied, "Forty-seven percent among the Poles. Thirty-one percent among the Germans. The probability rises to almost eighty percent for the Romanians and Bulgarians in the southern attack. Of course, the revanchist factor works in our favor in the north. The Bulgars and Romanians will want to abort their operations before their own homelands are attacked."

Koniev said, "But what about Soviet casualties?"

"In the Guards Army, light, of course. No more than a few hundred. In the Shock Army, the total is considerably higher because they are facing the power—such as it is—of NATO's Group North. The estimate is not exact, say four thousand killed, missing, and wounded. But in Vitebsk and Smolensk, much higher. It would be impossible at this moment to distinguish between military and civilian casualties. I think we would be safe in assuming 275,000 killed, 30,000 missing, and 400,000 wounded or suffering some degree of radiation poisoning."

"My God," Koniev said, shaken.

"The computer says that there is only a fifty-percent chance of reaching the Rhine without having this exchange escalate into a general nuclear war," Santorin said. "In which case we must then consider casualties in the high millions and the effective destruction of our industrial base. Of course, we could do much the same thing to the Americans, but as a practical matter this option is not a solution to the problem given me by Comrade General Galitzin. We are not here, after all, to turn the ruins of the planet over to the blacks and yellows of the Third World."

"Then what?" Koniev asked helplessly.

Santorin pressed a key on his terminal and a bell clanged in the frigid, echoing shelter. "Stop the simulation," he ordered his technicians. "Back the tapes to H-hour and stand by." He faced Koniev and said, "We have had these results or something very similar each time we have run a simulation. With the present deployment of NATO forces, there is no acceptable computer model."

Koniev said angrily to General Galitzin, "Is this why you have brought me to this forsaken place? To tell me a strike to the west is impossible?"

"It is, Comrade Koniev," Santorin said quietly, "as long as England is committed to the North Atlantic Treaty Organization. The United Kingdom is the staging base for all American reinforcements. It is the primary air and supply base for NATO forces. And the American nuclear forces based there can be used without compromising the main U.S. deterrent. We have tried to get these weapons removed as part of SALT, but President Demarest has refused to bargain for them in good faith. When Hugh Evans became Prime Minister of England, we hoped he would put pressure on Demarest. He has, but not enough. So you see, Comrade Koniev, that England is the key." He laid a caressing hand on the computer terminal. "I have another simulation for you to watch. In this one, Britain is not part of NATO. The Americans are denied the use of the British Isles for their warmaking. And what remains of NATO must face us with the bulk of American power three thousand miles away, instead of across the English Channel. You will see very different results, I promise you."

Koniev felt a surge of exasperation. The man had spent too much time playing with his electric toys. He was dealing in fantasy.

"I see you are skeptical, Comrade Koniev," Santorin said. His expression betrayed just a suggestion of contempt for the policeman's inflexibility of mind. "Don't be. It can be accomplished." He glanced at Galitzin questioningly. "May we now discuss Hastings, Comrade General?"

"Run the simulation first, Yevgeny Denisovich," Galitzin said.

Koniev felt he was being patronized and he did not appreciate it. "Never mind another shadow play. Get to the point. What is Hastings?"

"Hastings," Galitzin said, "is an American contingency plan. We have only just acquired it. I will brief you on the details after you have seen how it can serve us. The simulation will show you that the ends justify the means we shall have to employ."

"Is the Comrade President familiar with this . . . Hastings thing?" Koniev did not relish playing the fool, discussing with Nikitin some scheme that had been originated outside the KGB.

"No," General Galitzin said. "I think it best not to trouble him with it. He might be squeamish about another operation that requires the murder of a first minister of state."

Koniev had not become the chief policeman and spy of the Soviet Union by being easily shocked, but he was shocked now. There were killings and killings—sometimes they were necessary. Department V of the KGB's First Chief Directorate—the so-called Mokrie Dela—existed to perform these unpleasant chores. Nor were chiefs of state or first ministers immune. The shades of Moise Tshombe, Dag Hammarskjöld, John Kennedy, and a string of Afghan puppets could attest to that. But high-level assassinations were always extremely risky, particularly for the man who headed the organization which carried them out.

"The Prime Minister? Hugh Evans?"

Galitzin nodded.

Koniev said carefully, "Evans has always been a friend of the Soviet Union."

"A Socialist," Galitzin said. "Socialists dilute the appeal of Leninism. But that's of no consequence. Our need is paramount."

"Can we get to the simulation now, Comrade General?" Santorin asked impatiently.

"Wait," Koniev said harshly. To Galitzin he said, "It would be extremely difficult for the Mokrie Dela to perform such a killing cleanly, with no chance of it being traced to us. The investigation would not be performed by some presidential commission of amateurs or ignorant congressmen. The English have come down in the world, but in such matters they are professionals."

"I am glad to see that you do not reject the concept, Yuri Pavlovich," Galitzin said. "And I agree with what you say. But with a minimum of help from you, GRU can arrange the action. And with Hastings disclosed at the proper moment, the British will look west—not east."

Koniev was torn between bridling at the notion that Military Intelligence could do what KGB could not and relief at the lessening of a personal, direct involvement with something that could be very dangerous. He wondered if Galitzin had weighed the personal risks involved. Perhaps not. Piotr Ivanovich could be rash on occasion. And he had a tendency to buckle when the pressure came on. Still—Koniev performed a mental shrug—sometimes the GRU man's ideas, though they might seem outlandish, were sound. He asked, "Who can be found to do what must be done and not turn on us in a crisis?"

"That is the simplest part of the program, believe me, Yuri Pavlovich," Galitzin said earnestly.

Koniev considered. All of this sounded very hazardous, but if there was a plan, any plan, that could advance the Soviet timetable for the eventual occupation of the Western European industrial lands, a man would be a fool not to consider it. And if Galitzin and his computer-brained colonel had actually pieced together something remarkable, it might well be worth co-opting. If one could earn Pavel Nikitin's gratitude while letting another take most of the risk—why not?

"I'm listening, Piotr Ivanovich," the KGB man said.

"Hugh Evans has a son who will be happy to kill him," Galitzin said.

Koniev remained silent, his cold blue eyes steady on Galitzin.

"Now, Comrades," Colonel Santorin said. "May we get to the simulation?"

Galitzin looked questioningly at Koniev.

"Run it," Koniev said.

Santorin signaled his technicians on the floor below. The clocks, backed to H-hour, began to run again.

Beneath the frozen carapace of Severnaya Zemlya, the opening moves of the war for Western Europe began again.

2

Robert Brede, a slender, dark man in his forties, waited in the outer room of the National Security Adviser's suite of offices in the White House Executive wing. It was not yet eight in the morning of a humid summer day, but the traffic in and out of General Dracott's situation room was heavy. Among the early morning callers Brede had recognized Dwight Lamb, the Director of Operations of the CIA, and Chalmers Dodd, the Secretary of Defense. The two men had left together, preoccupied and in deep conversation.

Brede waited restlessly. For the last six months he had sat behind a desk in the Defense Intelligence Agency, doing a job of technical intelligence evaluation that was almost mind-destroying in its dullness. He had been delighted to be summoned to General Dracott's office. Any change at all, he thought, would be an improvement.

Katya Roth, ordinarily Paul Bruckner's personal secretary, had taken the early morning duty. She looked up and said, "Dr. Bruckner and the general will see you in a few minutes, Colonel."

Bruckner, an abrasive and unpopular man in Washington, was Dracott's deputy and assistant. The capital did not warm easily to brilliant men who were rude and outspoken, both of which Dr. Paul Bruckner made a fetish of being. But General Henry Dracott valued him for his mind, not his manners. And there was no man in Washington more loyal to the National Security Adviser than Paul Bruckner.

It was rumored in Washington that Paul Bruckner never slept. Brede could believe it. Bruckner had telephoned at five thirty in the morning to order Brede to attend on the general at seven—in civilian clothes. It was policy (Bruckner's policy, Brede guessed) for the general's military visitors to avoid wearing uniform to the White House. Henry Channing Dracott was the first retired general ever to hold the post of National Security Adviser to a President of the United States. It was an assignment that traditionally went to academics. Therefore, Bruckner, who knew only too well the criticism the appointment had aroused in Ivy League faculty senates, had let it be known that it would not do to give the impression that the office of the President's principal adviser on national security had become simply a White House annex of the Pentagon.

The administration of John Scott Demarest was a nervous coalition of doves, hawks, activists, and western conservatives. It existed as an administration only because it was held together by the force of the President's political magnetism. After too many years of blandness in the White House, John Demarest was beginning to revive some semblance of what had once been petulantly called "the imperial presidency." But no one knew better than Demarest himself that a truly imperial presidency was an impossibility. The adversary press and media and the hundreds of special-interest groups that dominated the capital would never allow any real challenge to their power over the nation's government. Between those forces and the sometimes intelligent but most often restless and puerile behavior of the Congress, John Demarest, the first westerner elected to the presidency since Richard Nixon, maintained an uneasy balance. He was an able man hard-pressed to serve what he took to be the best interests of a people swept this way and that by conflicting claims and ideologies.

His appointment of Henry Dracott had aroused a furious clamor from the left and some mutterings of dissatisfaction from the right. In the end, the President had his way, though he was forced to pay for it with the appointment of Orrin Blaine, an Ivy League college president who saw himself as a reincarnation of Woodrow Wilson, as Secretary of State, and another equally complaisant liberal, Elias Traynor, as SALT negotiator.

Traynor was endeavoring to breathe life into the corpse of SALT by falling back into the habit of making unilateral concessions. General Dracott had blocked the most egregious giveaways, but in so doing he earned the enmity of the Department of State and the always hopeful liberals in the Congress who wanted desperately to believe in the Soviets' peaceful intentions.

The wall clock moved to five minutes to eight and Katya Roth said, "It shouldn't be much longer, Colonel."

Brede nodded his acknowledgment. He was a naturally impatient man and it plagued him to wait, but he would have willingly waited far longer than this for a chance to escape his desk in the Pentagon. Brede had served on General Dracott's staff at NATO headquarters, the general's last military assignment before retirement from the Army.

Dracott had an easy manner with his juniors and Brede was sure that there was not one of his former officers who would not jump at a chance to work for him again. He did not know why he had been summoned to the White House, but he waited with some anticipation.

The communicator on Katya Roth's desk pinged and Brede heard Paul Bruckner's rasping voice. "Send Colonel Brede in now."

Brede entered Dracott's office and looked about. It was the first time he had been in this room, and he found himself in a warm and informal place that was yet not a sanctuary. The wall was lined with television receivers, silent now. Behind the general's desk was a stand of flags, one of which bore the four stars of his military rank.

General Dracott himself looked fit, but older than the last time Brede had seen him close-to. The short gray hair was neatly combed, as always, and he wore his well-tailored, conservative suit the way one would expect a general to do. The clear gray eyes were nested in fine lines and seemed tired. Brede wondered how long he had been at this desk, with the day just beginning for most of the people in Washington.

"I'm happy to see you again, Robert," Dracott said, "Congratulations on your promotion."

It was like him to be aware that Brede had recently been promoted to lieutenant colonel, even though the event had taken place far across the river in the deep warrens of the Pentagon.

"Thank you, sir. It's good to see you looking well."

"Sit, Robert." The general indicated a chair facing the large, uncluttered desk. "You know Paul Bruckner?"

"Yes, sir. We've met."

Bruckner gave him a froggy smile. His face was broad and his shoulders sloped to a thick body. Short arms and legs and protuberant eyes reinforced the amphibian appearance.

"I'm sorry we kept you waiting," the general said. "Paul and I have been arguing about something and it's taken time." He leaned back in his chair. "Paul has won the argument, so I'm going to let him brief you. But first, let me ask: how would you like to get out of the Pentagon for a while?"

"Very much," Brede said fervently.

"Tired of computer printouts, Colonel?" Bruckner asked.

"Something like that, Dr. Bruckner," Brede said.

Bruckner glanced at a file, which Brede surmised was his own. "You served as liaison to the Brits' Military Intelligence people in Brussels, Colonel."

Brede glanced at General Dracott. The general knew exactly what he had done on the NATO staff. He had done it directly for the NATO commander. Dracott nodded imperceptibly and Brede said, "Yes, doctor."

"Paul. I don't care for that 'doctor' bullshit." The bulging eyes regarded Brede unblinkingly. Brede was aware of Bruckner's continuing feud with the members of his own academic caste who found their way into government service. He was known to hate Brahmins, which made his devotion to Dracott remarkable. Henry Channing Dracott was the fourth generation of a family of military Brahmins. Bruckner, on the other hand, had come to the United States as a refugee child from Nazi Germany and had made his way through the academic maze solely by reason of his abrasive brilliance. Like so many immigrants, Bruckner was an extravagant patriot, convinced that the United States was the hope of the world—and not at all unwilling to say so. To anyone. The times did not favor flag-wavers, and Bruckner's academic colleagues tended to regard him as a troublesome hawk.

"Paul," Brede said politely. Even though Bruckner shared many of the same, out-of-time notions that Brede lived by, he was still a hard man to like.

Bruckner stared at the pale paneling of the room and the map cases, some open, some closed, that lined two walls. Abruptly, he said, "There's no way to tiptoe into this, Colonel. Let me ask you straight out. What do you know about a contingency war plan code-named Hastings?"

"Not a thing," Brede said. "Should I?"

"Think carefully," Bruckner said. "It's important."

"Nothing," Brede said. "But contingency planning isn't what I do across the river. I've been six months measuring calibers and the tread-width of Soviet-bloc tanks."

The general spoke quietly. "I had a personal call from Colin Farr, Robert. Have you heard from him recently?"

"Not for a couple of months, General. I saw him seven—no, eight—months ago when I was in England on the way here," Brede said with some curiosity.

Colin Farr had been his opposite number on the NATO command staff, a captain in the Welsh Fusiliers. They had been close friends, but, like most military friends, they saw one another only infrequently after Colin was posted back to London.

"You were intelligence officers together," Paul Bruckner said. "You know him well."

"We are good friends, yes," Brede said.

"It was remarkable to get a direct call from a former officer of mine like that," the general said. "Colin would never have done it unless he thought it absolutely necessary. Would you agree, Robert?"

"Yes, of course. Colin is a very proper type."

"Do you know what happened to him when he was posted back to the U.K.?" Dracott asked.

"No, not really. He didn't say much when I saw him last."

"He has been seconded to Defense Intelligence Five."

"Then he would not have said anything to me," Brede said. "Colin is discreet."

"Precisely so," Dracott said. "Yet he telephoned me three days ago—on his own—and asked about Hastings. When I said I knew nothing about it, he asked me if I couldn't arrange to send you to London. He's found something he wants us to know. Something that can't be discussed over an open telephone line or go through regular British-American channels."

Bruckner said, "We've had a computer search run done on the code name. There is nothing, Colonel. 'Code name reserved.' That's all we get from the Pentagon."

"What about the Agency?" Brede asked.

"Even less. Lamb was just in here with the code-name index.

There is nothing there at all. Zip." Bruckner handed over a sheaf of computer printouts. "What do you make of that?"

Brede glanced at the papers, frowning. It was peculiar that the Pentagon should carry Hastings as a reserved designation. It was stranger still that the Central Intelligence Agency computer should never have heard the name at all.

"Frankly, Colonel," Paul Bruckner said, "it stinks."

Dracott murmured, "Paul tends to be suspicious. But it is odd that a name carried as 'reserved' in the Pentagon data banks shouldn't even appear in the Agency's records."

"Carradine is a chicken-shit politician," Bruckner said. "The President took a hell of a chance when he appointed a trimmer like that as Director of CIA."

General Dracott ignored his deputy's harsh comment about the Director of Central Intelligence. He said, "The Agency lost a man recently. I'm sure you are aware of that."

Brede nodded. Earlier in the summer a low-level clerk at CIA had vanished—a supposed defector, or at worst, a longtime deep-cover agent gone home. The media had made a small circus out of it for a day or two and then dropped it. Despite the fact that it was a CIA blunder, it was a small one, nothing to drive the press into one of their famous feeding frenzies.

"Donald—no, Daniels. William Daniels," he said.

The general nodded. "Correct. Well, he turned up in England. Colin and some others were on to him."

"Did we get anything from them on him?" Brede asked.

Bruckner said, "Hell, no. Under the reign of good king Hugh Evans and his bolshie friends we don't get much cooperation anymore. Besides, the man asked for political asylum."

"Did they actually grant it?" Brede asked.

"They probably would have. But the elusive Mr. Daniels made a call or two in London and then slipped into the Polish embassy. He's living it up in Warsaw or Leningrad by now," Bruckner said. "He wasn't exactly the junior clerk our friends over at the Agency have been claiming, either. Lamb tells us he was a senior staffer in the contingency planning section. Lamb is furious, or so he claims to be, at being kept in the dark about Daniels's assignments."

"There is a possibility," the general said, "that the data banks have been purged. Whoever was responsible knew how to clear the Agency computer, but wasn't quite familiar with the Pentagon program, so the name was left in the computer bank, flagged for reassignment. The obvious choice of suspects is the missing Mr. Daniels."

"That is the charitable view," Bruckner said. "The general tends to give the benefit of any doubts. I don't. I put it to you that Hastings, whatever the hell it is, or was, was still alive and well in the Agency data bank after Daniels pulled a copy and departed. Then someone over at McLean decided it might be wise to check up on what Daniels had been doing with his time. When they found out, they purged the data banks to protect the political career of Davis Carradine, who has hopes of becoming a member of the United States Senate by this time next year."

"That is a serious accusation, Robert," General Dracott said. "But Paul's scenario has to be considered. I want you to go to London tonight. Colin will be waiting for you at Heathrow."

"I'll be on the one o'clock flight, General," Brede said.

"If you take the Concorde both ways you can talk to Farr and be back here by noon tomorrow. I don't want to go to the President with this until we know what Colin has turned up."

"What about the Agency?" Brede asked.

"Stay far away from them. From the Brits, too, if you can," Bruckner said, sprawling unhappily in his rumpled suit. "What you are, Colonel, is a plumber. You know nobody loves a plumber."

When Brede had gone, Bruckner asked the general, "What do you think?"

"He was good in Brussels," Dracott said. "He's had some rough times since then. His wife was killed in an air crash. It hit him hard." He regarded Bruckner thoughtfully. "Jessica, her name was. Lovely girl. With her, he might have gone all the way. She was Army, just like he is." He shrugged. "Without her—who can tell."

Bruckner grunted noncommittally.

"You aren't much of a sentimentalist, are you, Paul," the General said dryly.

You don't really know me, General, Bruckner thought. But he said, "If I were, I wouldn't be much use to you in this town." He gathered his papers and, without further comment, left the room.

3

Between Encarnación in Paraguay and Posadas in Argentina the Paraná River runs full and deep. The currents streak the muddy water as they carry the rotting debris of the deep forest toward the deeper sink of the Mato Grosso four hundred kilometers to the north.

The man calling himself Eisen sat on the porch of the dingy house overlooking the river. His thin, bearded face was protected from the sun by a dirty, wide-brimmed hat. He was sweating heavily in the wet heat, his khaki jacket stained at neck and armpits.

The visitor looked uncomfortable in his new linen suit, and the glass of caña, what the *campesinos* drank here, stood milky, warm, and untouched on the bamboo table. Inside the house the visitor could hear the native woman moving about behind the lowered blinds. He hoped she was not preparing a meal. He had not been able to eat anything except crackers and some bottled water since arriving on the flight yesterday from Buenos Aires. He hoped he would not have to try again before returning. This very afternoon, preferably.

The recruiter studied Eisen with interest. Small, dark, and wiry, he was well made to be a killer. Compact. His eyes seemed to have lost all color. They gave him a slightly mad look. Perhaps he was mad. The visitor knew a great deal about Eisen. He knew about Vietnam, about Angola and Rhodesia and South Africa. Under many names, Eisen had left a bloody trail across the world.

For two sweltering hours Eisen had listened to the visitor's soft, drawling voice. He had recognized the accent of the southeastern United States. He had had southerners in his units many times. It was a region that produced soldiers.

Eisen watched without interest as the police boat sailed sluggishly north. It passed his house twice each day. General Stroessner's government discouraged unregulated crossriver traffic between Encarnación and Posadas.

He regarded his visitor again and thought, *After the first death there is no other.* Eisen agreed with the poet about death.

"I'm sorry. I didn't quite understand." The round American face was puzzled. Eisen realized he must have spoken aloud.

"Dylan Thomas," he said. The man didn't seem to recognize the name. Unlettered clod, Eisen thought. He said, "What about equipment?"

"Whatever you require. We can get you anything within reason."

"Transport? Money?"

The man tapped his breast pocket. "Here. Tickets to Buenos Aires, then London."

Eisen squinted against the sun's watery glare. The police boat had vanished round the bend of the river.

"Money," he said again.

"As agreed, sir. One million dollars. U.S."

"To be deposited in Switzerland before the action," Eisen said.

The visitor hesitated. Then with a grotesque politeness said, "You do understand that there is a time limit."

Eisen said impatiently, "Yes, I understand that." His fevered eyes glittered. "The last Thursday in July. Will that suit you?" He could have added that he would kill the old man for joy, for all that was past. Hugh Evans badly needed killing. The surface of the river seemed to shimmer in the heat. Eisen put his fingertips to his eyes and squeezed.

"We have confidence in you. That is why I was sent down here," the visitor said expansively. "The last Thursday will do nicely."

Eisen suppressed an impulse to laugh. The man couldn't be the fool he seemed. But perhaps he was simply out of his element. A bloody clerk.

"All right," Eisen said, suddenly weary. He spread his hands on the rough surface of the table. It felt wet. He said flatly, "There will be no contact after I receive the ordnance."

"We expect that. In fact, we prefer it."

A river bird flew by, inches from the water. Eisen shivered with dislike at its shrill, repetitive cries. It sounded like a child screaming. Once, he had loved the sound of water birds.

The visitor put an envelope on the table. "Air transport tickets. And five thousand dollars for expenses." He stood to go.

Eisen was fascinating, the visitor thought. He had been thoroughly briefed on the mercenary's history and knew all that he needed to know. One could recognize a psychopath without help from the psychiatrists. It was amusing that he had taken the name of Iron. Here, among Germans, he called himself Eisen. Well, Josif Dzhugashvili had christened himself Steel. There were worse names for hard men. Stalin would have been at home here, hiding with the aging killers in the rainforest.

Eisen asked suddenly, "Why do *you* want him dead?"

"Policy is decided on a higher level than mine. Of course I have an opinion."

Eisen wanted him gone now. He turned rude. "I'm not interested in opinions." Who wouldn't want the old man dead? He betrayed everything: the Rhodesians, the South Africans, every-thing. Reason enough for the CIA. He didn't care about that. The CIA had done some betraying in its time. Eisen just wanted to get out of the sun. He picked up the envelope.

"Good," the visitor said. "The money will be deposited. There is a name in the envelope you can contact for ordnance. So I'll say good-bye and good luck, sir."

Eisen watched the broad back as the man walked down the river path to the road where the battered taxi waited. Careless, Eisen thought. To leave so clear a trail of witnesses who could identify him. But they were a clumsy lot, the CIA. He had learned that in Africa.

He went inside and stood in the sudden dimness, breathing deeply in the wet, fetid air. The woman came in and stood dumbly on her broad, splayed feet.

He should look in the envelope, count the money, make certain he had not dreamed it all out there in the white sun. He tossed the envelope on a table and gestured toward the alcove and the unmade bed under the mosquito netting.

The woman regarded him with opaque, expressionless eyes. He supposed she was terrified, but there was no way of knowing. Her broad-hipped, big-breasted body was like a statue carved from black wood. He gestured again and she bent, pulled her dress up and off, folding it carefully as she stood naked on the bare wooden floor.

He took it from her and threw it down, turned her toward the bed. She lay down without a sound. He stood over her. "Say something," he said.

"Cómo?"

How? What? She hardly understood Spanish, let alone English. He stripped off his sodden clothes while she watched out of those eyes that seemed to have no iris. Sweat trickled between her heavy breasts. The purple nipples lay inert. A fly landed on her belly and traveled jerkily down across her sparsely haired pubic mound onto her thigh. She didn't flick it away. She doesn't even feel it, he thought. It made him angry.

He dropped on her, spread her legs roughly. He held her wrists above her head. Her breasts were damp, they tightened as he stretched her arms. He felt himself rise and tried to enter her. He succeeded, but only for a moment. The hot wetness seemed to drain him in an instant and he went limp. He uttered a wordless cry of frustration and rage and reached for the pistol under the thin pallet. He came to his knees and held the pistol in both hands, pointed at her face. "Say something, damn you. Say something or I'll kill you."

The woman lay motionless, staring up at him. He could not even tell if she were feeling fear. She was alien; and even naked and beneath him, she was out of his reach.

He flung himself off the bed and scooped up his trousers and the envelope. He walked naked out onto the porch and pulled on his pants. The visitor's untouched caña was on the table. He picked it up and drank it down, throwing the glass far out into the river. It seemed to vanish without making a splash. Behind the blinds he could hear the woman dressing. She would be gone by nightfall, back to her people who had sold her to the crazy *inglés*.

He sat down and let the hateful sun burn down on his closed eyes. The light shining through his itching lids was like a vision of hell. His hand tightened on the envelope. "I'm coming back," he said aloud. "Do you hear me, damn you? I'm coming back to kill you."

4

The captain of the British Airways Concorde Mark III was on the public address system again. He had been chatting to the cabinload of passengers constantly since leaving Dulles, giving them descriptions of the flight plan, solicitous warnings about the acceleration to be expected when the flight crew engaged the "reheat," and lyrical descriptions of the dark sky and curved horizon that could only poorly be seen through the tiny, bottle-bottom windows in the passenger compartment. Now he was once again speaking in his north country accent, to explain (with a touch of smugness that Brede found slightly irritating) that "despite the current industrial action" that was stacking flights over Heathrow, the Concorde would be given priority to land at once. Brede realized that the preferential treatment involved both national pride and the rate at which the slender delta-winged aircraft consumed fuel. Even the militant wildcatters of the British Air Traffic Controllers' union would not care to be responsible for causing a Concorde to fall out of the sky with empty tanks.

In Brede's lap lay a copy of the *Washington Post* showing plastic bags of garbage stacked—neatly, to be sure—in Green Park across from Buckingham Palace. London dustmen were on strike for a thirty-percent wage rise, and members of Prime Minister Evans's party were saying in Parliament that a further cut in the military budget—and therefore in Britain's NATO forces—should instantly be made so that the dustmen could be paid. Despite his liking and admiration for the British, Brede found it a bit absurd to learn that the government of Hugh Evans considered the demands of London dustmen of equal importance with the maintenance of the Rhine Army. But then, he told himself, he was a professional soldier and probably not the person to make such judgments.

"There is ample transport to London available," the north country voice declared. "The labor action has not spread to the baggage handlers, and no Concorde passengers will be inconvenienced. We are now beginning our descent to enter the London approach corridor. Welcome to Britain."

Brede was looking forward to seeing Colin Farr once more. In

Brussels they had worked closely together and had become good friends. He was not surprised that Colin had been seconded to DI5. Counterintelligence work had always brought out the detective in Colin. He knew more than most serving officers about GRU and its efforts to penetrate NATO security. If Colin had breached his own security procedures to speak directly with General Dracott, he must be deeply agitated about something. His action could easily be interpreted as an offense, particularly now, when the climate of British-American relations had turned so chilly.

The Concorde, sloughing off speed, assumed its characteristically nose-high subsonic attitude and configuration. Through the open door of the flight deck Brede could see that the snoot had been lowered for better visibility. The air ahead and below was now hazy, but cloudless. London was in the grip of what the English liked to call a heat wave. The temperature in the summer twilight still stood in the mid-seventies.

The Concorde had destroyed the afternoon with its speed. It had been just after one Washington time when the aircraft had lifted off the Dulles runway. Faster by a bit than the Mark I airplanes that had inaugurated the Dulles-Heathrow flights, this Concorde had brought Brede to his destination in three hours. It was now 9:05, British Summer Time. Air Force people might be accustomed to plasticizing time this way, but to Brede, a ground soldier who could fly only lumbering helicopters, the Concorde's performance was still a source of some wonder.

He looked through the tiny window past the stub of the delta wing. Some few lights were coming on below, but the countryside was not dark, only tinged with the blue cast of imminent nightfall. Even the land around London was lovely from the air, patterned in shades of green, fields divided one from the other by hedgerows and narrow ribbons of road. To the east he could see the Thames reflecting the still-bright evening sky. London was coming into view out of the haze, with more lights now, and the shapes of

Saint Paul's and the Post Office Tower, so ugly that it was strangely appealing as it loomed over the city.

The aircraft banked gracefully, shivering a bit in the summer turbulence. Brede caught a glimpse of the green of Richmond Park and then the lights of Hounslow. The airport approach lights flashed under the wing and the airplane settled until the wheels squealed on the runway. Ten minutes later, Brede, small case in hand, was walking into the crowded terminal building.

The main bay was filled with passengers delayed by the air controllers' slowdown. People sat on luggage, sprawled on couches and chairs and on the stairs to the mezzanine. The Concorde passengers, separated from the rest by the glass partition of the bay leading to customs, hurried along, tinged with guilt over their special treatment.

Brede took his place in one of the lines leading to passport control and customs. The immigration officer at the desk opened the passport and frowned. "How long will you be in the United Kingdom, sir?" he asked.

"A day or two," Brede said patiently.

The officer glanced at the photograph and then at the information on the facing page. "You are a serving officer in the United States Army, sir?"

Brede nodded.

"Is your visit to the United Kingdom of an official nature?"

"Personal."

"Business or pleasure, sir?"

The pleasure was swiftly vanishing, but Brede said, "Just pleasure." The officer, he noted, wore service ribbons in the manner that was common among the British whose jobs required the wearing of uniforms. "The Military Medal," he said quietly.

For a moment the man's expression changed, became less fixed. "Yes. I was with your people in Korea," he said. "A long time ago."

The officer handed over Brede's passport. Without conscious

irony, he said, "Enjoy your stay in Britain, Colonel."

Brede walked on to the customs inspection thoughtfully.

He noticed that unlike the last time he had traveled through Heathrow, the customs' officers were examining Americans' luggage thoroughly. The new tariffs imposed by the Evans government were making petty smuggling profitable and the black-uniformed customs people were actually searching for such items as liquor and cigarettes. It caused delays and frayed tempers. Brede looked beyond the gates to the reception bay where people meeting flights waited behind a low fence. He caught sight of Colin's tall, angular figure and lifted a hand in greeting. He wondered why Colin didn't speak to the customs officials and speed up this maddening process for him, but it seemed that Colin preferred to wait. No special treatment for Robert Brede. No attention drawn. It made Brede even more thoughtful than before, this desire for anonymity on Colin's part.

It was another twenty minutes before Brede could open his small case for the customs inspector, a pale girl with freckles across her cheeks and pimples on her chin.

She rummaged in the bag suspiciously and said, "You're traveling very light, sir. How long do you plan to stay in the United Kingdom?"

"Not long," Brede said. Her manner was hostile and Brede wondered if all Americans were receiving this treatment or if there was something about him that she didn't like.

"No cigarettes, liquor, drugs, or reading materials?"

"Reading materials?" That was something new.

"That's correct, sir. Magazines or books."

He had heard of the government's restrictions on consumer magazines that depicted too many household luxuries that were no longer available in the United Kingdom, but he had refused to credit it. Apparently the government of Hugh Evans, unable to get enough production of such items out of British workers, had decided to prevent Americans from flaunting their trinkets to their Socialist cousins. American television shows were no longer being imported into England, either.

"No cigarettes, no liquor or drugs," Brede said. "But you can have this." He dropped the copy of the *Washington Post* on the table.

"I don't make the regulations, sir," the girl said unpleasantly. "I simply enforce them." She closed Brede's case and stamped it with a gummed label bearing the royal arms and the customs rubric.

Brede went through the gate into the concourse. The taxi rank lay beyond, and beyond that the multilevel concrete stack of the carpark. Colin Farr said, "Welcome, Robert. I'm glad you've come."

Brede smiled ruefully and said, "It looks as though you are the only one who is. What's happening here, Colin?"

The long, Anglo-Saxon face grew even longer. "Things are changing in England, Robert. We'll talk in the car, shall we? She's in the carpark just across there."

The greetings Americans were given in England might have changed since his last visit, Brede thought, but Colin Farr had not. He wore a Harris tweed jacket that Brede remembered as ancient even when they served in Belgium, baggy slacks and heavy walking shoes, a shirt of an atrocious blue shade, and his regimental tie Colin had never been a dandy about his civilian clothes, which went with his county background. His family still farmed an estate near the Welsh border. He wondered how they were making it these days with the new spate of laws intended to bring down the last of the old gentry.

"They gave you a time, did they? The rubber-stamp brigade back there?" Colin asked as they climbed the ramp into the second level of the carpark.

"Not really bad," Brede said. "Just not what I expected."

"I've had people tell me the East Germans ask fewer questions now," Colin said grimly. "How are things in Washington?"

Brede said, "You shook up the general, Colin."

"I thought about it for days," Colin said. "I didn't know what was the right thing to do."

"Are you in trouble, then?"

"About calling General Dracott? Not yet. Maybe not at all. We'll just have to see, won't we. It is a breach of security, certainly. I'm prepared to be burned for that."

Farr looked so preoccupied that Brede decided against pursuing the subject until Colin was ready to take it up himself, at a time of his own choosing.

They reached the top of the ramp to the second level and Colin marched along beside Brede, walking with the peculiar and slightly comical gait of the British officer, duck-footed with an exaggerated arm swing. I could see it from a thousand meters, Brede thought, and know it was Colin.

"Your man Daniels is—or was—in England," Colin said abruptly. "Our people identified him when he went to call on one of our more bolshie writers, a chap named Harald Langton." He walked in silence for a moment and then said, "We did a black-bag job on him, Robert. Or more specifically, *I* did. He had a copy of something called Hastings with him." He looked bleakly at Brede. "Does that name ring any bells with you?" His tone was odd, Brede thought, almost accusing.

"No bells, Colin. The first I heard of Hastings was this morning in General Dracott's office."

"Langton's a fool," Colin said. "I don't know if he realizes what he has in his hands. I photographed the lot." His eyes were hard and angry. "I want you to tell me that what I have is phony, Robert. It had better be. I have been stalling my people until you and I talk. I hope you have some answers."

"We'll talk, Colin. That's why the general sent me."

"How is he, Robert? Damn me, I love that old man. I wouldn't have broken security for anyone else in the world. Not even you."

"He's well enough. The President values him, Colin."

"Thank God for that," Colin said with feeling.

They reached the space where Colin's familiar old Peugeot stood and the Englishman exploded in uncharacteristic anger. "Some bloody clot," he said. "Look what the bastard's done."

A large, shiny American sedan had been squeezed into the narrow slot on the Peugeot's off side. The two cars were almost touching, making it impossible to open the passenger door of the Peugeot.

"Bloody rude," Colin said, fumbling for his keys. "Wait, I'll move the old crock so you can get in." He opened the right-hand door and slid behind the wheel while Brede waited by the facing row of parked cars.

There was a white flash.

The Peugeot seemed to bulge from within, the glass erupting outward in a rain of crazed bits. The sun roof flew into the air, followed by a blast of heat and shreds of the car's interior. The entire machine rose off the seared concrete to smash with incredible violence against the ceiling and then down again on splayed wheels. Brede felt a furnace flash of wind and the shock wave sent him sprawling across the roadway, spinning him under the car parked opposite. The cars on either side of the Peugeot half rolled with the force of the explosion, crashing into those parked next to them. The sound had deafened Brede and he lay with his head ringing and his cheek pressed against the oil-stained surface of the garage floor. When he could move his head to look, he saw through streaming eyes that the Peugeot was a roaring mass of gasoline-fed flames. Black smoke mushroomed against the ceiling and poured upward out of the opensided building.

One of Colin's heavy shoes lay wedged under the tire of the car that had protected Brede from the main force of the blast. The lace was still neatly tied.

Brede could hear shouting voices and people running, then the braying sound of an emergency vehicle. Filled with pain and anger and grief, he waited for the airport security police to arrive.

5

At the age of fifty-three, Davis Carradine, Director of Central Intelligence, was near to cashing in on the political IOUs he had collected in twenty-two years of government service. He was a stocky, rather florid man with the echoes of his Blue Ridge Mountain boyhood still in his voice. A lawyer by training, he had never worked for anyone except the federal government: first as a young lawyer in the Justice Department's antitrust division, then in a succession of bureaus ranging from the Environmental Protection Agency to the Department of Health, Education, and Welfare.

Over the years of his service he had taken care to develop a reputation for political loyalty, carefully screening the many requests for favors that were the currency of life in Washington and making certain that the most powerful men in the capital came to know him as reliable and worthy of advancement.

Carradine had accepted the post of CIA Director—the one job in the capital he had never coveted—as a favor to Senator Beauregard Curtis, the Chairman of the Permanent Oversight Committee on Intelligence. The President's original choice, a professional intelligence officer, had been unacceptable to Secretary of State Blaine. Blaine's own candidate, an academic, had been vetoed by General Dracott and the Joint Chiefs of Staff. The impasse had been broken by Senator Curtis's suggestion of Carradine as a suitable compromise. Privately, the Senator had assured Carradine that he need stay in the post only until the party powers were able to convince the President that General Dracott should be replaced—Curtis was never at ease with the austere Dracott—at which time Carradine could resign and be assured of Senator Curtis's support in seeking the junior senatorship from Virginia. The Curtises were a political dynasty in the state and very nearly could guarantee Carradine the Senate seat.

The offer had been impossible to refuse, even though Davis Carradine knew nothing about intelligence work and had no intention of getting bogged down in a learning process. He regarded himself as a caretaker for the CIA, and as a caretaker it was his task to see to it that the Agency behaved itself, did not embarrass the administration, did not anger the party Left, and did not—under any circumstances—engage the hostile interest of the national media. In his first press conference as Director, Carradine had told the representatives of the national press corps. "There will be no more horror stories from this Agency, gentlemen. I'll stake my future on that."

The defection of William Daniels had jolted Carradine. He had immediately ordered an investigation and a tightening of security. But because the fickle media might think that was a case of locking the barn door too late, Carradine had demoted Daniels, *ex post facto*, from a contingency planner to a low-level clerical position, and then ordered the data banks purged of all Daniels's projects. When that had been accomplished without becoming known, Carradine began to breathe more easily.

The press had nibbled at the Daniels story, but a decade of baiting the CIA had dulled investigative appetites. Small misfortunes in the intelligence community no longer attracted reporters with the true killer instinct.

Late this afternoon, however, Carradine had received a call from the Director of Operations that unsettled his peace of mind.

Now Davis Carradine heard the antique clock in the entryway strike eight. Upstairs, his wife Janice was dressing for a formal reception at the State Department for the new Soviet Ambassador, Dmitri Vukasin. They were going to be late because Dwight Lamb had not yet arrived. Still, Carradine did not think it wise to delay talking to Lamb, a man not given to false alarms.

Carradine had spent most of the day at Camp David with the President and Senator Curtis. The conference had been long and not entirely reassuring. Despite Curtis's persuasiveness, the President had not committed himself to endorsing Carradine's Senate candidacy. Beau Curtis, a man who was unaccustomed to having his political choices questioned, had grown increasingly annoyed with Demarest and had, at one moment, indirectly threatened to enter the early primaries next year in opposition to the President— "as a gesture of protest." The conference had broken up with nothing definitely decided and with the President's patience worn thin.

On the drive back from the Catoctins, Carradine had received Lamb's call on his car telephone asking for a meeting at the Carradine house in Georgetown. Whatever he had to say was not to be discussed over a radio link. Carradine found this ominous.

Dwight Lamb, the man who had been the President's original choice for the job of Director of Central Intelligence, was an old-line intelligence professional—one of the few left in senior positions at McLean. Like Carradine, he placed a high value on loyalty. But it was loyalty to the Agency that was the dominant force in Lamb's life. He had served the CIA for twenty-five years and it was only when Carradine's interests coincided with those of the Agency that Carradine felt Lamb could be completely trusted.

Carradine went to the bar built into a Georgian breakfront near the high, fanned windows of his study and poured himself a drink. He stood for a moment looking out into the narrow street. It was still suffocatingly hot in the Potomac basin and Carradine remembered with some envy the pines and cool breezes of Camp David. A man might even end up there, he thought, if he conducted himself with care and wisdom. John Goddamn Scott Demarest certainly had no lease on the place. He visualized himself standing before the great stone fireplace of the presidential cabin, but the memory of Demarest standing there this afternoon overwhelmed his fantasy. John Demarest was not a Carradine backer, that was plain. The President sensed the danger of a flanking attack from

Virginia and Carradine stood in a place where it might be easy to get caught in the crossfire. But only if ammunition came readily to hand. He glanced at his desk clock anxiously. It infuriated him that Lamb was keeping him waiting.

The house intercom on his desk buzzed and he said irritably, "Yes, Janice. What is it?"

His wife's voice, slightly aggrieved at his tone, came back. "It is getting late, Davis. Shouldn't you be dressed by now?"

"I'm waiting for Dwight. He's the one who's late, damn it," he snapped and turned the intercom off. He had married Janice Drury for her looks, her money, and her Washington society connections. But her Jeffersonian view of Washington as a place where American aristocrats governed with *noblesse oblige* in the name of the simple People (she always seemed to capitalize that word) struck her husband as maddeningly puerile. Carradine regarded the people with deep suspicion. His favorite quotation was from Franklin's *Poor Richard's Almanac:* "A Mob's a Monster; Heads enough, but no Brains."

He poured himself another drink and had returned to his desk when the black houseman announced the arrival of Dwight Lamb.

"At last, for Christ's sake, Dwight," Carradine said.

Lamb, a thin, dour man with short gray hair and a pursed, ungenerous mouth, was dressed in wrinkled seersucker and carried a locked steel briefcase. "I'm sorry to have delayed you, Director," he said primly, "but I believe you should see these cables." Carradine, who preferred everyone on his staff to use his given name, believed Lamb used his title to express disapproval.

Lamb unlocked the case and handed Carradine two cables from the London Station. The first reported a terrorist bombing at Heathrow believed to have been the work of Scottish nationalists. Carradine looked inquiringly at Lamb. "Now read the second cable. We received it at seven this evening."

The cable was once again from the London Station Chief and

contained more details on the bombing at Heathrow. A British army officer named Farr had been killed when a booby trap destroyed his car. And an American officer, one Lieutenant Colonel Robert Brede, of Washington, D.C., had been injured. Brede had been treated overnight in the hospital and was now being questioned by Special Branch of New Scotland Yard.

Carradine frowned at Lamb. "What is this?"

"Read on, please."

Carradine did so. WE ARE REASONABLY CERTAIN THAT FARR WAS AN OFFICER OF DI5 AND THAT IN THAT CAPACITY HE WAS INVESTIGATING STARSHINE—"

Carradine felt a sudden chilling apprehension. Starshine was the code name assigned to William Daniels in the course of the inhouse investigation of his defection.

"—AND HIS ACTIVITIES WHILE IN THE UNITED KINGDOM." Carradine said, "When did the London Station learn that DI5 had a line on Starshine? Why weren't we told at once?" He had thought he had heard the last of that damned Starshine business, had been willing to believe he had. And now this.

Lamb said, "London Station is trying to seem wise, Director. They had no idea until this Farr got himself killed."

Carradine returned to his agonized scrutiny of the cable.

The cable continued: "WE FIND THE PRESENCE OF AN AMERICAN DIA OFFICER AT THE SCENE OF THE HEATHROW INCIDENT VERY CURIOUS. SO DOES SPECIAL BRANCH. PLEASE INFORM US IF LIEUTENANT COLONEL BREDE IS IN ENGLAND ON AGENCY BUSINESS AND WHETHER OR NOT WE SHOULD COOPERATE WITH HIM. SIGNED: SIMONINI, STATION CHIEF."

Carradine's legal mind grasped the implications of the cable swiftly. "What the hell is London suggesting? Is he asking us if we sent this Brede on some sort of black-hat mission?"

"Interesting idea, isn't it, Director." Lamb shrugged his narrow shoulders. "London Station was deliberately kept out of the Starshine investigation. That might have been a mistake, since that's where Starshine surfaced."

"But this—this is insulting." Carradine held the cable in a trembling fist. "We are being asked if we sent an assassin to England to kill a British intelligence officer." When Carradine recalled the subject of the Hastings plan, he felt a coldness in his belly.

"Do you want Simonini relieved? Brought back here and disciplined?"

"Lord, no. What I want is the whole Starshine business buried. There is no reason at all to dig it up again."

Dwight Lamb's cold eyes showed his contempt, but he merely said, "It may not be possible, Director."

Janice Carradine, dressed in a summer evening frock that showed her smoothly tanned shoulders and breasts to advantage, appeared at the study door and said, "Good evening, Mr. Lamb." She disliked the Director of Operations and took few pains to hide it. "Davis, you really must dress," she said.

Carradine reined his urge to shout at her and said in a thin, stretched voice, "We're not finished here, Janice. Please leave us and close the door behind you."

Janice Carradine's face, lifted twice and somewhat immobile, managed to show her annoyance. Carradine knew that tomorrow she would discuss his rudeness in complaining tones to Monique Curtis and by cocktail time Beau Curtis would know that Lamb had brought some disquieting news to Carradine. Soon after that he would call the Agency and expect to be told what it was. Senator Curtis took his chairmanship of the Oversight Committee very seriously.

When the door closed behind his wife, Carradine said, "You were saying it might not be possible to keep the Starshine business buried. What exactly do you mean by that? It's done. The press has forgotten it."

"But apparently General Dracott has remembered it, Director,"

Lamb said. "He had me in early this morning with orders to bring the readout of a computer search on Hastings."

"Why wasn't I told?" Carradine demanded.

"You've been at Camp David all day. Should I have called you out of your political conference? I think the President and Senator Curtis would want to know why. Don't you, Director?"

God, Carradine thought, looking at Lamb's pale eyes. The son of a bitch really hates me.

"What happened in your meeting with Dracott?"

"Very little. I gave him a copy of the readouts on the name search. But there is nothing left in the data bank on Hastings. The Pentagon still keeps the name 'reserved,' that's all. Even Bruckner was convinced. The computer memory is clean."

"Yes," Carradine said distractedly. "I appreciate that you did a fine job on that, Dwight."

Lamb studied Carradine for a long, pregnant moment. Presently he said, "Actually, I did something I might end up being ashamed of, Director. But I don't want you, at least, to have any idea that I did a flush job for you because you ordered it and I was a good Nazi. What I did, I did because Hastings was a stupid, silly one-man plan that could never, under any circumstances I am able to conceive, ever be of the slightest use to the security of the United States. It deals with Great Britain as though she were some sort of banana republic and there is no possibility that it could ever be anything but a hot rock for the Company. Starshine planted it precisely so that some talkative 'source' could hand it to some left-wing reporter to use for still another attack on the Company."

The Company, Carradine thought. Only the old-timers still called it that—the dedicated, hard-line spooks who would do anything to keep their beloved Company safe from the press and from the budget-cutters on Capitol Hill.

"I understand why you did it, Dwight," Carradine said. "I appreciate your motives."

"I doubt that, Director," Lamb said. "But I will remind you of them when you are called to testify before the Oversight Committee about a cover-up on Starshine."

"It won't come to that, surely, Dwight?" It musn't be *allowed* to come to that, Carradine thought.

Lamb took a dossier from the briefcase and put it directly into Carradine's hands.

"What's that?"

"It is the life, times, and military career of Lieutenant Colonel Robert Brede, United States Army. The Colonel Brede the Brits are questioning. *The same Colonel Brede I saw this morning waiting in Henry Dracott's outer office.*"

"Jesus," Carradine breathed.

"I agree," Lamb said. "Brede is a paper-shuffler at DIA. But if you look at his 201 File you will see that he was on General Dracott's staff—as Brit liaison—at NATO headquarters."

He fished another sheet from the steel case and handed it to Carradine. "This is a cable from Brussels Station. It is an answer to a query I sent as soon as I read Simonini's second cable from London. You'll see that Brede's oppo on Dracott's staff was Captain Colin George St. Giles Farr."

He stood for a time, watching the color drain from Carradine's face. "I think, Director," he said, "if you are ever to be the junior senator from the Commonwealth of Virginia we are going to have to bury that Hastings memorandum all over again."

TWO

Councillors of state sit plotting and playing their high chess-game whereof the pawns are men.

—THOMAS CARLYLE,
Sartor Resartus

6

By ten in the morning Brede had been at New Scotland Yard for an hour, giving his statement to the Chief Inspector and a police stenographer. Now he found himself in a shabby, cramped office tucked into a corner of the Port of London Authority. The streaked windows overlooked Trinity Square and the Tower of London. Beyond the Tower Brede could see the water of the Upper Pool, where a half-dozen small freighters—two of them flying the Soviet flag—hung on their moorings to wait their turns to unload. Brede remembered the indignation of the British trade unions when the Soviets invaded Afghanistan. That all seemed forgotten now.

Inspector Thurston, the policeman who had escorted Brede here from New Scotland Yard, stood by the office door. He was a large man in ill-fitting clothes; he had a face that seemed cut from stone.

The man across the desk was a different sort. His gray suit fit perfectly—Savile Row tailoring, Brede thought. The Guards tie and the ruddy complexion gave a much grander impression. He seemed out of place in this dingy, temporary room.

"I am Major Hobbs, Colonel Brede," he said. "Alan Hobbs. How are you feeling?"

Brede's hands were bandaged. Somehow they had been burned. There was a bandage on his forehead, as well, where he had been cut by a shard of flying glass. His clothes were still oil-streaked from the floor of the carpark and the medics at the hospital told him the ringing in his ears would persist for a few days.

"Fair, Major," Brede said. "Considering my welcome to Britain."

"Unfortunate," Hobbs said. "Very." He took a silver case from an inside pocket and offered Brede a cigarette, which the latter refused. Hobbs tapped one on the case and lit it with a silver Dunhill. "I've never been quite able to shake the filthy habit," he said. His eyes, pale blue and steady, remained fixed on Brede. "You and Captain Farr were close friends, I believe."

The man was DI5. There could be no doubt about it. He had the style of a British counterintelligence officer: Sandhurst with an overlay of Oxford or Cambridge.

"I'm sure you know that, Major," Brede said.

"Yes. Do forgive me if I belabor the point, though. We are curious to know what business you had with Captain Farr. You did come to London just to see him." He glanced at a sheaf of papers on the desk before him. "The customs inspector says that when she made the customary inquiry about your length of stay in the United Kingdom, you told her that it would be only a short time. At passport control you stated that you would be here 'a day or two.' Am I correct?"

"You are."

Hobbs leaned back and regarded Brede steadily. "Could you then describe the nature of your business with Captain Farr, please?"

"I had a day or two of leave. I wanted to see Colin. Nothing very mysterious."

"I see." Hobbs searched for an ashtray on the desk, found none, and dropped the cigarette to the floor, crushing it with a polished black boot. It was obvious that the act offended a fastidious nature. It was also obvious that this office was a vacant one and that Hobbs was using it because he had not wished to have Brede brought to his proper office elsewhere, probably in the Defence Ministry. "We *are* still allies, aren't we, Colonel?" he said.

"I believe so, Major," Brede replied.

"One hopes," Hobbs said. "But one can never be certain these days." He glanced again through the papers on the desk. "Can we run through the statement you gave to the police just once again? You met Captain Farr at the barrier, is that correct?"

"Yes."

"And he had left his car on the second level of the carpark. Did he tell you how long he had been waiting for you to arrive?"

"No."

"How long would you say it was between the time you met Captain Farr and the time you arrived at the car?"

"Seven or eight minutes. Possibly ten. Not more."

"Are you certain about that?"

"Fairly so. We walked directly from the terminal building to the carpark and then up the ramp to the second level. It couldn't have taken more than ten minutes."

"You didn't stop or delay for any reason?"

"We made no stops. We walked directly from passport control to the carpark."

"The reason I question the time interval you gave us, Colonel, is that the explosive device—about two kilos of gelignite, by the way—was wired to the ignition system. As you may know, quite often these things are attached to a vehicle in a place of the terrorist's choosing and then detonated with a remote radio-controlled trigger—"

"Terrorist, Major?"

"That is what we think at the moment. The IRA is still active and now we have a new lot, the Caledonian People's Liberation Army. They always call themselves an army, don't they, Colonel. Like those blacks who used to be so troublesome to your people a few years back. Three college radicals and a felon who calls himself generalissimo or field marshal or some such thing. It really is tedious." Hobbs frowned his disapproval. "But I was explaining about the explosive device, wasn't I. It was not fired remotely. It went off when the ignition key was turned. A very old system, quite unsophisticated. But effective. Quite. The job of booby-trapping a car in a public garage is risky, but it must have been done that way. But I expect you know all about these things, Colonel."

"Only from the manuals, Major," Brede said dryly.

"Yes. You don't have many generalissimo field marshals about in the States these days, do you."

"Halcyon times," Brede said.

"Quite," Hobbs said. "You are fortunate, Colonel. Well, there is this to consider. Radio-triggering a booby trap allows one more or less to select the casualties. One can set the thing off when just the right people are in the vehicle, or the vehicle is in just the right place. Hot-wiring is another matter. It can be assumed that the bomber doesn't care who is in the vehicle—or, he wants the people he believes will be aboard killed without discrimination." He toyed with his cigarette case, then returned it to his inside pocket. "I trust I am not being obscure."

"You are telling me that the bomb was meant for both Colin and me."

"That seems to be what I am saying." He paused for a moment, not taking his eyes from Brede. "Could you tell me, perhaps, how it was that you were not in the car at the time of the explosion, Colonel?"

"It's in my statement," Brede said.

"Yes. But could you tell me again? We want to be perfectly straight on this point."

"The car next to us was parked too close. It would have been impossible to open the passenger-side door."

"So Captain Farr offered to drive the car out to you, is that it?"

"That is in my statement, too, Major."

"Do forgive me for all this repetition, Colonel. But you see where I am leading? You are extremely fortunate to be alive. It was purest chance that you survived."

Brede tried to ignore the throbbing headache that seemed to beat just behind his eyes. "I've thought of that, Major," he said.

"Under the circumstances, then, are you still so certain you don't want to tell us why you were meeting Captain Farr?"

"You know Colin and I served together in Brussels," Brede said.

"Yes, I was coming to that. On General Dracott's staff when he was in command there."

"Colin and I were good friends. I had some leave. I felt like seeing him."

"Soldiers' reunion. That sort of thing. I see," Hobbs said. "I do wish that were all there was to it, Colonel. But we both know that isn't so."

"I've told you why I came to London, Major. I'm sorry if it doesn't suit."

The ghost of a smile flicked across Hobbs's ruddy features. "Name, rank, and number, Colonel Brede. Surely, we can do better than that between allies?"

"I'm afraid I can't help you, Major Hobbs," Brede said, flexing his aching hands.

Hobbs sighed. "May I make a suggestion, sir?"

"Of course."

"Leave England. Go straightaway. Someone tried to kill you yesterday. Go home, Colonel."

"I'll think about it," Brede said.

Hobbs half smiled again. "Inspector Thurston thinks we should deport you. Put you back on the first flight to the States."

The big man at the door stirred disapprovingly.

"Albert thinks this is a police matter. If you stay, you are going to have company. Everywhere you go."

"Then I should be perfectly safe, shouldn't I," Brede said.

"Safe is a relative term at best, Colonel," Hobbs said.

He referred still again to the papers on the desk. "At the risk of sounding a cad," he said conversationally, "may I tell you that your friend Captain Farr had a lady friend? Have you ever met Miss Adanova?"

Brede said, "No." He felt that he might know the name from somewhere, but he could not recall it with his head still aching.

Hobbs passed a photograph across the desk. It had been taken with a telephoto lens on the concrete steps of the ugly block of flats where Colin had lived across the river near the National The-atre. The woman was slender, almost frail, unfashionably dressed. Her dark hair blew in an unseen wind. Her face was delicately made, with fine straight features and large, slightly almond-shaped eyes. It was an oddly touching face without much gladness in it.

"Larissa Andreiovna Adanova," Hobbs said. "She is called Lara—like the woman in *Zhivago*."

"Jewish?"

Hobbs, nodding, slid another photograph across the desk with a fingertip. "This might help the penny drop," he said. It was a glossy print with a UPI photocredit line stamped on the back. It had been taken in a television studio and it showed a younger Lara Adanova in a group with two swarthy young men and a minor American television personality.

"Remember her now, Colonel?"

Brede did. She had toured the United States five years ago, trying to get someone to do something about her father's imprisonment in Russia. Her father had sent her on a visit to Israel and then asked permission to emigrate. The Soviets had thrown him first into an asylum for a year, and then into the GULAG. They accused him of being a CIA spy, and his daughter an agent provocateur.

Brede remembered seeing her on television. She had seemed pitiable, even then, because John Demarest's predecessor had wanted to renew SALT far more than he had wanted a restoration of rights to Andrei Adanov. Such were the realities of politics, but she had never seemed to realize that. She had pleaded in her accented English with anyone who would give her house room or air time. And then the talk-show hosts and newscasters had lost interest in her and she had dropped out of sight.

"She turned up here in London six months ago, met Colin Fair at some party in Hampstead, moved in with him straightaway," Hobbs said.

Brede studied the Englishman. *You were watching Colin,* he thought. *You were watching him because he was DI5 and sleeping with a Russian woman.*

Suspicion brushed across his mind, a sick kind of surrealistic doubt of reality. *If you were watching him,* he thought, *why did you let him die?*

"Are you all right, Colonel? You look a bit peaky."

Brede said, "Are we through here, Hobbs?"

"I believe so, Colonel."

Brede stood up. He felt unsteady and slightly sick.

"Inspector Thurston will take you to your hotel, Colonel."

"I'll manage, thank you. Inspector Thurston can pay for his own cab," Brede said thinly.

His last view of Hobbs was of the man standing at the window looking, wistfully it seemed, at the ominous bulk of the White Tower in the pale English sunshine.

7

William Daniels sat on the bare pine bench in the empty room and waited. The chamber was windowless, and the light came from a single overhead fixture set into the wooden ceiling. The air was stifling. The summer heat had drawn the pitch from the raw pine and it ran down the grain in frosty globules that had left behind a sugary, crystalline trail.

Though he did not know it, Daniels was fifteen kilometers from the Polish-Soviet border, at the transit camp at Tuczna, one of the outlying islands of the GULAG archipelago.

In London, the Poles had treated him with the courtesy he had expected and with an efficiency that had surprised him. Within hours of his appearance at the Polish embassy he had found himself transferred to a locked cabin aboard an East German freighter. Five days later he had been gratified to see, from the scuttle of his cabin, the low skyline of Rostock. In an exchange conducted in German, a language he did not understand, he had been handed over to two uniformed officers of the Volkspolizei who had hurried him to the military airfield at Bützow where he was loaded (with less courtesy now) aboard a Soviet Tupolev twin-engine transport. His traveling companions were two Soviet captains wearing the field uniform of the Red Army with the shoulder boards of the GRU.

He had arrived at Tuczna in a state of increasing misgiving. The camp covered what appeared to be several square kilometers and consisted of blocks of new pine barracks, each group of three separated from the rest by an ominous double fence of electrified barbed wire.

Since crossing into Socialist Europe, Daniels had not been interrogated or debriefed. He had been given a change of clothes aboard the freighter, but nothing since then. He was bearded, dirty, and swiftly losing the buoyant confidence he had felt when he had walked into the Polish embassy in London.

Each day for five hours he had been held in this same bare room. Each night he had been returned to a barracks block inhabited by a group of dirty, sullen men, none of whom spoke English.

He still could not come to terms with the idea that he was a prisoner. The Soviets had bought him years ago. He had followed orders to the letter. It seemed incredible that he was now to be treated this way. He had begun to lose weight on the diet of tasteless, grainy black bread and thin soup that the inmates of the camp were given twice a day. He had not bathed for almost three weeks. The heat of summer on the flat-pitched roofs of the wooden buildings turned them into sweatboxes, filled with the smell of confined men. Each day a train arrived at the railhead and groups of men were herded aboard under the supervision of Polish police and Soviet officers. The trains departed east. When Daniels, in a mixture of pidgin English and sign language had tried to inquire from a fellow detainee about the destination of the human cargo, he received only phrases he did not understand, accompanied by gestures that were positively threatening. Life had become a nightmare for William Daniels.

Now, again, he waited in the windowless pine room for he knew not what. Sweating, he sat on the bare bench. He heard the sound of boots on the wooden floor of the corridor outside. It was too soon for his tormentors to be collecting him for the return to the barracks block.

The door burst open and a young man in the uniform of a GRU major stepped in. Behind him stood two Polish guards carrying AK-88 machine pistols. Daniels's mouth went dry and he felt his knees begin to tremble uncontrollably.

"Stand up and come with me," the Soviet officer said in English.

The sound of his own language made Daniels burst into a

stream of almost incoherent questioning. The Russian cut him short and gestured toward the open doorway.

They're going to kill me, Daniels thought suddenly, and his bladder leaked, staining his trousers. The Russian looked disgusted. "Out," he said.

Daniels walked between the guards out into the bright sunshine. It made his eyes burn. A Soviet Army staff car stood before the building, a driver and an armed soldier in the front seat.

One of the Poles opened the rear door and the Russian said, "Get in." Daniels complied dumbly. His heart seemed to be crowding up into his throat. He felt sick with fear.

The Russian climbed in after him and the car started. It swept past the guardposts at the gate without stopping, and onto the narrow tarmac road to the east.

The Russian took a pack of cigarettes from his tunic and lit one. The smell of the rich Turkish tobacco filled Daniels with longing. He had not had a smoke since stepping aboard the German freighter at the London docks. The Russian, about to return the pack to his pocket, thought better of it and extended it to Daniels.

"Thank you, Comrade Major," Daniels said. His voice sounded high-pitched and strange to him. He took a cigarette from the package. It was half cardboard and the tobacco was loosely packed in the paper tip. The Russian handed him a box of waxed matches and put the cigarettes back in his tunic pocket.

Daniels smoked. The tobacco was bitter-tasting but it made him feel slightly better.

At the border post, the driver merely sounded his horn and drove through the lifted barriers without stopping. The KGB border police stood at salute as the staff car drove by them. The Russian major acknowledged the courtesy with a gesture.

They rode in silence for the better part of an hour. The sun stood behind them in the west as they drove at a steady speed into the Soviet Union. Presently the officer spoke to the driver in Russian. At the next side road, the car turned south into the seemingly empty countryside. Daniels felt a renewed surge of fear. Perhaps they had brought him into the Soviet Union at last only to take him to a secluded place and shoot him. Images of the slaughter of the Polish officers in the Katyin Forest rose in his mind.

They drove through a forest of thin-trunked pines and emerged once again on the plain. Ahead of them was what appeared to be an immense military post. Low buildings and towers and a fence that seemed to reach to the horizon. As they drew nearer, Daniels could see vast parks with row upon row of T-80 tanks under thick camouflage nettings. Detachments of men in fatigues were working around the buildings. Other parks contained camouflaged mobile rocketry and artillery pieces and what seemed to be thousands of trucks and armored personnel vehicles. He estimated that an entire Soviet Army group occupied this base within a dozen kilometers of the Polish border.

The staff car slowed as it drove deeper into the base, approaching a fenced-off area studded with radar dishes and radio antennae. The car stopped at a guarded gate and armed militiamen wearing KGB uniforms stood in the roadway with their weapons ready while another checked the identification papers the major offered.

Daniels saw still another KGB man telephoning inside the concrete block gatehouse. The soldier replaced the telephone receiver and signaled for the car to proceed.

They drove toward a mound of earth and concrete into which the road descended steeply toward a massive steel door, which opened as they approached. The staff car rolled slowly down a narrow, curving driveway lighted with sodium vapor lamps and covered with armored television cameras until Daniels estimated they were at least fifty meters underground. Here the car stopped at a blastproof door. The major said, "Get out here."

Daniels did as he was told and stood before the door while the major punched what Daniels took to be a code into the small panel in the wall. Two television cameras watched.

The door slid back and the major urged Daniels ahead into a tunnel of stressed concrete studded with retracted blast dampers. The entire installation, Daniels realized, was hardened against nuclear attack.

Twenty meters beyond the outside door, the corridor became a T. The GRU major guided Daniels to the right, into a passageway lined with steel doors. The officer stopped and once again punched a code into an electronic lock. The door opened and William Daniels caught his breath, staring into the room beyond.

He found himself in a large underground television studio, complete with lights, scenery, sets, backdrops, and a battery of video cameras. Uniformed technicians paused in their tasks for only a moment to glance up as the major led Daniels toward a group of men in uniform.

One of them, a bulky man of medium height with light hair and what seemed to be a heat rash on his white cheeks, came forward with a broad, welcoming smile. "Mr. Daniels. It is good to meet you at last. I've been anxious for the opportunity to work with you."

Daniels continued to stare, numb with surprise. The man, who wore the shoulder boards of a lieutenant colonel in the KGB, spoke with the softly drawling cadences of an American southerner. There was something clownish about his easy, outgoing cordiality. Daniels had the impression of a Rotary Club greeter or a red-dirt county politician.

"I'm Alek Kadogan, Mr. Daniels. Colonel Kadogan, actually. Welcome to the Soviet Union."

An Aleksandr Kadogan had served as Consul General of the Soviet Union in San Francisco, then as Ambassador to the United Nations, and finally for years as Ambassador in Washington. He had only recently been replaced by a new man. But Kadogan would have to be in his sixties. This man was no more than thirty.

"I see you recognize the name, Mr. Daniels," Kadogan said in that easy southern drawl. "Y'see, I'm Aleksandr *Aleksandrevich* Kadogan. The Ambassador is my daddy." His smile grew even warmer. "I was born in the United States. Went to Staunton and The Citadel. Loved it there, Mr. Daniels. Really did. Why, if my daddy hadn't had diplomatic status, I'd be an American citizen, isn't that right?"

Daniels nodded mutely. Colonel Kadogan spoke swiftly to the GRU major who saluted with great punctilio and withdrew.

Kadogan indicated the studio with a gesture. "What do you think of all this, Mr. Daniels? Rather grand, ain't it?"

"Yes," Daniels said. "Grand, Colonel."

"Why don't you call me Alek, all right? And I'll call you Bill. Or would you prefer William?"

"Yes," Daniels said stupidly. All his professional life in Washington he had worked with people who looked and sounded just like this. And here was another one, inside a Russian military base and wearing the uniform of a lieutenant colonel in the KGB.

Kadogan put an arm familiarly around Daniels's shoulders and said, "Now, I suppose you're wondering why we brought you down here, aren't you, Bill? Well, let me explain what we're going to do." He called to a young man in a sergeant's uniform and spoke to him briefly. The soldier studied Daniels from several angles and made a number of comments.

"This is Senior Sergeant Bunin, Bill. He's worked with the State Theater, the Bolshoi, all sorts of theatrical things like that. He's doing his military service just doing what he does best, you see. Makeup. He's really very good. We're going to let the sergeant work a bit on you. You *do* look a bit seedy, Bill. No offense. Then we're going to make some video tapes. You're going to do a little speech we've prepared for you about that Hastings memorandum you brought over. . . ."

Daniels, recovering himself slightly, said, "I'm not in any shape to. . . ."

"You'll be fine, Bill. You'll see how well you'll do," Colonel Kadogan said. "You just leave it to us."

The man's cordiality began to reassure Daniels. He prepared to voice some complaints about the way he had been treated.

But Kadogan rambled on, his arm still about Daniels's shoulders. "We'll make these tapes and send them around to the Western press to back up the story our journalist friend Mr. Langton is going to tell, y'see? And then, when the right time comes, we're going to send you back to London, so that you can back up the story in person. How's that strike you?"

Daniels drew a breath and said, "I don't think so, Alek. Not until we get some things settled. I don't think you understand how I've been dealt with—"

"You feel you've been treated poorly, Bill?" Kadogan asked, squeezing Daniels's shoulder.

"Yes, of course. I've been confined and treated like a prisoner."

Kadogan reached into a trouser pocket and took out a packet of Gelusil tablets. He chewed one apologetically. "I've just come back from a place where you wouldn't believe the food, Bill. Now, you say you don't want to make the tapes?"

"I didn't say that exactly, Alek," Daniels said. "The tapes are all right, I suppose. But I really don't think it would be safe for me to go back to England."

"You won't be going until Langton is ready to break the story he's doing on the material you gave him," Kadogan said reasonably.

"Even then. It would be risky for me to go back there," Daniels said positively. It was really time to put this incredible clown in his place and take command of his own destiny.

Colonel Kadogan smiled pleasantly. "Well, now, Bill," he said. "Let me explain the situation to you again so that you can understand it better. First, the sergeant here will do what he can to make you look like an American intelligence officer again. Then you are going to read the script we have prepared for you about Hastings and American troops occupying London and all that. Then when the proper time comes, and it won't be too long, you are going to get on an airplane and fly to Britain, where you will do as you are told." As the litany progressed, the soft accent vanished until Colonel Kadogan was speaking with the clipped precision of a Marine drill instructor. "Or else," he concluded in a voice that seemed to come through breaking ice, "I shall personally put a bullet in the back of your treacherous neck. Is that clear?"

"Colonel—" Daniels's knees were suddenly watery again.

"Is—that—clear?"

Daniels nodded, unable to speak.

The warm smile and the accent returned. "Good, Bill. I'm real pleased we understand each other now." He signaled the sergeant to take Daniels in hand.

As he watched the defector and the soldier disappear in the direction of the makeup studio, he took another Gelusil tablet from his pocket and popped it into his mouth. The people one had to deal with in this work, he thought contemptuously. Psychopaths and pants-wetting traitors. Where would it end?

8

Harald Oliver Cromwell Langton, author, lecturer, and economist, had long been aware that he was not a physically brave man. Even on the playing fields of his minor but well-regarded public school, he had always had a tendency to avoid contact with his boisterous schoolmates, and to break into tears when violence was forced upon him. During his time at Oxford in the early fifties, he had used every legal and medical device to evade his national service obligation—a duty that might have exposed him to the hazards of the war in Korea.

To balance this tendency toward pusillanimity and maintain his self-regard, he compensated by displaying what he sincerely came to believe was the greater, moral and intellectual, courage. In a time of strong anticommunism in Britain, he became a Marxist.

It seemed to him only just that having chosen to swim against the political tide of the 1950s, he found himself lustily floating on the prevailing current of the 1960s. His Marxist mentor at Balliol had once promised him that the Red-baiting fever would pass and that the British worker would come to his senses and reward the steadfast. Harald Langton had not really believed that this would happen and he had resigned himself to a life of hostile readers, abstruse discussions about dialectic materialism, publication in arty little magazines, and vodka in paper cups at sit-on-the-floor parties in Hampstead.

Even when the permissiveness of the flower children's generation brought him into vogue and he found himself regarded as an advanced thinker, he held himself in readiness for the inevitable pendulum swing back into middle-class bourgeois values. To his amazement, when it came it failed to touch him. The conservative years under Margaret Thatcher and the Tories were a wonderful time for Langton. Despite the bitterness of the Left's reaction to Tory rule, Langton enjoyed a visiting lectureship at the London School of Economics, a respectable London publisher, a guest professorship at an American West Coast university, and ready access to the media. And when the political pendulum swung again to Labour, his celebrity increased. He frequently appeared on the BBC and even on American talk shows, indulging the American taste for self-inflicted wounds.

Langton's most recent book, a historio-economic study of American exploitation of Europe entitled *Plastic Imperialism: The End of the American Century,* stood number four on *The New York Times* nonfiction best-seller list, selling well three months after publication. His works sold less well in the United Kingdom, a circumstance that often caused him to comment on the fate of the prophet's honor in his own land.

Among the thinkers of the Labour party Left, Langton had been a strong supporter of old Hugh Evans. The man's personality was abominable, of course, as could be expected in one who had clawed his way into politics and up the ladder from beginnings as a miner in the coalpits of Wales. "Old Hugh," Langton had used to say, "is a Marxist at heart. Wait until he's Prime Minister and you'll see him coming out of the closet."

Though "Old Hugh" had eventually become Prime Minister, he had, to Langton's chagrin, failed to show himself as any sort of Marxist. While swiftly becoming a nemesis to anyone who favored a continuation of the traditional American connection, and, while making overtures of trade and friendship to the Soviet-dominated East, he had given no sign whatever of being anything but what he had always been: a British Socialist with iron ties to the left wing of the trade union movement, a hater of armies and navies (American armies and navies, for choice), and militantly, almost exhibitionistically, working class.

For Harald Langton this was not nearly enough. One could bear with the Prime Minister's lower-class manners and behavior if one could hope that he would eventually lead the nation into the Marxist-Leninist sunlight. But this Old Hugh gave no sign of doing and Langton had lost faith in him. Recently Harald's friends—writers, critics, artists—the people who mattered in London's intellectual life—had been urging him to go into politics, to stand for election to the House of Commons. He would be, they told him, a voice of sanity in that nest of pretended Socialists. He was seriously considering it.

Langton was a large man: six feet and a fraction. But the fat that had plagued him as an adolescent had not hardened as he had hoped into muscle, the thin brown hair that had hung over his eyes had receded, fading into a pale biscuit color streaked with gray. He still wore it long enough to curl fashionably over his collar, but the fierce beard of his college days had been trimmed back to muttonchop sideburns and a moustache that left his chin bare. He regretted the loss of the beard, but his skin had always itched and pimpled under it and he had made the sacrifice in the interests of hygiene.

He knew that he was a far from handsome man, but he could be eloquent, and he had accumulated an encyclopedic knowledge of other men's work in the fields of political science and economics. He wrote in prose that had been widely praised for style, if not for content, and he liked to think that he had remained faithful to his youthful principles even into the years of his maturity. No un-gallant man, he thought, would have done that. A timid one would have recanted, frightened or outraged by the Soviet crush-ing of the Hungarian uprising in the fifties, the suppression of the Czechs in the sixties, and the invasion of Afghanistan in the seven-ties. Instead, Langton had remained steadfast.

He was the son of minor academics, both of whom had taught in red-brick universities. He regretted that he was not of genuinely working-class origins, and for many years had tried hard to live as though he were. But his innate snobbishness and a certain de-bilitating love of comfort always seduced him. In the early seven-ties he had acquired a Swiss wife who bore him no children and died quietly after eight years of marriage. Not being a strongly sexual man, he was secretly relieved to have Greta gone. She had never been an intellectual companion for him, refusing to involve herself in his political interests. But she had left him quite a de-cent legacy which, with a touch of guilt, he accepted and con-verted into a weekend house in Rye, the lease on a flat in Belgravia, and a Mercedes.

It soothed Langton's conscience when he visited the Soviet Union and saw how approved poets and writers lived there, with their ZIL automobiles and their dachas and their Western household appliances. He told himself that there was nothing wrong with a British Marxist living at least as well as they.

His view of privilege in the West was somewhat harsher. That he counted himself among the enemies of the British monarchy was only to be expected; he wrote and spoke scathingly of the Queen, the Royal Family, and the aristocracy. Each time a peer's daughter was reported to have taken up with a rock star or an American, Harald Langton put pen to paper—or rather ribbon to typewriter—to produce a suitably contemptuous piece for the liberal journals. The gentry were an anachronism, he believed, only slightly less preposterous than Britain's dowdy royalty. He lauded each increase in the wealth and capital gains tax, though he sequestered a substantial amount of his foreign earnings in a Swiss bank account "as an escape fund against a Fascist future."

More than any people on earth, he disliked Americans. His enmity toward the people he had once called "the greedy transatlantic Assyrians" was rooted in his Marxism and in a barely remembered childhood memory of having discovered his mother in bed with a Yank airman during the war. In his early days in Hampstead, a young psychiatry student had suggested this to him, elaborating grandly on the Freudian implications of the Oedipus legend. The resident was now a respected and affluent Harley Street analyst and Harald Langton still cut him dead whenever they chanced to meet.

Harald Langton was an introspective man. In fact, no subject in the world so commanded his devoted attention as did the Langton talent, intellect, and social conscience. Over the years he had come to realize that the activist personality must always be completely untroubled by that foolish consistency Emerson (one of the few Americans Langton admired) had said was the hobgoblin of little minds. His own nature had made him receptive to many concepts that men of lesser vision would have considered mutually exclusive. He had no difficulty in regarding the collective state as an instrument of perfect democracy, or the conspiracy as the suitable means of bringing about changes in public policy. He professed a love for the common man, a creature he found repellent in his habits and lacking in intelligence and sensibility. In his writings he described his ideal state as all-powerful yet compassionate, peace-loving yet capable of striking terror in the hearts of its enemies. It was a measure of his skill with words that these contradictions were always made to seem reasonable.

Part of his hatred for America was rooted in his innate dislike of disorder. The Americans, he thought, were ungovernable yet possessed by an inner drive toward fascism. Despite the fact that they had been, for a decade, involved in a self-motivated purging of racism from their society—the only nation in the history of the world ever to undertake so remarkable a process—he noted with contempt that the effort had not been completely successful. Americans still discriminated against minorities. It showed their inability ever to reach the higher levels of true nationhood.

And in a country where the police and the intelligence community labored under the most stringent restraints ever enacted into law, he felt himself watched, endangered, and suspected. He was certain that each time he crossed the borders of the United States (which he did often, being a celebrity and a best-selling author there), the FBI and the CIA surveilled him. (When writing and thinking about Americans he indulged himself in many such neologisms.)

New York made him think of blacks rampaging in blackouts, looting stores and being shot down by FBI men for stealing television sets. Sometimes he dreamed of leading those looters in the streets of that American Gomorrah. Washington brought to mind Salvador Allende, dead in a pool of blood shed by DINA agents armed by the CIA. In his fantasies he stood tall on the barricades, protesting the death of the martyred Marxist. He disregarded the anachronisms and contradictions in these daydreams. What was important was that Harald Oliver Cromwell Langton stood in the vanguard of the Movement that was, at last, seventy-odd years after the Russian triumph, once again on the move across the world.

When the American Daniels appeared with the documents on Hastings, Langton almost missed the opportunity of a lifetime. He would now, after three weeks, like to think that his investigative journalist's instincts had been only momentarily dulled by the dreary familiarity of the American's story. To be sure, the man had presented the correct credentials. But turncoat CIA agents had become commonplace in the last few years. Betraying CIA confidences was a cottage industry among ex-Agency men.

Possibly—just possibly—he told himself, he should have been intrigued by the man's insistence that he hold his information until "something important" happened; that he, Langton, would know the proper moment to break the story. A less disciplined worker than Harald Langton would have succumbed to curiosity. But Langton considered himself made of sterner stuff. Besides, there was little in the American's story that Langton had not heard before from other ex-CIA people promising the exposé of the century. Daniels had recited all the clichés: that he could no longer stomach being a part of an organization that threatened world peace; that his defection was an act of conscience; that he was (like Langton himself) a citizen of the world and an enemy of American imperialism.

Harald Langton had found himself growing weary with the pro-testations that repetition had reduced to banality. He had soothed the man with a drink, a promise to "look into it at once," and then had ushered him firmly from the flat.

But he had not "looked into it at once." Langton's work habits were as rigid as his personality. He took one project at a time, and one only. It was the central tenet, he liked to say, of his "methodology."

For seven weeks he had been mewed up each day at Kew, in the Public Record Office basement where he had access to a terminal linked to the Post Office computer. He had been working on a government-funded study of the effects of coal production on the purchasing power of the pound sterling for the last half-century. It was a labor of stultifying dullness, but it was lucrative. The study had already run to two hundred pages of text, graphs, and tables, all calculated to prove that nationalization of the mines had increased the purchasing power of all British citizens. Since coal production had fallen steadily since nationalization, it required all of Langton's creativity to make the results acceptable. Langton was a skilled programmer and systems analyst and his touch with the computer was delicate. He could make the computer do tricks, and he did.

But the task was demanding and he was deeply committed to it when Daniels arrived in Belgravia. Consequently, he had put the Hastings folder aside for nearly three whole weeks. Now he cursed the rigidity of his working habits. When he had at last begun to study the documents, he had received the shock of his life.

The Hastings papers were not the ordinary run of old reports of sin and wickedness inside the CIA. They were something quite different. As he read, he felt the thrill that comes to an investigative journalist only when he has in his hands the makings of a real bombshell. Now he wished he had Daniels on hand to be probed and prodded for these juicy morsels which make a great story into a sensational one.

But the man was gone and there was nothing to be done about that. He must now make do with what he had in his possession. And what he had was a very great deal, indeed.

Langton had often dreamed that one day he might come upon material like the Pentagon Papers, or an informant such as Deep Throat, who had made Woodward and Bernstein rich and destroyed an American President and cut his successor's power to govern by half. Now he had such a story in his hands.

It would be dangerous, he told himself excitedly. The documents were most secret American memoranda which the Americans might take extraordinary measures to retrieve. But it was clearly his duty—and it would be his pleasure—to write the story that would drive the damned Yanks out of England.

He drove straight to his house in Rye and buried himself there. He often dropped from sight when he was working on a project and was reasonably sure he would not be missed in his customary haunts. The work at Kew was government work and could wait. This was far more important.

He set himself to study, in his methodical way, the outrageous proposals in the American document and began to outline the article he would write to form the hard core of his attack. Never having been a soldier, he understood almost nothing about such things as troop movements, supporting echelons, and amphibious landings. A great deal of research was needed to make clear to him the actual operation envisioned in the memorandum. With the patience that marked all of his research, he sorted it out. What the Americans proposed to do was land on the south coast near Hastings under cover of a NATO maneuver. With a task force in support and a strike force of two Marine divisions and one Army division, they would occupy London almost immediately, and all of England up to Hadrian's Wall by month's end.

Langton was a political rather than a military commentator. But he understood at the outset that the memoranda described a contingency plan that would be implemented if and when the militarists in the Pentagon decided, in all their arrogance, that England had finally leaned, or had been pushed, too far to the Left and was becoming neutralist.

The audacity and overbearing insolence of the plan was astonishing, Langton thought after his first incredulous reading. But his careful research on the subject of the British defense establishment told him plainly that militarily the plan was sound. If the Yanks ever became irresponsible enough to put Hastings into operation, it would succeed.

The thought of living, even for a day, in a country occupied by the American military, filled Langton with horror.

For a day or more he read and reread a section of the plan that was written in strangely ambiguous terms for so straightforward a military document.

The British people have always conducted themselves with fortitude and resourcefulness in times of crisis. A vital factor in this conduct has always been the coalescence, around one or more personalities, of a powerful will to resist. This historical fact is one that should be given careful consideration by the agencies assigned to the task of covert preparations for Hastings, and suitable responses formulated.

With the sound of gulls and the smell of the summer fog blowing in through his open window, Langton brooded over these strangely elliptical phrases. Were they an injunction to seize the Royal Family? Sequestering the sovereign was so obviously a necessity that it hardly required special attention from those assigned "the task of covert operations."

Then what was meant by "suitable responses"? At whom would these responses be directed? He closed his eyes thoughtfully and remembered his childhood, that bleak first summer of the war. Dunkirk. The fall of France. The Battle of Britain. Winston Churchill had been the pillar of strength around which the English had rallied in those days. Not Parliament or its ordinary members, not the labor unions, not the generals and admirals who had hashed things so badly, not the few Communists who still withheld their support from the war until Russia should be attacked. Churchill. The Prime Minister. No other.

Langton's mouth pulled down into a hard frown. That's what the Yank contingency planner was saying. Before Hastings was implemented, "suitable responses" would be formulated.

Langton bared his uneven teeth in a sudden, excited grimace. By God, he thought, *the Yanks are talking about killing the Prime Minister.*

For the next five hours Langton was almost beside himself with delighted excitement. The bloody Yanks had actually concocted a plan to do away with a British Prime Minister—and at the moment that meant Old Hugh and no one else. For a time Langton felt as though he held the fate of the world in the palm of his hand.

He worked furiously on his outline, arranging the damning evidence in the way most calculated to bring the average Englishman to a boiling rage by the time he had completed reading the first installment. Langton saw the piece as a syndicated, four-part exposé, saving the threat to Hugh Evans's life for the final, climactic chapter. On its publication, relations between Britain and the United States would be at the breaking point. The final disclosure would bring them down in ruins. The government might even, he thought, have to ask the Soviet Union for protection. The possibilities were staggering.

At six, nearly exhausted by his excited labors, he took a short break for a cup of tea and the early evening television news.

What he saw on the screen dampened his exuberant spirits and brought on a terrible apprehension.

The lead story was about a bombing at Heathrow. The pictures were chilling: they showed a car blasted apart by a gelignite bomb of savage power. The blackened ceiling, the twisted remains of the car, the white fire-fighting foam still frothing on the wreckage, the ghoulishly clear pictures of paramedics removing the mutilated corpse of the victim in a too-small plastic body-bag made Langton's blood turn cold.

The commentary was worse: "The victim was the single occupant of the car, Captain C. Farr, an officer of the Welsh Fusiliers. . . ." Langton had a passing acquaintance with Captain Farr, whom he had met briefly at a Mayfair cocktail party. More to the point he had been identified by a journalist close to the Home Office as probably a member of DI5.

". . . An American, whose identity was not disclosed, was the only eyewitness. He has been temporarily detained for questioning."

The presence of an American at the scene of the violent death of a British counterintelligence officer held an ominous meaning in Langton's conspiratorial mind. Was it possible that the Hastings plan was already being put into operation? Langton immediately thought of the CIA. They must know by now that their damned Hastings memorandum had found its way to England. Where else would it have been taken but to the country they intended to wrong? Were they searching already, killing when necessary, as they always did? And worst of all, did they guess to whom their defector might have delivered their property and were they even now coming to collect it?

Langton considered this for a time and found himself sweating. The documents on his worktable could be his death warrant. And yet he remained true enough to his self-image to refuse to take them to the authorities. What questions would be asked? Were such things as this covered by the Official Secrets Act? He did not think so, but he was damned sure he didn't want to risk handing the Hastings papers over to the police. Who knew how deeply into the police force the CIA had already infiltrated?

He needed time, he thought. Time to think, to make sure it was safe to continue. And he needed a place for the Hastings papers. A place where they would be safe and where only he could retrieve them.

By dark he had made his decision. He gathered the several sheets of the memorandum, a handbook of computer operations, and his special pass to the computer terminal room at Kew.

From the stack of books on his worktable he took a copy of the collected journalism of Ernest Hemingway, a writer he thought overly macho but one he read for style. He leafed swiftly through the book, glancing at the dozens of passages he had underlined in pencil. At random, he selected a page with one phrase underlined and tore it from the volume, adding it to the pile of documents in his briefcase. Then he discarded the book, gathered his light mackintosh, and left the house.

He hurried down the cobbled slope of Mermaid Street in the thickening fog toward the carpark where he kept his Mercedes. The nape of his neck prickled, but he did not look back.

He hesitated a long time before turning the ignition key. His hand shook so badly that he had difficulty getting the gear selector lever into reverse. At last he managed it, and the car's silky turbo-diesel came obediently to life. He allowed a sigh of relief to escape him and sat for a moment organizing his thoughts.

It was a pity that the Mercedes was so conspicuous. He considered the wisdom of hiring another car in London, but he didn't want to take the time it would require—and there were probably hundreds of Arab-owned Mercedes in the Home Counties, anyway.

Presently, he backed the car around and drove out of the carpark and onto the high road to the north. He was by now convinced that he was running for his life as well as for the survival of an English Britain.

9

The man calling himself Richard Iron sat behind the wheel of his hired car staring emptily across the gray water of Tremadoc Bay. He vaguely remembered coming here with his mother on what he supposed had been meant as a holiday. The memory should have been a pleasant one, but it was not. There were no happy memories of Wales for Richard Iron.

A bank of fog lay motionless on the water, masking the peninsula on the far side of the bay. The sands that he remembered as white were gray, streaked with oil. The seabirds were gone. He had liked the sound of the birds when he was young.

There was a legend about Tremadoc. Long before Columbus, a Welshman named Madoc ab Owain Gwynedd had sailed from this bay for the New World. He never returned, but the harpers who still remembered the old songs claimed that he reached the golden land and founded a tribe there, a tribe of golden-throated singers. Or so Iron's mother had told him. He remembered that: the cold dark miner's terrace house, one of a long, grimy row, dimly lit (with the light of oil lamps? It was hard to remember that clearly), and his mother who called herself Bronwen Evans but who wasn't entitled to that name because she had never married, had been Hugh Llewellyn Evans's fancy woman, the villagers said. But she told the son stories and said that one day he would leave Wales as Madoc ab Owain had done, and find a golden land.

He had left Wales, right enough. He had buried Bronwen in the cemetery between the mountains, bare mountains lightly dusted with green in springtime but in winter black as the coal that had been taken from them. The villagers had not come to the burial and neither had the father. The boy had not expected that. He had imagined that Hugh Evans would come for his son when he knew that Bronwen was dead. So the boy had buried his mother and left the coal-black land for the New World.

My God, he thought, it is like something out of the seventeenth century. The bastard son, forgotten by his father, the rising man gone off to Cardiff become a power in the union organization. But that was the way things still were in this country. A man could grow with the ancient feuds still in his heart.

It was a mistake to come back here, Iron thought. But he had wanted to see Wales again. Or was it that he needed to touch the native land to draw some strength from it, something to feed the old anger?

The car stood on the road-verge near the shore. The black ribbon of asphalt curved away to the south, riding the shoulder of the mountains that came down almost to the placid bay. Beyond those mountains, somewhere in a narrow valley roofed over tightly with the low clouds, was the village where Iron was born. There would be slag heaps, some old enough to be covered with grass, and those miner's terraces, and the chapel with its neglected burial ground, and Bronwen, the mother. His eyes felt the unaccustomed dampness of a renewed grief. Why had his father done that? Why had he gone off without heart or conscience, leaving his woman and a bastard son?

In America the boy had lived thin, but he had managed. He had been fifteen when he slipped off the Liberian ship on which he had worked his way across. At sixteen he had lied about his age and nationality and enlisted in the U.S. Army. The Vietnam war was being fed men in small increments by an administration that was too dishonest to tell the people what was happening in Southeast Asia.

He made a good soldier. His officers sensed that he was full of anger, but unlike the conscripts who had been unable to find a way to evade the draft and so were angry, too, Private Evans (he was using his father's name then) directed his fury at the enemy. By the time the war was lost, he had become a sergeant and a Ranger. He was developing a taste for killing.

Once he wrote to his father, who was becoming a power in the

British Labour party. The letter had been composed in a jungle hooch with the rain hissing in the thatch and a radio blaring rock music from the Armed Forces radio station in Saigon. He had received no reply.

Young Evans was twenty when the Army discharged him with a Bronze Star for thanks. He returned to the United States and was infuriated by what he saw and how returning soldiers were treated. He had been back for only a month when he answered an advertisement in a Texas paper asking for young men with recent military experience. The ad was for a mercenary commando being formed to fight in Angola.

He had stopped calling himself Evans now and never would again. In the CIA-organized-and-equipped mercenary force, he called himself Snowdon, deriving a certain ironic amusement from telling his mates that he was a black-sheep member of an ancient Welsh family distantly related to the Royal Family.

Only once, drunk and on leave in Salisbury, where members of the commando were assured of a welcome among the Rhodesians, he confided to a comrade that he was the son of a man who would one day be Prime Minister of England. The soldier, a KGB plant in the commando, did not believe it for a moment, but the information was included in his report to his superiors after the remnants of the commando were dispersed when CIA support was withdrawn.

Snowdon collected his pay in Salisbury and remained. He watched the guerillas come in from the bush and from the sanctuaries across the borders when the Thatcher government's peace plan was put into operation. He watched these same guerillas destroy the peace and begin fighting among themselves. He was glad to see it, but by then the white cause was lost in Rhodesia.

He crossed the border into South Africa and lived there for a time in a colony of ex-mercenaries, casting about for employment. He was approached by some anonymous men to form a small death squad to attack and kill the members of a Red action group operating along the so-called Namibian border. The engagement was so successful and so savage that he began to develop a reputation and a following.

Twice, KGB assassins, members of Department V, the Mokrie Dela people, made attempts on his life in the slums of Capetown. One of the assassins was left floating in the scummy harbor waters, his larynx shattered by a blow from the edge of a hand. The second hovered between life and death for weeks in a Port Elizabeth police hospital, his liver punctured by the point of a commando knife. He was worthless to the KGB when he finally recovered.

In Moscow, the officers of Mokrie Dela began to take a stronger interest in the young killer who claimed to be the son of the man about to become Prime Minister of England.

A second raid into Namibia resulted in such a slaughter of innocents, along with a small Red cadre, that the authorities in Johannesburg were alarmed by the publicity. Colonel Snowdon, as he was now known, was paid off and advised to seek sanctuary in Paraguay, since it was unlikely that one more war criminal would attract attention there.

It was in Encarnación that Colonel Kadogan found him.

Richard Iron looked with cold, aged eyes at the waters of Tremadoc Bay and the bleak mountains of his homeland. He was thirty-four, but tropical illnesses and killing had made him old. There was nothing here for him, he thought. He started the car and headed east for England.

10

On a day barely two weeks after Larissa had moved into the flat, while Colin was at his office, the first telephone call had come. It had been straightforward to the point of arrogance. In this, at least, these calls did not surprise her.

"Citizen Adanova. You know, as do we, that your—companion"—they were still as puritanical as she remembered them being from her Komsomol days—"is a counterintelligence officer. Whatever information you can obtain for us will ease your father's confinement." And they gave her a telephone number in Kensington to call.

My God, but they were sure of themselves. The thought of their pale Russian faces and steel-chip eyes filled her with rage. She had sat for a full minute, the telephone receiver still in her trembling hand. Mixed with her anger was fear: of course they knew that. Everything they did was laced with threats and menace for someone with a relative in the GULAG.

Still shaking, she had dialed Colin and reported the call. She knew that her presence in his life was already causing problems for him. One rainy evening he had taken her to the window and pointed out the Burberry-coated man standing miserably in the wet, watching the front of the flat. People from Colin's own Service. She hadn't understood that, couldn't believe that simply taking up with a Russian émigrée could cause him to be suspected. What did they think would happen? And then the first call came and she understood perfectly. When she reported the call to Colin, she hoped that they were all listening: Colin's people and the others, so they would know that they could not use her fear for her father that way.

"If they call again," she had asked that night as they lay in bed, "what shall I tell them? I'll tell them anything you say." She had a vague notion of helping Colin in his work, of being useful to the country that had taken her in and allowed her to live among its own people. But she had no real idea of the kinds of things Colin and men like him did for a living. Sometimes she thought of them as policemen of sorts, but she didn't like to think of them that way. To her, policemen were stolid militiamen or bullet-headed officers of the KGB. Actually, she had very little experience of Soviet police. She had been out of the country, in Israel, when the KGB became the most important thing in the life of Andrei Adanov.

Colin had said gently, "Perhaps they won't trouble you again." She hadn't thought he believed that. He just wanted to soothe her. She knew that there was a strong element of pity mingled with the sexual attraction he felt. Three weeks ago, he had grown preoccupied with something in his work. He brought home darkroom equipment, a thing he had never done before. He did not come home at all for two or three nights. Larissa asked no questions. She was still a Russian and he was an intelligence officer. She did not think it good to ask him anything. What I don't know, she thought with a touch of drama, they cannot force me to tell them.

He sometimes said, "I worry about you, Lara."

"There is no need, I am a survivor," she replied. Perhaps that was truly so, she told herself. But she was tired. More than anything in the world she wanted to be lonely no longer.

She had come to believe that Andrei Adanov might die in Russia. If they never let him go, it would have been, in part at least, her doing. She had taken her complaints abroad, to the Americans. She had let herself be shown on television. She had pleaded for human rights. She had been an embarrassment to the Soviet state. They would never forgive that.

Such thoughts filled her with melancholy. I am a Jew, she thought, but I am a Russian, too. A sad, gloomy Slav. She loved her country, but she hated the men who ruled it.

She did not love Colin, but she needed him desperately. She had been alone, even while people had surrounded her, for too many years.

She was nearly twenty-six years old.

The evening Colin was blown to bits at Heathrow she lay awake through the night, shivering in the too-large bed. She found that she could not cry. Her eyes ached and burned, but there were no tears. She was drained and empty.

The men from Colin's department had come, of course. They had dealt with her as gently as they could. They said kind things about Colin and seemed to understand that Colin had been fond of her—perhaps that he had even loved her, though their British restraint didn't allow them to use such a word as *love* to a stranger.

She wondered if they would search the flat, perhaps ask her to leave. Nothing here belonged to her except her clothes and a few memories.

They went away and she sat in the dark, not knowing what she would do.

On the following night the second call came. The same cold voice, the same arrogance. "Farr was investigating something called Hastings. You will look through his effects, please, and bring them to us." They gave an address as she listened, her heart beating heavily.

A white-hot certainty seemed to explode in her chest. She said, "You killed him."

"That is absurd. Please do as you are told. Your father is still in need of your help."

She began to tremble with an almost hysterical rage. "*You killed him,*" she screamed into the receiver.

"Kindly control yourself and pay attention, Citizen Adanova."

She broke the connection and sat for a moment, her breath

coming in short, shallow gasps. They would come now, she thought wildly. They would come and seek for themselves what they knew they would not get from her. They would come and she had to be ready for them.

She went into the alcove where Colin kept his photographic materials. She gathered all the dry prints, all the negatives hanging in strips from clips on the wall. She gathered all the typed pages of the report he had been preparing.

These things she carried to the cold grate in the fireplace. She struck a match and touched it to the pile, but it refused to burn. She cast frantically about the flat, rummaging in drawers until she found a bottle of lighter fuel. She hurried back to the fireplace and soaked the pile of papers and photographs in the grate. Then she touched a match to them and they blazed.

She remained on her knees, watching the burning, and realized that she was weeping at last. Tears streamed down her cheeks and she breathed in deep, shuddering sighs.

She heard a noise out in the passageway and stood. She was barefooted, dressed in a sweater and a pair of denim trousers, and the room was warm with the heat of the summer night and the fire in the grate. She felt as though she were freezing.

She was filled with grief and anger and fear. She went into the tiny kitchen and took a long meat knife from the drawer. Then she went to the door and stood for a moment, listening. There was no sound out there now. She unlatched the door and opened it slowly. There was no one in the passageway.

She would leave the door open, she decided, so that she could hear them when they came. She thought about the cold, commanding voice on the telephone and held the knife handle in both small hands, squeezing it until her knuckles whitened.

She went back to the fire that was dying into black ash and embers. Let them come, she thought. I have had enough. Just let them come to me now.

She heard a footstep in the passageway. Slow. A man's step. She closed her eyes and tensed, trembling in the heat, her body damp with fear and hatred.

The steps came closer. Then there was a knock on the doorjamb. The breath whistled in her throat and she held the knife even tighter.

A man stood leaning against the doorframe. She had the crazy impression that he was wearing white gloves and then she realized that his hands were bandaged.

He spoke in a low, persuading voice. "Miss Adanova? Lara? Will you put down the knife, please. I am Robert Brede."

11

Katya Roth's day had been long and difficult, with urgent messages coming and going from the National Security Adviser's office from early morning until late in the evening. It was one of Katya's duties to keep the communications log and another to route the material to wherever her employer might be at any given moment—a far from simple task with a man as active as Dr. Bruckner.

Today he had accompanied General Dracott to a meeting of the National Security Council staff, he had attended a briefing from the scientists at the National Security Agency, and had testified before a House subcommittee on government operations. At ten in the morning a report on the bombing at Heathrow had arrived and Katya had had to hand-carry the papers to him at the Capitol and stand by while he composed a reply to be sent back to Colonel Brede in London.

Katya had been horrified by the colonel's near-disaster in England. She did not know him personally, but since he was on a particular mission for the general, she regarded him as a colleague, and the thought of his having nearly been blown to bits in some terrorist's protest outraged her.

It was almost ten thirty in the evening when Katya reached the apartment she shared with Julia Tamayo in Silver Spring. She had had no time to shop for dinner, but Julia, a computer programmer at the Department of Health, Education, and Welfare, was never late and Katya knew that she would have dinner waiting and a cold pitcher of iced tea standing by to ease the discomfort of the apartment's poor air conditioning.

Katya had grown up in New York, the plain daughter of a symphony cellist and a schoolteacher. The discovery that she was absolutely devoid of musical talent had been a disappointment to her parents, who had spent far more time and money than they should have done in the hope that she would one day become a concert pianist. It had taken them a long while to accept the fact that their only daughter was not a prodigy. But when Katya had passed her eleventh birthday, her teacher informed them that she was a competent pianist and nothing more. Their silent disappointment filled young Katya with a guilt that was to remain part of her personality.

To make up to them for her failings as a musician, Katya became a determined student, and by the time her father died (of a heart attack during rehearsal for an all-Wagner program) she had won a scholarship to Hunter College and was well on the way to graduating *cum laude* at the age of nineteen.

Despite the attention of a loving and concerned daughter, her mother—now retired from teaching—lost interest in living, and by the time Katya had moved on to Columbia to study for a master's degree in public administration, she, too, was dead. Alone now, Katya became obsessed by the notion that her parents would have lived into their nineties (as other Roths had) if only she had achieved what they had expected of her.

The plain girl had become an even plainer woman. Katya was

short, slightly overweight, with thin, dull hair and rather coarse features. She was shy and did not make friends easily. She thought herself unlovable. In actual fact, those of her acquaintance who took the trouble to know her regarded her as kind, dedicated, and reliable—a good woman.

Her career began in New York City's administration, but soon moved on to Washington. Her first internship was with the Department of the Interior and she would most probably have remained there doing routine work had not a fortunate chance brought her an in-grade transfer to the Department of State, where she attracted the attention of Dr. Paul Bruckner, who was then merely a consultant. The people at State would remember her as the unusual sort of government employee who could always be counted upon to do more than her share, to cover for an absent colleague, and to perform every task with conscientious efficiency. Workers like Katya were rare in the bureaucracy, and they made personnel administrators suspicious. If it had not been for Paul Bruckner—who had, characteristically, come to Washington without a personal assistant—Katya would have remained a low-level employee forever.

Bruckner, a man who regarded even Cabinet members as possible security risks, trusted Katya Roth implicitly. He had once said to General Dracott: "Katya would turn into a pillar of salt if she were ever indiscreet."

This was true. Katya Roth considered the secret information, to which her sensitive position in the National Security Adviser's office gave access, sacred. She believed it was all she possessed of value. In a city of enormous egos, Katya Roth was an anomaly.

By the age of thirty-eight, she had been on exactly three dates. Two of these occasions were outings with Roth cousins who had been forced ("kicking and screaming," she told Julia Tamayo) to escort her to approved family functions. The third had resulted in a brutish near-rape at the age of sixteen that had left her shaken and revolted and was never to be forgotten. Except for that, until Katya met Julia, she was totally innocent.

Julia had come into her life shortly after Katya had taken up her position as Paul Bruckner's assistant and secretary in the National Security Adviser's office. A tall and slender girl of mixed Spanish and Negro ancestry, Julia had come into the United States in the last wave of refugees from Castro's Cuba. She had been twenty when she stepped off the airplane in Miami with the others who had been given Fidelista permission to go in an effort to bring about some Cuban-American normalization. She was now twenty-five and a beautiful woman with large dark eyes, shining black hair, and a skin that was, Katya Roth thought, the color and texture of brown velvet.

Julia Tamayo was intelligent; she had benefited more than most from the educational preferments bestowed by her minority status. She had come straight to Washington from the University of Miami. At HEW she did her job well and gracefully avoided the approaches of her male co-workers. She seemed intensely feminine and this alerted the macho hunters of Washington women, but she rebuffed their advances with calm disinterest.

In the early days of their friendship, Katya did not understand how it was that a woman with Julia's attributes—so much greater than her own—remained unmarried. In the Roth family, marriage as a career had ranked only slightly below being a professional musician and even ahead of being a doctor or lawyer.

The discovery that Julia was a lesbian came as a shock to Katya. Julia had told her one night only days after they had moved into the Silver Spring apartment. "If it troubles you, Kat," Julia had said over after-dinner coffee, "I'll go, of course."

Katya was too loyal, too good-hearted, and too much attracted to the Cuban woman to consider such a thing. But she found herself wondering about her own tendencies. Sexually, her relations with men had been unfortunate, and virtually nonexistent.

Julia Tamayo was the only person with whom she had ever had even the semblance of a warm personal relationship. And Katya Roth, though no one knew it—except possibly Julia—was a woman hungry for love.

The night Julia and she first slept together, Katya wondered if she had somehow bought herself an immediate passport to hell. In tears, she confessed her doubts to the Cuban girl and was soothed and reassured.

Katya Roth was not, in fact, a true lesbian. She was an extraordinarily sensitive and loving woman. If a man had ever loved her, she would have accepted his affection with joy. But no man ever had, except her father—whom she had bitterly disappointed. Katya's relationship with Julia Tamayo grew in fertile, but unseeded, ground. She even came to believe that no man had every truly loved her because men had sensed that her natural sexual preference lay elsewhere.

On this night when she drove into the apartment carport in Silver Spring, Katya had been sharing living quarters—and her life—with Julia Tamayo for more than a year. She still had moments of concern. But Julia was kind, considerate, and her perfect lover.

She was also a good listener, a person to whom Katya felt she might safely confide anything. To Julia Tamayo, Katya Roth could talk freely. And she did.

By midnight, Katya was feeling much better than she had all day. The dinner dishes were put away. Julia had insisted that she let her do it all, concerned that her friend had had a hard day. Then there had been brandy and coffee—dark and strong, made the Cuban way. And now the two women were in the bedroom, and Julia was rubbing the tiredness out of Katya's back, a thing she did with consummate gentleness and skill.

At dinner they had watched the eleven o'clock television news. Julia had been aghast at the film clips of the wreckage at Heathrow and she had asked if Dr. Bruckner was terribly upset about the DIA man—Colonel Brede, wasn't it?—being injured in the terrorist attack.

Now, in the dimly lighted room where they slept, with Julia's surprisingly powerful fingers kneading Katya's weary muscles, they carried on a fitful, lazy conversation about the day's events.

"Nothing ever really happens in my shop," Julia said easily. "The Secretary is going to make another speech about smoking and health at the Commonwealth Club in San Francisco and I am supposed to dig up all the gruesome statistics I can find in the data banks. It isn't like working for someone like Paul Bruckner, Kat. Not at all."

Katya, her eyes closed and drowsy, murmured, "It sounds peaceful, Julie."

Julia gave Katya a caressing stroke along her flank. "It's boring, Kat. Boring." She rolled Katya over and began to massage her shoulders and the swell of her breasts. She was dressed in a short nightgown open down the front so that Katya could see her small, hard nipples. Katya felt the flush of blood in her cheeks. She could never be as unaware of herself as Julia. The brandy had warmed her.

"Is he the one you told me about yesterday?" Julia asked.

"He?" Katya had allowed her eyes to close again.

"The man who was hurt in London last night. The one who was working on—Hastings, was it?"

Katya nodded drowsily.

"He sounds nice—interesting," Julia said with a catlike smile. "I would like to meet him."

Katya was appalled at the flash of jealousy she felt. She kept her eyes closed and said, "Well, you can't. He will be staying in London now. Indefinitely."

Julia laughed delightedly. "Kat, dearest. I believe I struck a nerve."

Katya, incapable of deception, opened her eyes and said sadly, "You did. It doesn't take much, Julie. I'm sorry."

"Kat, Kat. Don't you be sorry," Julia murmured. She opened the cotton nightdress until Katya's large breasts were exposed, and lay down with her lips against them. "I'm mean to tease you and I shouldn't ever do it. You're so very sensitive, my dearest."

Katya held the other woman's head against her and said ruefully, "I'm sorry. And I *am* sorry, Julie. I know you don't need Colonel Brede or any man." She paused for a moment and then said uncertainly, "Julie? Isn't that so?"

Julia Tamayo shrugged out of her own light nightgown and reached for the light. "Of course that's so, Kat darling. Of course that's so," she said.

At seven thirty in the morning, Julia Tamayo pulled her new Mustang out of the commuter traffic on New Hampshire Avenue and into the parking lot of an all-night franchise pancake restaurant. She locked the car and walked across the parking area to the glass and concrete building. The sun was already hot on her face. The sky was clear blue-white. She wore dark glasses against the glare.

In the restaurant she found a seat at the counter and ordered black coffee and a doughnut. She ate only half and quickly finished the coffee. She left fifteen cents for a tip on the counter and carried her check through the crowd to the cashier, a dark, smooth-skinned young man with long, straight hair. She looked at the wall clock and asked, "Is that the correct time?"

The man's eyes met hers impersonally. "It's a few minutes fast," he said.

She took a folded five-dollar bill from her purse and placed it on top of her check on the rubber mat by the cash register. The young man brushed it to the floor as he reached to ring up the sale. He stooped, retrieved the money, paused, then straightened. He gave Julia Tamayo a brief, blank smile and made change.

Julia glanced at her wristwatch, which showed a time that almost exactly matched that on the wall clock, and hurried out of the restaurant.

The young man at the cash register called to a waitress. "Cover for me a minute, Janie?"

The girl, who thought the dark young man handsome as Robert Redford—though in a sort of Latin way—stepped behind the cash register. The young man went through the door into the steaming heat of the kitchen, through to the storage area, and finally into the employee's toilet.

When he had locked the door he took a thin paper from his pocket and smoothed it against the mirror. It was covered with tiny, precise writing. The young man grunted with satisfaction, memorized what was written on the paper, and then crumpled it into a tiny ball and flushed it down the toilet.

His shift ended at ten. At ten fifteen he would be on the dry grass in front of the Washington Monument. At ten twenty, he would be reporting to his Control, and at ten forty his information would be transmitted, in hyperspeed microbursts, from the sophisticated transmitters in the Soviet embassy to a satellite in space, and thence to the receivers at 2 Dzherzhinsky Square in Moscow—the headquarters of the KGB.

12

Brede watched in silence as she packed Colin's things into two heavy leather cases. She was angry and afraid, but it was her anger that was in control and held her hysteria in precarious check.

While Lara worked, she talked. Her voice was pitched higher

than it normally was, he suspected, and it trembled from time to time as she folded Colin's clothes to fit into the battered, hand-made cases. The room was badly lit by a single lamp. Beyond the windows, Brede could see the city and the summer night.

"There is nothing they won't do," she said, looking down at the open case. "There is nothing they won't twist, or break, or kill. They say history is on their side and that makes everything logical and right—" She stopped for a moment, as though to catch her breath. She held a uniform tunic to her breast. Colin's Service dress. She said, "I'm sorry about the knife. I said that, didn't I?"

"Yes," Brede said.

"I thought they were coming. I wanted to do something, any-thing. I think I could have used it. The knife, I mean." She put the folded tunic into the open case. "These things. They all have to be sent to Colin's people, you see. They will want them, don't you think?"

"Yes," Brede said again, watching her.

In the shadowy room he could not see her features clearly. She bent over the cases, her dark hair hanging about her face. The clothes she wore made her look like a small boy. Colin's personal things were stacked on the floor all around her. There was no way that she could get them all into the two cases, but she worked on as though packing them away were the most important thing in her life. Shock was like that, Brede remembered. It made trivial things vital, compelling.

He looked regretfully at the fireplace. What she had burned there was cold now, and gone beyond recall. He would have to get a message to Bruckner and tell him that. But he didn't want to leave Lara Adanova alone.

She said, "I knew his work was dangerous. He told me that and I would have known it even if he hadn't. But what they did to him—" She broke off, drew in a ragged, shuddering breath. "I could have used that knife on them, you know, I really could have done." She looked at Brede bleakly, shock and grief making her eyes cavernous. "They should pay. I want them to pay for what they did." She sank back on her heels, her hands limp in her lap. She was near to breaking now, Brede thought.

It wasn't the same, of course, for him. But Colin had been a friend and so he felt some of what she was feeling. Some of the anger and less, but enough, of the grief.

"Tell me about the telephone call," he said.

"They said I was Russian," she said in a thin voice. "They called me Citizen Adanova."

"And then you burned Colin's papers."

"Yes. I thought they were coming for them. I wasn't thinking clearly."

Brede looked at the silent, blank-eyed face of the television set. No, one didn't think too clearly when one saw one's lover being carried away in a body bag.

"I'm sorry," she said. "I didn't know it was a friend of Colin's who would come." She brushed the strands of hair back from her face. "The English—Colin's own people, the ones he worked for—they were spying on him. Did you know that?"

"Yes," Brede said.

"Because of me. Because I am Russian."

"They had to do that," he said gently.

"Colin loved his country."

"They had to be sure, Lara," Brede said. "It's a war. It has been for years. Nobody will call it that, but it's a dirty war."

"First my father and now Colin," she said. She regarded Brede with those deep, shadowed eyes. "Why didn't your people help me when I asked? I begged them to do something." She was letting her images of Colin mingle with the old ones of her father now, Brede thought. How much could she remember about Andrei Adanov after so many bad years? Enough to give her pain. Everyone had used her: the Israelis, the politicians who wanted to show themselves as advocates of human rights, and the media with their false concern and short memories. Lara Adanova had been given more than her share of the secret war to carry. It made him angry as hell. Because he had to use her, too.

He said, "When they called, Lara, did they mention Hastings?"

"I can't be sure."

"Try to remember. It's important. Did they use the word?"

She let her head fall forward wearily. "Maybe—yes—I think so."

"Try to remember exactly."

"They said—'Farr was investigating something called Hastings.'" She looked up at Brede and asked, "How would they know what Colin was doing? How *could* they know?"

"They could. They did."

"Did they kill Colin because of that? Because of what he was doing?"

"Yes. I think that was the reason. It is important to them."

"Is it important to you?"

"Very," Brede said.

"I can hear that voice now," she said, her own voice thin again and trembling. "'Farr was investigating something called Hastings. You will look through his effects and bring them to us. Please.'" Her shoulders shook slightly with a terrible, mirthless laughter. "They said please. They had just killed him and they were so polite to me."

The hysteria was very near the surface now. Brede could hear it in her voice. He had to rein her in or he might lose her completely. "*Lara*," he said.

Her body was shaking again and her breath was coming in broken, jagged sighs. He knelt at her side and put his arm about her. She twisted, buried her face against his chest, and gripped his jacket with surprising strength. A drowning person might hold on like that.

His voice was flat. "They will be coming, Lara. They can't afford to stay away. They have to know."

He could see her shudder as she asked, "When?"

"Soon. Tonight. They won't wait."

"What should I do?"

"Nothing. Let them come. I'll wait with you."

"No."

He wanted to see one of his enemies face to face. It was suddenly the most important thing he could think of to do.

"You want them to come, Robert," she said. "My God, *why?*"

He held her by the shoulders and spoke with cold honesty. "I need to know about them." He paused and then looked at her with eyes as hard as agate. "And I want to do something about Colin. They ought to pay something."

They waited in the darkness now, the light extinguished. Beyond the glass of the window, London's light reflected on the waters of the Thames. Brede could see excursion boats on the river. He remembered that people sang and danced and drank on the boats. Normal people, he told himself, to whom the Cold War was a phrase and not much else. They slept at night, and made love and lived ordinary lives and read about the dirty little skirmishes on the back pages of their newspapers. Or, once in a while, saw the battlefields on the television news, never knowing the terms of the battle or its costs.

He unwrapped the bandages from his hands and flexed his fingers. The skin was red and angry and it hurt like hell when he closed a fist. He sat and thought about Colin.

The girl was silent. In the glow from the city he could see her pale, luminous face. He wondered if her anger would sustain her against the fear she was still feeling. She seemed vulnerable, touching. He wondered if Colin had loved her. He tried to put all that out of his mind

"What if they don't send anyone?" she asked.

"They will," Brede said.

"I suppose so," she said in an almost inaudible voice.

"Tell me how it was when you were in the United States," he

said. He wanted to keep her talking. Silence could give her time to think too much.

"I thought your people would help me," she said. "You all talked so much about human rights, and about the way everyone should be free. I thought you could do for my father what you did for Bukovsky and the others."

"Not very many others," Brede said.

"No. That's true. But I thought it would all be made right. I was very young."

"Twenty? Twenty-two?"

"Twenty when it began. The Israelis said that they would take me to America and that I would speak to the people on television and then it would be all right; the Russians would let my father and the others go." She drew a deep sighing breath. "That was all they ever wanted, my father and the others. Just to go out. But they said he was a spy. For the CIA. It wasn't true. My father never betrayed Russia. He only wanted to be allowed to go out. He knew nothing about the CIA." She paused, and then asked, "Are you from the CIA, Robert?"

"No," he said.

"But the work you do. It is like the work that Colin did. Isn't that so?"

"Yes. And no, not exactly. It is hard to explain, Lara. I am a soldier, like Colin was. We served together."

"I know. He spoke about those times. He was happy then. He said they were good times." The silence came on her again and Brede could not break it. She was, after all, entitled to her grief.

The sound of the buzzer from downstairs broke the stillness. Lara started fearfully.

"Open the door," Brede said. How many would they send? They didn't need to send more than one to intimidate a sorrowing woman.

Lara spoke into the intercom. "Yes?"

"Miss Adanova?"

"Yes."

"May I come up please." It wasn't a request. Lara looked at Brede and he nodded. She pressed the latch button. Brede stood and moved across the dark room to stand behind the door.

They heard steps in the hallway.

A wait, and then a pair of confident raps on the panel. Lara looked at Brede and he gestured for her to open the door.

A man stepped into the flat. He was of medium height, dressed in dark clothing. That was all Brede could see. The man said: "Larissa Adanova?"

The lack of light made the man wary. Brede slammed the door and the man turned, startled. He spun and reached inside his coat, aware now that he was being ambushed.

Brede said, "No," and hit him with the side of his hand. He dropped silently and Lara made a sick, frightened sound. Her anger hadn't quite prepared her for the reality of violence, he thought. It made the memory of her holding that foolish kitchen knife almost pitiful.

"Turn on a light," Brede said.

"Have you killed him?"

"No," Brede said. Thinking of the scene in the Heathrow car park he was almost sorry. But this man was a messenger, nothing more. He hadn't been within miles of Heathrow when Colin died.

The lamplight illuminated a pallid face, longish blond hair, workingman's clothes. Brede felt the carotid pulse. It was strong enough, though the man would have a headache for a day or so from the chop across the temple. And maybe a new caution about entering dark flats.

Brede searched swiftly through the man's pockets. Ten pounds and a few pence. A wallet with a gasoline ration book, a membership card of the Transport and General Workers Union, a driving license in the name of James O'Rourke, a British passport for

James Lasky, and in a shoulder holster a silenced Colt Woodsman. Brede jerked the weapon out of the leather, not gently. Larissa Adanova looked at the pistol with wide, frightened eyes.

Brede wanted to smash the unconscious face. The intensity of his feeling startled him. He flexed his burning hands and took the clip from the pistol and emptied it, slipping the bullets into his pocket. He unchambered a round and added that bullet to the others. "Get me a lamp cord," he said.

Lara looked at him without understanding. "A lamp cord. Any one of them. That one." He pointed to a lamp beside a shabby love seat. Lara brought him the lamp and he ripped the cord free, using it to truss the man, Vietcong style, elbows drawn back and tied to his ankles.

Brede slapped the man's face until the eyes opened. They were watery blue and confused. "Who sent you?" Brede asked.

The man stared back blankly.

Brede said to Lara, "Ask him in Russian."

The girl spoke to him and the man shook his head. Brede took the pistol and held the tube of the silencer against the man's eye. "Who sent you, you son of a bitch?"

There was terror in the pale eyes, but he didn't speak. Lara turned away.

Brede felt his hands trembling, and it wasn't from the pain in them. He wanted to savage the man. It was what he had thought about earlier: a dirty little skirmish in an even dirtier war.

Lara said in a strangled voice, "Robert—*don't*—"

Brede forced himself to relax. We're no better than they are, he thought. We fight just as cruelly, with the same ugly animal inside us. It was only what the war was *about* that made a difference. He jerked the man over, jammed the pistol back into the holster under his arm. A thick smell of fear came from him but he made no sound at all.

Brede stood up and walked to the telephone. Holding it, he asked Lara, "Is there a back way out of this building?"

She nodded.

He grunted, "Good," and dialed the police emergency number. When someone came on the line, he said: "Listen carefully. I want to speak to Inspector Thurston of the Special Branch."

The woman on the other end said in bureaucratese, "If you will tell me the nature of the emergency, sir, I will connect you with the proper person."

"I said Inspector Thurston. You will probably find him in a police car somewhere in Southwark or Bermondsey. I want a radio patch. Now."

"One moment, sir."

Brede said, "There is no need to trace this call. This is Colonel Brede. Now patch me through or I'm hanging up."

"We are trying to locate Inspector Thurston now, sir."

The man on the floor stared. Brede turned and said to him, "What you came for is gone. Burned up. Too bad, Comrade."

Brede heard the sound of a computer trace on the line. They couldn't help themselves. They were policemen. They lived by procedures. He wondered if Major Hobbs did that, too.

He heard Thurston's voice on the line. "Colonel Brede? Is that you?"

"Listen carefully, Inspector. If you will come straight up to Colin Farr's flat you'll find a package on the floor. I don't know for certain who he belongs to, but you can find out soon enough. He will be carrying a silenced Woodsman, which I believe is illegal in Britain. He has been harassing Miss Adanova. Have you got all that?"

"*Colonel Brede. Stay where you are.*"

"Good-bye, Inspector," Brede said, and broke the connection. He turned to Lara. "Now, quickly. We get out of here. Now."

He took her unprotesting by the arm and led her from the room into the hallway. He closed the door to the flat and said, "It has to be fast, Lara. Thurston can't be far away. He'll be here in minutes. Lead us out of here."

"Where are we going, Robert?" Good. She was holding together. She had to do that.

"Colin mentioned the name Harald Langton to me before he was killed. We're going to find him."

Langton's flat stood in a side street off Pont Street, one of a row of refurbished Victorian houses that reminded Brede of something in a BBC television series of some years back. He parked the hired Volvo at a distance and sat for a moment studying the silent houses.

It was after nine now and he and Lara had taken the long way round to reach Belgravia. The street was quiet. The soft light of the streetlamps shone through a row of carefully tended trees in concrete tubs.

"Will anyone be watching?" Lara asked.

Brede was pleased with the girl. She was quick and there was real strength in her. She had hated what he had done to the man in her flat, but she held herself in control and that was important now. He had put them both outside the law.

"It's possible," he said. Colin had mentioned Daniels's contact with Harald Langton, but Hobbs had not. That did not necessarily mean that Hobbs didn't have Langton under surveillance. He had been dogging Colin. He might well have been watching Harald Langton as well. "We'll sit and wait for a time," he said.

A couple walked slowly down the street. A man and woman ambling together like lovers. London, despite all its troubles with strikes and terrorists, was still a city where a man and woman could walk together on a street at night without looking over their shoulders. Respect for the social contract was still very much a part of British life.

Lara said, "That young man back at the flat. He will be all right?"

"He'll have a headache for a day or so," Brede said.

"And you?" Lara sounded concerned. "Are you all right, too?"

Brede flexed his fingers. The burns were not that bad, but his hands hurt. He began to remove the bandage over the cut on his head.

"You shouldn't," Lara said.

"They'll be looking for it," Brede said. "They'll be looking for this car soon, too. We'll need to get another."

"How, Robert?"

Brede essayed a meager smile. "With a little help from our friends," he said.

"There are no friends," she said bleakly. "Not now."

Brede sat frowning as he thought about the silenced pistol the man at the flat had carried. The more he considered it, the more it troubled him. If Hobbs had been watching Farr, how was it that his people hadn't monitored Lara's telephone? Or had the watchdogs been pulled off the moment Colin died? The notion that the man who had come to the flat was not what he seemed was growing.

"Let's go now," he said. A man and woman together at Langton's door would be less threatening than a man alone. He said, "Did we pass a telephone back there?"

"I think so, yes," Lara said.

"Good." Brede locked the car and threw the keys under the front wheels. In response to Lara's questioning look, he said, "We won't need it again."

They walked to Langton's door, painted black and trimmed with gilt around the brass knocker. Brede rapped. Through the fanlight they could see a light.

Presently the door was opened on a chain and a woman's voice, pure Cockney, asked, "Who is it, please?"

"Is Mr. Langton at home?"

Brede could see only a strip of face between the door and the jamb. "Mr. Langton is in the country, at Rye," the woman said. "There's no one here. I'm the housekeeper."

"Could you tell me where in Rye?" he asked.

"His place," the woman said. "Where else?"

"His address? It is important," Brede said. "The street number?"

"There's no numbers in *Rye*," the woman said, pityingly.

Brede said patiently, "Can you tell me how to find his house?"

"Mr. Langton goes to Rye to do his writing. He don't like being disturbed by people," the housekeeper said severely.

"We must see him," Brede said. "It's *about* his writing."

The woman said, "Cadman's Blue in Mermaid Street just down from the House Opposite," and slammed the door closed. Brede heard "owse hopposit" and looked at Lara.

"Did you understand that?"

For a brief moment her thin face came alight with a real smile. It nearly made her beautiful. "I thought Americans spoke English," she said.

"Only just," Brede said.

"She said 'Cadman's Blue'—a blue house, I suppose. In Mermaid Street, 'down from the House Opposite.' I think that's a house opposite the Mermaid Inn."

"No numbers," Brede said.

"None I've ever heard about. Not in Rye. Everything has been there so long everyone knows where it is, you see."

"Almost everyone," Brede said dryly. He took Lara's arm and led her away from the house toward Brompton Road. A car passed and Brede put his arm around Lara's waist and slowed to a lover's saunter. Her waist was willowy. She came to Brede's shoulder as they walked.

When they reached a telephone box, Brede went inside and dialed a number.

A voice said, "Yes?"

"Get me Simonini. This is Brede."

The voice came alert. "Wait."

After a moment, Brede heard a telephone somewhere else being lifted. In the background Brede could hear children's voices. The London Station Chief was a good family man.

Simonini sounded agitated. He had cause to be, Brede thought.

"Colonel Brede? You have the cousins in an uproar. Jesus Christ, you've put us in a hell of a situation here."

In the background over the sound of a television set, Brede could hear a child's voice shrieking with laughter. Simonini must be a permissive parent, he thought inconsequentially, to let his children stay up this late.

Brede said, "I need a car, some money, and a change of clothes." He was still wearing the suit soiled by the explosion at Heathrow. "Size forty-two regular," he said, thinking about the look on Simonini's face now. He glanced at Lara. "And a woman's coat. Something light. Size—uh, medium."

The CIA man sounded as though he were strangling. "Who the hell do you think you are? Do you know what you're doing? Who sent you here, for Chrissake?"

"I'm here to try to paint over a Company screw-up," Brede said evenly. "And if you want to know who I am, check with Bruckner in Washington. Now quiet down and tell me how long it will take to get what I need."

Simonini's voice went flat. "We check this line every day, but you had better not get too specific."

"Then answer me and I'll get off the line," Brede said. He'd hated to use Bruckner's name, but there was no choice.

Simonini said, "Give me an hour."

"All right."

"Can you get to Euston Station?"

"Too far. I don't want to use a cab."

"The London Air Terminal then."

"Yes."

Simonini said, "Wait one. I have to use another phone."

Brede listened to the children and the television set. He wondered in which London suburb Simonini lived. Woking, perhaps. Woking would be just respectable enough for one of the new breed of CIA men.

Presently Simonini came back on the line. "Okay. Yes. Look. There will be a blue Spitfire in the A-section of the terminal carpark. The ticket and keys will be in a magnet box under the passenger door. The rest of what you want will be behind the seat. You can make the pickup any time after eleven."

"Thanks," Brede said.

"Look, I don't want to know what you are going to do. But for Chrissake, Colonel, be careful. You've already put one of the cousins in the hospital with a concussion," Simonini said. He sounded aggrieved. "Hobbs is pissed off, I can tell you."

Brede's eyes went dark with anger. "That was one of Hobbs's men?"

"Colonel, you're an amateur. You shouldn't be so damned surprised."

"That bastard," Brede said with cold fury in his voice.

"I take it she's with you right now?" Simonini said.

"Yes."

"Then watch yourself. Hobbs's people have been trying her ever since she shacked up with Farr. They want to know where she stands."

"He was carrying a silenced Colt," Brede said.

"He might have needed to scare her a little," Simonini said. In the background, the children were still laughing.

"You're something of a bastard yourself, mister," Brede said quietly.

"Don't let her charm you, Colonel," the CIA man said. "Remember she *is* a Russian, after all."

Brede broke the connection.

Once well clear of London, Brede turned off the motorway and into a warren of narrow roads leading generally south. The Spitfire that Simonini had provided ran poorly on the low-octane fuel that was all one could buy in the West since the last Arab oil embargo, and the closed space under the raised top smelled of stale cigarettes.

Lara sat huddled against the left-hand door, her face hidden by the upturned collar of the Burberry they had found rolled into a bundle behind the seats.

"What time is it, Robert?" she asked. She sounded faint with weariness. Brede sympathized. His own eyes were beginning to feel as though they had been rubbed with sand.

"Two thirty," he said. A sign caught by the brightness of the headlights said: TONBRIDGE 8 KM. His hands hurt and his head ached and he wished almost unbearably for a bed and time to rest, but he couldn't think of that. By this time Hobbs had surely alerted the police and they would be looking. If it took them a few hours to find the hired Volvo. . . . But it wouldn't take them long at all. Colin had known about Daniels's visit to Langton. There was no reason to think Hobbs didn't know as well. The police would find the car near Langton's flat without any delay.

He thought about how Hobbs's people had treated Lara and his anger rose again. Intelligence work was turning over wet stones. If you didn't like what lived under them, you should take up another occupation. But he was still angry and afraid for Larissa.

Traffic on the side road was light. Only occasionally did they pass a car or truck as they drove between the dark fields and patches of woodland.

He had changed clothes in the terminal's men's room. The suit Simonini had found for him was gray and too tight across the shoulders. Brede wondered whose clothes he was wearing and to whom this tired Spitfire belonged. Some poor sod working in the embassy, Brede guessed. Someone Simonini could lean on who would keep his mouth shut.

"Are you all right?" Lara asked. "Do your hands hurt?"

"They're all right," Brede said shortly.

"I can drive," she said.

"Try to get some rest."

"Yes," she said. "I'd like that. But I don't think I can. I keep thinking."

"That's the hell of it, isn't it," he said. He had told her that it was Hobbs who had sent the man to the flat. She had taken in the information silently. She was accustomed to being suspected.

Brede's eyes wanted to close. He said, to keep talking, "Tell me about your father."

She shifted in the narrow seat. The lights of an approaching car limned her fine features against the darkness. The scent of her hair was clean and fresh even in the stale air under the canvas top.

"He never worked for the CIA," she said. "He was never a spy the way they said."

"Your family?"

"There was no one but my father and me. My father is a poet. Did you know that?"

"I remember you saying so, I think, on some television show." He noted that she was mixing up her tenses, past and present. He supposed you did that when the person of whom you were speaking might be alive or dead.

She drew a deep, deep breath and said, "The secretary of the Soviet Writers Union testified against him. He said that Andrei Adanov was a CIA spy. The secretary of the Writers Union. Can you imagine something like that?"

"No," Brede said. But he could imagine it. Easily. Sholokhov denounced Solzhenitsyn before they expelled him. A Nobel laureate denouncing a man who would become a Nobel laureate. Marxist logic.

"Why do they do it?" Lara asked. "Why do they try to destroy Russia's soul?"

What a Russian thing to say, he thought. And yet that was what Marxists did. They did a job on their own souls, too. Back in 1953, the Chilean poet Pablo Neruda had called the American hydrogen bomb "infamous," the Soviet bomb "grand as the sun." And in 1971, *he* was given the Nobel Prize for literature. How could you explain that to a person like Larissa, who wanted sanity and order and peace in her life?

She rested her head against the seat back and in the dim illumination from the instrument panel Brede could see tears glistening under her long, dark lashes. "We are Jews," she said bitterly. "It wasn't that we did not love Russia, it was that we wanted to help our own people in our own land. Nothing more than that."

Andrei Adanov may have loved Russia, Brede thought, touched by her pain, but he had committed the unpardonable sin. He had not loved the regime and he had asked to leave it. Surely by this time the girl understood this. He reached for her hand and held it for a moment. It felt cool and still against his singed flesh.

"Colin and I were friends," she said. "We were lovers in a way, but mostly we were friends. He was a kind man, Robert."

A kind man in a cruel business, Brede thought. He paid a big price for that. The biggest a man could pay.

The road bypassed Tonbridge. They drove on under a waning gibbous moon that shone through the trees by the side of the highway. They passed through a sleeping Tunbridge Wells and took an even narrower road that led to the village of Wadhurst. Lara slept fitfully for a short time, murmuring in her sleep.

Brede forced himself to keep his eyes open. Shadows flitted across the road, shadows of nothing real. Presently he could drive no farther and he pulled the car onto the grassy road-verge and turned off the engine. In the distance he could see the dark shape of a lonely farmhouse. The low, amber moon cast a faint light over fields and hedgerows. There was no traffic at all on the road now. It was after three.

Brede extinguished the lights and rested his head against the seat. Larissa sighed and put her face against his shoulder. He held her. He felt as though he had been running for days and nights without end.

He closed his eyes and slept.

A flashing blue light woke him.

He sat up and shaded his eyes against the glare of a hand torch. A white police car was parked ahead of the Spitfire and a man in a dark uniform was standing outside the car, bending to point the flashlight he held into Brede's face.

"I'm sorry to disturb you, sir. But you really shouldn't sleep by the side of the road like this. It could be dangerous."

Larissa was waking now. She said, "Robert? What is it?"

He cautioned her to silence with the pressure of his hand.

The policeman shone his light on the license disc on the near-side of the windshield. Satisfied, he brought it back to Brede. "May I ask you for some identification, sir," he said.

This was the test, Brede thought. Hobbs and Thurston must be looking, but had their bulletin reached this country constabulary yet? he wondered. He handed the officer his driver's license and the folder containing his Adjutant General's Office card.

"Stationed in Britain are you, Colonel?"

Brede let his breath escape in a silent sigh of relief.

"Aldershot, Constable. Temporary duty," he said.

"You are a bit off the track for Aldershot, sir," the constable said.

"We've been up to London," Brede said. "My wife wanted to have a look at Winchelsea before returning to the post," Brede said. "She fancies medieval towns."

"You really should get a British driving license, Colonel. If you will be stationed in this country long, that is." He returned the documents and snapped off the flashlight. "And do remember that the law requires you to keep your sidelights on when you stop on the verge. Unlit cars can cause nasty accidents, sir."

"I'll remember that, Constable," Brede said. He turned on the headlights and reached for the ignition switch. "We got a late start and I stopped for a rest. I'm afraid I dropped off. Is there anything else, Constable?"

"I should give you a summons," the policeman said. "But I'll let it go this time, sir." He touched the peak of his cap to Lara and said, "Enjoy Winchelsea. You'll find it quite historic."

He walked back to his patrol car and turned off the blue emergency flasher on the roof. The car made a U-turn across the road and disappeared back in the direction of Tunbridge Wells.

Lara began to shiver. "Even after all this time," she said, "policemen frighten me."

Brede started the car and let in the clutch. The first faint suggestion of dawn was in the sky. The moon had set and the stars came down to the horizon. He looked at his watch. It was nearly five.

Rye slept in the morning twilight. Brede drove the Spitfire to the foot of Mermaid Street and stopped. The steep hill street was lined with restored houses and buildings that looked like illustrations in history books and fairy tales. Some of them had stood in Rye since the fifteenth century.

"It must be up there," he said.

"That's the Mermaid Inn," Lara said, indicating a building well up the street on the left. "Colin and I stayed there once."

Brede parked the Spitfire near the estuary that reached into the town at the foot of the hill. Small yachts lay to moorings in the glassy water.

The air was cool and smelled of salt water. The sky was now the color of smoke. The stars were fast fading and there was a growing brightness behind the point that separated the town from the Dover Strait. Sea gulls perched on the masts of the small boats in the anchorage. It was still too early for them to fly.

Brede and Lara began to climb the cobbled street. "They do have numbers," Brede said.

"Yes," Lara said, "but no one ever notices them."

"There," Brede said.

They stood before a half-timbered house trimmed in blue. A sign on the narrow gate read CADMAN'S BLUE. The house was silent, dark.

"What now?" Lara asked.

"We wake Mr. Langton."

"If he isn't there?"

Brede said, "I think maybe you should wait in the car."

Lara shook her head and held his arm. "No. I don't want to do that. I will stay with you."

They went through the gate and stood at the door. There was no bell or knocker. Brede rapped at the blue-painted panels.

Nothing. In the distance a dog began to bark. A black and white cat appeared in the window of the house next door and examined them with a profound interest.

Brede rapped again. They waited, but there was no activity inside Cadman's Blue.

There were mottled glass panels on either side of the wooden door. Brede looked about, found a stone and picked it up.

"You aren't going to break in?" Lara asked.

"Yes."

She looked frightened. He said, "Go back to the car."

"No," she said. "I will stay with you."

Brede removed his coat and wrapped it around the stone. He gave a window panel a sharp blow and the glass cracked, but did not fall out. The cat in the window next door looked disapproving.

Brede hit the window again and the glass shattered, falling into the house. He reached in and opened the simple latch.

Lara was looking up the street nervously, but there was no movement anywhere. The distant dog fell silent and the black and white cat vanished from the windowsill with a flick of his tail.

Brede and Lara stepped into the dark house and Brede closed the door behind them.

The interior of Cadman's Blue was very dark. Some light came through windows at the rear. They stood in a small hall that opened onto a cluttered sitting room. Brede reached for a light switch. He snapped it on. All the curtains were drawn in the sitting room. He saw that the room in the rear was some sort of workroom. There was a large Spanish table to serve as a desk, a smaller table with an electric typewriter on it. Books stood everywhere in stacks. A narrow stairway disappeared into the gloom of the second story.

"Wait," he said, and went up the stairs. He found only a tiny bedroom under the eaves of the house. It was furnished with a bed, a wardrobe, and a table. It was neat enough to stand an inspection. Not even a newspaper or a book. Langton was a man of carefully compartmented habits, Brede thought, comparing the tidiness of the sleeping quarters with the workroom below.

He went back down the stairs to Lara.

"I am sorry," she said.

"For what?"

"If I hadn't burned Colin's papers we wouldn't have to be here, would we."

"It doesn't matter. Just help me look."

"What are we looking for?"

"I'm not sure. Computer printouts, for one thing."

"What do they look like?"

Brede told her. But he had a feeling that they would find nothing. He had wanted to find Langton. Searching his house was a poor substitute for finding the man.

The sitting room was overfurnished, decorated with bad paintings and some good Japanese scrolls. They went into the workroom and looked at the clutter. It seemed hopeless.

Brede went through the papers on the worktable. They were pages of a typescript, an econometric study of British coal production.

Lara said, "Are these something important?"

Brede felt a surge of excitement when he saw the folded computer sheets in her hand. It died when he examined them. They were printouts of coal-production statistics. Pages of them, going all the way back to the early 1900s. They bore the imprint of the Public Record Office's data processing service. Apparently Langton used the computer at Kew for much of his research.

"Sorry," he said, and shook his head.

Outside it was becoming daylight. They had to leave. And do what? Brede thought. They were at a dead end. Langton could be anywhere, miles from here. And Hastings with him.

He stood in the center of the workroom and looked about, frustrated. Bruckner was going to be delighted to learn that his agent was breaking and entering in England, where they took such things rather more seriously than they did at home. And all for nothing.

He stepped on a book and picked it up. It was a copy of Ernest Hemingway's collected journalism and it had been thrown to the floor in a rush or a fury, one or the other. The pages were bent and the spine of the book was broken, loosening the leaves.

It seemed an odd book for a Yankee-hater like Harald Langton to own.

Brede riffled through it. It was filled with heavily underscored passages. And one page was missing. It had been ripped out.

Code book? Brede thought. Or was that too melodramatic.

Using a commonplace book with passages underscored was a simple way of creating a key for a substitution code. And Langton was a Marxist—the genuine, card-carrying sort. They seemed to love to play at being spies. Some of them were not half bad at it, at least at home, where spying was all too easy.

Brede put the paperback in his pocket.

"There's nothing," he said. "Let's go, Lara."

They went back to the hall and switched off the light. Brede opened the outside door and searched the street. It was much lighter now. The sky was turning red and gold and far up Mermaid Street a man was delivering something from house to house with a handcart.

He stepped outside. It was after six now. Lara followed him and he closed the door carefully.

From around the side of the house came the hulking form of Inspector Albert Thurston. He said heavily, "You may be a proper colonel, Mr. Brede, but you are certainly a very bad burglar."

13

On the tennis court at Annandale, the Pimmet Hills estate of the Curtis clan, Janice Carradine stretched to return a hard volley from Monique Curtis. She struck the ball on the wood rim of her racquet and sent it feebly into the net.

"That's game, set, and match," Monique said, her tone clearly indicating what she thought of the level of competition Janice had been able to supply this blazing hot morning.

Monique Curtis was Beau Curtis's wife of eleven years, a wiry woman of thirty-five with sun-bleached blonde hair and skin burned the color of mahogany by hours of tennis and sailing in summer and skiing in winter. She had been a Long Island deb when she first met Beauregard Curtis, and immensely ambitious to marry a man with both money and ability. The handsome Beau, heir to a political dynasty, fit the bill precisely.

Eleven years of affairs and liaisons had soured her view of her husband as an ideal man, but she still remained ambitious and there had never been any serious talk between the Curtises about separation. Divorce, of course, was impossible. Both were practicing Catholics.

She had borne five children in eleven years, none of whom she regarded with any particular affection. Fortunately, the immense Curtis resources made it possible to maintain an almost entirely separate children's household staffed by governesses, two tutors, and a full-time nurse. Monique was left free to amuse herself and to host the Senator's political parties at Annandale, which were legendary for their size and opulence. It was said that the Curtises did not entertain—they held court.

The Curtis money came from politics. In the 1920s, the patriarch of the clan had held the Senate seat that was to become almost hereditary. By means that in a later time would have surely landed him in federal prison, Old Beau (as he was generally known) amassed a fortune of truly staggering proportions. This wealth was distributed by the old man into trust funds of several million dollars for each of his seven daughters, and into a far larger one, of hundreds of millions, for his heir, young Beauregard.

With a foresight amounting almost to prescience, Old Beau had funded the family trusts with tax-free securities, thus effectively protecting his descendants from the depredations of the Internal Revenue Service and the voracious government it struggled to feed.

When the elder Curtis died shortly after the end of the Vietnam war, young Beau was still too unseasoned to step into his father's place. The Senate seat was therefore given to a distant cousin of no great ability or ambition, but possessed of the famous Curtis name.

Senator Marcus Curtis served for one full term and one-half of another before the party machine decided that young Beau was sufficiently seasoned to take over. Cousin Marcus was prevailed upon to resign—"for reasons of ill health"—and Beauregard Curtis II became a United States Senator at the age of thirty-six.

Now in his forties, Beau Curtis was considered the most likely presidential candidate to be prepared against that time when John Scott Demarest should complete his second term in the White House. Since becoming Chairman of the powerful Senate Intelligence Oversight Committee he had also become a spokesman for the populist elements in the party.

The polls showed Beauregard Curtis to be the favorite of the party's left wing. His detractors said that it was easy enough for him to support the party's Left in such matters as income redistribution schemes, since he and his sisters would remain as rich as ever due to Old Beau's prudent funding of the family trusts. The argument left the people unconcerned. Young Beau had Old Beau's touch with the common folk.

Despite the Senator's many infidelities, Monique Curtis still held him in some esteem. She no longer loved him: she wasn't even sure she liked him very much. But Monique nurtured visions of one day becoming the First Lady, and she felt reasonably sure that if she endured, her ambition might be realized. Beau Curtis, for his part, had learned to be tactful and discreet about his personal behavior. He understood that Monique would never embarrass him unless he put her in a position where her pride demanded retaliation. In addition to this assurance, Monique was a useful ally. She was, he sometimes said in not-quite-jest, his own personal intelligence service. The gossip exchanged among the guests at Annandale was carefully screened by Monique Curtis, who passed the best of it to the Senator.

Now Monique walked across the hot clay of the court with Janice Carradine toward the umbrella-ed table where the black houseman had set a tray with a frosted pitcher of Moscow mules and iced glasses. As she walked she swung her racquet to and fro in the practice motion her tennis professional had recommended. Janice was drenched with sweat, her tennis dress sodden. Monique noted this with quiet amusement. She had run Janice hard and she not only enjoyed winning, she liked to know that her opponent had tried hard to beat her.

The two women sat down and the houseman poured their drinks. The ice tinkled enticingly in the glasses. The Moscow mule was making a comeback as The Drink this summer in Washington.

"How is Davis?" Monique asked.

Janice Carradine, wiping her face and neck with a towel, said, "Oh, Davis." She always opened any conversation about her husband this way, as though nothing he did was really worth discussing. But Monique knew that Janice would talk about Davis and what he did. She had very little else to talk about.

The sun burned down with a suffocating intensity. The greenery around the tennis court exuded moisture, so that the air smelled of thick-leaved plants and chemical fertilizers. Monique stretched her long, brown legs and studied them with genuine interest. Her thighs, hard and athletic to any casual observer, seemed a bit heavy to her. She resolved to do something about firming them up a bit. The Curtises were planning a sailing vacation on the *Demelza* soon and it wouldn't do to show bad thighs to the guests on the boat, all of whom would be important to Beau's presidential hopes.

She had almost forgotten that she had asked about Davis when Janice said plaintively, "Davis can be very rude, you know."

"Davis? Rude?" That was not Monique Curtis's vision of Davis Carradine. He tended toward obsequiousness, if anything.

"I'm serious, Monique. That nasty little man Dwight Lamb came to the house last night with some sort of bad news for Davis and he all but ordered me out of the room."

"Dwight Lamb did?" asked Monique Curtis, deliberately mis-understanding.

Janice Carradine said, "No, good heavens, *Davis*. That Lamb person kept us waiting for I don't know how long—he made us late for the Soviet Ambassador's reception—and then he put Davis into the filthiest mood you can imagine."

"That isn't at all like Davis," Monique Curtis said. "He's usually so calm and steady."

"I did hear them mention General Dracott and that revolting Bruckner person who works for him. You know him, of course? Everyone knows Paul Bruckner. He looks like a rabbi," Janice Carradine said with a touch of self-conscious anti-Semitism.

"I've met him," Monique Curtis said. She was curious about Paul Bruckner, who was one of the very few men in government ever to refuse an invitation to Annandale. Beau called him a Fascist in public, but she had a standing order to try to bring him out to Pimmet Hills for private consultations. Beau thought that the way to General Dracott's trust was through Bruckner.

"They were arguing about something called Starshine and how General Dracott and Bruckner were interfering in some way. I know I shouldn't have listened, but I really *am* so tired of all this cloak and dagger business. Grown men behaving like children," Janice Carradine said exasperatedly. "And then, of course, it turned out to be a simply ghastly evening. The new Russian isn't at all like the last one. He wears starched shirts and has bad breath. And Orrin was really foul about our coming in late. So Davis just sulked all evening." She sipped at the melting ice in her glass. "The men oughtn't to bring office problems home. It's too awful, really. The President doesn't like it, you know."

"I've heard," Monique murmured into her glass.

"Anyway, when my tiger left for McLean this morning he was still in a state."

"Poor Davis," Monique said thoughtfully.

"I hope that by this time next year he is out of that job," Janice Carradine said meaningfully.

"Perhaps he will be, love," Monique Curtis said, standing. "Have the time for another set or would you like to change?"

"I have a thousand things to do today. You don't mind?"

"I don't mind at all."

"I'll go shower and dress then," Janice Carradine said.

When the other woman had gone into the cabana between the tennis courts and the pool, Monique rang for the houseman and said, "Bring the telephone, Samuel."

Starshine, she thought. *Starshine*.

Samuel placed an instrument on the table and plugged it into a jack in the terrace coping. When he had retreated out of earshot, Monique Curtis dialed Beau's private number at the Senate Office Building and waited for her husband to lift the phone.

14

The road from the military airfield at Simferopol to Yalta is one of the best in the Soviet Union. Its four concrete lanes run through the Krymskije mountain range, following the Selgir River to the Black Sea coast at Alusta where it joins the main route around the Crimean Peninsula from Sevastopol in the west to Feodosiya in the northeast.

This coast is the favored location for the summer dachas of seventy years' worth of high-ranking Soviet officials, so it is hardly surprising that the road through the mountains is kept in better condition than any other mountain highway in the USSR.

Marshal Leonid Petrovich Kunavin, Minister of Defense of the Union of Soviet Socialist Republics, sat in the rear seat of the armored ZIL limousine supplied by the Red Air Force at Simferopol, looking worriedly at the stands of conifers and the white water running in the narrow bed of the Selgir some twenty meters below the level of the road. Ahead of the limousine, two motor-cycle outriders led the way to warn off any civilian traffic, but they were hardly necessary. Ordinary Soviet citizens seldom, if ever, traveled this particular stretch of road. Marshal Kunavin was on his way to the seaside dacha of his friend and patron, Pavel Grigorevich Nikitin, President of the Soviet Union.

The visit was not a social call.

Leonid Kunavin was the first Soviet Minister of Defense to have been too young to serve in the Great Patriotic War. He had served his military apprenticeship in guerrilla wars in Africa, as an adviser to the Arab states in their many wars against the Jews, and to the Vietnamese in their border war with the Maoists. At forty-three, he was a high-ranking party member as well as supreme commander of all of the armed forces of the USSR.

The small motorcade emerged from the mountains and turned northeast on the coast road. The weather was sparkling clear, with a bright summer sun turning the blue sea to a carpet of diamonds. So sharp was the visibility that Kunavin could see the dark shapes of the Caucasus Mountains far to the east across the water of the Black Sea.

He never visited this peninsula without remembering that it was here, in the Crimea over a century ago, that the Western powers first combined to fight against the Russian motherland. What happened then could easily happen again. The nation and the revolution were surrounded by enemies.

He lit a cigarette and stared moodily at the glistening sea. In the front seat with the driver sat Bukov, his soldier-servant and personal bodyguard, an immense man with the personality of a mastiff and the curiosity of a stone. Marshal Kunavin had deliberately left his aides and staff behind in Moscow. The information he was carrying was volatile. The fewer who knew of it, the better.

Like most Soviet soldiers, Kunavin was absolutely convinced that the Soviet Union must eventually dominate all of Europe. For a nation whose history was one of bloody invasions from the West, no other long-term doctrine was possible. To allow hostile ideologies to exist in the space between Russia and the North Atlantic was suicidal.

But before the USSR could safely strike against NATO, Kunavin believed, it was essential to complete the domination of what the Americans called the "crescent of crisis" from the Horn of Africa to Pakistan. So far the master plan had gone well. Despite continuing insurgency the Red Army ruled in Afghanistan and the KGB in Iran. To dominate the "crescent" meant to control the world's oil. Without oil, NATO became meaningless. It was even probable that the people of western Europe could be brought to their knees with the oil weapon alone. Kunavin envisioned the Red Army rolling to the Channel coast cheered by Europeans believing that the Russian presence would start the oil flowing again.

For more than ten years the Soviet Union's policy in the "crescent" had been taking shape. Soviet bases now dominated the outlet of the Persian Gulf. Soviet-sponsored governments ruled the southern coast of the Arabian Peninsula. Iran, divorced from the West by the Ayatollah Khomeini's revolution, was steadily being subverted by native Marxists and, appropriately, the remnants of an intelligentsia trained in American universities at the former Shah's expense. Afghanistan was, to all intents, a part of the Soviet Union.

The geomilitary master plan begun by Marshal Kunavin's predecessor and wholeheartedly endorsed by President Nikitin and by Kunavin himself, had been running as though on rails since Brezhnev's time. It was not a scheme for impatient men, but the Soviet Union had not been governed by impatient men for a generation. The nation, the party, and the military were all subject to world-historical forces that required them to work carefully and in harmony to ensure the final victory. Whether that victory came tomorrow or in the next century was relatively unimportant. What *was* important was that the inevitable triumph of the world revolution should be achieved without the risk being run of destruction of all that had gone before. The Soviet Union would in time dominate all the world, but this prize had to be won slowly and with great care. Any serious miscalculation anywhere along the line could bring down a rain of nuclear missiles and that would make the concept of victory meaningless.

But now, Kunavin thought angrily, impatient men were interfering with the plan. People highly placed in the government were tampering with the slow—but steady—process. When a member of the Politburo had brought him the tape, he had been furiously tempted to order the immediate arrest of Colonel Santorin and General Galitzin. Fortunately for his own safety, he had waited for calmer consideration. It was only then that he learned that Yuri Pavlovich Koniev had thrown the weight of the KGB behind Santorin's dangerous planning.

Instead of taking precipitous action that could be dangerous to himself, he had decided to fly at once to the Crimea, where the President was vacationing, and lay the problem in *his* lap. It was simply too risky to take any chances, Kunavin told himself. There was no certain way of knowing how far Yuri Koniev might go to protect and support this insane shortcut into Western Europe created by Santorin and his computer.

One thing was plain: to have triggered the deep cover agent in the CIA to expose Hastings was a considerable act of commitment. Kunavin supposed that operation had been conducted with skill and finesse: Koniev was no fool. The trail left behind by Hastings would lead straight back to Washington, and to the CIA—that was a reasonable certainty. But there was something odd about the picture Kunavin had so far pieced together, something incomplete that made him very uneasy. It was bad enough that the KGB, GRU, and an overly ambitious war planner were, in effect, trying to speed up what amounted to a twenty- or even fifty-year plan for conquering the West. What was even worse was the arrogant risk-taking involved.

If this affair went sour and became common knowledge, the best that one could expect would be a delay in the revival of détente, so dear to the hearts of European and American liberals. The second possibility was what had brought Marshal Kunavin hurrying south to see President Nikitin. The worst case could mean the wrong war, fought at the wrong time and with the wrong odds.

Ten kilometers before the President's dacha came into view, Kunavin's ZIL stopped at the first checkpost. A pair of concrete blockhouses flanked the road. Across the pavement stood a pair of steel lift gates.

The blockhouses were manned by KGB militiamen, a senior lieutenant and six enlisted men. Their uniforms were immaculate and the officer wore white gloves, but their weapons were not parade issue. They were new AK-88 assault rifles. Atop the block-houses, the muzzles of a pair of antitank guns protruded from deep slits.

The officer examined Kunavin's identification carefully, despite the fact that the Marshal's face was known to every uniformed man inside the Soviet Union. Kunavin wondered if security around the President were not tighter than he remembered from previous visits to the dacha.

The second checkpoint, two kilometers from the house on the beach, was certainly new, as was an electrified fence that closed off access to the water for as far as one could see in either direction.

The dacha itself was as Kunavin remembered it, a white stucco palazzo in miniature that had been commissioned by and built for Nikita Khrushchev many years ago.

Kunavin was met on the steps of the house by Colonel Voroshilov, the President's military aide, a handsome officer of twenty-nine who owed his post to the fact that he was the grandson of a hero of the Great Patriotic War. Kunavin liked Voroshilov well enough but he found himself wondering if the Soviet hierarchy was not falling into the old, royalist ways of nepotism and privilege.

"Where is he?" Kunavin asked.

"On the beach, Comrade Marshal. Do you want to change into something more comfortable before you go out? It's hotter than blazes."

"No," Kunavin said. "I'll go as I am." He did not fancy stripping down to a bathing suit to present bad news to Nikitin.

They went through the house. Kunavin noticed that Nikitin had ordered a lunch prepared. On the terrace overlooking the white sand beach, a feast of cold meats, iced caviar, Crimean wines, and vodka was being assembled on a glass-topped table. He had not eaten since leaving Moscow, but the sight of the food did not stir his appetite.

He asked, "Has the security force been increased, Voroshilov?"

"Comrade Koniev recommended it, Comrade Marshal. There are plenty of Muslims on this peninsula and Comrade Koniev takes no chances."

Kunavin restrained his bitter comment. There was no way this puppy could know, of course, just how big a chance Yuri Koniev was in the process of taking at this moment, as the tape in his briefcase would soon disclose to the President.

The Marshal wondered if Koniev was not also planning something else, something special and unpleasant for the President if the discovery of what he had been doing should arouse opposition. Koniev was a policeman, and policemen had a bad history in the

Soviet Union, as the shades of Beria and a number of others could attest.

Still, it was true that the ethnic minorities were giving more and more trouble in the country—particularly the Muslims. It was possible, Kunavin thought, that he was being overly suspicious.

Voroshilov stood by the steps leading down to the sand and pointed. "There, Comrade Marshal. He said that you should join him. Tell him, please, that the vodka is being iced and the staff is ready to serve whenever he wishes."

Kunavin, his case firmly under his arm, plodded through the fine, hot sand toward the man reclining on a canvas chair at the water's edge. Voroshilov was right. It was like an oven out here in the direct sun. Sweat began to run down his back under the heavy dress uniform.

Pavel Grigorevich Nikitin had been dozing. He awoke at Kunavin's approach.

He was a fat man and the rolls of flesh around his waist hung glistening with sweat over the waistband of his trunks. His mottled skin never tanned and, strangely, seldom burned, even in the hot Crimean sun.

He was in his middle sixties and, except for his weight, was in good health. He had, he liked to think, all the stamina of his Great Russian peasant ancestors: men who could work all day in the fields, eat and drink until surfeited, and then make love most of the night. It had been a good many years since Pavel Nikitin had allowed himself such a routine, but he knew that, under the proper circumstances, he could certainly live that way.

He was married to a large and dumpy wife whom he kept secluded in Moscow. He regularly picked young mistresses from the various Bolshoi companies, enjoyed fast automobiles (as his predecessor had done), and in general lived a fulfilled and busy life.

He came regularly to the Crimea in summer because it gave him a chance to get far away from Moscow and all that it contained, and to lie in the scorching heat of the sun, which he thoroughly enjoyed.

He sat up to watch his Minister of Defense slogging through the sand in his polished boots. Briefly he wondered if Leonid Kunavin ever relaxed as other men did. He was certain that he had never seen the man without his medals. He signaled for him to sit on a canvas sling at his side. "You should get out of that uniform and into something more suitable, Leonid Petrovich," he said. "You look as though you are about to have a heat stroke."

Kunavin dismissed the pleasantries and came directly to the point. "I am sorry to break in on your holiday, Comrade President, but something has come up that needs your personal attention."

Nikitin's somewhat clownish face lost its welcoming smile and became something quite different. Behind the heavy sunglasses, the pale eyes narrowed and the slack mouth turned hard. "Explain, Comrade Marshal," he said.

Kunavin, uncomfortably seated on the low canvas sling, opened his leather case and extracted a video tape cassette. "I would rather you see this for yourself before I make any comment. This is something Koniev and Galitzin have done with the help of an officer in the War Plans Directorate and without my knowledge or consent."

"What officer in the Plans Directorate?" Nikitin asked. If anyone else had asked, Kunavin would have thought the question stupid, but Pavel Nikitin literally knew on sight every member of every planning unit in the government. He had an uncanny memory for names and faces.

"Colonel Yevgeny Santorin, sir," Kunavin said.

"Computer specialist. Chief of the War Plans Directorate of the General Staff. One of your appointees, Kunavin."

Kunavin's expression hardened. "Quite so, Comrade President. I am sorry to say "

"That bad?"

"If we can go back to the house and play this tape," Kunavin said heavily, "you can judge for yourself, Comrade President."

In the President's study, a white-walled room decorated with photographs and paintings and lighted by a single large window facing the sea, Kunavin asked, "What Red Army personnel are here besides Voroshilov, Comrade President?"

Nikitin, now wrapped in a voluminous toweling robe, looked startled at the question. "No one, Kunavin." The entire staff was KGB, from the cooks and stewards to the troops manning the perimeters. He found the Marshal's question ominous.

"A moment, Comrade President," Kunavin said. From his case he removed a small black box with a wire loop antenna. With this he carefully examined the walls and baseboards. As he swept the detector over one of the photographs above the desk, a red light flashed on the box. In total silence, he took a magnifying glass from his case and examined the surface of the picture. Satisfied, he opened a small penknife and scraped a corner of the glass with the point. When he had done this he held the penknife up for Nikitin to examine. A tiny black dot lay on the surface of the steel. Kunavin crushed it on the desk top. "Microdot transmitter," he murmured.

Nikitin's face reddened, but he said nothing.

"That seems to be the only one," Kunavin said. He walked to the door and called for Voroshilov. When the young colonel appeared, he asked, "Colonel, have you a sidearm in that shiny holster?"

The young officer looked startled. "Why, yes—of course, Comrade Marshal." He fumbled at the pistol on his belt. Kunavin wondered how long it had been since he had fired the weapon. Years, probably. Not since his training days.

"The President and I are not to be disturbed, Colonel. If anyone attempts to come through that door, shoot him."

"*Sir?*"

"Did you understand what I said, Colonel Voroshilov?"

"*Sir!*"

"Good," Kunavin said, and closed the door.

Nikitin said in a rush, "Leonid Petrovich, what in hell is all this about? Are you suggesting that this house is not secure?"

"It is secure enough, Comrade President. That microdot transmitter is not a CIA plant."

"*Koniev?*"

"If you were in his place, sir, wouldn't you do the same? I am sure if you accuse him he will deny it, but again—wouldn't you? Here you are absolutely in the keeping of the KGB. It would be too much to expect of a policeman not to plant listening devices here."

Pavel Nikitin had spent too many years in Russian politics not to acknowledge the unhappy logic of what Kunavin was saying. But he was angry and frightened, and he did not like being frightened. Yuri Koniev would pay for this.

Kunavin was inserting the video tape into the Japanese player standing next to the television set. Without comment, he turned it on.

For fully fifteen minutes, a ravaged-looking man spoke and read in English. Interspersed with his description of something called Hastings were close-ups of documents on CIA stationery and computer readouts, all bearing a red TOP SECRET stamp. Nikitin watched and listened in dumbfounded fascination as William Daniels described in great detail a contingency plan for nothing less than a military occupation of Great Britain.

When the tape had run out, Nikitin looked at Kunavin, "Is that *genuine?*"

Kunavin shrugged. "It may be. It may be something Daniels

was instructed to create. It may even be a total fabrication. The point is that these tapes—there are several copies—are being shown to a number of Politburo members by Koniev and General Galitzin. They are being told, most privately you may be sure, that these Hastings documents—if disclosed—will cause the British to drive the Americans out. Without the Americans in NATO, according to Koniev and Galitzin, we can advance our timetable for the drive into western Europe. They are being told the move can be made immediately. And they are doing all of this, Comrade President, without your permission or knowledge—and most certainly without mine." He rewound a portion of the tape. As it was running, he said, "But that's not the worst of it. Please listen again to the last part of the document as read by this American defector."

Daniels's image appeared once again on the screen and he spoke deliberately and with little expression: "The British people have always conducted themselves with fortitude and resourcefulness in times of crisis. A vital factor in this conduct has always been the coalescence, around one or more personalities, of a powerful will to resist. This historical fact is one that should be given careful consideration by the agencies assigned to the task of covert preparations for Hastings, and suitable responses formulated."

Kunavin stopped the tape. "Your English is even better than mine, Pavel Grigorevich. What does that mean to you?"

"Assassinations?"

"Of course. And I believe Galitzin and Koniev are planning to implement this section of the American plan to give the disclosure—verisimilitude. I believe that is the word."

"Good God," Nikitin said. "Who?"

Kunavin shrugged. "At least one, possibly more, people in the government. The obvious choice is the Prime Minister."

Nikitin sat down in a chair abruptly, the folds of his robe bunching on his bony knees. "Dangerous. If it went wrong—"

"Precisely, Pavel Grigorevich. If it should go wrong, what then?"

"Who was directly responsible for this tape?"

"A Colonel Kadogan. Aleksandr Aleksandrevich. KGB."

Nikitin reached for the telephone on his desk. His hand stopped in midair, as though the instrument were too hot to touch.

"Yes," Kunavin said quietly. "You see."

"We must return at once to Moscow and take this business in hand."

Kunavin said, "Forgive me, Comrade President, but we must take care. I will go back now. You can follow tomorrow evening as planned. Keep to the routine, sir. I will have troops at Sheremetyevo. An honor guard we can trust."

"You think it is as bad as that, Kunavin?"

"I can't afford *not* to think it, sir."

"Of course. You are right." Nikitin came to his feet, in command of himself again. "Very well, Comrade Marshal. I will see you again in Moscow tomorrow. Then we will have Galitzin and Koniev and their game-playing Colonel Santorin in for a private interview. In the meantime, we go quietly. Very quietly, indeed."

15

At four thirty in the afternoon the level sun burned through the windows of Senator Beauregard Curtis's conference room in the Senate Office Building. The room, expensively paneled and furnished, designed for meetings of as many as two dozen staffers, was occupied only by the Senator and David Halloran, his administrative assistant.

The Senator was a thickset, handsome man with regular features and hair curling over his shirt collar. Halloran's appearance contrasted sharply with that of his employer. He was angular, with a lumpy face and brilliant red hair. His eyes were as shrewd as any pawnbroker's. He was five years out of Harvard Law, all spent on Senator Curtis's staff.

It was Halloran who made all the important assignments among the fifty bright young men and women who served the Senator from Virginia and the Senate Oversight Committee on Intelligence he chaired. Halloran did much of the staff's legal research, helped to write the Senator's speeches, and coordinated the Senator's political finances. He also supervised the Curtis public relations team, one of the best in the capital, and contrived to obscure the media's view of Beau Curtis's personal vices—which mainly centered on women and liquor.

David Halloran had no overt political ambitions, but he was clearly a power in the capital. Beau Curtis was a clever and charismatic politician, but one woefully short on application. To his credit, he recognized this failing and used his immense wealth to gather about him a private army of researchers, pollsters, public relations people, speechwriters, academics, lawyers, and hardworking pols. At the head of this formidable phalanx stood David Halloran, the best, the brightest, and the most devoted of the lot.

Through one window of the paneled room Senator Curtis could look down the Mall to the obelisk of the Washington Monument and beyond. From the other he could see down the length of Pennsylvania Avenue to the White House. He liked to keep an eye on the Executive mansion. As a future tenant, he felt he owed it to the country.

The two men were conducting their regular Wednesday afternoon private briefing and discussion of future projects, the latest polls, strategy, and whatever else either man felt was important enough to be included on the agenda.

Halloran put away the notes he had made on a number of legislative proposals he had been studying to determine the Curtis position. The Senator had accepted two of them as suitable to his image. Halloran and the staff would now prepare position papers and projections of the support the bills could expect from minorities and feminist groups, which were to be exploited as important constituencies for a Curtis presidency. Halloran's constant purpose was to present Curtis to the nation in such a way as to make his presidential future a preordained certainty.

From an inside pocket of the tailored denim work jacket he wore, Halloran took the black book in which he kept the cryptic entries on the more sensitive and confidential projects he handled for the Senator.

He said, "I stopped by Davis's office to see him as you asked, Beau. I'm not quite sure what to say about our conversation."

"You asked him about Starshine?"

"Yes. I didn't beat about the bush much. I saw no reason to. I came straight out and asked him 'What is Starshine?' "

"And?"

"Frankly, Beau, I had the feeling I scared the shit out of him. I didn't startle him—at least that was my impression. He seemed almost to expect me to ask the question. But he looked green when I did."

Curtis stroked his closely barbered cheek thoughtfully. "Did he give you a satisfactory explanation?"

"He gave me an explanation. Let's leave it at that. But I think you are going to have to talk to him yourself. He didn't want to give me anything but bare bones."

"Which are?"

"Starshine is the Agency code name for that clerk they lost a while back."

"Janice Carradine told Monique there was something about the business that was upsetting Davis badly. It's just women's gossip, of course, but Monique has an instinct. She thinks it could be something important."

"I agree with your lady." Halloran always took pains to speak of Monique Curtis with southern courtliness. The Senator liked that. "There's something about the Starshine affair that has Davis on a bed of nails. I think that clerk was a bit more than just a clerk."

"Has the Agency located him?"

Halloran shook his head. "Davis says not. He got as far as England and then vanished in a puff of smoke. I had the impression Davis would just as soon that be the end of it. A minor defection of an unimportant paper-shuffler without much access to sensitive material. Every time I pressed him he became very evasive."

"Did he pull national security on you?"

"He wanted to. I could see it in his beady little eyes. But if he had done that, Daniels would suddenly seem much more important."

Curtis drew a finger across his lips. "What's he up to, David? Has he got himself into some trouble that can rub off on us?"

"He did mention that Simonini in London sent in a report that they suspected Daniels would ask the British for political asylum. And that they considered granting it before he skipped off to the East."

"Jesus," Curtis said sourly. "What the hell is happening to England?"

"They're having a reaction to Maggie Thatcher's conservatism. And anything they can do to screw us, they'll do."

The Senator recognized Halloran's bogtrotter prejudice and sympathized with it, though as a southerner he did not share it.

"The government over there is just reflecting the Prime Minister's anti-Americanism, one supposes," Halloran said. "He's next to a Commie, after all."

"So they gave Davis no cooperation."

"Damned little. Daniels was allowed to run free wherever he pleased. Until he disappeared, that is. He's probably in Russkiland by now, eating fish eggs and drinking champagne."

Senator Curtis grimaced. "More probably black bread and stale water if he's as unimportant as Davis claims."

Halloran spoke with emphasis. "That's my point, Beau. I can't believe he is so unimportant as all that." He stood and walked to the window to look down on Pennsylvania Avenue where bumper-to-bumper traffic moved at a crawl despite the gasoline shortage. "I think we had better do some careful investigation, Beau. In the public eye we are very closely tied to Davis Carradine. We got him the appointment at Central Intelligence. We are practically on record as supporting him for the Senate seat next year. If he's gone and caught his dick in his zipper it could make us look very bad. We've dug up too many political snakes in other people's back-yards to let ourselves be bitten by this one. We could get poisoned real bad."

Beau Curtis frowned thoughtfully. What Davis said was per-fectly true. The opposition would love to incite another Water-gate investigation if they got scent of something rotting under a rock. Find the Cover-up had become the great Washington game. In Congress it even took precedence over legislating.

"Monique said Janice told her Davis and Dwight Lamb were discussing Bruckner and Dracott," he said. "Did he say anything about that?"

"Not a word."

"It would be useful to have something we could use against the Basement Hawks," Curtis said.

"Davis didn't offer anything," Halloran said. "But I came up with one bit of interesting information about that American who was almost blown away at Heathrow. He works for DIA."

"Doing what?"

"I don't know, Beau," Halloran replied with a touch of impa-tience. "Sharpening swords or loading crossbows—what does it matter? What *is* important is that my source at the Pentagon tells me that this Brede—he's a light colonel—used to serve on Dracott's NATO staff as an intelligence officer. And so did the Limey captain who got blown up. I find that interesting."

"What's the connection with Davis's trouble?"

"I don't know. But I'll bet you a month's pay there is one," Halloran said.

"I had better have a private chat with Davis. And soon."

"Not here, Beau," Halloran said. "And not at Annandale. In case this starts to come unraveled and it becomes necessary to dump Carradine, we had better start putting a little distance between us. I wouldn't go over to McLean, either."

"Agreed," Curtis said. "All right. Monique and I are going to take the *Demelza* south when Congress recesses. The boat and crew are at Newport finishing up a refit. We'll fly up Saturday for a sail to Block Island or the Vineyard."

"I'd make it sooner, Senator," Halloran said.

"Tomorrow afternoon, then. You can shift my schedule to fit."

"Davis will say he's too busy. Believe it."

"Then remind him that the state finance committee is meeting at Annandale next week to discuss the Senate seat. I don't think he'll ignore an invitation. Tell him Janice, too, of course. Monique can keep her busy."

"All right," Halloran said, dreading what he knew would come next.

"You'd better plan to come along, David. I want you in on this."

Halloran nodded, already feeling slightly ill. There were few pastimes in the world that he loathed as much as screwing about on a sailboat.

16

Hugh Llewellyn Evans walked slowly through the deep summer grass under a sky the color of blue porcelain. He was a small man, once slender but now running to fat, with the broad, sloping shoulders of the miner he still remained at heart. His face was deeply lined and dominated by dark and opaque eyes that were capable of lighting up with the fires of an almost religious intensity, a thick and misshapen nose (broken long ago in a battle between strikers and soldiers and still worn like a badge of defiance), and a mouth that seemed carved in granite.

He was three months past his sixty-ninth birthday, but he had the strength and bearing of a man twenty years younger. The thick, slightly drooping moustache gave him a non-English look that he cultivated with the racial pride that was one of the mainstays of his personality.

Hugh Evans was Welsh and he was determined that no man or woman in the British Isles should ever forget it. He had a well-developed sense of history and he was never unaware that the Welsh were, in fact, the remnants of the true Britons, while the English were the descendants of invaders and exploiters.

It was his habit, when at Chequers, his official residence, to walk in the fields in the early morning, alone and armed with a malacca stick that he used to slash at the wild grasses as he thought his private thoughts.

Since becoming the first minister of the Crown (an institution Hugh Evans held in not so silent contempt) he had done his best to finish for the nation the work begun by all the previous Labour governments. His socialism was more than an ideology, it was an article of religious faith, although the attempts by his government to turn Britain into the country of the common man had been only partially successful. It was still possible, though just barely, for an heir to inherit money and property he had not earned with his own sweat; there were still Public Schools, though for some years they had been accepting both government subsidies and pupils from the slums and industrial and mining constituencies; and there were still British soldiers on the Rhine. As a politician, Hugh Evans understood that a perfect society was, and probably would always be, beyond the reach of a democracy. But this realization did nothing to reduce the zeal with which he pursued his vision of a new Britain.

He turned to look back at the beautiful façade of Chequers, reddish brick and mullioned windows against the green of the Buckinghamshire countryside. Beyond the house lay a forest of beech and larch and holly alive with birds and wildlife. On the near horizon he could see the soft rise of Beacon Hill, a grassy knoll as gently curved as a woman's breast.

As always, the vista filled him with conflicting emotions. An intelligent and sensitive man, he could not help being touched by the tranquillity and grace of the scene. As a Welshman and a Socialist, he was troubled by the contrast between what he saw before him and the imprinted memory of grim mining valleys, and towns streaked with coal dust; and thin, malnourished children.

Hugh Evans believed that the engine of a politician, the force that had to drive any true Socialist, was the sense of outrage. Wherever injustice existed, there was the fuel he needed to keep age and complacency at bay. From Chequers, he never failed to return regularly to the London or Cardiff slums to keep alive the contrasts that drove him.

He appreciated the irony of his presence on a guarded estate that had been owned by members of the aristocracy since the Conquest until the second decade of his own century. Chequers was listed in the Domesday Book—as "an estate of fourteen and one-half hides of land held by one Maigno the Breton," a freebooter who had come with Duke William to kill, to exploit, and finally to settle. In nine hundred years much had changed in these islands, he thought, but there were still foreign soldiers on British soil, and if they did not own great estates, they still owned far too much of British independence.

As if to confirm his thought, the pale blue air of summer was streaked with the condensation trail of a high-flying American aircraft from one of the American-British bases in the south.

The Prime Minister slashed with renewed vigor at the barley heads that surrounded him, swaying in the warm breeze.

He glanced at his pocket watch. It was nearly eight. He had been up since five thirty. Daylight was not the clock he lived by. His early years in the mines had taught him that time was not regulated by the position of a seldom seen sun, but by clocks and watches and colliery whistles. He had been tempted by his black sense of humor to install a mine whistle at Chequers, but the staff had been so shocked by the heresy that he had reluctantly abandoned the idea.

At eight o'clock he had an appointment with General Sanday-Maclean of DI5 and one of his officers, a Major Hobbs. Evans guessed that he was being maneuvered into receiving this Hobbs person because Hobbs had been at Winchester with Blaylock, the private secretary. Ian Blaylock was a typical upper-class Socialist, with feelings of guilt, yet convinced that the members of the lower orders needed well-born true believers to run the world for them. Evans glumly expected Alan Hobbs to be much the same sort of being. It added to the Prime Minister's ill-temper that Blaylock had given a valuable morning appointment to any sort of intelligence people. They, and the security types, reminded Evans of the injustices suffered by himself and too many others at the hands of policemen and informers. Even after nationalization of the mines, political activism had led, more than once, to jail terms and broken heads. Time had not weakened Hugh Evans's prejudices. He had no intention of allowing it to do so.

He turned and walked slowly toward the house. He was certain that there were security people watching him from the forecourt. He had long ago made it clear to them that he did not need protection from the people, and that they were to keep their distance from him. If he could have dismissed them completely he would have done so, but the National Executive of the party would not hear of such a thing.

He regarded the house as he walked. It was built from the native brick whose color had mellowed to a warm, pinkish red. The soft tone brought out the sweet lines of the gray stone stringcourses and window mullions. In the parapet of the easternmost double-storyed bay he could make out the weathered carving of a panel bearing the heraldic insignia of the Hawtrey family who had acquired the house in the fourteenth century. The Prime Minister never looked at the coat of arms without feeling a sharp stab of resentment against the class system that had dominated his country since time out of mind. The destruction of such entrenched privilege was the task of more than a lifetime and the bitter fact that the end was not yet in sight made Hugh Evans burn with a zealot's anger.

In the halls of the house were dozens of portraits of men and women who had lived and died in surroundings like these, never knowing the weariness of a day's hard manual labor or the ache of an empty stomach. One painting in particular, a portrait that Marcus Cheeraerts the Younger had done in 1620 of the last Hawtrey to own the property, aroused something like real pain in Hugh Evans's breast. The woman in the painting had a narrow, delicate face and dark eyes that reminded him vaguely of Bronwen. But the lace and jewels and brocade that the long-dead heiress wore were worth a thousand times the money it would have taken to support Bronwen for all of her days.

Her days had been short enough, Evans thought. Now that he was getting older, he thought of the girl much more often. He had done a dishonorable thing to Bronwen Thomas. But he had been a rising young politician then, without money, his progress watched by the powers in the Labour party. He had been certain that the affair would spoil the one chance he had to get out of the coal valleys and into public office. And so he had simply run away from the town, from the mines, and from sweet Bronwen. He remembered her that way, a sweet-tempered and loving girl. But her pregnancy had panicked him and he had gone off, away, to England. Years later, when his position had been more secure, he had gone back to find her. But by that time there had been nothing but a cheap headstone in a chapel burial ground overgrown with weeds.

He remembered Bronwen when he looked at the portrait of the last Hawtrey and he often told himself he would have the painting removed, put away in storage. But he never had because it, too, fed the fires inside him. In a different kind of social order he might have lived out his life with Bronwen beside him. Instead of that, he had never married. He had become, he admitted in moments of introspection, an angry, lonely, forbidding man.

General Gordon Sanday-Maclean, waiting with Ian Blaylock and another officer, stood and said, "Thank you for receiving us, Prime Minister. This is Major Hobbs."

Evans regarded the man sourly. It was as he suspected, and possibly worse. There was not only Winchester but Sandhurst in Major Hobbs's bearing.

Sanday-Maclean seated himself in a straight chair. The head of DI5 was a white-haired, erect officer of Evans's own generation. He had the body of a retired rugby player and a complexion ruddy as roast beef. As a Black Watch subaltern during the war, he had won a Victoria Cross. The Prime Minister, who had spent the war years digging coal, supposed this made the general a bona fide war hero. He belonged to the same class as Hobbs, though in Sir Gordon's case, it was Eton and Sandhurst. Most political offices were in the hands of working-class men at last, but the civil service, the military, and the intelligence services were still run by men like these.

Evans did not deny his prejudice, but he was willing to admit that these people did their jobs well enough. The pity was that jobs like running DI5 had to be done at all. In the Britain of Evans's vision there would be no use for such an instrument.

Evans took an armchair in the sunlight under the painted bay windows at the end of the Long Gallery. He stoked his rank-smelling pipe and lit it with a wooden match. He raised his hooded eyes to Blaylock and said, "That's all, Ian. Tell the Home Secretary I shall join him shortly in the Great Parlour."

The private secretary withdrew and Evans said to his visitors, "My time is limited, so please begin. And be brief."

General Sanday-Maclean said, "I had better let Major Hobbs do the talking, Prime Minister. This is his line of country."

Evans looked at Hobbs through a cloud of acrid pipe smoke. The major wore a Guards tie and a suit of clothes that cost what a miner used to make in two months.

"The day before yesterday, Prime Minister," Hobbs said, "we lost one of our men in a bomb explosion at Heathrow."

"Yes," Evans said impatiently. "The Caledonian People's Liberation Army or some such. I have read the preliminary report from the police."

"We have reason to belive, sir, that this was not a CPLA attack. At least not completely."

Evans frowned. He sympathized with the Caledonian separatist movement, but he disapproved of their methods. There was no longer any need for violence, and terrorism only strengthened the right-wing opposition who attacked the government for failing to take measures to protect the public.

"Explain yourself, Major," he said.

Hobbs glanced at General Sanday-Maclean, who said, "We have discussed this before, Prime Minister. The connections between the CPLA and agents of the Soviet Union's intelligence activities in Britain are of deep concern to DI5."

Hugh Evans felt his temper growing shorter. He had heard this sort of thing from Sanday-Maclean before. "Proof, General. Have you any proof of these allegations?"

"The evidence is circumstantial, Prime Minister, but—"

"Her Majesty's government can't go about accusing a friendly power on circumstantial evidence, Sir Gordon," Hugh Evans said. He knew that these people would bridle at classifying the USSR as a "friendly power" and he did not entirely disagree with their view of the matter. But for Britain, good relations with the Russians were absolutely essential if it were ever going to be possible to rid the country of the Americans, who were a continuous provocation to the Socialist nations.

Major Hobbs said, "To go on, sir. We have received information—hearsay, to be sure—that the planting of a bomb in Captain Farr's car at Heathrow was done in support of some planned action by the KGB."

It was always possible, Hugh Evans thought. The Soviets were a brutal lot and it might be as Hobbs said. But wasn't it far more probable that the killing at Heathrow had been aimed purely at DI5? That would make it quite a logical act for the fanatics of Scottish independence to have committed. Why was it always considered necessary to bring in the specter of the KGB? People such as Hobbs and Sanday-Maclean always saw the Communists as the ultimate enemies of their own class values. That made it impossible for them to be objective. They saw the Red Menace everywhere they looked. It destroyed their powers of discernment.

"Some weeks ago, Prime Minister," Hobbs said, "the Americans lost a CIA man. They gave out that he was strictly low-level and that his loss was unimportant. But we have picked up rumors in Washington that he was not quite so low-level—that he was, in fact, a supervisory grade contingency planner. This man, William Daniels, turned up in Britain directly after leaving the CIA. . . ."

"And did you notify the Americans, Sir Gordon?" Evans asked.

The general flushed. "No, sir. You will recall that you instructed us not to rush to share sensitive information with the Central Intelligence Agency."

Hugh Evans said dryly, "That is rather stretching my directive, General."

"There was some talk about the man seeking political asylum, Prime Minister. Your instructions on *that* were quite specific."

In fairness, Evans thought, one had to give him that. He had made it clear that dissenters from the United States would always at least be considered for asylum if they should request it. It was a matter that had caused a great deal of anger across the Atlantic. President Demarest had made it very clear that he considered any such policy an affront to the government of the United States. The point, however, had been moot—until now. No one from the United States had requested asylum in Britain—apparently until this Daniels person.

"We tried to keep track of him, sir," Hobbs said. "We felt that we should at least do that. He visited only one person in this country before he went to the Polish embassy and was lost to us."

"Lost, Major Hobbs?"

"We have reason to believe that he was put aboard an East German ship bound for Rostock. In any case, he is now outside our jurisdiction."

"Major," Hugh Evans said, "can you get on with it? It seems that if the man is gone he is no longer our concern."

"It is not quite so simply forgotten, Prime Minister," Hobbs said with a touch of asperity in his tone. "The man he visited while in Britain is Harald Langton."

"Yes? What of it? Langton would probably want to hear whatever a defector had to say about the CIA," the Prime Minister said. "The Americans have been publishing horror stories about their intelligence operations for years now. You can't blame Langton for wanting to hear—and probably write about—whatever this fellow would have to say."

"Langton is a known Marxist, Prime Minister," General Sanday-Maclean said.

That again, Evans thought. If one were to believe DI5, the Red Army was on the streets of Putney these days. "It is not against the law to be a Marxist, General."

"No, Prime Minister. I realize that."

"But? There must be a *but*, surely, General?"

"Our information from Washington indicates that the Americans lost a contingency plan along with Daniels, sir. In fact, we understand he was largely responsible for the plan to begin with. The name of the plan is Hastings."

Hugh Evans gave his visitors a bleak smile. "So they are even stealing our history, gentlemen?"

"The name has a peculiarly aggressive sound to us, Prime Minister," General Sanday-Maclean said.

To Evans the general sounded pompous and a bit absurd. He decided to use his gift of irony to deflate the bastard. "Should we fortify Pevensey, General? Send the army to Battle Abbey?"

"I did not mean to be facetious, Prime Minister," General Sanday-Maclean said, his ruddy cheeks darkening "It was merely a passing comment."

Major Hobbs now looked impatient. He said, "When our man was killed at Heathrow, he was meeting an American, sir. An officer with whom he had served in NATO. They both worked for General Henry Dracott, who is now President Demarest's National Security Adviser. We find this peculiar, to say the least."

"Why peculiar, Major? If the men were friends?"

"Captain Farr had been investigating the visit of Mr. Daniels and gathering what information he could on the nature of Hastings. It was his particular assignment to obtain a copy of the memorandum, or the plan, whatever it was."

"And had he obtained a copy?"

Hobbs shook his head. "That is the peculiar thing, sir. He had been on the assignment for several weeks and yet he had reported nothing." He paused and then added: "One more thing, sir. Captain Farr has—or had, rather, a Russian mistress. A Miss Adanova. An émigrée with a close relative in the GULAG."

The Prime Minister scowled and said, "If you are suggesting that we had a potential defector or traitor of our own in this Farr person, it is your responsibility to correct the situation. It scarcely needs my attention."

General Sanday-Maclean said, "There is no evidence of that, Prime Minister. But be assured that we are investigating. We are trying to find the American, as well. One Colonel Brede."

"Trying to *find* him, General? Does that mean you've lost him as well as Daniels?"

General Sanday-Maclean's cheeks flushed again, his face reddening with contained anger.

Hobbs said quickly, "The police are searching for him, Prime Minister. For him and for Miss Adanova, who is also missing."

"Good God," the Prime Minister said. "You have dropped a clanger, haven't you. And you see some sort of *Soviet* plot in all this? Gentlemen, it seems to me that what we have here is a proper balls-up in DI5 and damned little else."

Hobbs said doggedly, "What you say is most probably true, Prime Minister. I quite accept the responsibility for any laxness. But that is neither here nor there at the moment. What we need is some cooperation in Washington, and we believe it should be requested at the highest level."

"Meaning what, precisely, Major?"

"We would like you to speak directly to President Demarest and ask—in the strongest possible terms—for a complete disclosure on Hastings. Only if we know what it is can we make a judgment about its effect on British security."

"You astonish me, Major," Hugh Evans said tartly.

"Forgive me, Prime Minister, but why?"

"You should know that President Demarest and I are not on the best of terms. The asylum matter we talked about—and there are other things. The policies Her Majesty's government have been seeking to implement have not exactly pleased the Americans."

General Sanday-Maclean said, "That is understood, Prime Minister. But we feel that this is important enough to justify involving you. If there *is* a Soviet connection here, we cannot judge the seriousness of the situation until we know precisely what is contained in that Hastings memorandum."

Evans studied the two men carefully. Though he disliked them because they were his class enemies, he knew the British soldier and civil servant class well enough to know that they would never ask such a thing from the Prime Minister unless they thought it essential.

He rose from his chair and thrust the now-cold pipe in his jacket pocket. "Very well. I shall be returning to Downing Street tomorrow. I will consider it and notify you of my decision. Now good morning to you."

Major Hobbs seemed about to protest, but General Sanday-Maclean warned him off and said, "Thank you, Prime Minister."

The Prime Minister left the two DI5 men standing in the Long Gallery and walked to his next appointment with the Home Secretary in the Great Parlour. As he passed the portrait of the last Hawtrey, he paused for a moment and looked up at the narrow, delicate face and the questioning dark eyes. Then he thrust his big hands into the pockets of his jacket and hurried on.

As the two intelligence officers settled into their black car for the drive back to London, Major Hobbs said, "We can still lean on Harald Langton a bit, sir."

General Sanday-Maclean snorted. "Don't think of it, Hobbs. It's far too risky. The man can make incredible trouble for us and is just waiting for the chance."

Major Hobbs shrugged and stared out at the green countryside of Buckinghamshire. "He may do it in any case."

"That's as may be," General Sanday-Maclean said, "but at least let's not provoke him." There was a time, he thought, when DI5 was better regarded by the government it served and men such as Harald Bloody Oliver Cromwell Bloody Langton could be made to toe the line. He sighed heavily and muttered, "Bloody bolshie." Was this, he wondered angrily, what we fought and won the war for?

17

At forty minutes after two in the morning General Galitzin was awakened by the ringing of the special telephone beside his bed. Even in his stuporous state he recognized the unique sound of the instrument that connected his quarters on the Leninskij Prospekt with the operations room at GRU headquarters in Arbatskaya Square.

Beside him his wife muttered something and turned her back. Galitzin opened his eyes and swung to a sitting position on the large bed. He snapped on a small light on the telephone stand and reached automatically for a cigarette.

There were no lights on anywhere else in the apartment. The special telephone did not ring in the servants' quarters.

Beyond the windows overlooking the Prospekt and the University Park the night was quiet. No traffic moved on Moscow streets after midnight except for official cars, city services, and the police. A sagging, yellow moon in its last quarter was rising. It made a puddle of brackish light on the floor of the cluttered bedroom.

Galitzin picked up the receiver and said, "What is it?"

A youthful voice said, "Duty officer, Comrade General. Lieutenant Zaytsev. We have a call for you from Comrade Koniev."

Galitzin glared at the timepiece next to the telephone. What was the man thinking of, he grumbled silently. And why was he calling on the line through the operations room? There was only one reason the policeman could have to call at this hour. "Put him through," Galitzin said.

He heard the musical tones of an encoding program and then Yuri Koniev's voice, harsh and deep. "Galitzin?"

"I am here."

Koniev spoke without preamble. "A problem is arising with the man we hired for the London action."

"What problem?" Galitzin forced the sleep from his brain. One did not deal with Koniev under handicaps.

"The ordnance was purchased from the Irish as planned, and delivered to the address in London. But when the London *rezident*'s man went to set up an observation post in the building opposite, there was nothing to watch. He had gone."

"Gone? Gone where?"

"Perhaps you can tell me, Piotr Ivanovich."

"I? How can I tell you? The selection of the man was left entirely in the hands of the KGB. It was not a military operation."

"GRU gave us much of what we have on him. Almost all his background. Perhaps you know him better than we do."

Galitzin felt a mingled thrill of anger and fear. Whenever Koniev and his KGB killers became involved in anything, it became something dangerous for everyone else participating in the operation.

"He is a professional," Galitzin said. "He probably prefers not to be watched by anyone. What does Kadogan say?"

"Kadogan says there is nothing to worry about, but I don't like it. If I am holding an electric wire, I want to know if the other end is connected to anything."

"He took Kadogan for an American?"

"Of course."

"That may be the explanation, then. Perhaps he thinks Americans are too indecisive. They complicate things."

"Possibly. Sometimes I think Kadogan is too American for his own good. The tapes are like American television commercials. Hastings must be believed."

Galitzin could not remember Koniev ever sounding so uncertain. It troubled him. "Are you having doubts, Yuri Pavlovich?"

"It is too late for doubts. That is what troubles me about having lost the man in London. There is no way we can change the plan if it should become necessary."

Galitzin felt a slight shivering chill down his broad back. Of course, Koniev was right. It followed that never, under any circumstances, could it become known that the Soviet Union was in any way involved with the implementation of any part of the Hastings plan. And now the plan was moving like a runaway train. Somehow these thoughts had not taken hard shape at the Severnaya Zemlya meeting. It had all been clean and sterile and controlled: a war game.

"Did you know that Kunavin made an unscheduled flight to Simferopol to see the President?" Koniev asked.

As it happened, Galitzin did know. The information on the whereabouts of the Minister of Defense was always logged at GRU headquarters. Galitzin had been notified of the Marshal's flight and he had not given it another thought. Ministers were always flying down to the President's seaside dacha. It was a standard joke among the junior officers at Arbatskaya Square that the old men liked the dancing girls Comrade Nikitin invited down for sun, sand, sea, and sex.

"I heard," Galitzin said.

"There was a conference there on which we have no data."

Galitzin suspected that Koniev spied on everyone in the regime, not excepting the President, but he had never heard him come so near to admitting it.

"Kunavin may have come into possession of one of the Hastings tapes," Koniev said. "He will need watching until we are ready to brief the President."

We could do it now, Galitzin thought bleakly. It is a *fait accompli.*

"Well," Koniev said suddenly. "I am sorry to have disturbed you, Piotr Ivanovich. I was having trouble sleeping. I often do."

He sounds as though he wants sympathy, Galitzin thought. The man who commands a half million policemen and three hundred camps of the GULAG has trouble sleeping. Little wonder.

"Good-night, Comrade," he said.

"Good morning, Piotr Ivanovich," Koniev said and rang off.

General Galitzin lay awake until dawn. He was beginning to wish that he had not lent himself to this Hastings thing. But it was too late for regrets now.

18

The study of General Dracott's house at Fort Myer was lit by a single lamp. It cast a dull light on the Persian carpet, the Chinese chests, the memorabilia gathered by Henry and Mary Dracott in a lifetime of moving about the world in the service of the United States.

The two men were alone in the warm room and there was an unaccustomed tension between them. Paul Bruckner had been pacing restlessly and he stood now at the window, looking out at the sloping lawn and the dark road beyond. General Dracott sat at his desk, his slender, oddly fragile hands spread out on the dispatches before him.

"I don't like it, Paul," he said.

Bruckner turned to face Dracott with a deep frown creasing his broad, ugly face. "I don't like it either, Henry. In fact, I like it less than you do. But I intend to know who in our office is responsible."

"Are you so certain the information came from our unit?" Dracott had never lost the habit of speaking in military terms.

Bruckner said, "One. We send Brede to England." He ticked off his point on a lifted thumb. "Two. We are the *only* people who knew where he was going and whom he was to meet." The index finger pointed accusingly at the ceiling. "Three. Farr is bombed at Heathrow." The index finger was joined by a spatulate second. He closed the hand into an angry fist. "That bomb was meant for Brede, too. There isn't a doubt in my mind about that. It's a damned miracle it didn't get him the way it got Colin Farr."

The general's Brahmin face couldn't hide the personal loss he was feeling. "That fine young officer," he said. "To be killed that way."

Soldiers, Bruckner thought. What archaic creatures they were, actually. If Farr had been killed in some battle against Russian armor, the general would feel regret, of course. He had always been a commander deeply involved with his troops. But he would not be experiencing this peculiar grief. What people like Henry Channing Dracott never seemed to understand was that death was simply death. However it came, it was revolting, wasteful—and final. Perhaps it took someone who had been through the Holocaust to know that. To know it down in the gut, where it counted.

"Farr was killed because he was on to something that he was going to share with us, Henry," Bruckner said. "The information that there was to be a transfer had to come directly out of our office. I mean to find out how that happened and see to it that it doesn't happen again."

Henry Dracott's compressed lips showed his feelings, but he remained silent.

"General, we have a leak in the Adviser's office. There is no other explanation," Bruckner said.

"Yes," Dracott said reluctantly.

"Then I have your permission to take steps?"

"To spy on our own people, Paul?"

"There is no other way."

"I don't want the law broken, Paul. I am deadly serious about that."

"Time could be important," Bruckner said.

"We will have to risk that."

"I will go to Judge Grant in the morning and ask for a court order."

Dracott nodded unwillingly. The notion of disloyalty in some member of his own staff was offensive, revolting.

Bruckner watched his chief speculatively. Henry Dracott was the product of generations of men and women to whom public service was a matter of honor. That was the one trouble in dealing with genuine aristocrats: when the fight left the field and descended into the gutter, their own sense of decency shackled them. Paul Bruckner had decided that the staff would be watched and bugged. If Judge Grant issued the order, fine. But even if he would not—and that was a possibility because he was one of those who would defend the Constitution if the Russians were on the steps of the Supreme Court building—the job would be done anyway. Bruckner intended to know who in the Adviser's office was betraying his trust. The risk to himself was of little moment to Bruckner. He would take larger risks than this one to protect the country he loved.

General Dracott said, "I will have to brief the President."

Bruckner had expected that. He thought it premature and possibly unwise, but it was that question of Henry's honor again. He would not put the administration in jeopardy by running an unauthorized operation.

"I suppose you must," Bruckner said. "When will you see him?"

"As soon as I can get an appointment. He is still at Camp David."

"He won't like it, Henry."

"*I* don't like it, Paul. Colin Farr was killed like some *mafioso*. The President has a right to know what is going on."

"The trouble is we don't really know yet," Bruckner said. "If you could wait a day or two—or at least until we hear from Colonel Brede—we might have more to say to the President." We might know, too, he thought, who is leaking our moves to the damned KGB.

"We know enough," General Dracott said. "We know that someone in the CIA is covering up something. We know that we have taken it on ourselves to send Colonel Brede to England. And we know we've managed to get Captain Farr killed. The President should be told so that he can take whatever action he deems appropriate."

Bruckner's bulging eyes flashed angrily. "Like firing you, Henry?"

"If that is what he decides. Yes."

"Brahmin," Bruckner muttered tightly.

"What is that supposed to mean?"

"It means that if you don't take the gloves off, Henry, you are apt to end up on the scrap heap."

The lamplight etched Dracott's long, finely made face. He looked like a Dutch portrait, his eyes hooded, his expression masked and composed.

"I appreciate your concern, Paul. But I can't lie to the President. We have deliberately exceeded our authority by sending Colonel Brede on what amounts to an intelligence mission. I understood that when we dispatched him. I felt it needed to be done. I still do. But now matters are getting beyond our control and if the President feels I have done wrong, I must take the consequences. One way or another, he must be told."

Bruckner shrugged and returned to the window. The parklike atmosphere of the old military post depressed him. It made him think of dress uniforms in the style of the mid-1800s, white-gloved officers waltzing with their ladies. It had no relevance to the world as it was now, armed with nuclear bombs and missiles and boiling with racial and national hatreds. Henry Dracott was an archaic man, his brilliance constrained by a morality that had no place in the last half of the twentieth century. And yet, he thought, isn't it that quality that binds me to him? No matter how ugly the world became, one had always to hope that there was a place for a man like Henry Channing Dracott.

He asked, "Will you mention Hastings?"

"I will tell him what I think. That something with that name has been purged from the intelligence data banks."

"Carradine won't thank you for that."

"Carradine may not be responsible."

"I don't believe that," Bruckner said.

"I am sorry to say I don't believe it either," Dracott said. "But he will have a chance to defend himself. The President is a fair man."

"You'll make a bad enemy out of Senator Curtis."

A thin smile appeared on the general's face. "We are not exactly friends as it is, Paul."

Bruckner shrugged his sloping shoulders again. "All right. I'll set up a chopper to take you to Camp David when your appointment is confirmed." He moved toward the door, paused, thought better of continuing the discussion, and put his hand on the knob.

"Paul," the general said.

Bruckner turned.

"Is there anything you would like to tell the President personally?"

The froggy face crumpled into a grimace that might have passed for a smile. "I'd like to be there to back you up, General."

"All right. You can come along and keep me honest."

"You are too honest for your own good, Henry," Paul Bruckner said. "I'll go along to obfuscate and confuse. Good-night."

When Bruckner had gone, Henry Dracott sat for a time in the silent room. He was thinking that Paul would go through the motions of legality because he, Henry Dracott, demanded it. But if the judge failed to authorize the desired surveillance, Bruckner would order it anyway. When Paul Bruckner thought that the national security was endangered he would take any risk, break any law, to protect it.

Henry Dracott was fond of Bruckner, admired his intellect, sympathized with his patriotism. But he could not escape the thought that men almost exactly like Dr. Paul Bruckner sat in Whitehall and the Forbidden City and the Elysée Palace and the Kremlin. And that, in the final analysis, was why the world was in danger.

19

Thurston rode in the rear seat beside Brede. Two Special Branch detectives occupied the front. Behind the black Triumph, three more Special Branch plainclothesmen and Lara Adanova followed in a gray Jaguar. Brede disliked being separated from Lara, but there was nothing to be done about it. Albert Thurston rode in almost total silence.

Brede had expected that he would be returned directly to London and another interview with Major Hobbs, but he soon saw that he was mistaken. The small caravan drove north, away from the coast into Kent, keeping to secondary roads.

By midmorning they were in an area that had the green, closed-in feeling of a land that time had passed by. A mile or two beyond one of the villages, the driver left the road for a graveled single-lane track that wound through a wood of beech and elm trees. Brede estimated that they had traveled a half-dozen kilometers when they reached a brick wall, moss-grown and ancient. The road led around this obstacle to a wrought-iron gate set between two stone pillars. On one of the pillars was a squarish scar where a plaque of some sort had been removed. The verdigris of old bronze still stained the stone.

The car pulled up and the detective in the front passenger seat dismounted and pressed a bell-button mounted below a speaker grid. Brede could not hear the exchange, but presently the gate was unlocked electrically and the detective pushed it open to allow the two cars to drive through. He closed it with care when the gray Jaguar was clear and returned to his place beside the driver of the Triumph.

The cars rolled up a long straight drive toward a red-brick Victorian house of surpassing ugliness that could be seen through the trees of the park.

When they pulled up before the house, Major Alan Hobbs was standing on the steps.

Thurston opened the rear door and stepped out. "If you please, Colonel," he said.

Brede alighted and looked for Lara. She was pale and silent and he said, "All right, Lara?"

"All right, Robert," she said. She looked up at the three-story façade of the house. "What is this place?"

"One of our places, Miss Adanova," Major Hobbs said. "What we call a safe house. When we are being melodramatic, that is." To Brede he said, "I do wish you had taken my advice, Colonel, and gone home."

"I couldn't do that, Major," Brede said. "I expect you understand that."

"I do, of course. But now it gets a bit difficult. For all of us," Hobbs said and led the way inside.

The house echoed emptily. The broad hallway and the rooms

Brede could see beyond it were unfurnished. The elaborate parquet floors were scuffed and worn. A soldier with sergeant's chevrons on his sleeve sat at a wooden table on which were three telephones and some sort of government-printed directory. Hobbs said, "Call Mrs. Danvers down, Sergeant, there's a good chap." While the soldier used the telephone, Hobbs turned to Brede and Lara and said, "That's our private joke—a little tribute to *Rebecca*. Her name isn't Mrs. Danvers at all. It's Fletcher. And she is a police matron."

"Are we under arrest?" Lara asked.

"Let's say you are 'detained,'" Hobbs said. "You are guilty of breaking and entering, at least."

"But you are not a policeman," Lara said.

"This is Major Hobbs," Brede said. "He works for the same people Colin worked for."

Lara's eyes flashed angrily. "You were the one who was spying on Colin."

"I must plead guilty to that, Miss Adanova," Hobbs said. To Thurston he said, "I'll want you here, Inspector. The others can return to London." Thurston turned and went out. Brede heard one of the cars start up and drive away.

A plain-faced woman in a police uniform appeared from somewhere in the rear of the house. Hobbs said, "Mrs. D., would you see if you can organize some sandwiches and something to drink? Our guests have probably not eaten for some time. We'll be in the drawing room."

The matron went back the way she had come and Hobbs said, "Come with me, please. Let's find a comfortable corner where we can chat."

Brede and Lara followed Hobbs down the hallway. They passed an open door that led to a room filled with communications equipment. Two uniformed soldiers looked up briefly as they passed. Hobbs said, "Yes, we are rather well off for signals gear.

We can even tap into the satellite circuits." He went on down the empty, echoing hall to an arched, sliding door which he opened. Inside was a room with carpets and furniture, all Victorian. Brede guessed that they were part of the original furnishings of the house. There were tall windows behind drawn velvet drapes that looked dusty. The room was illuminated by lamps that cast a yellow light on the low table and chairs where Hobbs indicated that Brede and Lara should sit.

He closed the door behind them and then took his place facing them across the empty table. "Now," he said. "Welcome to Nameless House. Ghastly, isn't it? It was left to the nation by a crotchety old gentleman who claimed Disraeli once lived here. Personally, I find that very hard to believe."

He fumbled in the pocket of his tweed hacking jacket for his tobacco and pipe. Brede wondered, as Hobbs extracted them, how he managed to carry them without marring the line of the impeccably cut coat. Somehow Hobbs managed to be as well dressed as a tailor's dummy without looking like a male model. It was something that came with generations of practice, Brede thought wryly.

Hobbs looked at Lara over the packed pipe and lighted Dunhill and said, "You don't mind, Miss Adanova?"

"Do what you like," Lara said brusquely. She was thinking that this man, who should have trusted Colin Farr and helped him, had spied on him instead.

"I am sorry," Hobbs said, puffing the pipe alight. "But really, Miss Adanova, if you had not burned Captain Farr's papers none of this would have been necessary."

Brede said, "And if you hadn't harassed her with your stupid loyalty tests, she wouldn't have thought it was the opposition who wanted them. You blew it, Major. Don't blame her for your own bloody-mindedness."

"Touché, Colonel," Hobbs said. "Perhaps I misjudged her. But I'll remind you that we are in a rather bloody-minded business.

Just for my own satisfaction, would you like to tell me why you sat about waiting for Sergeant Lasky to appear?"

"I knew someone would show."

"I hadn't quite counted on you being there so soon, old man," Hobbs said. "We waited a quite decent interval before troubling Miss Adanova. We assumed you'd be even more considerate—being a mate of Colin's."

"That's bull, and you know it," Brede said. "You wanted to know if she'd call the Russians. When she didn't you decided to prod her a bit."

"Well, yes," Hobbs murmured. "One could interpret things that way. As it happened, you turned it into an ambush, Colonel. Old habits are hard to break, aren't they. You see we did some research on you. Omega—in Vietnam, wasn't it?"

"Convey my regrets to Sergeant Lasky. And tell him to take care walking into dark flats."

"You are a dangerous man, Colonel," Hobbs said speculatively.

Lara said, "He was Colin's friend. He had a right to be angry."

Hobbs nodded. "True. Unprofessional, but true. But then you aren't a professional, are you, Colonel?"

Brede remained silent.

"So perhaps now you'll tell me why you are here in England, dashing about committing illegal acts and causing a bloody lot of trouble."

"We've been through this," Brede said.

"No. We have progressed a step since last I saw you. Now, at least, I know the proper question to ask," Hobbs said. He leaned forward and said, "Do try to remember that we are supposed to be on the same side, Colonel."

He put the pipe down on the table carefully and said, "Now tell me. What is Hastings?"

"I don't know," Brede said.

"Please, Colonel. Let's not go back to name, rank, and number. That simply won't do any longer."

"It will have to, Hobbs. Because I don't know the answer to your question."

"You were looking for Hastings when you broke into Harald Langton's house, Colonel."

"Was I?"

"You were. What did you find?"

"Thurston searched me. Ask him."

Hobbs went to the door, opened it, and spoke to someone in the hall. He returned with a folder. He put it on the table and exposed the contents of Brede's pockets, taken by the Special Branch detective outside Cadman's Blue.

"Nothing very remarkable, is there," Brede said.

With a fingertip Hobbs separated Brede's wallet, passport, money, identity folder. "Hardly the stuff of spy novels," he said. He lifted the book of Hemingway journalism. "You always carry something like this to while away the quiet hours, Colonel?"

Brede said, "There haven't been many quiet hours since I reached England."

"Does it belong to Langton?" He leafed through it thoughtfully.

"It did," Brede said.

Hobbs examined the underlining. "Code book?"

"Pony, more likely," Brede said.

"I don't understand." Hobbs put the book back in the folder.

"Handy quotations. Significant phrases. He's a writer, isn't he?"

"And a great deal more," Hobbs said dryly.

The policewoman appeared with a tray of sandwiches and a pot of coffee.

"Serve them out, please, Mrs. D.," Hobbs said.

The girl placed the tray on a sideboard and poured the coffee. It smelled strong and rich. She brought the food and drink to the table.

"Help yourself," Hobbs said. "You must be starved."

Lara picked up a sandwich and took a small bite. Brede helped himself to the coffee. It was dark and bitter, but it warmed him and drove some of the tiredness from his mind.

"Your hands are better?" Hobbs asked solicitously.

"Better," Brede said. The lift from the coffee was swiftly vanishing. The room seemed oddly proportioned. It began to tilt slowly. He put the empty cup down with a crash on the table.

He was having difficulty focusing his eyes on Hobbs.

Hobbs said, in a conversational tone, "What is Hastings, Colonel?"

Brede tried to rise to his feet but couldn't. He fell back into the musty-smelling chair. "You bastard," he said.

"Yes," Hobbs said, regretfully. "Quite so. But then, you see, I *am* a professional."

The last thing Brede heard was Lara, alarmed, calling his name.

20

Even through the distortion of the scrambler circuits, the voice of the London Station Chief was harsh and angry. Davis Carradine held the telephone tightly, as though he feared it would escape his grasp and broadcast Simonini's complaints everywhere in the building.

"I want to be put in the picture, Director," Simonini said. "I feel like a goddamned idiot sitting over here with a time bomb ticking in my lap and not even knowing who owns the bloody thing."

"Where is Colonel Brede now?"

"I think the cousins have him. I've been asking them and they keep putting me off."

Carradine hunched in the large chair behind his desk. The office felt oppressively hot, though the air conditioning was working perfectly and the temperature inside was thirty degrees cooler than it was out in the green Virginia countryside he could see from his window. His forehead was beaded with sweat and he felt clammy.

"Maybe you shouldn't involve yourself, Sim," Carradine said. "Brede is nothing to us."

"I don't see how you can say that, Director. We *are* involved. He came here to investigate Starshine, I'm certain of it. When he called me last night for a car and some money I had to get them for him. There wasn't anything else to do."

"You should not have done that, Sim," Carradine said.

"Shit, I had no choice!" Simonini exploded. "He put a British counterintelligence agent in the hospital, for Chrissake. I thought he was going to run for it. It was a judgment call and I made it. But I made it on damned little information, and that's a fact."

"I'm not faulting you for it," Carradine said. "Brede is Dracott's man and he had no business mixing into Agency operations. You did the best you could, under the circumstances."

"I'm still not getting across to you, Director," Simonini said. "I want to know why in hell there is suddenly some amateur working in my territory without me knowing what he's doing. It *is* Starshine, isn't it?"

Davis Carradine wiped his face with a Kleenex from the drawer of his mahogany desk. This was a bad morning and it seemed that it was going to be an even worse day. Only ten minutes earlier, David Halloran had called to deliver what amounted to a royal summons from Beau Curtis. To fly up to Newport and go sailing, for God's sweet sake. Only it wasn't just a social command, Carradine was sure of it. The Senator was picking up rumors and gossip and what awaited on the *Demelza* was not an afternoon of sun and sea, but an interrogation.

"Yes," he said. "I think it may have something to do with Starshine."

"Why should the National Security Adviser suddenly develop

an interest in that business, Director?" Simonini demanded. "I thought we all agreed we'd take it no further."

Information given to the London Station had been deliberately limited to Daniels' and the fact that he had defected. Even then Simonini had been made aware that Daniels had been in London only after he had made good his escape to the east.

"We did agree," Carradine said. "General Dracott is overstepping his directive."

Simonini said suddenly, "What is Hastings?"

Carradine's face drained of blood. The temperature in the room seemed to have plummeted. "Where did you hear that word?"

"I had a conversation with Alan Hobbs of DI5. He asked me if I could enlighten him. He seems to think it was the designation of some memorandum Starshine brought to England." That last was said with a kind of angry emphasis intended to let the Director know what he thought of the Agency having kept the London Station in the dark about the defector's track.

"Daniels was working on something with that code name when he ran," Carradine said.

"And I had to hear it from the cousins?" Simonini asked bitterly.

"You had no need to know, Sim."

"Bullshit, Director. Excuse me but bullshit again. An Agency defector comes into my territory with a secret memorandum and I have no need to know?"

"Calm down, Sim," Carradine said. The last thing he needed at this moment was trouble, perhaps even a resignation, from the London Station Chief. His mind raced, searching for some method of papering this over, at least until he had spoken with Curtis and knew how much support he could expect. "I am going to send someone to London to brief you."

"It is a bit late, isn't it?"

"No, it is not. I'm going to send Dwight. He can tell you exactly what the situation is."

"Lamb? The DOO?"

"Yes."

Simonini fell silent. Carradine realized that he was thinking that the thing had to be very important if the Director was willing to send the Director of Operations on such a mission. Well, Carradine thought, it was. Dwight would have to tell Simonini that Hastings was a contingency plan that could embarrass the United States and that Simonini would have to cooperate in every way to keep it from the British. The thought of old Hugh Evans reading a summary of the Hastings memorandum was enough to make Davis Carradine sick to his stomach. The explosion would be heard from Whitehall to Pennsylvania Avenue. No matter how slighted Simonini might feel at having been left out of the original Starshine investigation, he was a professional and he would listen to another professional, such as Dwight Lamb.

"Dwight will be on the next flight out," Carradine said.

"What do I try to do about this Colonel Brede?"

"Dwight will instruct you personally," Carradine said.

There was a long pause on the scrambler line. Then Simonini said, "Director."

"What is it, Sim?"

"Did the Agency have anything to do with the reception Brede got at Heathrow?"

Carradine was genuinely shocked. "Absolutely not," he said. Simonini was one of the few old-timers left in the Agency. Like Dwight. It was frightening to get so clear an indication of the way their minds worked. He said again, "No. The Agency was not involved in any way." But knowing Dwight Lamb, he shivered. Could he be so certain? For the first time since taking the post of CIA Director, Davis Carradine the careerist had a sharp, clear insight into what espionage and intelligence work could really demand of a person. He resolved to be rid of this job as quickly as he could possibly manage it.

21

At twenty minutes past four in the afternoon the young man who had been admiring the Queen Victoria Monument turned and picked his way through the crowd of sightseers and into the shade of the trees that grew by the side of the lake in Saint James's Park. He was dark, thin almost to the point of emaciation, and dressed casually in khaki trousers and an open-necked shirt.

He had been taking pictures of the park, the monument, and Buckingham Palace with an instant camera. Now he slipped it into the pocket of his shirt and leaned against the trunk of a tree while he smoked a cigarette.

The tourists flowed across the Mall between Saint James's and Green parks. Several tour buses had paused nose to tail along Birdcage Walk. The thin man watched them disgorge a load of Japanese tourists. They trotted in a group across the roundabout to join the other vacationers who stood along the iron fence of the palace aiming their cameras at the bear-skinned Guardsmen in the striped shelters that stood at intervals along the façade of the building.

Richard Iron glanced at his wristwatch, a complicated steel chronometer that seemed too large for his slender, brown wrist. He walked slowly across the grass, threading his way between idlers lying in the late sun to a refreshment stand where he bought a cola drink and stood sipping the cool, sweet stuff as children ran by, shouting and laughing.

He finished his drink and dropped the plastic cup into a trash bin by the side of the stand and looked again at his watch. It was now twenty minutes to five.

He moved easily across Birdcage Walk and stood for some time at the fence enclosing the parade ground of Wellington Barracks where soldiers were drilling. He watched them with professional interest. A pair of navy-blue-uniformed police officers strolled up the street through the dappled sunlight.

At ten minutes to five Iron walked slowly toward the round-about and the intersection where Birdcage Walk joined Buckingham Gate. He took a pair of dark glasses from his shirt pocket and put them on, peering with apparent interest at the royal standard flying from the flagstaff on the roof of Buckingham Palace.

A group of East Germans wearing *Spartakiade* badges rushed by him, cameras ready. Their tour leader was issuing orders in a peremptory fashion and his instructions were being obeyed with military precision. Iron smiled to himself as the platoon jogged past.

He checked his watch again. Four fifty-five. He turned to look down Birdcage Walk. From the direction of Whitehall a black Austin Princess had appeared. It approached at a sedate pace. Iron measured the distance between the place where he stood beside a barrel-shaped pillar box and the left-hand gate into the palace forecourt. He judged it to be 120 meters.

He noted that cars were discouraged from parking along Birdcage Walk, though earlier a red Post Office van had stood for several minutes while the driver transferred the mail from the pillar box into the rear of the vehicle.

He walked up to the head of the street and waited. The black Princess drew nearer. It was driven by a chauffeur wearing a peaked cap. A Special Branch plainsclothesman sat in the left-hand seat. Iron observed this with the interest he had displayed in watching Vietcong on the jungle trails of Southeast Asia.

He looked again at his watch. It was now four fifty-eight. When the Princess passed him he started the stopwatch. He only glanced at the slope-shouldered, gray-haired man in the rear seat.

He timed the interval between the moment the Austin passed the post box and it stopped at the gate to the palace forecourt. When the car pulled up, he started the interval timing function of his watch afresh.

He watched the policeman on duty check the Special Branch detective's warrant card and then briefly glance into the rear seat. When the policeman saluted and the car started to move again, Iron stopped his watch. The limousine disappeared from his field of vision into an archway across the forecourt. Iron's hands felt damp and sweaty. It had taken the Prime Minister twenty-one seconds to travel from the pillar box to the forecourt gate. The car had paused there for precisely seventeen seconds.

Time enough, Iron thought.

He turned and began to walk back across the roundabout. At the head of Birdcage Walk he encountered the patrolling policemen.

"Pardon me," he said. "That was the Prime Minister, wasn't it?" He spoke English like an American. His years in the U.S. Army had forever destroyed the Welsh inflections in his speech.

"That's correct, sir," the taller policeman said cheerfully. "That's our Old Hugh. Back from Chequers."

"On his way to see the Queen?" Iron spoke with a tourist's ingenuousness.

"That's right, sir. Every Thursday, when she's in London."

"That's really great," Iron said in the same voice. "And I didn't even get a picture of him. I would have if I'd known it was the Prime Minister."

"Ah, well, sir," the policeman said. "Perhaps next week."

"He does it every week?"

"Regular as clockwork, sir. Every Thursday at five. It is a tradition, sir. We set great store in tradition, sir."

"That's wonderful," Iron said. "I'll sure try to be here next week. And be ready."

"Do that, sir."

The two policemen smiled pleasantly, and then strolled on through the late afternoon heat.

Richard Iron watched them with eyes cold and dead as ball bearings.

22

Harald Langton had spent a sleepless night and a harrowing day. He had driven from Rye to Woolwich, a place where no one who knew him would ever expect to find him. He had spent most of the day in a hotel room of revolting dinginess, but he had no intention of venturing anywhere near his Belgravia flat.

By three o'clock he had completed the work on his computer program and he waited nervously until nearly four before retrieving his Mercedes and driving to Kew.

This, he knew, was the point of danger. If the CIA or DI5, either or both, was after him, there was an outside chance they would know that over the last few weeks he had been working with the computer terminal in the basement of the Public Record Office. But it was a risk he must take: the computer was essential.

Oddly, he took no satisfaction from the fact that he was performing a genuinely brave act now. He was too frightened to think about it in such terms. His integrity as a radical journalist sustained him, but only just. When he finished his work at Kew, he was sweating with fear.

At five twenty he tapped out the "finished with computer" code on the terminal and gathered the Hastings documents into their folder. He walked quickly to the wastepaper chute and fed the pages one by one into the opening. Wastepaper from the bins was collected each day and pulped each week for recycling. When he had dropped the containing folder into the waste system he felt as though a weight had been lifted from his chest.

At five twenty-five he walked up the stairs past the public restaurant and the registration desk. It was now after hours and the space behind the desk was empty.

The attendant at the door of the main entrance watched with time-serving disinterest as he hurried out of the building and into the carpark.

The late afternoon was still heavy with the heat of the day. The smell of the river was thick in the air. He got into his car and drove out of the carpark, across Kew Bridge, and through the city traffic to the northwest.

He was not firmly decided about what to do now. The idea of leaving the country for a time occurred to him but he discarded the notion. He was convinced that he was well known and would be recognized. Nor did he want to risk going through a passport control point.

Instinctively he was drawn north, toward Oxford, where he had spent so many safe and self-important years. It was there, he decided, that he would hide and rest and try to think what he must do.

Harald Langton was not a decisive man. In all of his life his only straightforward commitment had been to the ultimate triumph of world revolution. Yet now that he was in possession of information that he was certain would advance that cause, he was confused and uncertain about how he should go about exploiting it.

His nerves were raw and jangled. He saw a CIA killer in every passing car, a cold-eyed British plainclothesman in every shadow. He hated this feeling of exposure and vulnerability.

Time, he thought. That's what was needed. Time to think, to organize. And if it came to the final, terrible confrontation with his imperialist enemies, he needed the support of people who both shared his ideological devotion and had the power to protect him.

Thinking this, he drove north through the summer-sere countryside of the Chiltern Hills.

23

At the presidential retreat at Camp David in the Catoctin Mountains the President of the United States was also having a difficult day. He had spent the morning in discussions with Orrin Blaine, the Secretary of State, and Chalmers Dodd, the Secretary of Defense: men with such diametrically opposed views on almost every subject that agreement was rare and cooperation rarer.

Dodd, a man brought into the administration from industry, had been berating Secretary Blaine about the most recent decisions made by Elias Traynor, the SALT negotiator, relating to American naval bases in Israel and the Indian Ocean. Traynor, a man so devoted to his task of arranging a third SALT treaty that he was willing to bargain away anything his Russian counterparts thought "provocative," was Orrin Blaine's man in every way. And Blaine considered it his manifest destiny to be the Secretary of State who achieved final and complete Soviet-American amity.

John Scott Demarest, who was too astute a politician to entertain any such sanguine ideas about Soviet ambitions, had no intention whatever of abandoning the American bases at Elath and Diego Garcia. He was only too aware of the imbalance of forces that existed between the United States and NATO and the Soviet Union and its Warsaw Pact satellites. But he was willing to allow Traynor to hold out the hope of such American fecklessness in order to freeze the historically aggressive behavior of the USSR in the crisis-ridden region.

It was to be expected that Dodd, whose responsibility it was to maintain American military power in the face of adversaries who had achieved parity in the 1970s and were now, so he believed, well on the way to conventional and nuclear superiority, would react like a spurred horse to the suggestions of Blaine and Traynor. It was equally to be expected that the Secretary of State, an academic to his fingertips, would regard the Secretary of Defense as an unregenerate hawk, Cold Warrior, and servant of the "military-industrial complex."

The result, for President Demarest, had been a trying and unpleasant morning.

His mood had not been improved by the intelligence précis presented to him at lunch. The CIA reported that satellite recon confirmed another bad year for crops in the Soviet Union. This meant that the Russians, in order to compensate for their need to buy grain from the West, would be even more provocative than usual elsewhere. The Agency also reported that there were Muslim uprisings being put down with great severity in Kazakhstan and portions of the Turkomen Soviet Republic. Internal pressures in the USSR were always dangerous for the West, since they caused the people around President Nikitin to become adventurous elsewhere in the world, looking for successes with which to impress the Socialist-bloc nations.

A special intelligence study done by the embassy staff in London predicted that the government of Prime Minister Evans was contemplating a further reduction in the manpower of the British Rhine Army, and the Ambassador had added a personal note warning that his private talks with the Foreign Secretary had led him to believe that Evans was preparing to make a number of very tough demands as the price of renewing leases on the bases being used by the United States Air Force in Great Britain.

By one in the afternoon, the President had been brought to the point of snapping at Della and the children, who had asked for nothing more than his company on their daily afternoon walk along the hiking trails that wound through the grounds of Camp David.

Now he sat on the veranda of the presidential lodge, smoking his pipe guiltily (he had promised Della that he would stop smoking) and watching the helicopter carrying Henry Dracott approach

from the direction of Washington. His affection and admiration
for the general was strong and genuine, but he heartily wished that
Henry had not seen fit to ask for a special appointment this afternoon. John Demarest and his family had come to Camp David for
a rest. It appeared that there simply was no rest for a President of
the United States.

The Marine Corps helicopter slowed and descended behind the
trees with a flurry of whacking sounds. Within minutes, a car
appeared and pulled into the circular drive of the presidential
quarters. Demarest watched while Henry Dracott and his deputy,
Paul Bruckner, walked up the log-lined path to the lodge veranda.

The President, a large man dressed in denim trousers and an old
bush jacket, stood to greet his National Security Adviser.
"Henry," he said. "And Paul. Nice to see you."

Bruckner was carrying his ever-present attaché case. People said
it was part of his arm. The seersucker suit he wore was wrinkled
and none too clean. His bushy hair needed combing.

By contrast, General Dracott's linen jacket and trousers were
pressed and spotless, managing to look more like a uniform than
what Dracott called, in archaic fashion, "an ice-cream suit."

"It is good of you to see us, Mr. President," Dracott said.

"Sit, sit, gentlemen," the President said. His politician's affa-
bility was so ingrained, after twenty five years of public life, that it
had become his normal demeanor. "Can I offer you something to
drink? Take the edge off the heat?"

Henry Dracott said, "Thank you, no, Mr. President."

"I can use something," Paul Bruckner said. "I feel as though I'm
going to melt into a puddle of sweat."

The President rang a call bell in the veranda post and when the
steward appeared he ordered Moscow mules for himself and Paul
Bruckner.

The three men arranged themselves around a redwood table
and the President said, "All right, Henry."

Dracott immediately began with a statement of his decision to send Colonel Brede to London. He described Colin Farr's telephone call without comment. "It was apparent to me, sir," he said finally, "that Captain Farr had learned something about our defector and wished to share that information with us. He obviously did *not* desire to deal with the Central Intelligence Agency. And so I dispatched Colonel Brede to London to meet with him."

The President's face showed his disapproval. "You didn't feel it necessary to coordinate your activities with Davis at CIA?"

Bruckner stirred and shuffled his feet, wanting to answer that question instead of letting the general take full responsibility.

"Frankly, Mr. President," Henry Dracott said, "the Agency's handling of the Daniels defection did not make me confident about disclosing Captain Farr's conversation to them. In any case, he made it quite clear he would talk to no one but Brede."

"If you'll forgive me, Mr. President," Paul Bruckner interjected. "Let me say what the general is too goddamned polite to say. The Agency buried the Daniels defection. There is no reason to assume that they would not do the same to any information that turns up now and is inconvenient."

The President's eyes flashed with dangerous anger. John Demarest was loyal to the men in his administration, to all of them. It was a loyalty that had caused him political pain on numerous occasions. "Are you saying Davis has swept the Daniels affair under the rug?"

"I am saying plainer than that, Mr. President. Davis Carradine inherited a rotten apple in Daniels, but when Daniels decided to go east Davis covered it up for purely political reasons."

"That is a very serious accusation," the President said. "Do you back Paul's statement, Henry?"

"Yes," Dracott said. "Without equivocation." He paused while the steward brought the drinks and put them, frosty and wet with condensation, on the table in front of the President and Paul

Bruckner. Bruckner drank his thirstily. He had an almost childish relish for sweet things and a seemingly total immunity to the effects of 150 proof vodka.

Henry Dracott continued, "Unfortunately, we've been remiss ourselves. Somehow, the information about the meeting between Farr and Robert Brede leaked. I think that without question the leak was in my office. . . ."

"That is being taken care of, Mr. President," Paul Bruckner said promptly. "By me. Personally."

Dracott said, "I have to accept at least partial responsibility for what happened at Heathrow."

"You think the Soviets engineered that bomb?" the President asked. The idea was far from strange to him. He was a realist where KGB activities were concerned.

"Not directly, Mr. President," Paul Bruckner said. "But they have a working arrangement with the Caledonian People's Liberation Army now just as they've had for years with the Provisional IRA. For some reason it was important to them that whatever information Farr had not be passed on to one of our people."

"What could he have had that was worth a bomb attack?" John Demarest asked.

Dracott said, "Mr. President. Have you ever heard of a contingency plan code-named Hastings?"

The President said, "Never. Should I have?"

"Well, damn it," Bruckner exploded, "*someone* should have, Mr. President! Colin Farr specifically mentioned Hastings in connection with the investigation he had been conducting concerning our defecting Mr. Daniels. We asked Dwight Lamb to run the name through the CIA and DOD computers. He came up empty."

The President, frowning, regarded Henry Dracott. "Cover-up in the Agency, General?"

"Yes. I think so, Mr. President," Dracott said.

"Damn it, Henry, I thought we were all through with that sort of thing."

"Hastings existed, Mr. President. Whatever it was, it existed and probably still does. I could almost guarantee that the Soviets know what it was—or is. And someone here must know. Davis, perhaps. Dwight Lamb, almost certainly."

"How could any plan or operation be limited to so few, Henry?"

"It is the old 'need to know' gambit, Mr. President," Paul Bruckner said. "If you use that one just right, you can limit information to the point where no one but the originator hears anything about it. It makes no real difference how high a security clearance you have, you can still be kept in the dark on any given project. Why, back in 1941, after we had cracked the Japanese codes, even President Roosevelt was kept off the distribution list for secret intercepts dealing with Japanese fleet movements. We were not at war, and so someone reasoned that the President of the United States had no 'need to know.' Insane, but there it is."

John Demarest's frown deepened. "I think maybe I ought to have a talk with Davis Carradine."

The President's naval aide, Captain John Steinhart, appeared at a run from the direction of the message center. He stood at the bottom of the veranda stairs and saluted. "Mr. President, there is a priority-one call for you. Shall I have it patched through to the house?"

"Won't it keep, Jay?" Demarest asked impatiently. "I'm busy here."

"No, sir."

The President got to his feet. "All right, then. Put it through." To Dracott he said, "Stand by, Henry. Let me see about this and then we'll carry on with this business."

Dracott and Bruckner stood. The President walked into the house.

Steinhart said to General Dracott, "Have you any word on Colonel Brede?"

"He was slightly injured in the blast, Captain. That's all we know."

"Bloody brave heroes," Steinhart said bitterly. "It really takes guts to plant bombs, doesn't it."

"They murdered a good soldier," Dracott said heavily.

"Are the Limeys doing anything about it?"

"One presumes they are trying, Captain. It isn't a simple matter."

"No, sir," the captain said. He nodded to the general and returned down the path toward his duty station at the house where the communications gear was kept.

Dracott and Bruckner sat down again and waited for the President to return.

John Demarest appeared out of the house, his face flushed and angry. He said, "Goddamn it, General, did you set this thing up?"

"Sir?"

"I have just spent fifteen minutes on the telephone with the Prime Minister in London. Do you have any idea what he asked me?" The President's voice was still thick with anger.

"Should I, Mr. President?"

"Mr. Evans wanted to know if I could enlighten him on an American operational contingency plan code-named Hastings."

Paul Bruckner's breath exploded in a surprised snort. "Shit. Pardon me, Mr. President."

"Good God," General Dracott said softly.

"Well, gentlemen?" the President demanded.

"In answer to your question, John," Henry Dracott said evenly. "The answer is no, we did not set this up. You have my word of honor on that."

The President sat down abruptly. "I believe you, Henry. I was just knocked off my feet for a bit." He looked first at Dracott and then at Bruckner. "I had to tell the Prime Minister that I was not *immediately* current on any such plan, but that I would certainly investigate and get back to him." He compressed his lips and then said, "Do you have any idea what it cost me to admit to that old bastard I didn't know what was going on in my own intelligence community? He thinks Americans are dangerous to begin with. Now he is going to think that we don't have any control at all over our war planners." He fixed his visitors with a steely glare. "And goddamn it, he'll be right."

Bruckner said to Dracott, "Should I call General Sanday-Maclean and try to pick his brains?"

"No," Henry Dracott said. "Definitely not. The request undoubtedly originated with Sanday-Maclean." He turned to the President. "I think we should get Davis Carradine up here on the double, Mr. President. I think," he added with heavy irony, "that we all have a 'need to know' now."

Bruckner murmured, "Davis is away, Henry."

The President snapped, "Away? Where, for Chrissake?"

"I tried to reach him before we came up, Mr. President. I was told that he flew up to Newport early this afternoon on Senator Curtis's personal plane. I believe he was going sailing with the Senator."

"*Sailing?*" The President's face had gone livid.

"I'm sorry, Mr. President. That's the story I got from his deputy at McLean," Bruckner said with an ill-concealed enjoyment. Paul Bruckner considered Davis Carradine the worst sort of empire-building opportunist and a personal toady to young Beau Curtis.

"By *God!*" Demarest said furiously. He stood and shouted into the house for one of the stewards to call the naval aide.

Alerted by the President's tone, the steward transmitted the urgency of the situation to Captain Steinhart, who appeared once again at a run from the communications room. "Mr. President?"

"Jay, what's the closest Coast Guard helicopter station to Newport, Rhode Island?"

"Why, Block Island Coast Guard, I think, sir," Captain Steinhart said.

The President wheeled on Bruckner and Dracott. "What's the name of that goddamned barge of Curtis's?"

"The *Demelza*, sir," Paul Bruckner said.

The President turned back to the naval aide. "Send a message to Block Island Coast Guard to find that boat, Jay. I want Director Carradine taken off and flown here. Right *now*. If he gives the Coast Guardsmen any trouble, they have my permission to bring him here under arrest."

Captain Steinhart's handsome face had difficulty masking his surprise, but he said, "Yes, Mr. President," and ran off down the path to the message center.

"Now," John Scott Demarest said, "let's see if the President of the United States has a *need to know* about Hastings."

24

It was after 2200 hours and no time to come snooping, Captain George Percival thought. He sat in a stuffy temporary building at the new Royal Ordnance Depot at Shrewton, on Salisbury Plain. It was late, and the CID man across the desk made him nervous, as most civilians did.

Percival was a stout young man whose round face was made almost ludicrous by the immense and bristling Guards moustache that seemed to explode in the space between his girlish mouth and his button-shaped nose. He rapped nervously on the littered desk with his swagger stick to emphasize his disclaimer.

"This is an unfinished installation, Inspector," he said. "Our facilities for providing proper security are very limited. On the night of the incident I had fewer than twenty men here."

The CID man, a middle-aged Yorkshireman with twenty-five years of police work behind him, said with weary tolerance, "I am not here to assess blame, Captain. That will be handled by the Army in proper fashion, I am sure. I simply want to go over the list of missing items once again."

"I sent a complete inventory to Battalion in my report, Inspector," Captain Percival said.

"Can we go over it again, sir? If you please?"

"Well, of course. Certainly. If you wish." Captain Percival hoped that his nervousness came across as the brusqueness of a soldier, but he suspected that the Inspector was not deceived. The theft from the depot had well and truly put the cat among the pigeons. Captain Percival considered his next efficiency report with dismay. The colonel had already torn a strip off him and now, it seemed, the CID was going to keep everyone in an uproar.

He opened a file folder and began to read a list of the stolen items. "Six FN nine-millimeter automatic rifles, twelve nine-millimeter Browning automatic pistols, one case of American-made M1 chain demolition blocks—"

"Describe those, please," the CID man said, notebook in hand.

"The individual chain demo block is two inches square by eleven inches long and weighs two and a half pounds. It has a tetryl booster pellet cast into the end of the block, and eight blocks, about seven inches apart, are cast onto a single line of detonating cord which passes through them. Each chain is packed in an O.D. cloth bag with a carrying strap. The whole package weighs about twenty-two pounds. Two bags like that—sixteen blocks of Tetrytol—are packed in a wooden case. The blocks can be separated, of course, and used individually."

"Splendid," the CID man said dryly. "What else was taken?"

"A case of nine-millimeter ammunition. And the TOW."

"TOW?"

"Target on Wire, Inspector," Captain Percival said, fingering his swagger stick. "An antitank weapon designed to be used by infantry."

"Describe it, please, Captain," the CID man said. "Your report to your colonel isn't specific."

"The colonel knows what a TOW is, Inspector. It wasn't necessary to explain it to *him.*"

"Well, it is to me, Captain. If you would, please?"

"Well, I will keep it simple. . . ."

"Yes," the CID man said ironically, "in civilian language."

Percival's moustache quivered and he knocked the swagger stick off the desk. It hit the wooden floor with a clatter and rolled out of reach. "A TOW is rather like the old-fashioned bazookas which you probably remember, Inspector." The CID man acknowledged the thrust with a lifted eyebrow. "It consists of a shoulder-held tube the way the bazooka or German Panzerfaust did, but there is an optical sight and a reel of very fine, very strong wire attaching the launcher to the missile. That's a shaped-charge, rocket-propelled projectile with an armor-piercing nose cone, by the way. The beauty of the TOW is that the missile is guided by signals from the sight. All one needs to do is keep the sight reticule centered on the target after firing, and the missile homes, trailing the wire behind. There are more sophisticated shoulder-held weapons now to use against tanks—laser-guided, heat-seekers, that sort of thing, of course. But the beauty of the TOW is that it is compact, light, and can be fired by one man."

"Lovely," the CID man said. "And one of these things was taken?"

Captain Percival, his professional enthusiasm fading, nodded wordlessly.

"That's the lot?" the CID man asked.

"Yes, that's all of it," Percival said. "Was it the IRA, Inspector?"

"We believe so, Captain." He stood and put his notebook into his pocket. "I'll get this description of the items off to CID-Ulster. That's where the stolen goods will likely surface."

The captain stood and straightened his uniform over a rather too-prominent stomach. "Is there any chance any of it will be recovered, Inspector?"

"It will turn up, Captain," the CID man said grimly. "And we'll get it all back. One way or another. You can be sure of that."

25

Heeling gently to a light summer breeze, the fifty-seven-foot Sparkman and Stephens–designed sloop *Demelza* moved through the gentle swells of Block Island Sound.

Kirk Caldwell, one of the two professional crewmen aboard, stood at the wheel in the helmsman's cockpit. Dudley Frazier, the second crew and foredeck boss, straddled the coaming, trimming the drifter sheet. In the spacious cockpit, Janice Carradine and Monique Curtis reclined in the warm sun, drinks in hand. On the foredeck, leaning against the base of the spar, David Halloran looked longingly across the glittering sunpath at the low-lying Rhode Island coastline and nursed a worsening case of seasickness. He knew that he should be below, in the salon with the Senator and Davis Carradine, but he could not face the horror of descending into the teak and mahogany cavern belowdecks with all its mingled smells of food, strange woods, fiber glass, and bilge. He raised his eyes to the curving acres of white and red nylon over his head. The masthead made slow corkscrewing movements against the pallid sky. Halloran closed his eyes and tried to swallow the bilious taste in his throat. Through an open hatchway in the fore-deck he could hear the murmuring of voices. The Senator sounded angry. Davis Carradine, Halloran thought, probably feels worse at this moment than I do. He leaned his salt-laden, uncombed red head against a halyard winch and wished he were on shore.

"I did what seemed best, Beau," the Director of the CIA said anxiously. "After all, this was a situation I inherited."

Senator Curtis's heavy, handsome face was dark with anger. "You should have talked it over with me before letting Lamb go into his act. Don't you realize there are six other committees of the Congress besides mine looking over your shoulder? How in hell did you think you were going to get away with it?"

"I didn't want to shove a stick into the hornets' nest in my first year as Director, Beau. For Chrissake, try to see it from my point of view. Lamb as much as promised me that all the old spooks would cooperate with me if I let him handle Starshine in-house. There was no need to go to the committee and spill my guts about it. How would it make us look?"

The Senator's eyes flashed dangerously. "Not *us*, Davis. You. You are the Director of Central Intelligence."

Carradine's stomach griped painfully. He regarded his surroundings and thought bitterly that the setting was appropriate for a man who was about to be made to walk the plank.

"I was thinking of you, too, Beau," he said artfully.

"I wonder if you were thinking at all," Curtis said. "I went to bat for you at the confirmation hearings, Davis. But let me make this perfectly clear. If this thing gets any farther out of hand, I'm going to shop you. I'm telling you straight out. I'll get you in front of the Oversight Committee and I'll skin you. I'm not getting splattered with shit for you or anyone." He removed his sailing hat and wiped the sweat from his broad, tanned brow. "So let's just see what can be done to salvage this situation." He regarded his protégé coldly. "You sent Dwight Lamb off to London. That was probably smarter than you realize."

Carradine bridled. "I knew exactly what I was doing, Beau. Dwight is the only one at McLean who has actually seen the Hastings memorandum whole. He is the man who purged the data banks."

The Senator stretched his legs across the companionway, bracing his feet easily on the opposite settee against the gentle heel of the boat. He said sourly, "What I don't understand is how anybody in the Agency could be allowed to spend his time dreaming up a plan like Hastings in the first place. What the hell do you people do over in McLean? Invent games?"

"Daniels was a deep-cover agent, Beau. He was in place long before I took over."

"That doesn't answer my question," Curtis said.

Carradine said, "Lord, Beau, there are contingency plans for *everything*. War against Libya, revolution in India, invasion of Canada, Mexico—you name it—everything and anything."

"But a military occupation of *England?*"

"Why the hell not? Since the Tories got the boot, the government has been lurching to the Left. Old Hugh Evans hates our guts. He's been hinting he wants us out of there. So why not? Is it really so improbable?"

"I can't imagine an American administration contemplating such a thing, Davis. It's absurd."

"There are plenty of things that are absurd, Beau," Carradine said with some heat. "It's absurd that for a quarter of a century we have tolerated an *actively* hostile Communist dictatorship ninety miles off the coast of Florida. It's absurd that we've sat on our cans and let the Soviets just about encircle the oil supply for all of Western Europe and half the United States. It's absurd that under an act of Congress a KGB *rezident* in Washington can write to the Agency and demand a copy of our budget. Jesus, Beau, don't use absurd as a defense against the ridiculous. Nothing is all that absurd anymore."

Curtis stared at Carradine and said, "Maybe absurd was the wrong word to use. Maybe I should have said it was criminal that a deep-cover agent was allowed to compose something like the Hastings memorandum while holding down a sensitive post inside our intelligence agency, and *then* was allowed to skip off to England with it. Sweet Mary Mother of God, don't you people know an agent provocateur when you work with one for ten years? Isn't that how long Daniels was a CIA spook?"

"Yes," Carradine said miserably.

"Can you think of any way to stop the Limeys from finding out about the games you've been playing?"

"I don't see any way," Carradine said resignedly.

"Marvelous. Simply marvelous," the Senator said. His expression grew more pinched and suspicious. "What else, Davis?"

"Else? I don't read you, Beau."

"What else was *in* the plan? I mean besides picking beaches for the Marines and whorehouses for the occupation troops."

"I told you. I never actually saw the memorandum. Dwight thought it best."

"Dwight did, did he? And so where are we? Over Dwight Lamb's barrel?"

"Dwight Lamb is totally loyal, Beau."

"To you? To me?"

"To the Agency. He'll do anything to protect it from another ten years of savaging by the Congress and the media."

"And I'm to be satisfied with that?"

Davis Carradine said, "For the time being. Yes."

"And what about that DIA brass hat Henry Dracott sent over to snoop?"

"There's no way he can make trouble. I don't think Henry Dracott would want Hastings to become public knowledge. Not if he knew all the implications."

Curtis's eyes narrowed. "What does that mean, exactly?"

"Dwight can handle Colonel Brede, Senator," Carradine said.

"You aren't being clear, Davis. Put that in plain English."

For the first time Davis Carradine's tone held a glint of hidden steel. "Dwight Lamb and Simonini are old hands. If Brede turns into a real problem, they will know what to do."

Senator Curtis's fleshy face went slack with astonishment. "What the hell has come over you, Davis? Do I understand you correctly?"

"I think you do, Senator," Carradine said.

"My God. Suddenly you frighten me a little. You begin to sound like one of *them*."

Carradine spoke harshly—more harshly and more honestly than he had ever spoken to Beau Curtis before, "I want to be a senator, Beau. I want that more than I have ever wanted anything. I don't intend to be screwed out of that by something that isn't my fault. If I have to lie, I'll do it. If I have to commit perjury, I'll do that, too. And if I have to order Colonel Brede terminated to keep a lid on this Hastings business, well, I won't back away from it. Is that plain enough for you, Senator?"

For a long while there was no sound in the boat but the murmur of feminine voices from the cockpit, the creak of the running rigging, and the rippling of the water along the hull.

Senator Curtis stared at Davis Carradine with new respect that was well mingled with an even newer fear. The man had become more than a liability. He had become a threat.

Young Dudley Frazier's face, sunburned and topped by a tangled mop of streaked blond hair, appeared in the hatchway. "Coast Guard helicopter coming, skipper," he said. "They're hailing us to heave to."

26

The clock in the Ivan Bell Tower was striking midnight when Marshal Leonid Kunavin entered the office of the President in the Kremlin. The room was huge, with tall windows overlooking the inner courtyard and the new buildings housing the vast administrative staff that served the Politburo. There were lights still burning in those buildings and a heavy concentration of soldiers patrolled the yard below the President's windows.

Pavel Grigorevich Nikitin sat behind his huge desk at the end of the long, empty room. Far above his head, painted cherubim floated on painted clouds. The figures of the old tsarist decorations were faded and almost invisible in the shadowy heights of the room. It was a chamber meant to impress visitors with the size and space of the country that was ruled from there. Marshal Kunavin had chosen the President's office for the confrontation, rather than one of the smaller and more comfortable rooms on the floor above, for good reason. The men Nikitin was about to interrogate were among the most powerful in the regime. It was imperative that a sense of hierarchy be instilled in them. To that end, Kunavin had instructed the soldiers who had collected Koniev and Galitzin to present themselves heavily armed and wearing full uniform, including the medals all Soviet citizens revered. It would always be difficult for a Russian, no matter how highly placed, to attempt to subvert soldiers wearing the badges of Heroes of the Soviet Union.

Kunavin marched across the echoing floor and stood before President Nikitin's desk. "They are here, Pavel Grigorevich," he said.

Nikitin's round face looked hard as a moonstone. "Send in Koniev and Galitzin. Let the others wait."

General Galitzin had been arrested in the middle of a Guards

Regiment officers' mess party at which great quantities of vodka had been drunk. But Galitzin was quite sober now. To be arrested by men of the President's honor guard and driven across Moscow under the guns of soldiers young enough to be his grandchildren had been a humiliating experience. It had been meant to be and Galitzin knew it. He also knew that the next ten minutes would determine whether Piotr Ivanovich Galitzin would continue to live as a general of the Red Army and Chief of the Military Intelligence Directorate of the General Staff, or be dead with a pistol bullet in his neck in the cellars of Lefortovo Prison. His heavy face showed the mingled anger and anxiety he was feeling. His hands, held rigidly at his side as military courtesy demanded, were trembling.

Koniev, whose position as head of the KGB was even more politically sensitive than that of the Commander of the GRU, felt his danger acutely. Traditionally, the man who headed the secret police *apparat* was both the most powerful and the most vulnerable man in the regime. Russian history was strewn with the corpses of the men who operated the state police. They were buried under a mountain of victims, but they were just as dead. From the time of Feliks Dzerzhinski, who founded the Cheka and was killed by it, to his own time, Yuri Koniev understood how two-edged was the instrument that was now the KGB.

He had reached a critical moment. There had been excesses, as there always were, but it had not been his intention to challenge Nikitin for the leadership of the state. That challenge, if it was ever to be made, lay in the future. What was absolutely vital at this moment was to convince Nikitin that no action taken by any member of the KBG's high-level policy planning committee was intended to do other than advance the cause of world revolution as mandated by Nikitin and the Council of Ministers.

Details were unimportant. Intentions, loyalty, and devotion to the state were all. Koniev prepared himself to answer any charges on this single basis: what served the state served Comrade Nikitin, and anyone who suggested otherwise was either a fool or a traitor, or both. Koniev was resolved not to defend himself, but to attack, attack, attack.

He turned a cold and unfriendly eye on Kunavin. Perhaps it had been a mistake not to include Kunavin in the planning stages of the Hastings operation. But Kunavin was a stodgy soldier. He did not really believe in any modern technology that did not result in bigger bombs or longer-range cannon. Colonel Santorin, presently sweating with fear in the President's outer office, was a new sort of soldier, one that Marshal Kunavin neither loved nor appreciated. Kunavin, therefore, must be neutralized. He must not be allowed to serve as prosecutor at this midnight trial. For that was what was taking place here. Koniev, Galitzin, and quite probably Santorin and young Colonel Kadogan were on trial for their lives.

If Koniev had had any pity in his makeup, he would have felt sorry for the two colonels. They were not policy makers. They had made no decisions. Santorin had simply done his job, showing the way to Soviet hegemony in Europe a generation ahead of schedule. Kadogan had only done what his training had made possible and his orders had made imperative. He had recruited a suitable instrument and had manipulated another, less perfect, but still essential to the Hastings plan.

He did not feel sorry for the two younger men. But he did intend that they should be saved tonight, if it was possible to save anything at all. So much depended on what Pavel Grigorevich Nikitin chose to believe.

Koniev stood beside General Galitzin and waited. There were no chairs placed for them. Kunavin stood by the President's chair, his hard-hewn face a mask of cold suspicion.

Nikitin said, "Look at you. Look at the two clowns who thought they could subvert the state."

Koniev thought, It is going to be like that, then. Hard and accusatory, using irony to make us seem the fools, and treacherous as well.

"You first, General Galitzin," Nikitin shouted suddenly. "Explain to me how it is that you approved an operation that endangers almost thirty years of sound, careful planning?"

Galitzin flushed at the tone. Full generals of the Red Army were not accustomed to being spoken to as though they were schoolboys. He said, "Please forgive me, Comrade President. But it is my judgment"—he glared at Kunavin—"my *military* judgment—that the Hastings plan offers us a chance to speed up the timetable of our advance to the west by years—if not by decades. It was worth doing. It *is* worth doing. It can save time and possibly millions of Soviet lives."

"That is your military judgment, is it?" Nikitin said angrily. "Does it interest you to know that your superior, the Minister of Defense, does not agree?" He leaned forward in his great-backed chair that made Galitzin think of a throne. "Not only does he not agree, Galitzin, he is of the opinion that a premature attempt on the North Atlantic Treaty alliance could be disastrous. Did you bother to *ask* him before creating this *stew*?" He took a video tape cassette from the desk top and threw it at Galitzin's chest. It struck him and clattered to the bare hardwood floor. Galitzin's cheeks grew dark with resentment. It lessened his fear.

"The Minister of Defense is too conservative," Galitzin said.

Kunavin glared back at him. Things were being said tonight, the Commander of GRU thought, that would never be forgotten. That will only matter, he warned himself, if we survive this inquisition.

Nikitin spoke in that master-to-schoolboy voice again. Galitzin smoldered. "Pay attention to me, General," Nikitin said. "You were once an officer cadet at Frunze, were you not? Then try to remember what you were taught. For more than thirty years, since Dzhugashvili's time, the Soviet Union has had one basic aim. Can you remember what your instructors told you it was, General?"

Galitzin tried to protest, but Nikitin silenced him with a gesture. He lectured on, his voice filled with a scathing irony. "Lenin taught us that the aim of the Soviet state must be world revolution. By any means. By any means, that is, that do not threaten the existence of the Soviet state. You do understand that, General? Good. We are making some progress, then. In support of that doctrine we remained in Eastern Europe after the Great Patriotic War. We encouraged client states to fight against the client states supported by the imperialists. In thirty years of doing this, we have not lost *once*. Not once, General Galitzin. Does that suggest to you that possibly we have been doing something right? In Korea, in Vietnam, in Hungary, in Czechoslovakia, in Afghanistan. *We*, not America, are the dominant power. We have operated with aggressiveness when the situation permitted, with other methods when aggressiveness would not do. *And we are winning, Comrade Galitzin*. Are you with me still?"

Galitzin said stiffly, "Yes, Comrade President."

Nikitin looked at Kunavin and said, "Excellent. The general has mastered the essentials of a first-year military cadet's political indoctrination." He turned back to Galitzin, still ignoring the silent Koniev standing at the general's side.

"In recent years, General Galitzin," he went on, "since the Americans clasped defeat to their bosoms in Southeast Asia, we have been free to press a little harder. We have established our selves in Africa, in Afghanistan, in Yemen. Not only have we placed ourselves in a stronger position against our Chinese enemy, but we have all but encircled the sources of the imperialists' oil. We have kept the Americans bemused with détente and SALT talks while we have placed our conventional forces in positions of vital strategic importance in the Horn of Africa, Malagasy, and Jamaica. As chief of our Military Intelligence Directorate, this all may not come as a shock to you, General. Or is it news? Are you unaware of what has been happening in the world recently?"

"I am not unaware, Comrade President," Galitzin said through stiff lips.

"Very *good*, Piotr Ivanovich. Perhaps I need not despair for you, after all. You have now reached the level of understanding we demand from a *third*-year military cadet. Did you also know that parties sympathetic to the Soviet Union are now strong in Northern Ireland, in the Irish republic, in Belize and Guyana as well as in Iran, Greece, and Turkey? Excellent, General. You are nearly to the level of a graduating student." Nikitin's voice rose, growing harsher and more bitterly accusing. "The *plan*, General. *Our* plan, the plan that we have followed like a religious document since Khrushchev's day, through Brezhnev's time, to this very night. For world revolution. Slowly. Carefully. Without ever risking nuclear war. It has been working, General Galitzin. Perfectly. We *own* sixty-five thousand armed Vietnamese and two hundred thousand Cubans. In Asia we are keeping the Maoists in check. In Africa we are near to toppling the reactionary regimes in Egypt and South Africa. *We are doing very well*, Piotr Ivanovich. And you want to risk this all for some crazy concoction that comes out of a machine nobody understands run by a soldier who has never fired a shot? Are *you* crazy, Galitzin? Or are you only a fool?

"Comrade President," Galitzin said woodenly. "Comrade Koniev has convinced me that we can advance the timetable—without appreciable risk—by exposing the Americans' contingency plan to occupy the British Isles if the government swings farther to the left. It is a good plan, sir, and one that will be understood and believed by the English. It may—no, I will go farther than that and say that it *will*—cause the English to reevaluate their entire military relationship with the United States." In spite of his anger and chagrin, Galitzin could not avoid showing his anxious enthusiasm. He understood only too clearly now that a vote against Hastings would be a vote against a long life for Piotr Galitzin. "It will destroy NATO, Comrade President. And that will make it possible for us to move to the Rhine—or beyond—when and how we choose." He turned to face Kunavin. "I should have discussed this with you, Comrade Marshal, before any implementation. That was an error, for which I am very sorry. *But the plan is working.* In less than a week now, we will see the results of it." He turned back to speak directly to Pavel Nikitin. "There is *no way* in which the Soviet Union can be embarrassed by the disclosure of Hastings, Comrade President. The USSR has been protected every step of the way. The Hastings memorandum is genuine, sir. It comes directly out of the Central Intelligence Agency. Furthermore, the Americans themselves will believe it. They have been conditioned by their free press to think the worst of their intelligence community. In America the people have been led to believe that the CIA and the FBI and the other secret intelligence and police organizations are more dangerous to their precious liberties than *we* are. The disclosure of Hastings is in our vital interests, Comrade President. It was those interests I was serving when I gave my authority to this operation."

Nikitin spread his hands on the desk and looked at the Minister of Defense. "He is unregenerate, Leonid Petrovich. What am I to do with him? A post on the Amur River?"

Galitzin sensed a change in the atmosphere. It was slight, but promising. He looked across at Koniev and said urgently, "You are more eloquent than I, Yuri Pavlovich. *Tell* them that it is for the best."

Kunavin said brutally, "I don't know what one is expected to believe of a traitor who places spy devices in the quarters of the leader of the Soviet state."

Koniev said, "If that is an accusation against me, Comrade Marshal, I shall demand a trial before the Politburo. And I shall demand that you prove your slander!" His voice had the ring of steel in it. He was sure of his ground here.

"The Comrade President saw the microphone," Marshal Kunavin roared.

Koniev fixed Nikitin with a steady gaze. Not the gaze, he thought inwardly, of a guilty man. One did not reach the top of the KGB hierarchy without some acting talents. "Did you see a microphone, Pavel Grigorevich? Did you actually see a spying device of any kind?"

Nikitin said, "I was shown a microdot transmitter. It was secreted in my study in the dacha."

"A microdot transmitter? And what, exactly, is that? Describe it to me, Comrade, I beg you."

Kunavin was stunned. Only six months ago Koniev himself had shown him a microminiaturized transmitting device from the laboratories of the KGB.

Nikitin said, "A tiny instrument. The size of a period on a printed page. Kunavin scraped it from the glass on a photograph."

"There is no such device, Comrade President," Koniev said calmly. "A half year ago I showed the Minister of Defense some of our efforts to perfect such a tool, but as I made it clear to him then, the scientists have not yet been able to make it work properly." He looked at Kunavin with a glint of triumph in his eyes. "What the marshal showed you must have been a scrap of paint, a bit of ink. I assure you that no such device exists, inside the USSR at least."

Nikitin turned to look at Kunavin. "Could you have been mistaken, Leonid Petrovich?"

"There was a device," Kunavin said grimly. He knew beyond a shadow of a doubt that if he were to investigate further among the technicians in the KGB laboratories he would find out nothing. It took true spies to spy on spies. The twisting, sickly logic made him ill.

"The Minister must have been overwrought," Koniev said coldly. "The KGB does not spy on the elected chief of our government." The use of the term *elected* was deliberate. It was one of Pavel Nikitin's favored fantasies that he was the democratically elected leader of the Soviet state.

Kunavin found himself in a minefield. There was only one way through, and it was a humiliating one. He knew that as surely as Yuri Koniev stood before him he also spied on the chief of state as a matter of course. Nikitin must know it, too. He wasn't a fool. If he was being deceived, it was because he wanted to be. And there could be only one reason for that. He had listened to Galitzin and he had been moved by the GRU man's arguments. Hastings was beginning to tempt Pavel Nikitin.

Kunavin said painfully, "Perhaps I was mistaken." He stared hard into Koniev's eyes. Koniev met his glance with wintry assurance. The man was cold and inexorable as a glacier.

Yuri Koniev spoke forcefully now and his words were aimed directly at Nikitin. "In this company I think it is no secret that the regime has serious problems. The minorities are restless. The crops are bad and will get no better. We will have to continue our purchases of wheat from the West. Our supply of foreign exchange is low, and *that* will get no better. There are still *refuseniks* making trouble despite all the disciplinary methods we have put into effect." He looked at Kunavin. "Thanks to you, Comrade Marshal, and your predecessors—*and* the failure of nerve that has afflicted the Americans since their disaster in Vietnam—we have, for this moment in history, a slight nuclear superiority over the West and an immense superiority in conventional forces. Our navy is new, theirs is old. For this one moment in time, we have advantages that will not recur again. Not in our lifetimes. The Americans are slowly waking up again. Demarest is not like the last man in the White House. He will not allow this imbalance of forces to continue for long." He returned his attention to Nikitin, who must make the decision Koniev was seeking. "Lenin said: 'Grasp the moment!' Well, Pavel Grigorevich, this is the moment. We have running a plan that will surely weaken the NATO alliance, perhaps destroy it altogether. It may be that Galitzin and I and the others should not have set things in motion without the approval of the Politburo. But think for a moment, Pavel. Could we afford a debate, with all the argument, delay—with all the probability of security leaks? I admit my error in not discussing it with you personally—I know your devotion to democratic discussion and collective leadership. . . ."

Marshal Kunavin's stomach surged at the flattery, and at the calm acceptance of it by Nikitin.

"If it was an unforgivable fault," Koniev said, "I accept the responsibility. Completely. I offer to resign my post here and now, Pavel Grigorevich. But I beg of you not to interfere with Hastings. It will open our door to the West."

President Nikitin sat silently, his fleshy chin sunk into his collar, his eyes thoughtful.

Koniev decided here and now to "grasp the moment." He said, "In order to back the Hastings memorandum's disclosure, we have set one other operation in motion, Comrade President. We have put an assassin into England to kill the Prime Minister."

Nikitin sat bolt upright. "You have done *what?*"

"On Thursday next, the Prime Minister will be killed by a CIA assassin, Comrade President," Koniev said.

Kunavin's face was a mask of alarm and horror. "Koniev, you've gone mad. What have you done?" His surprise was false, but the fear was genuine.

"What must be done, Leonid Petrovich," Koniev said calmly.

Nikitin's hammerlike fist came down hard on the desk top. "*No! By God, no!* This is too much! You must put an end to this at once!"

Kunavin was impressed again by the President's histrionics. It was as though he had never thought of the killing before. As though it were not inherent in the plan.

"That is not possible, Comrade President," Koniev said.

"What do you mean 'not possible'? I order you to call off your murderer. Now. *Immediately!*"

"Pavel Grigorevich, I understand your concern," Koniev said.

"We have had some frightening experiences as a result of some inefficiencies in the past. In Andropov's time the KGB took some dangerous risks. I would be the first to admit it. The man Oswald was almost traced back to us. He was a weapon that came near to turning in our hands. It was only corrected by Andropov's fortunate contacts with the American underworld, who produced Ruby. But the situation is in no way comparable now, Comrade President. Let me prove it to you. One: in the Kennedy case, Khrushchev had been recently humiliated over the missiles in Cuba. That was the motive and it was there for all the world to see. And two: Andropov used as an assassin a man who had ties to us, who had lived here in this country, who thought of himself as a Marxist, and who had connections with the Cubans." He spoke with renewed emphasis. "But even from that near-disaster, we have learned valuable lessons that we can now apply to the present situation. We learned that the Americans did not wish to believe that we were responsible for the killing of their President. They simply refused to follow the investigative pathways that were there—available to anyone who really desired the truth. We learned that if the Americans—and this applies to all the West— were given any opening, any slight opportunity to *avoid* learning the truth, they would seize it. To do otherwise would commit them to war, sacrifice, to all manner of things that they simply would not—*will* not endure.

"The imperialists never face facts. When we sent a hundred thousand troops into Afghanistan, they threatened to stay away from the Olympics. They are small men, Pavel Grigorevich. Timid men.

"The risk we face now is minimal. The man who will kill Hugh Evans is not a Russian, not a Marxist, has never been in our country—has, in fact, spent most of his adult life fighting against us and our surrogates. He served in the American Army, and in the Rhodesian Army. He has been a mercenary and he has killed well before. The man who recruited him is just outside this room, Pavel Grigorevich. Have him in here. Speak to him. I defy anyone here to identify him by his speech, manner, or appearance as a Russian. He was educated in the United States. He is, in fact, eligible under their own laws to be a citizen of the United States. He recruited the assassin as an American. The assassin believes him to be an American, an officer of the Central Intelligence Agency. There is no way, Pavel, that this country can be implicated in the murder of Hugh Evans. And when it is accomplished, and then the Hastings memorandum is exposed—" He shook his head positively. "NATO will be finished. We can move west within months." He appealed to Kunavin now. "Possibly even weeks. You cannot deny that, Leonid Petrovich. You know—as a soldier—that it is so."

Nikitin sat staring hard at Koniev. The KGB man realized that his own life was hanging by a spider web.

Nikitin said, "But Hugh Evans is a Socialist. A friend of the Soviet Union."

Koniev's breath escaped in a whistling sigh. Safe. *Safe.*

He said, "We all know that the Socialists have traditionally been the worst enemies of the revolution, Pavel Grigorevich. They temporize and compromise and waste the momentum of the armed struggle. They must always be liquidated in the end."

Kunavin said, "This man, this assassin. How was he selected?"

"According to the rules set down years ago by General Sudoplatov when he commanded Spetburo Number One of the NKVD. I know his instructions well enough to quote them to you verbatim. He said, 'Go search for people who are hurt by fate or nature—the ugly, those suffering from an inferiority complex, craving power and influence but defeated by unfavorable circumstances.' He said much more, but that is the measure of the political killer, Leonid Petrovich. We have such a man. He is in England now."

"Who is he?"

"It doesn't matter *who* he is," Koniev said. "It is *what*."

"Explain yourself, Yuri Pavlovich," Nikitin said.

"Hugh Evans will be killed by his own bastard son."

There were chairs grouped around the President's desk now. Outside, under the thinning moon, the Ivan Bell Tower's chime struck two. The remains of a late snack littered a side table and a carafe of iced vodka stood on the edge of Nikitin's desk.

Kunavin asked, "KGB-London knows nothing about the operation?"

"I thought it best," Koniev said. "The fewer who know, the safer for all."

Nikitin addressed General Galitzin. "And GRU?"

"No one in London," Galitzin said. "For the same reason. We cooperated with the Poles in moving the American defector, but only as a"—he shrugged and half smiled, vodka and relief combining in him to produce a small joke—"only as a courtesy. The military attaché knows nothing whatever about Hastings."

Koniev said, "Our *rezident* in London has been told that a British journalist will soon make some remarkable revelations, and he has been instructed to give any help requested—but only within reason. The exposure of the Hastings memorandum must be a purely British action. It must not come from us."

"Yes, that's a wise precaution," Nikitin said. "But it troubles me that there is no one in London who can report directly to us."

Koniev said, "We can send someone, Comrade President."

Galitzin said, "Kadogan?"

"The obvious choice, I think," Koniev said. "The President's suggestion is an excellent one."

"The man who recruited Evans's son?" Nikitin asked, frowning.

"Yes," Koniev said.

"Send him as—as a commercial attaché. Something like that," Galitzin suggested. "Who is the London *rezident?*"

"Stepan Lykov. A good man. Clever enough to know Kadogan is someone special."

"Very well," Nikitin said. "Send your Colonel Kadogan. He is to report directly to *me*. Is that understood, Yuri Pavlovich?"

"Of course, Comrade President."

Nikitin continued to take over the operation. All present were aware of what was happening. "I want your Colonel Santorin sent back to Severnaya Zemlya. Under close arrest. Incommunicado. I want no talk *anywhere* about this. Not even under the Arctic ice. Is that clear?"

Kunavin said, "Yes, Comrade President."

"The American Daniels will *not* be sent to England. It is far too risky. He is to be sent away." All present understood the euphemism. It meant that Daniels was to be buried in the GULAG.

"The tapes are to be retrieved and held by you, Kunavin. We will decide later what is to be done with them."

"Yes, Comrade President."

"You will take all military precautions. In case of trouble, I want our forces positioned and in a state of readiness."

"That may alert NATO, Comrade President," Kunavin warned.

"Let it. Say that we are conducting maneuvers, mobilization practices, whatever you need to say. But I want the armed forces ready for any eventuality."

"There will be no military moves in the West, Comrade President," Koniev said. "At least none directed at *us*."

"We shall hope so," Nikitin said. "But we will take precautions anyway. Now I think that is all. We will drink a toast and go home. It is late and I am tired."

The four men lifted small glasses and drank.

"To Russia."

"To the revolution."

"To you, Comrade President."

When General Galitzin and Yuri Koniev had been escorted out of the office, Marshal Kunavin said, "Congratulations, sir. You gave no sign that the killing of Evans was not a strange idea to you."

Nikitin turned to Kunavin with a steely stare. "It may work. We shall see." He glanced at the door through which Koniev and Galitzin had left. "Those two," he said. "I want them watched. All the time. And when this affair has run its course I want them arrested and shot. They will have to learn that there is only one President in the Soviet Union."

27

The sun, setting through the pines, touched the rim of the Catoctin Mountains. For the first time that day a cooling breeze had begun to blow, but the men sitting on the veranda of the presidential lodge were hot, tired, and angry.

They watched the car carrying Davis Carradine back to Washington vanish down the road toward the main gate. In the distance they could hear the President's children playing with their Secret Service guards. It was a strangely anomalous sound under the circumstances.

"By *God*," President Demarest said, "I'll have that man's guts for garters before we finish with this."

"Give him credit for nerve, Mr. President," Paul Bruckner said. "Frankly, I didn't think he had it in him."

"He was against the wall," General Dracott said. "It wasn't a confrontation he could avoid."

The President glared angrily at Dracott. "Well, Henry? What in hell do I do now? What do I tell the Prime Minister?"

"You will simply have to put the best possible face on it, Mr. President. So Hastings was a contingency plan. An *old* plan. Every country in the world does contingency planning."

"Somehow," John Demarest said in a dry voice, "I doubt the British have a plan to occupy Washington, D.C."

"Well, we don't know that, do we, Mr. President."

"Be serious, Henry. This is no goddamned joke."

"I'm not joking, sir. Somewhere in Whitehall there is probably a file spelling out military and political options that could even include something as outlandish as Hastings. There has to be. It is the way the military mind works. It is the way intelligence organizations work, too. The Prime Minister is a reasonable man. He will see the truth in that."

Paul Bruckner said, "I'm sorry, General. But I don't think Hugh Evans *is* a reasonable man. Certainly some of the demands and conditions he has been laying on us about renewing base leases are hardly reasonable. He wants us out of England and England out of NATO. That, I submit, is not the attitude of a reasonable man."

"Whether or not," the President said. "I have to tell him something. And it has to be before he finds out for himself. He wouldn't have asked if his people were not on to something."

"Davis's actions have cost us valuable time," Dracott said. "If we had known about Hastings the moment Daniels ran, we could have handled it. We could have kept it in perspective, at least."

"Carradine will pay for it," the President said grimly. "His resignation will be on my desk Monday morning. Or I'll fire him and let Curtis's committee hear the whole story."

"I don't think the Senator will hold still for that, Mr. President," Paul Bruckner said.

"Carradine is Curtis's protégé," the President said viciously. "I'm going to feed him to the Senator piece by piece. He is going to choke on Davis Carradine." He turned on General Dracott and said, "Did Curtis know what Carradine was doing? What is your estimate of that, General?"

"I doubt that he did, Mr. President. Beau Curtis wants to be the next President too much to risk being part of a cover-up."

"I promise you one thing, gentlemen," the President said in a voice ribbed with iron. "Young Beau will become President over my dead body. There is no way in the world we can permit this business to remain secret. The media may cherish Beau Curtis, but even they won't make a love pile for him when the facts come out. And they must, you know. *I'm* not taking Nixon's way. You can count on that."

"It's going to make quite a stench, sir," Paul Bruckner said. "It can't help but reflect on your administration as a whole."

"I can face that. Hell, I'll have to face it. I appointed the bastard CIA Director."

"I don't like what it will do to the Agency, sir," Dracott said. "Another year or two of horror stories in the press. I can imagine the treatment the network news organizations will give it. Story after story about the black gang out at McLean—"

"Hands off plucky little England," Bruckner said dryly. "Well, we should have looked into it when the Agency lost Daniels. But that's as may be. Do you want a suggestion from me, Mr. President?"

"At this moment," President Demarest said, "I'll listen to suggestions from anyone, Paul. I've got my tit caught in a wringer."

Bruckner glanced covertly at General Dracott to see how his aristocratic and rather puritan chief reacted to the President's vulgarism.

"Stall, Mr. President," Bruckner said.

"That's it, Paul? That's your forty-thousand-a-year advice?"

"I am quite serious, sir. We have a man in England right now Exactly *where* in England, I can't tell you. But he's a good man and he's not an Agency man. His loyalty is to the White House, not the spook house. Before you speak to the Prime Minister again, at least let's hear from Colonel Brede and see how much the British actually know about Hastings."

"Can you reach him?"

"I can have my office call the embassy. We could do it from here, but I think it best we don't use presidential channels. It would just make things look bigger and worse than they already are."

"You think that's possible," the President said grimly.

"Yes, sir," General Dracott said. "I agree with Paul. Let's see what Colonel Brede has found out. We need to know specifically what Daniels did in England. If he gave the Hastings documents to someone there, we need to know who it was. I don't think the British are going to tell us. At least not right away and not until they are fully informed about the nature of the Hastings memorandum."

The President stared out at the darkening forest. The branches, against the brassy sunset, looked like black coral. It was criminal, John Demarest thought, to be so angry in such a beautiful place.

"Damn it, Henry," he said. "*We* are not fully informed about Hastings. We only have Davis's description of what the plan entailed. And he admits—he *declares* with such great self-righteousness—that he never actually saw the plan."

"I believe him, Mr. President. It is like Davis to make sure he never saw the plan."

"That's what will cost him his job, Henry. I can live with a certain amount of incompetence. What I won't stand for is deliberate self-deception for blatantly political reasons."

"But for the moment," Paul Bruckner said, squatting froglike beside the President's chair, "it serves your purpose not to be fully informed. In point of fact, Mr. President, you *can't* give the Prime Minister any hard information because you have nothing but hearsay. So stall, sir. Stall until you can speak from firsthand knowledge. Hell, that ought to be good for four or five days. Maybe a week."

"Dwight Lamb was the man who actually flushed the data banks," the President said.

"And he's in London, sir. Out of touch."

"I can have him back here in six hours. You know that, Paul," John Demarest said.

"To do what, Mr. President? To fire him? You can do that anytime. First let's see just how bad it really is in England. Let's find out if Daniels gave the information to anyone."

Henry Dracott looked sharply at his subordinate. Paul knew, or thought he knew, that Daniels had seen a journalist named Langton. He had given the name to Brede. But he was exercising the well-known Washington principle of cutting off information before it reached the man with the ultimate responsibility. For a moment General Dracott was moved to stop this, because it offended his sense of what was right. But almost immediately he checked himself. If a committee of the Congress ever asked the President to depose about the Hastings affair, the most important question would be "What did the President know and when did he know it?" The answer to a similar question had already cost the nation one chief executive. It was not in Henry Dracott to risk another. Politics, he thought sadly, sometimes made terrible demands on honor.

But Paul was playing for time, hoping that somehow Colonel Brede—stung as he must have been by the brutal killing of a friend—would track down Langton, or at least learn what Langton planned to do with the bombshell dropped into his lap by the defecting Daniels.

"What Paul says is correct, Mr. President. We don't have any hard facts yet. Let's see what the next day or two brings us. Even Hugh Evans can't quarrel with us on that one."

Paul Bruckner caught General Dracott's eye gratefully. He

knew what it was costing the old Brahmin not to expose this sin of omission. He said, "I'll put through a call to Katya, General. She can send a cable to the embassy in London to locate Colonel Brede and have him report in without delay. Does that meet with your approval, Mr. President?"

"God, yes," the President said wearily. "Let's see if we can't get some hard information for a change."

"There is one thing we must consider," Henry Dracott said.

"Something else?" the President asked. "Nothing good, I'll wager."

"Daniels was a deep-cover agent more than a true defector, Mr. President. He was the originator of the Hastings plan. Have you considered the possibility that it might be something that comes out of KGB Department A?"

Bruckner came to his feet. "*Desinformatskaya*. By God, Mr. President. There's an out with the Prime Minister, sir. Hastings was composed and planted by the KGB as a disinformation scheme. Why not?"

"Because we do not know that, Paul," Dracott said severely. "The President can't lie to the Prime Minister. And that isn't why I mentioned the possibility. What comes to me is that the Soviets could be planning some major political or military move somewhere to coincide with the uproar that will surely follow the disclosure of a plan like Hastings. At the very least, they should expect NATO to be in disarray at that moment."

"Jesus, Henry. You make my blood run cold," the President said.

"I am sorry, Mr. President. But we should be prepared."

The President pinched the bridge of his nose and closed his eyes for a moment. "Yes," he said presently. "You're right, Henry. But I don't want a crisis atmosphere. We had better get back to Washington tonight. And I shall want a meeting of the National Security Council scheduled first thing Monday morning."

28

Edward Simonini's office did not overlook Grosvenor Square. At one time the Chief of the CIA's London Station would have commanded enough prestige and status to rate select quarters in the United States embassy, but no longer. The suite of rooms occupied by the Agency staff were interior offices on the top story into which sunlight came only through the dusty skylights.

Dwight Lamb looked about with something bordering on distaste. Not because he was a particularly status-conscious man, but because he was only too aware of how the Agency had fallen into disrepute over the last decade among the men who made these minor, but telling, decisions.

The preweekend quiet had fallen on the embassy. A minimal staff was on hand to handle the routine business, but for the most part the halls and offices were empty. Even the Ambassador, Clement Samuelson—an industrialist with heavy financial commitments to the party—was away on leave in Chicago. Presumably, Lamb thought, he was inspecting the factories producing the wealth that had won him this prize plum among political appointments.

Lamb sat across from Simonini in the noisily air-conditioned room. His dour face was held in that expression of masked neutrality that he had cultivated in the many years he had served the Company. Simonini, on the other hand, was a more volatile man, and his demeanor was that of one who feels ill-used.

For the past ten minutes the London Station Chief had been listing his grievances and stating complaints about the handling of the Starshine affair.

"I should have been told at the outset that Starshine was in England," Simonini said. "I feel like a damned fool learning about it this way. What sort of operation are you people running?"

"No operation, Sim," Lamb said evenly. "It was decided that it would be in the best interests of the Company to keep Starshine's defection as much under wraps as possible. You know what the media are and what they would do with the story. They gave it a fair try even without any facts."

"You say 'it was decided,' Dwight. I've heard that kind of crap before. *Who* decided. You?"

"As DOO, that was my responsibility," Lamb said.

Simonini's mobile Italian face showed his skepticism. "You're snowing me again, Dwight. A decision like that would have to be made higher up. By the DCI, at least. Maybe even by the President."

"Carradine concurred," Lamb said briefly.

"The President?"

"The President has not been informed."

"Jesus," Simonini said. "You flushed Starshine's project out of the data banks on Carradine's authority?"

"On my own and Carradine's. Yes." Lamb's neutral expression failed to suppress completely the intensity of his feelings. "We had to protect the Company. It can't take another ten years of shelling from the bleeding hearts.

"You," Simonini said, "are out on one hell of a skinny limb, Dwight."

"I made the decision freely and after careful consideration. If it was a mistake, I'll be around to take the heat."

"What about Carradine?"

"He's a timeserver, Sim. Lightweight. He wants to be a senator, that's all."

"Okay, so you're on the limb alone, or almost alone if Carradine is with you," Simonini said. "So what's gone wrong? You wouldn't be here if something weren't coming unglued. The DOO doesn't pay social calls."

"Carradine had to meet with Senator Curtis. He didn't say so, because he doesn't have the balls, but he wanted me out of the country. I suspect Dracott will have talked the President into asking Carradine some questions, too, by this time."

"Better and better," Simonini said gloomily. "I think you'd better tell me what Starshine carried out of Langley, Dwight."

"A contingency plan to occupy this country if the government goes any farther left."

Simonini's mouth opened. "Oh, my *God. That's* why Dracott has Brede snooping around over here?"

"That," Lamb said primly, "is a fair assessment."

"Sweet Jesus," Simonini said.

"I flushed the computers and tried to bury Starshine's defection because I was certain that he would go straight to the Russians. It wouldn't matter at all if the Soviets got hold of Hastings. They could broadcast it all over the world and who would take it to be anything but a disinformation scheme?"

"But he didn't go straight to the Russians, did he," Simonini said. "He came here first."

"Yes. I should have foreseen that," Lamb said.

I would have, Simonini thought bitterly. But then I'm only a field hand. I don't live in that Washington Wonderland. He said, "I'm sorry to pile more on your back, Dwight. But I have to tell you that the cousins are suspicious that something's not kosher."

"Was it Dracott's man appearing that stirred them up?"

"They were on to something before he arrived."

"I would like to know *why* he arrived. Why did Dracott and Bruckner send him?"

Simonini rested his knees on the edge of the gray GI desk and said, "The guy who got blown away at Heathrow Tuesday served with Brede in Brussels. They both worked for General Dracott when he was NATO commander. Is that enough of a connection for you?"

"Yes. It had to be something like that," Lamb said. "Then they *were* really on to something."

"I think they picked up on Starshine when he arrived in this country."

"And didn't tell you."

"Shit," Simonini said angrily, "who tells *me* anything?"

"Is noncooperation an official policy now?"

Simonini shrugged. "Maybe not official. But Old Hugh Evans hates our guts. I mean he hates Americans and he particularly hates the Company. He's been reading American newspapers and seeing American newscasts for a long time. The power of the press has reinforced what he always knew about us—that we tend to screw up too often."

"That's not the Company's fault," Lamb said harshly.

"I know that, Dwight. For Chrissake, who should know it better? I was in Chile, remember? The media and the academics managed to turn a win into a loss. That bastard Allende is a hero now."

"We can't have another show-and-tell, Sim. The Company can't take it."

Simonini looked at Lamb speculatively. "How do you propose we prevent it?"

"Who did Daniels see while he was in England?"

"A writer named Harald Langton."

"The Marxist."

"If he was looking for someone to expose Hastings, who else would he turn to?"

Lamb frowned. "Even a Tory wouldn't take kindly to what was in that memorandum, Sim. It was just a stupid, goddamned contingency plan. That's the irony of it all. If anyone but a mole had ever looked at it, it would have been deep-sixed immediately and that would have been the end of it. But Daniels was senior. He worked alone. He classified the hell out of it. Now we have to bury it, Sim. Finally and completely. Can we find Langton without too much trouble?"

"And do what?"

Lamb stared at Simonini.

"Come *on*, Dwight. That won't work."

"All we want is to recover the memorandum. I wasn't implying anything else."

Like hell, Simonini thought. He said, "Dracott's man Brede has been looking for Langton. I'm reasonably sure that whatever Farr had, Brede has now. Farr's lady is with him. I had to get him a car and some money."

"He is an amateur," Dwight Lamb said.

"Yes. DI5 has him, I'm afraid."

"How do you know that?"

"We still have some sources among the cousins."

"Where is he?"

"I don't know that."

"Find out," Lamb said. "It will be a safe house somewhere near London."

"I know of two. One in Aylesbury and another down in Kent. If they have Brede at either, I can find out. But it will take a day or two."

"We need him more than DI5. So let's get him back."

"We don't know he's found anything, Dwight."

"You said it yourself. He has Farr's lady. We'll need her, too."

"The cousins may get sticky about letting us have her."

"She's a Russian, I believe. Tell them we'll deal for her. Full cooperation."

"If we make a contract like that and then give them nothing, I'll be through here," Simonini said.

"I'll give you Rio. You like South America."

"I like it here."

"Or would you prefer Paraguay?" The threat was implicit.

"I'll talk to Alan Hobbs," Simonini said.

"Good. And let's see what we can do about Langton."

"Brede may have spooked him."

"All the better. A frightened man doesn't think clearly."

"He could run," Simonini said. "KGB is strong in London these days."

"If he runs to them, our troubles are over. His value as a British voice for Hastings is finished."

"So let's herd him along to them, then."

"I'd rather have him myself," Lamb said.

"Dwight," Simonini said, "I won't help you to hammer a British citizen here." He glared at his superior's masked face. "Even for the Company, Dwight. No go. You can have me relieved if you want, but that's the last word on the subject."

"I was saying what I would rather do, personally. If he runs to KGB-London that will be just fine with me. Is Stepan Lykov still the *rezident* here?"

"Yes. Do you know him?"

"We've met. He's an ideologue. If Langton asks for asylum or help, Lykov won't turn a fellow Marxist down."

"Then we spook him?"

"If that is your best offer," Lamb said, with a thin smile. He stood. "Call me at the Britannia when you have something."

Simonini flushed, embarrassed for the country for which he had come to feel affection. "I may have trouble getting through to you by phone from my house. The switchboard operators are starting a slowdown over wages."

"Let's hear it for socialism," Lamb said dryly. "All right. Send a messenger. But get on all of this right away. We don't have too much time."

29

The medical officer was a physician with twenty years' experience of medicine, and eighteen of those years had been spent in the service of the Defense Intelligence establishment. He should have been inured to this sort of thing, he thought, but somehow, one never really became accustomed to it. One served a democratic state with all the best intentions, believing—or wanting to believe—that police-state methods were not really necessary. Yet one used such methods and salved the pangs of conscience by saying that in some cases the end truly did justify the means.

He looked down at the man on the bed, refusing to dwell on the restraints across his chest and on his wrists. The I.V. drip tapped into his vein was exactly the same piece of equipment one would find in any hospital: a saver of life. Yet in this case the solution was laced with sodium amytal and the purpose was something very different.

He did not know, and did not want to know, the identity of the man on whom he was practicing this outrage. He hoped that he was, at the very least, an enemy of the country. To know that he was otherwise would be more than conscience or medical ethics could support.

Major Hobbs and a young woman in police uniform came into the room. Hobbs asked, "May we proceed, doctor?"

The man on the bed stirred. His resistance to the drug was remarkable. It was almost impossible to keep him balanced between unconsciousness and sufficient awareness to permit the questioning to continue.

"You have perhaps fifteen minutes, Major, before the amytal puts him under again. The effect is cumulative, you know."

The DI5 man ran thumb and forefinger over his upper lip. He looked far less smoothly barbered and self-assured than he had when all this began twelve hours before. For some reason, the medical officer found this reassuring. Hobbs was, in the final analysis, a professional soldier. And this was not soldiering.

"He has stamina," the medical officer said. "Even with the amytals, a certain amount of cooperation is necessary for successful interrogation. He has to have at least a subconscious desire to impart the information you are trying to take from him."

"Thank you, doctor. I know how narcosynthesis works," Hobbs said wearily. "May I continue?"

"Forgive me, Major. But has it occurred to you that he may not have the answer to your questions?"

"It most certainly has, doctor. But we must be quite sure." Hobbs looked down at Brede's flushed and sweat-soaked face. The eyes looked cavernous, as though there were no irises in them. He was wondering if he had made a mistake dealing with Brede this way. It was beyond question that General Sanday-Maclean would not approve. But that was why there were majors under generals: so that the majors could take the rockets that came their way before they reached the generals.

One had to know some things and in this case there was no quick way to get the answers that were needed. What made this so bad and so risky was that the rape was being performed on an officer of a friendly nation, not on an enemy. And worse still was that the rape was not working. Either Brede did not know the nature of Hastings or the treatment was not able to pull the information from him.

Hobbs thought about the Russian girl, presumably sleeping in one of Nameless House's upstairs rooms. Damn the bird. If she hadn't panicked, they would have the information Colin Farr left behind. But that had come about directly as the result of another bad decision. It had been a stupid mistake to try to test her with Sergeant Lasky's visit.

The thought of the sergeant, still in hospital with a monstrous headache, gave rise to another thought: whether or not this interrogation succeeded, Brede would awaken an angry and dangerous man.

To which bleak thought Major Alan Hobbs added another: I don't blame him. If I were Brede, he told himself, I'd be killing mad.

He looked at the policewoman and said, "Are you ready Mrs. D.?"

"Quite ready, sir," she said. Nothing bothers Mrs. Danvers, he thought. If the Soviets were ever to take over Britain, she would serve them with the same calm dedication and lack of discernment. Not like the sawbones here. He was revolted. And well he should be. But there are no real ends, doctor. Even after you convince yourself about ends and means, you find that one does not stem from the other. Means lead to means lead to means. Torquemada himself must have wept when he discovered that. He pulled himself up sharply. You're getting tired, old son, he thought. And bloody sick of the Great Game. "Start the recorder, please, Mrs. D.," he said.

When the machine was running and Mrs. Danvers had notebook and pen in hand once more, Major Hobbs sat on the bed beside Brede and said softly, "We'll begin again, Colonel. Please tell me about Hastings."

30

Mrs. Emma Boatwright stood by the window peering curiously at the young man working in the lean-to garage behind the house. It was a bit odd that one should spend the better part of a summer weekend at the task of repainting what appeared to be a new van that already had a perfectly satisfactory coat of paint.

Mrs. Boatwright was fifty years old, the widow of a chemist (dead these five years, now, and still missed), and a staunch Conservative. In twenty years she had never voted Labour, a fact that made her something of an anomaly in the working-class neighborhood where she lived.

Emma Boatwright's assets consisted of a small annuity and the semidetached house where she and her husband had lived for most of their married life. It was not large and was unsuitable for a proper boardinghouse. She had only two rooms to let and she had never fancied cooking for guests, but she still managed to rent her rooms occasionally. Ordinarily, these were let to middle-aged persons much like herself, who were reliable and respectable.

But this summer had been difficult for Mrs. Boatwright. The roof had required repairs, the government had required new licenses, and her income tax had risen though her income had not.

When young Mr. Carter had arrived in his new van, asking for accommodations, she had been tempted to send him on his way. In the first place, he was American—his speech identified him immediately. Not that Emma Boatwright disliked Americans. She did not. She had pleasant childhood memories of the Yank soldiers who came to Britain to help defeat Hitler. But in recent times, and this to Emma Boatwright meant from the 1960s onward, Britain had suffered an influx of loud, hairy, impolite, and badly dressed young Americans who were most definitely *not* respectable. She had no desire to be subjected to loud music, marijuana-smoking, and bad manners in her own house.

But Mr. Carter was not the ordinary sort of young American. In fact, he was not all that young. It was his dark complexion, dark eyes, and slender figure that had first given her that impression. On closer examination he was probably nearing thirty-five or more. That, after she had decided to rent the room and the garage to him, rather made her feel better.

He was in London, he said, to study at the London School of Economics when the fall term began. He was extraordinarily polite and reserved. Emma Boatwright found that she approved of his manners, even though he looked rather like a spiv. With Americans, of course, one could never be quite certain.

He had arrived two days ago with that shiny new van loaded with crates. He had been generous about renting the garage, telling her that he realized it would inconvenience her to store some of her own goods elsewhere, but he planned to repaint his van and it would not do to spatter her belongings with red paint.

The personal luggage he had moved into the rear room consisted of one single, small suitcase. In the garage, he had unloaded several crates and a small compressor. This morning he had attached that to the house power and had begun to spray the van red. The exact red, Emma Boatwright noted idly, of the vehicles of the Post Office. A cheerful choice, she thought, resolving to charge him for the extra electricity he was using to accomplish the change.

He worked swiftly, with neat, economical movements of his compact body. It was hot, even in the open garage, and he had removed his shirt. Mrs. Boatwright, peering through the machine lace of the curtains, felt an unaccustomed tightness in her throat. It had been a long while since she had seen even that much of a man's body glistening with sweat in the sunlight. She was tempted to call out to Mr. Carter and ask him to cover himself, warn him that the sun might do him an injury. But his skin was burned brown by far stronger sunlight than England's. She realized that she would sound a fool.

31

At eight o'clock on Sunday evening, Lieutenant Colonel Aleksandr Kadogan, traveling as A. A. Kadogan of the Soviet-British Trade Mission, deplaned from the Tupolev just arrived from Leningrad and Moscow. He was met at the Aeroflot terminal at Heathrow by a driver from the Soviet embassy and taken directly to the home of Stepan Lykov in Chelsea.

As the black Mercedes left the airport complex, Kadogan noted the smoke-stained side of the multilevel carpark. An entire story had been blocked off for repairs and even from the road Kadogan could see police vehicles parked in the floodlighted, damaged area.

"It looks as though there has been some trouble there," he remarked to the driver.

The chauffeur, a very junior member of Lykov's KGB staff at the embassy, pleased to make conversation with what was quite obviously an important visitor from home, said, "Yes, Comrade Kadogan. It seems hooligans planted explosives in the automobile of some member of the British secret police. Scottish nationalists, the news media say."

Kadogan shook his head with a rueful smile. "Such a thing could never happen at home."

"I should say it could not," the driver said vehemently, guiding the Mercedes skillfully into the traffic on the motorway to London.

Kadogan regarded the cropped blond head in the front seat with a tolerance that was almost affectionate. How wonderful it was to be so absolutely certain that black was white. But then the boy probably had had the very best of a homegrown Soviet education. In Kadogan's own case, he had had to grow up without such conditioning. To have been raised and schooled in America was to have been cursed with an unruly flexibility of mind that required the most stringent intellectual discipline to control.

Kadogan leaned back against the luxurious leather cushions of the car seat and looked broodingly at the darkening English countryside. The motorway was jammed with cars and trucks. One had to call on a kind of discipline to compare this abundance with the economic bleakness in Russia and still retain a proper sense of superiority, but Kadogan could manage it. He had performed a similar, but even more demanding, trick in America where every indication of material well-being was a direct affront to Marxist-Leninist economics.

Still, as a man of the world, he was able to appreciate the bourgeois comfort in which he was traveling. The fact that he had just come through some very dicey moments in Moscow simply served to increase his sybaritic appreciation of the opulence of the German car and the easy libertarianism of the people one encountered in the West.

He thought about Colonel Santorin back at Severnaya Zemlya under arrest. Was the game-player being allowed to continue his work? Kadogan wondered. It was quite possible. Santorin was not exactly in disgrace—yet. Actually Santorin was in a kind of limbo. Whether or not it changed for better or worse depended entirely on the success or failure of the Hastings operation. And though he, Kadogan, was not under arrest and was, in fact, riding comfortably toward London in the back of a seven-passenger capitalist Mercedes, his situation was exactly comparable to Colonel Santorin's.

He was under instructions to report directly to President Nikitin on any matters concerning Hastings, and to make himself available and useful for any action that the furthering of the plan might require.

Stepan was not going to be pleased. As head of KGB-London, Lykov had arranged for the destruction of the British counterintelligence agent at Heathrow. But he had been given no explanations. It had been his task simply to obtain the services of a suitable group of what the driver so quaintly referred to as "hooligans."

Kadogan was acquainted with Stepan Lykov, and he knew him well enough to expect many questions.

Kadogan, of course, had no intention of answering any of them. Nor would Lykov expect it.

Kadogan was empowered to give instructions and make decisions, but his recent nightmare hours in the Kremlin, not knowing whether he would leave the President's outer office for duty or for a short trip to Lefortovo Prison, were not forgotten. He intended to be very cautious with anything relating to Hastings.

By special agreement with the government led by Hugh Evans,

the Soviet Union had acquired a block of property in the Chelsea district. It had been an expensive purchase, because Arab oil millionaires had by now succeeded in bidding up the price of British real estate to an almost prohibitive level. But once having made the buy, the Soviets had embarked on an extensive "renovation and beautification" program that had successfully isolated the block from the rest of the city, sequestering the houses and flats behind high—pseudo-Georgian—fences and gates. Within the block there were now masses of sophisticated communications equipment, a substantial cache of files and document storages, and a number of microwave devices useful for monitoring British civilian telephone lines. The senior members of the embassy staff, including members of the KGB *rezidentura*, all lived in the block, which was familiarly known to the not so pleased neighbors as Little Leningrad.

One of the best of the dwellings, facing a pleasant, tree-dotted square beyond the spear-topped fence, housed Stepan Lykov. It was a house suitable for a man with a large family, but Lykov was a widower whose children were all in Russia, his two daughters doctors in Siberia, and his son a pilot at the Red Air Force base at Tyuratam. It was a measure of the importance of KGB in London that Stepan Lykov had never been asked to surrender his quarters to embassy family men, even those who outranked him.

It took the better part of an hour to reach Chelsea from Heathrow, but Kadogan enjoyed the drive. He supposed that his pleasure in riding about in fine automobiles was a result of his American upbringing. But perhaps not, he thought; Brezhnev and Nikitin were collectors of cars—and one could not exactly call them the bourgeoisie.

The limousine rolled through the gates to the compound and pulled up in front of the *rezident*'s quarters. The driver alighted and opened the door for his passenger as a servant in a dark suit appeared from the house to take Kadogan's luggage.

Kadogan stepped from the car and found himself on the ground, his ankle sending him pain messages. He had struck the unaccustomed extra height of the curbstone, twisted his ankle, and sprawled in a heap. He was furiously embarrassed. The servant and driver leaped to help him to his feet but he shoved them aside impatiently, hobbling up the stairs to the door.

"Comrade, are you all right?" The damned doorman's face, pale as a cod's belly, was a mask of servile concern.

"Yes, yes," Kadogan said. "I twisted my ankle, that's all."

Stepan Lykov appeared in the entryway. "Comrade Kadogan. What happened?"

"I stumbled, that's all. Let's not make so much of it, Stepan." In times of stress, Kadogan's Russian acquired a strong American accent.

"Let me help you." Lykov put his arm around Kadogan and the two men limped into the house.

Lykov gave instructions to summon the resident doctor and then assisted Kadogan into his private study. He drew up a chintz-covered ottoman and placed it where Kadogan could rest his injured ankle.

Kadogan's chagrin faded and he laughed. "I have arrived in style, Stepan Efremovich."

"Does it hurt?"

"Yes, it does, rather," Kadogan said. "It would hurt less if you offered me a drink."

Lykov went to a sideboard and returned with a tray of bourbon, glasses, and ice. He poured two large drinks.

Kadogan drank with relish. "Your information is extensive, Stepan. How did you know I had a taste for bourbon? And with ice?"

Lykov's eyes rested steadily on his guest. "You are our resident American, Alek. Everyone here knows that."

The doctor hurried into the room and began to worry over

Kadogan's ankle. The two KGB officers regarded each other warily, but did not discuss anything until the doctor had bandaged the injured ankle and extracted a promise from Kadogan that he would report to the infirmary for X rays as soon as he and Comrade Lykov were finished.

When the doctor had closed the door behind him, Lykov said, "All right, Alek. What questions can I ask?"

Kadogan's round face assumed its best expression of innocence. "You can ask anything you like," he said.

"But I shouldn't expect too many answers, correct?"

Kadogan shrugged. "I will do the best I can."

"Then why are you here?"

"As an observer, Stepan. That's all."

"An observer of what?"

"I'm not here to spy on *you*, Stepan. You can be assured of that much."

Lykov's expression masked his anger imperfectly. "You are here to run an operation. In my territory. And I am not to be told what it is?"

"I am not running an operation," Kadogan said firmly. "Or perhaps I should put it another way. An operation is being run, but not by me. By Comrade Koniev. Directly from Moscow. Does that answer your question?"

Lykov retreated before the mention of Koniev's name. Even the head of the London *rezidentura* did not probe and prod at an action controlled from home by the number-one man in the KGB. "I see," he said.

"I hope you do, Stepan," Kadogan said. "I am to see all communications traffic designated *Hastings*. My decisions concerning these messages are to be accepted without question."

"On Koniev's authority?"

Kadogan fixed his pale eyes on the London *rezident*. "From higher up than that, Colonel Lykov," he said.

The sternness left his jowly face and he smiled dazzlingly, show-

ing a set of teeth that had benefited from years of American ortho-
dontia. He held out his glass and said, "So, now, Stepan
Efremovich. If you'll sweeten this a bit—as we say in Yankeeland—
we'll drink a toast to you and then hobble on in to the infirmary
and keep your physician happy."

Stepan Lykov did as he was told, wishing all the while that it
had been Kadogan's fat neck and not his ankle that needed the
doctor's attention.

32

With mingled feelings of anger and pity, Paul Bruckner
watched Katya Roth leave his office. He leaned back in his chair
and half closed his eyes. He was bone weary, as much from the
emotional drain of his interview with the woman as from the
strain of the last few days. He looked at the line of clocks on the
wall facing his littered desk. It was nearly midnight in Washington, five in the morning in London. In Moscow the day was well
begun, the *apparatchiks* all at their nasty Monday morning tasks.

The anger Paul Bruckner felt was not directed at Katya. It was
aimed, instead, at the bastards who used her and people like her,
taking advantage of their needs, their vulnerabilities, their loneliness. Paul Bruckner knew something about loneliness. He had not
been much loved in his lifetime; it was but for the grace of God, as
the Scriptures had it, that their positions were not reversed.

He rubbed a hand across his stubbled chin, frowning. He looked
again at the FBI report on his desk. The evidence was clear. Julia
Tamayo was systematically transmitting information into a con-
duit that led directly back to KGB-Moscow. The Bureau had not
gone so far as to suggest that Katya was an agent or an informer,
though the possibility was certainly not denied. It was the opinion
of the FBI, however, that Katya was an extreme security risk—

"due to her friendship with Julia Tamayo." How cautiously, how primly, that was put, Bruckner thought. It was as though those proper young men of the Bureau, still conscious of the ghost of J. Edgar Hoover, declined to discuss in plain language the lesbian relationship they were implying.

Bruckner had met Julia once or twice. He remembered her as a slender, dark woman whose mixed ancestry gave her a look that connoisseurs of such things would describe as "interesting." Bruckner himself did not fall into that category. Even in Washington, where female flesh was available everywhere for the asking, Paul Bruckner's sexual needs had always been handled by discreet professionals.

At this moment he allowed himself the luxury of hating Tamayo's guts. She had come to this country as he had himself. A refugee. And she had benefited from all the opportunities an opulent, benevolent society could provide. In her case, as in his, the promise of the Golden Door written on the Statue of Liberty had been fulfilled in abundance. And her response had been to take and take and then to betray. She had been faithless to the country that had taken her in, to the government that had employed her, and finally, to Katya, who had loved her.

Bruckner was sure that Tamayo, when she came before the bar, would claim that she was being accused unjustly. That her transgressions were not betrayals at all. That she was being accused because of her race. There would be endless justifications in the name of Freedom, anti-imperialism, the People. And the hell of it was that she might just get away with it. The courts had a way of allowing the color of a person's skin to slip into the scales of justice. That, Bruckner supposed, was the price a democracy paid for the sins of its fathers.

But by God, he thought, she'd play a useful part in this Hastings mess before she came to plead her case. He had seen to that. If only Katya remained firm.

He could see even now Katya's stricken face as she read the FBI report. She hadn't wanted to believe it—who would have, in her place? But he had sensed immediately her shifting dependence. Though she refused to accept the fact that Tamayo was an enemy, the truth was there—in a hard knot beneath her heart. And she had turned, as he had known she must, back to him for the strength to survive the shattering of her life.

And then, he thought, *I* used her. That was an unpleasant truth that knotted his own belly. But there it was, and there it would always be.

"I want you to tell Julia," he had said, "this one thing. Tell her: 'Langton is coming over.' "

"I don't understand."

"Don't try. Just tell her that. 'Langton is coming over.' "

He wondered if she could—or would—carry it through. She had better. It would make a very great difference when the case came to trial. He asked himself if he would help to condemn Katya Roth. He answered himself in flinty bitter terms. Yes. He would. If she failed to do as he instructed, he would not turn a hand to save Katya.

He closed his eyes and listened to the late-night sounds of the White House: the soft humming of the clocks, the whisper of the air conditioning.

The hell of it was, he told himself sadly, that in a quiet, secret sort of way that had never come to anything and now would never come to anything, he was a little bit in love with Katya Roth.

Julia Tamayo could see that Katya was upset. Her eyes were red and her face tired and strained. Over the remains of a late supper, she said, "Oh, my dear, you do look terrible. What have they been doing to you in that place?"

"It's nothing," Katya said. "I've had a long, bad day."

"Dr. Bruckner?"

Katya nodded, pressing her fingertips to her temples. Her head was aching and her eyes were on fire. It wasn't true. It couldn't be true. Not Julia. She wouldn't say what Paul wanted her to say. It was some kind of trap and she wouldn't demean Julia by doing such a thing.

"You work too hard, Kat." The slender brown hand touched Katya's.

"Things have been happening—" She broke off. I won't say it, she thought. I can't do this. "All weekend. There's never time to catch one's breath. And you never really know when the least little mistake—" She broke off, feeling hysteria bubbling up inside her chest. I'll tell her about the FBI report, she thought. I'll tell her they have been watching, spying on us. She looked about the room and wondered where the listening devices were, the hidden cameras. It was all so sick, so terrible.

Julia began to clear away the dishes. Katya thought, She waited for me. She waited for me on a Sunday evening when she could have been off on her own or with friends. She waited here for me because she loves me. Julia would never, never betray me.

Julia's luminous brown eyes were soft and understanding. "Do you want to talk, love? Or do you just want to get some rest?"

"It was just a bad day," Katya said. Her voice sounded thin and reedy to her. How was it that Julia didn't notice it? How was it that she didn't understand what was happening? "There were so many messages coming in. And then. . . ." She limped to a stop, looking at Julia as she moved so gracefully across the room to the kitchenette. "Julia?"

"What happened, love?"

Katya said, "We learned that a man named Langton is coming over."

"Is he someone important?"

Katya's heart seemed to turn over inside her. *She doesn't know.*

She doesn't care. It means nothing to her. Katya could feel relief flooding warm and safe over her. It was all right. They were wrong about Julia.

"No," Katya said. "I don't know if he is important. Dr. Bruckner thought so."

Julia moved about the apartment, graceful as a shadow.

Katya closed her eyes and breathed, "Oh, Julie, Julie. . . ."

"You're so tired, love. Why don't you just take a warm bath and slip into bed?"

"Why? What are you going to do?"

Julia's smile was dazzling. "Why, I'm going out to the pancake house and buy us some dessert. We'll have a feast in bed—like we used to do."

Katya's voice grew reedy again. She felt the fear come surging back. "I don't want anything. It's late."

"A bath and to bed for you, love," Julia said. "I won't be a minute. Here, I'll even run the water for you." She went into the bathroom and Katya heard the tap being turned on. Steam and the sweet smell of bath oil came into the living room.

"Julia," she called. *"Please,* Julie. I don't want anything."

Julia reappeared, still smiling. "It's running hot. You slip into it and I'll be back before you know it."

Katya sat looking at her lover with eyes that were flat and lifeless. Julia picked up her purse and went to the door. "I won't be ten minutes, love," she said, and slipped out.

Katya Roth's voice was like a plea for mercy. "Julia—*don't go!*"

It was only midnight when Julia Tamayo parked her Mustang in the apartment carport. She sat for a moment, collecting herself. Katya, she thought, was growing suspicious. Her behavior tonight had been unstable. It was possible that this relationship could not be maintained much longer.

She had weighed carefully the wisdom of coming out for a special contact so late at night. But she had been instructed most specifically to report immediately any mention of a person named Langton. One did not ignore such instructions, no matter what the risk to future information. Julia Tamayo was not only dedicated to her cause, she was disciplined.

She got out of the car and locked it. Then, holding her purse and the paper bag containing a quart of ice cream in her hands, she walked up the ramp to the open veranda onto which the apartments opened. She was uneasy, but she was satisfied, as well. She had been instructed to report any information about Langton, whoever he might be, and she had done it. By now the information was on its way to wherever it was sent, to whomever found it important. There was a deep pleasure in doing whatever one could do to injure this plastic Sodom.

She stood for a moment on the veranda before her apartment. She looked out over the Maryland countryside, quiet now in the deep summer night. Americans had owned slaves here, not so very long ago. They had not grown much more kind or tolerant in the years since their slaves were taken from them, either. She thought about the woman waiting beyond the closed door. One could pity a Katya Roth, but one could not, actually, respect her. She was a warm and giving person and in other circumstances one could possibly love her. But what was love, anyway? One loved a cause, an idea. Not a foolish, dependent, middle-aged Jewess. . . .

She opened the door and called out. "I'm back, love."

There was no reply. She wondered if Katya had gone to bed. The door to the bathroom was open. Had she fallen asleep in the tub? Julia wondered. She had looked tired enough to do something like that.

She put the ice cream in the small refrigerator and walked to the bathroom door. "Kat?"

Katya Roth was in the tub. The water was the color of wine. There was a rich, sweet sickness in the air. It mingled with the scent of bath oil. Blood streaked the white sides of the tub. It puddled on the tiled floor. Katya's bare breasts were like small islands of flesh in a burgundy sea. Her mouth was open and so were her eyes. They regarded Julia with the flat, glazed indifference of death.

Julia Tamayo's stomach surged and she hunched over, spewing. She braced herself on her knees, hands slipping on the bloody tiles. She saw the safety-razor blade Katya had used, and vomited again.

Panic rose in her. She struggled to her feet and stumbled out into the living room, her feet tracking pink on the light-colored carpet. Out. She had to get *out*, get *away*—

She went to the kitchen tap and splashed her face with cold water. She clawed the blood on her hands. It was a trap, she thought. It was something *they* had done to trap her.

She ran into the bedroom and dug into a bureau drawer. She found the cache of money she kept there against an emergency. She stuffed it into her purse with trembling hands and ran back into the living room. She looked again at the open bathroom door but she was afraid to touch it.

She hurried out onto the veranda and closed the apartment door behind her. She ran, her heels clicking, down the ramp to the carport. She was fumbling with the locked door of the Mustang when the two men appeared out of the shadows.

"Julia Tamayo? FBI. You are under arrest, Miss Tamayo."

33

The Bureau man's voice was correct and impersonal, but Bruckner could sense the overtones of shock and—yes—disapproval. It was as though the scene the FBI people had discovered in the

Silver Spring apartment were somehow improper. But death, the death of innocents, was always improper, Bruckner thought.

There was a bitter taste in his throat as he returned the telephone to its cradle. He felt numb, as though his capacity to feel anything at all had slipped away from him. Poor Katya, he thought. I didn't expect this from you.

But what right had he to have expected anything different? If he had had only a fraction of the sensitivity and understanding he should have had, he would have known that she would do something desperate, something terrible. He closed his eyes and imagined her lying in the water, the life drained from her. There was something almost biblical in her action: *If thy right eye offend thee, pluck it out.* Oh, Kat, he thought. I've lived too long with the compromisers. I forgot that there were still people who believed that the wages of sin are death. Tears streaked his broad, ugly face, glistening in the light of the single desk lamp.

Presently he picked up the telephone and dialed the duty officer at McLean. "This is Paul Bruckner. Put me through to the Director on a secure line."

The Washington clock showed that it was nearly three, but Davis Carradine picked up his telephone on the first ring. Davis was not sleeping well, Bruckner thought bitterly. He had probably lain awake all through the night worrying about his disintegrating career.

"Carradine? Bruckner." Paul's voice was ragged and even harsher than his normal rasp. "Listen carefully. It may just be possible to salvage you—for a while at least. May I assume you are interested?"

"The President wants my resignation on his desk in the morning," Carradine said in a hopeless tone.

"I may be able to get Henry to delay his acceptance. It might give you time to save something out of this situation. So say right now whether or not you are willing to cooperate with me."

"Anything. Jesus, anything at all."

None of this would have happened but for you, Bruckner thought bitterly. It was you who let all the pieces fall apart so that when they were reassembled they became a juggernaut, with scythes on the wheels to cut down the innocent. He believed that he could kill Carradine at this moment.

"Henry sent Colonel Brede to London on my recommendation," Bruckner said. "How much do you know about Brede?"

"Nothing. I don't know the man."

"I'll tell you about him. Listen carefully." Bruckner drew a deep, shuddering breath. He felt as though he were dabbling in filth, dealing this way with Davis Carradine. But that was because Katya Roth lay dead on a slab in the Washington morgue tonight. In the cold light of morning he would have himself under control again, doing what must be done. No, he told himself, that is a lie. Things will never be the same again for me. "Are you listening to me, Carradine?"

"Yes. Of course I'm listening, Paul." Carradine's voice was anxious, probing for any ray of hope.

"Brede once commanded a Project Omega team in Vietnam. Do you know what Omega was?"

"No."

"If you were worth a damn at your job you would know," Bruckner said. "Omega teams were sent into North Vietnam and Cambodia to retrieve important POWs, collect defectors, and eliminate high-level cadres. All of those things. Brede was good at his job. Very good. I want you to understand that. He isn't a man who will let up on any job he is given to do. That's why I picked him to retrieve Hastings. Do you understand me?"

"Yes, Paul. But what—"

"Shut up and listen," Bruckner said. "The one thing that you had better get through your head is that the British must not learn the contents of the Hastings memorandum. The results could be catastrophic to the alliance. And to you, personally. I'm not just talking about resignation now. I think the Senate's Oversight

Committee would go to the Justice Department for an indictment on you. In fact, I'll see to it that they do if it comes to that. Am I getting through to you?"

"Jesus, Paul—"

"I said *listen.*"

"Yes. All right. Go on."

"I think British intelligence has Colonel Brede right now. I have had nothing from him. He wouldn't stay out of touch if he were able to communicate. So far, it's all right. I don't think he's found out what's in the Hastings plan. But the British are going to have trouble holding him for very long. And when he's free, he's going to find Harald Langton. And then he's going to sweat Hastings out of him. Take my word for it. Brede can do it."

"That's why you sent him," Carradine said. "What can I do now?"

"If I could reach Brede, I might be able to call him off. And maybe not. General Dracott could do it, but I don't want the general involved in any more of this shitpile. He stays clean, is that understood?"

"I still don't see—"

"I'm telling you, so listen. The President is going to order you to get Dwight Lamb back here. You are going to sit on that order for forty-eight hours or so."

"You want me to disregard a direct presidential order? With my resignation sitting on his desk? Good God, Paul."

"God has nothing to do with this," Bruckner said bitterly. "It's between you and me. We understand each other. I wish it were not a fact, but it is. We are corner-cutters and we are going to cut one now. Or would you rather hang up and forget this call?"

"No, Paul. Go on—anything."

"I can't just go to the British and ask for Brede. But your man Lamb can do it. He's a professional, so I would be surprised if he hasn't thought of it already. *He* knows what's in the memorandum." Bruckner paused to catch his breath. His anger was making his chest ache. "I want you to tell Lamb to get Brede and see to it that he leaves England *at once*. If he can't make Brede agree, he is to use whatever means he has at his disposal to see to it that Brede does not reach Harald Langton. Langton is the only Englishman who knows what's in that damned Hastings plan. I want you to make certain that's as far as it goes."

"Go on, Paul."

"The Prime Minister has picked up rumors. He's been on to the President asking about Hastings. You weren't told that at Camp David."

Carradine's voice was near to breaking. "Oh, my God."

"Get hold of yourself, damn it. Now listen carefully. What I want is for Langton to run to the KGB. We are sending them a message that he's coming over to us. If he runs, he's discredited. If they buy our story, he's dead. The Soviets don't leave loose ends lying about the way we do."

"I don't see how I can arrange that, Paul. Even if the President lets me stay on."

"You don't have to. I already have," Bruckner said. And you'll never know at what cost, he thought bitterly, the grief still thickening his speech.

"I simply want you to have Lamb collect Brede and get him out of England. We don't need him breaking Langton. There's too much chance the British will hear of it."

"Yes. Yes, I can see that. I can reach Lamb tonight."

"Then do it," Bruckner said. "There's one thing more. The President is going to have to have something to give the Prime Minister. I want you to put the Company's contingency planning section onto it."

"Yes. I'll do it tomorrow."

"You'll do it *now*. I want a Hastings plan that concerns the American role in a *defense* of the British Isles in case of a Russian amphibious attack. Something far out, something imaginative."

"That could take *days*, Paul."

"It had better take hours, Carradine. Think about what you'll have to say to an investigating committee. That should keep you alert."

"All right, Paul. Yes. Whatever you say."

"I don't make any promises. But I think the President will use a tricked-up Hastings plan on old man Evans." Henry Dracott would never do such a thing, Bruckner thought. But Henry Dracott and John Scott Demarest were two very different people. And it was Demarest who sat in the Oval Office. "But understand this," he added, "it won't work unless Brede can be kept away from Langton. So get Lamb working as soon as you can reach him."

"It's three here," Carradine said. "Eight in London. I'll talk to him right now."

"Do that. And keep me informed," Paul Bruckner said and broke the connection.

He sat for a time at his littered desk, staring at nothing. He was sickened by what he had done, but convinced of the need for it. He had to follow through, or Katya Roth's death would be meaningless.

He stood and walked out into the night-lit outer office where Kat had worked. He looked at her desk and chair, waiting for the wave of guilt. But he felt nothing.

The duty officer, a young staffer who had drawn the Sunday night dogwatch, looked into the office. "Is there anything I can do for you, Dr. Bruckner?"

"Nothing," Bruckner said. "I'm going home now. Good-night."

34

Dwight Lamb's haggard face showed the effects of a sleepless night. It was not in his character to slouch in a chair, but the effort it cost him to keep from slackness was apparent to Simonini. He had just replaced the telephone in its cradle. The call to DI5 had taken some time to complete, despite the fact that it had gone through the special exchange.

"Well?" Simonini could not completely disguise the annoyance he felt at the way in which this business was being guided by remote control from McLean. "What did he say?"

"You could have listened," Lamb said.

"What for? This is your show. Yours and Carradine's."

"I think you were right about the safe house. They used the Delta code to locate him."

Simonini smiled mirthlessly. "We aren't supposed to know about those procedures." It was a measure of how cooperation between allies had deteriorated that the London Station now had to rely on informants within DI5 to obtain such routine information as the locator codes for shunting secure messages about within the United Kingdom.

"He said he would come. He's willing to talk."

"Will he deal?"

"I think so," Lamb said. "Maybe not for the girl. But he'll give us Brede in return for a summary of Hastings."

"McLean won't have Hastings Two ready for another three hours," Simonini said.

"We'll stall for a bit. We'll take him out and buy him a fancy lunch. That will take a couple of hours."

Simonini shook his head disgustedly. "Take a British counterspy to lunch today. Good God, what a tangle."

"He said he'd be here before noon."

Simonini glanced at a clock. It was, as the cousins said, going on for ten. "Alan Hobbs is a good man. I don't like screwing him this way."

"We have to get Brede out of England. It doesn't matter too much to Davis how we do it."

"If the lid comes off this, Dwight," Simonini said, "I'm through here. You know that."

"I mean what I said about Rio."

"Fuck Rio," Simonini said bitterly. "This is what happens when an operation is run from three thousand miles away. And by a politician."

"Laundering Starshine was my assignment," Lamb said grimly.

"That's very noble of you to take the blame. But don't snow me, Dwight. It was Carradine's idea to cover up Daniels's defection."

Lamb's expression was bleak. "I didn't do it for Carradine, Sim. It was for the Company.

"Whose idea was it to send KGB a message about Langton? That doesn't sound like Davis Carradine."

"All I know is that I got the word from Davis. And I think it's a good move. If the message gets delivered," Lamb said.

"If? Dwight, Washington is so full of leaks that sensitive information gets to KGB here before I receive an action bulletin."

"Why not?" Lamb said bitterly. "We can't put a surveillance on anyone without getting permission from a judge. Even then, they insist that we let the Bureau do the job instead of doing it ourselves. And the press watches the Federal Courts Building like a bunch of hungry hyenas. You wonder whose side they are on." He stirred stiffly in his chair. "Maybe this will change things, but I doubt it. Not as long as Henry Dracott advises the President. He's as bad in his way as Orrin Blaine is in his." He pressed his thin cheeks with the heels of his hands. "Jesus, I need some sleep."

"Do you want to sack out in the duty officer's quarters until Hobbs shows?"

"No. I have to keep on the contingency plan section's tail." He stood. "I'll be in the commo room."

"Dwight," Simonini said. "Is Carradine in trouble with the President?"

"I think so. He said the President pulled him off Senator Curtis's yacht and had him flown to Camp David. That sounds like trouble to me."

Simonini regarded his superior steadily. "And are you in trouble?"

"If the Director is in trouble, so is the DOO, Sim. It's a bureaucratic axiom."

"Will you appeal to the President directly? Will you make a case?"

"There is no case for a man who covered up an Agency error, Sim. No case John Scott Demarest would understand."

"I think he'd listen to you, Dwight."

"He might. And then he'd hand me my head on a dish. It wouldn't make any difference to him that I did it to keep the media off the Company's back. That's the way it's going to be, Sim."

"Will he cooperate with Hastings Two?"

"You mean will he feed it to the Prime Minister? I don't know. Maybe giving it to Hobbs will take the heat off."

"If Hobbs buys it."

"If. Yes."

"Alan is a long way from stupid, Dwight."

"If KGB takes the bait and goes for Langton, it won't seem so improbable. They've been known to embellish existing plans and try to turn them on us. At least we'll have a case to make in the goddamn press when it comes out."

"KGB might take Langton out," Simonini said speculatively. "Lykov is a very pragmatic Russian."

"If they do, wonderful," Lamb said. "I wish we could do it ourselves and make sure. But it's a long shot. They don't want him dead, you can be reasonably certain of that. They want him alive and shouting from the rooftops about the imperialist Yanks and their plot against Albion. I think all the message from Washington will do is buy us some time while they check to see if he really has any idea of coming over to us. I can't speak for Lykov, but I know Yuri Koniev. He won't waste a useful man unless he is absolutely certain he's gone bad." Lamb stood leaning against the door out of Simonini's office, his white, blue-veined hand on the knob. Simonini was struck suddenly by the fact that Dwight Lamb was old. That he had grown old in the service of the Company. He found himself feeling sorry for the sour-faced intelligence officer.

"How long do you think we have, Dwight?" he asked.

"A day. Maybe two or three. Not a week, that's sure. If the Brits buy Hastings Two, we'll have the week. But they aren't going to, Sim. As you reminded me. They aren't stupid."

"Maybe they'll pretend to buy it."

"Maybe they will. But sooner or later we are going to have to level with them."

"Better later than sooner," Simonini said fervently.

"That's why we have to get Brede out of our hair. He's like a wild card in a poker game. He won't take orders from us."

"Can't we collect him from Hobbs and show him a recall?"

"Davis spoke to Paul Bruckner. The Frog Man doesn't want the National Security Adviser's office involved any longer. He doesn't want Henry Dracott having to testify before a Senate committee on why he interfered in the first place and then pulled his man out before the job was finished. If you go around turning over rocks, you can get nailed by something crawling out of the hole you turn up. It is strictly up to us to get Brede out of the country. In a crate, if we have to."

"You know, Dwight," Simonini said with feeling. "This is a shitty business we're in."

"I've often thought so, Sim," Dwight Lamb said with that frozen smile. "But it's for a good cause."

Simonini watched the door close behind Lamb.

I hope so, Dwight, he thought. I'd hate to believe I've spent my life in the sewer to no purpose.

THREE

Knight nor Bishop can resist
The pawns of this Antagonist
Whose countenance is dark with mist.
The game goes on and will not wait,
Caesar is gripped in a deadly strait—
What if the pawns should give checkmate,
Iscariot?

—FRANK BETTS,
"The Pawns"

35

Brede opened his eyes and stared at the ceiling. His brain seemed clogged with images: a montage of memories that had no anchors in time or space. His body felt slimy with the heat of the Mekong Delta, yet he shivered with the night cold of the Laotian highlands. He was remembering things he had buried long ago. The spurting of blood that soaked a hand holding a commando knife. The hunger and thirst of a long forced march through a hostile territory. And there were images that had no meaning in that time or place: Colin's blasted body, legless, smoldering. General Dracott, his Brahmin face stern and serene behind a desk. Flags standing against the wall of a Washington office, and more flags whipping in the wind on the plain at West Point.

Then he remembered Jessica's long hair blowing in that same wind, but that was quite wrong. That image came from another time. He bade his wife good-bye and watched her vanish into an airplane at Bruxelles National, homeward bound. How could that be, Brede wondered. Jess was dead. Everyone who boarded that airplane was dead in the cold waters of the wintry Atlantic. Jessica didn't belong in the same dream with Henry Dracott and Paul Bruckner.

Someone had kept repeating the word *Hastings* to him and he had wanted to make it clear that he, too, wanted to know its meaning. But it had somehow been impossible to get that simple idea across to his inquisitor.

There was a long crack in the ceiling, and a stain in the plaster. For a moment they fascinated Brede. The stain was shaped like the head of a horse. The crack made the reins. Duke William's men rode horses at Hastings. And that wasn't quite right. The battle had been fought inland, not really at Hastings at all. And King Harold Godwinsson had remained behind the English shield wall and might have won the battle if a Norman arrow had not pierced his eye.

That was all he knew about Hastings but he should know more. He had been ordered to find out more. It had taken a long time, but the inquisitor had finally accepted that.

Larissa. God, what had happened to Lara Adanova? Somehow he had lost her somewhere in this spinning confusion. He felt himself growing angry again. He had been angry for a long while now. He shivered and worked at the restraints on his wrists. They were looser and he could almost free his hands. The stain on the ceiling didn't resemble a horse anymore. It was only a stain made by leaking water.

Hobbs, he thought. I'm going to kill you, Hobbs. His fingers curled around the handle of a nonexistent knife. The old skills were not forgotten, only buried beneath a veneer of civilized behavior. He closed his eyes and drew deep breaths into his lungs. There was a bitter taste in his throat. Amytal. That bastard Hobbs had pumped him full of sodium amytal.

How long had he lain here? Brede wondered. Hours. Days. He

had no accurate way of judging the time. The drug deadened the temporal perceptors in the brain even as it loosened inhibitions. His eyes felt wet with tears as he remembered Jessica again. It was almost as though she had died minutes ago. He had to go through all of that again: all the grief he had learned to forget. You'll pay for that, too, Hobbs, he thought.

Painstakingly, he began to reorder his memories. He had gone to Rye with Lara Adanova. They had been searching for a man named Harald Langton. He reconstructed in his mind the littered workroom at Cadman's Bluc. Books everywhere. Work sheets. Notes. A book of journalism on the floor. That must be here, somewhere in this mausoleum of a house to which Thurston had brought them. *Them.* Yes, Lara Adanova was here, too. Had Hobbs drugged her, as well? No, not likely. She knew even less than Brede himself knew about Hastings. Back to Rye. There was something, something. . . . Computer readouts. Pages of them. All about coal production. Why should he care about that? Langton was an economist by training. He must use computer data constantly. Was he a programmer, too? Brede's mind wanted to keep twisting away, back to the Mekong Delta and the Belgian airfield and Henry Dracott's White House office. He forced himself to concentrate on the *here*, the *now*.

He turned his head and looked about the bare room. He lay on a bed, still fully dressed except for his jacket. Beside the bed stood a stainless-steel stand holding an I.V. drip. The rubber tube was coiled and stowed. In the crook of his elbow there was a small bandaged patch. Hobbs had given up, then. He had satisfied himself that Brede didn't have the information he seemed so desperately to want.

Brede began to work again at the restraints on his wrists. They were of heavy gauze. Improvised. He applied all of his strength to the right-hand side. The gauze tore at the burned flesh, but he persisted. The pain helped to keep his mind clear.

His right hand was free. For a moment he lay still, feeling the beat of his pulse in the throbbing fingers. Presently he loosened the left-hand restraint and untied the gauze strap across his chest. From somewhere outside the room he heard someone climbing steps. Hobbs. Or the medic. There had been a doctor, or at least someone with medical training. He remembered seeing him during one of his sessions with Hobbs. Brede bared his teeth in an almost animal grimace of anger.

He took the neoprene tubing from the I.V. drip and stretched it between his hands, testing its strength. His right hand was bleeding, smearing the pale tubing with red. He lay back with the tubing hidden under his body. The footsteps approached the closed door.

Brede waited for the door to open.

A tall, gray-haired man entered. Brede studied him through half-closed eyes. The man approached the bed and leaned over, reaching for Brede's wrist.

He saw the loose restraints then and an expression of alarm leaped into his face. Brede drove his hand upward, knuckles bent, into the man's throat. As he staggered back, Brede was upon him, the neoprene tubing stretched between his fists. He spun the man before he could fall, and looped the garrotte around his throat.

The man struggled soundlessly, his larynx paralyzed by Brede's blow. Brede wound the tubing around his hand, making a halter of it. He shoved the man ahead of him to the open door.

They stood on a balustraded landing above the empty entrance hall to the house. Below, the sergeant Brede remembered sat at the same table staring up at him in astonishment. Brede said, "Hobbs. Get Hobbs or I'll kill him." He yanked the medic's head viciously, allowing him only enough freedom to breathe.

The policewoman Hobbs had called Mrs. Danvers appeared at the foot of the stairway. Her face was pale and frightened.

"*Hobbs,*" Brede said again.

"Major Hobbs isn't here," the sergeant said. His hand stole toward a telephone.

Brede tightened the halter around the medic's neck and said, "Don't do that, Sergeant." The sergeant's hand stopped.

"Major Hobbs has gone to London," the policewoman said. "Please don't hurt Doctor Macrae."

Brede stood unsteadily for a moment and then said, "Where is the girl?"

As if in answer to his question, a door behind him was kicked and pounded. He heard Lara's voice calling, "Robert! Robert, is that you?"

Brede said to the policewoman, "Come up here and let her out."

She climbed the stairs cautiously, her eyes fixed on Brede's.

Brede said, "Sergeant. You come up here, too. Slowly."

The soldier did not move. Brede snapped the doctor's head forward and back again, sending his longish gray hair flying. "*Move*, Sergeant."

The sergeant followed Mrs. Danvers up the stairs.

To the policewoman, Brede said, "Let the girl out."

She took keys from her uniform pocket and unlocked the door to Lara's room. Lara, her clothing wrinkled and her hair untidy, came out, her eyes wide. "Are you all right, Robert?"

Brede ignored her. He watched the sergeant come toward him. "That's close enough," he said. "Now I'll have your side arm. Take it out of the holster with your fingertips, Sergeant, or I'll break this man's neck."

The medic made croaking sounds, his eyes pleading.

The sergeant looked at the policewoman, who nodded. "Do as Colonel Brede says, Sergeant."

"Lara, stay behind me," Brede ordered. To the sergeant he said, "Put the side arm on the floor."

The soldier did as he was told.

"Now move away from it."

"There is no need for any of this, Colonel Brede," the police-woman said. "Major Hobbs has gone to London to arrange for you to go back to your own people."

"Move away from the pistol," Brede told her. "*Do* it, damn you."

When she had backed across the landing, Brede shoved his hostage forward until Lara could reach the heavy automatic on the floor. "Get it, Lara," he said. He took it from her.

"Now, everyone. Downstairs. Very carefully," he said.

"Colonel—"

"Shut up, Sergeant," Brede ordered.

At the base of the stairway, Brede kicked open the door to the communications room. The radio gear and switching consoles for the secure telephone lines were untended. Brede said, "Who else is in the house?"

"No one, Colonel," the policewoman said. "Major Hobbs took the signal staff back to London with him."

Brede gave a sharp tug on the tubing halter around the doctor's neck. "Is that true—*doctor?*" His anger burned in his voice. Dr. Macrae nodded, speechless.

"Who else is on the estate?"

"No one, Colonel," the policewoman said again. "We were closing down. I told you Major Hobbs is with your people—"

"Lara," Brede said. "Look outside."

Lara went to the door and opened it a crack.

"What's out there?"

"A military vehicle and two others."

"Is one of them yours, doctor?" Brede emphasized his question with the rubber halter. The doctor nodded again.

"Take the keys out of your pocket and hand them to Miss Adanova."

The doctor complied. His hands shook so badly that he almost dropped the leather key case.

"Sergeant," Brede said. "Unlock the gate to the road."

"Colonel, if you'll just wait—"

"*Do* it, Sergeant. I'm getting impatient."

The sergeant touched a wall switch.

"That had better not be an alarm, Sergeant."

"It isn't, Colonel Brede," the policewoman said. "Please don't harm Doctor Macrae," she said again.

"I'll be as good to him as he's been to me," Brede said. He lifted the sergeant's heavy service pistol and fired four shots into the communications gear in the side room. The shots were deafening in the empty hall. Lara flinched at the noise and Brede said to her, "Go out and start the doctor's car." He tugged the halter again and said, "Which is it?"

The policewoman said, "The gray Austin."

"Go, Lara," Brede said. The girl ran out the door.

"Now you, Sergeant," Brede said. "Those telephones on the table. Pull the wires out of the wall box."

The sergeant, his face wooden now, complied with Brede's instructions.

"Now get my papers and belongings. All of them. Everything I had in my pockets when I was brought here. You, Mrs. Danvers. Quickly," Brede said.

She opened a cabinet and removed a bundle.

"Now we will all go outside. Let's do it quietly," Brede said.

Still holding the doctor by the neoprene noose, he followed the other two out into the daylight. The flat white of an overcast sky almost blinded him. The bitter taste of amytal in his throat made his mouth water. He staggered and would have fallen if he had not braced himself against his prisoner.

Lara was in the driver's seat of the gray Austin. The engine was running.

"Open the rear door, Sergeant," Brede said.

The sergeant did as Brede ordered. Brede pushed the doctor up against the side of the car, released the noose, and turned with the sergeant's pistol lifted. He fired one shot into each of the front tires of the khaki-painted Army sedan, reaimed and did the same to the white police car. Then he fired two more shots. One into the radiator of each car. Coolant began to puddle on the brick pavement. Ten shots fired, Brede thought. Two remaining.

He shoved the doctor into the rear seat of the car and said to the sergeant. "If the gate is unlocked, you'll get him back alive."

"Colonel Brede, sir. Please be careful," the policewoman said anxiously.

"I intend to be, Mrs. Danvers. From now on," Brede said. "Put that bundle in the front seat."

The woman complied. Brede climbed into the rear seat beside the doctor and said to Lara, "Let's go. Drive."

She let out the clutch with a jerk and the car lurched down the drive onto the tree-lined road to the gate. Brede, looking back, could see the sergeant standing, looking after them. The police-woman was inspecting the immobilized cars. It would take the sergeant perhaps fifteen minutes to repair one of the telephones. Or if he could not manage that, he might walk to the village in thirty. Time enough, Brede thought.

Lara pulled up at the gate. Brede opened the car door and said to the doctor, "Open the gate. Don't run or I'll shoot you."

The medic's eyes were wide, terrified. He nodded wordlessly.

As the gate swung open, Brede changed into the front seat. "Go, Lara," he said. The Austin pulled out onto the road.

"Which way?" the girl asked in a breathless voice.

"Go right," he said. They had come from the opposite direction and his instinct told him that whoever missed killing him at Heathrow could be watching the roads around Nameless House. It was essential to rid themselves of this car and break through to London. He said, "Stay on this road to wherever it meets a major intersection. We'll find a town where we can lose this car and catch a train to London."

Lara's face was strained as she concentrated on driving. "Will they be after us?" she asked.

"Yes," Brede said. He didn't elaborate on his suspicions that there must be others searching the country around Nameless House to finish the job they had begun at Heathrow. The girl had enough to worry about with a groggy fugitive from DI5 on her hands.

Lara asked, "That man. Would you really have killed him?"

Brede, his eyes closed, said, "I don't know. Maybe I would have."

"They drugged you. I could hear you calling out," Lara said.

"Yes," Brede said. He didn't want to talk about it. To be interrogated under amytal was like being violated. It made him tremble with fury when he let himself remember it.

"Who is Jessica?"

Brede opened his eyes, remembering again. "My wife," he said curtly.

"Oh."

"She died in an airplane crash," he said.

"I'm sorry, Robert," Lara said. "I didn't mean to pry."

Her remark struck him as suddenly, hysterically, funny. He gave a harsh laugh that was like shards of broken glass. He said, "I may kill Hobbs for that."

"You aren't one of them," Lara said, as though she were trying to convince herself. "You wouldn't do that."

"You're wrong, Lara," Brede said. "I am one of them. Just like Colin was. You'd better know that."

"What are we going to do, Robert?"

"We're going to do what I was sent over here to do," he said shortly. He sat up and looked at the gray, flat sky. The air was cooler than it had been before his stay at Nameless House. "What day is this?" he asked. "What day of the week?"

"Tuesday, I think."

"Did they trouble you back there?" he asked.

"They asked me questions. About what Colin had been doing. I would have told them, Robert. But I didn't know."

Brede lay back again. He felt as though he were going to be sick. "Stop the car," he said.

Lara pulled onto the road-verge. He opened the car door and swung his feet to the grass. The amytal lay like a coating of bile in his throat. His cheek, when he ran a hand over it, was stubbled. Suddenly he retched. It was as though a hand were gripping his guts and trying to rip them out through his throat. He hung his head low between his knees until he could breathe again. Presently he turned back into the car and closed the door. "All right now," he said hoarsely.

Lara began to drive again.

He said, "You'll have to buy me a razor and a necktie somewhere. I can't get on a train looking like this."

"Yes," she said. "But the police?"

"We'll have to take our chances. They know we'll head for London. Hobbs will look for us there." He thought again of the workroom in Rye—the computer printouts. There was something there, something he should be able to put right in his mind. But he was too tired. He said, "Drive slowly. I have to close my eyes. If a policeman stops us, wake me. I'll give myself up. You will say I forced you to come with me. I don't want you involved in this anymore. . . ."

His voice trailed off and the girl was sure that he did not hear her reply. It was as well, she thought. This was no time to speak about what she was feeling.

36

From his place at the large table that dominated the Cabinet Room, General Henry Dracott could look through the windows in the east wall to the rose gardens. The White House grounds were beautiful at this time of year. The brilliant summer sun blazed on the stands of roses, heliotrope, lilies, and nicotiana that bordered the west wing of the Executive mansion. Beyond the flower gardens, the lawns lay green and sloping toward the bustle of Connecticut Avenue.

The city was less lovely than the grounds of the White House in summer, Dracott thought. It was the protest season and the parks were filled to overflowing with demonstrators who littered the grass and defaced the trees in the name of every cause from free marijuana to Malaccan independence. It was their right to behave so, Henry Dracott thought, but he longed for the more decorous times he remembered from long ago.

The atmosphere in the Cabinet Room was hardly less acrimonious than that in the capital's parks. Of the dozen men who had gathered to attend the meeting of the National Security Council, only the military commanders seemed agreed on a course of action.

Admiral Stephen Winfield, the current Chairman of the Joint Chiefs of Staff, backed firmly by General Cassius Price, the Army Chief of Staff, and by Admiral Oliver Bocke, the Chief of Naval Operations, was insisting that the President authorize a third-level alert of the American forces in Europe and the Middle East. Admiral Winfield had put the case with characteristic bluntness. Within the last twenty-four hours, the Russians had made a number of military dispositions that could be considered threatening. They had done this under the guise of a massive training exercise, but Winfield found their explanations wanting.

"Under the terms of the Kabul *rapprochement* we signed with them after Afghanistan," the admiral said, "they must notify us of any unscheduled major redeployment of forces, and they have done so, Mr. President. But our satellite surveillance indicates that the movement of armor into the forward zone facing NATO is much more extensive than Marshal Kunavin's notification suggests." He referred to documents handed to him by his aide and nodded. "The Soviet First Shock Army is now established within ten kilometers of the border of the Federal German Republic. And the First Guards Army is moving out of its bases on the Priara Plain toward the Iranian frontier. A number of Bulgarian and Romanian units, up to division size, seem to be joining up."

Dracott watched the thin, deeply lined face of the Secretary of State as Admiral Winfield spoke. Any discussion of military movements tended to bring an expression of cold disapproval to Orrin Blaine's sour features. He looked like a born-again preacher listening to improper language.

Dracott stirred restlessly. This meeting was not accomplishing anything really pertinent to the situation in England. At least, not yet. At Paul Bruckner's insistence, Dracott had managed to delay the President's public acceptance of Davis Carradine's resignation as Director of Central Intelligence. Dracott had reluctantly agreed that a precipitous firing of the DCI would give credence to any sudden disclosure, in England, of the Hastings memorandum. Paul wanted time to collect the various pieces of the situation in London and make them into an acceptable whole.

Given what was already known about the deplorable handling of the Daniels defection and the loss of the Hastings documents, Henry Dracott found it difficult to believe that the situation could be retrieved without serious damage to Anglo-American relations. But he was willing to make the gesture if Paul thought it would help.

General Dracott was profoundly depressed by the shock of Katya Roth's suicide. He was even more distressed by the assumption that she had taken her life because of an unwillingness to face the consequences of being involved in an improper relationship with a woman who was, apparently, part of a Soviet spy network. He had not known that Katya was a lesbian—the thought had never occurred to him. In Henry Dracott's world such relationships were the stuff of textbooks on abnormal psychology, not everyday happenings. Dracott knew that he should not allow his depression to affect his performance at this meeting or at any other task to which the President might set him. But for the first time that he could remember, he felt old today, and anxious to retire and leave this city.

The President had handled the Hastings situation with skill, Paul Bruckner was thinking. He had told the assembled members of the Council simply that documentary proof of a contingency plan affecting Anglo-American relations was missing and feared to be somewhere in Britain. The Daniels defection, he said, was more damaging than had at first been believed. At this he had fixed Davis Carradine with so frigid a stare that it was plain to all present who—in the President's view—was responsible.

It would be necessary, the President had said, to take precautionary action against the possibility that Anglo-American cooperation might be minimal for some time in the future.

It was, Bruckner thought, a masterful piece of political understatement. And it was a measure of the force that John Demarest could exert on the members of his administration that it had not resulted in a flurry of alarms and excursions.

Bruckner glanced at the ship's clock on the mantelpiece below the Matthew Jouett portrait of Thomas Jefferson. It was ten twenty. The day was well advanced in London by now. He expected momentarily to hear that Colonel Brede was safely diverted from his search for the Hastings material. Once that was accomplished, there would be time enough to paper over this dangerous tangle.

The Secretary of State was speaking now, contradicting all that Admiral Winfield had been saying. "It seems to me, Mr. President, that the moves the Joint Chiefs are recommending are highly provocative. Even granting that Her Majesty's government take the view that we have been at fault in this abominable affair—and we have been, I might add—it bears not at all on our direct relations with the Soviet Union. Admiral Winfield seems to want us to prove the theory of the self-fulfilling prophecy. We have mishandled some documents which should never have existed at all; therefore we assume that the Soviets will take advantage of the situation; therefore we behave provocatively in order to assure that they will do so." He looked down his long nose at the ribbon-bedecked admiral across the table. "Why do you find it so difficult, Stephen, to believe that the so-called military moves by the Soviets are exactly what they say they are—simple training exercises?"

"If they are innocent training maneuvers, Mr. Secretary," the Chairman of the Joint Chiefs said, "they are far more extensive than anything they have undertaken since Marshal Kunavin became Minister of Defense." He turned to the CNO and said, "Can you give the Secretary an update on naval movements, Oliver?"

The Chief of Naval Operations, a pale-complexioned man with smooth dark hair, accepted a sheaf of computer readouts from a commander wearing an aide's aiguillette. "In the last twelve hours, there has been a heavy concentration of Soviet forces in the Gulf of Oman. The ships are being tracked by Nathan Hale satellite. I have ordered air surveillance from Diego Garcia. So far we have identified the helicopter assault ship *Moskva*, the amphibious force carriers *Togliatti* and *Allende*, and four missile cruisers of the *Admiral Gorshkov* class."

He looked up and addressed himself to the President, rather than to the skeptically frowning Secretary of State. "The entire flotilla is steaming toward the entrance to the Persian Gulf, Mr. President."

President Demarest looked across the table at Secretary of Defense Dodd. "What about it, Chalmers? Do you consider that a threatening gesture?"

The former industrialist spoke carefully, but with emphasis. "If the concentration that includes the Guards Army were going to cross the border into Iran, they would certainly support the move with a strong naval task force in the Persian Gulf, Mr. President."

"This is absurd, Mr. President," Orrin Blaine said forcefully. "We pretend to support the doctrine of freedom of the seas, yet when the Soviets avail themselves of this freedom, we begin to get itchy trigger fingers. There is absolutely no reason to assign some dark motive to what is obviously a routine cruise by Russian naval vessels exercising their privileges in international waters." He fixed Chalmers Dodd with one of his most Wilsonian stares. "Has the Pentagon any firm information on the status of the Soviet strategic forces? Their missiles and submarines?"

"None," Dodd said reluctantly.

The Secretary of State looked down to the end of the table where Davis Carradine sat, hunched and gloomy. "And has the CIA anything to indicate bad intentions on the part of the Soviets? *Even assuming*"—he added with transparent malice—"that the misconduct of an officer of Central Intelligence creates an unfortunate situation between the United States and Great Britain?"

"There is no evidence of an imminent attack, Orrin," Carradine said sullenly.

The Secretary of State looked at the President and shrugged his shoulders. "I rest my case, Mr. President."

General Lescher, the Air Force Chief of Staff, shifted impatiently in his chair. The Secretary of Defense said, "You have something to add, Bob?"

"Only this," the airman said. "Our surveillance inside Russia has been seriously curtailed ever since the revolution in Iran." His tone became slightly edged with disapproval. "We are not allowed to fly SR-71s near the Soviet border for fear of provoking an incident. The only thing we have to look with are the satellites—which we have reason to believe are being interfered with—and some old U-2s which give us a slant range of possibly four hundred kilometers. What I am saying, Mr. President, is that we cannot be *sure* that some of the Soviet missile force isn't in a touch-and-go configuration."

"This entire discussion." the Secretary of State said, "is typical of the sort of speculation SALT is intended to end."

"The SALT process is a long way from being revived, Orrin," the President said dryly. "What I want from this meeting is some recommendation on what our posture should be for the next week or ten days. Until this tangle in England is resolved one way or another. I have a gut feeling that the Soviets are positioning themselves to take advantage of any rupture in the NATO structure. Therefore, I shall act accordingly. Chalmers, I want all American units in Europe and the Middle East put on standby alert. Keep the moves low-key, but let the Soviets see that we are reacting to their actions. Let's get a carrier into the Indian Ocean. How long will that take, Admiral Winfield?"

The admiral consulted with the CNO and then said, "The nearest we have is the *Dwight Eisenhower*. She's cruising in the China Sea. Under forced draft we can move her into the Indian Ocean by Friday morning. She'll have to leave her escorts behind. They can't keep up with her when she travels at full speed. But that will at least give us a full air group to reinforce the wing at Diego Garcia."

"If that's the best we can do," the President said, "very well."

He stood to indicate that the meeting was ended. "General Dracott, will you and Paul remain, please." He turned to Davis Carradine. "You, too, Director Carradine. We have further matters to discuss."

When the room had cleared, President Demarest, standing under the Jefferson portrait, said, "I have given you a reprieve, Davis. Not a pardon. On Henry's recommendation, I am delaying accepting your resignation until some more suitable time. But I don't want this decision to give you the impression that I am pleased with your performance in office. What you have done is unforgivable, and now—in a sense—we are all co-conspirators in suppressing knowledge of an illegality inside the Central Intelligence Agency." His voice was brittle with contempt. "There was no need for this, Davis. You were not responsible for allowing a deep-cover agent to remain in the planning section. There was no way you could have been expected to know about his activities. I blame your Director of Operations. But once having lost the man, you committed what I regard as an unpardonable sin. You tried to make it appear that nothing significant was involved. The potential for damage to the national security is enormous—and it is only because General Dracott and Paul, here, think something may be retrieved out of this mess that I am allowing you to stay on until you can resign more gracefully. Have I made myself clear?"

Davis Carradine looked at Paul Bruckner, who returned his gaze impassively. "Yes, Mr. President," he said.

"For your information," the President said, "this morning I received a telephone call from Senator Curtis. He told me that he has been suffering a crisis of conscience, or some such political malady. He is withdrawing his support for the Senate seat from you and searching for someone more, as he put it, suitable."

Carradine flushed angrily. How like Beau Curtis to bail out

quickly. He thought for a moment of all the scurrilous information he had at his disposal to use against Curtis: the drinking parties, the womanizing, the smart cocaine parties at Annandale and on the *Demelza*. He promised himself that he would use it all to see to it that young Beau Curtis never became President of the United States. He looked hard at John Demarest. The President's eyes were hard and shiny as chips of blue ice. He knew exactly what Carradine was thinking now, and he derived a frigid, bitter satisfaction from it.

"If I were you," President Demarest said, "I would begin to make plans now for early retirement, Davis. In the meantime, I expect you and your man Lamb to give Paul—and the general—your wholehearted cooperation."

Bruckner said, "Have the contingency planning people come up with something reasonable?"

Davis Carradine opened his attaché case and extracted a file folder, flagged with red, stamped SECRET, and sealed.

"Is this in the data banks?" Bruckner asked, taking possession of the file.

"Yes. Agency *and* Pentagon," Carradine said.

"I think that's all we need trouble Davis about now, Mr. President," Paul Bruckner said.

Carradine's lips tightened. The Jew-bastard was dismissing him.

The President said, "Yes. That's all for the moment, Director."

When Carradine had walked stiffly from the Cabinet Room, General Dracott said, "I disapprove of this, Mr. President. Most vehemently."

The President took the folder containing Hastings Two from Bruckner and said, "I'm sorry, Henry, I don't like it either. But I have to give the Prime Minister something."

"Hugh Evans isn't a fool, Mr. President. He'll know it isn't genuine," Henry Dracott said heavily.

"Of course he will, Henry," the President said. "It gives us all a fig leaf, nothing more."

"If you think it necessary, Mr. President," Dracott said. It was ending for him now, Henry Dracott thought. A lifetime of public service was winding down to a disgraceful, whimpering, dishonest ending. After this he could never stay on as National Security Adviser.

"I don't think we need to discuss this any further, gentlemen," the President said. He departed, taking the red-banded folder with him.

Dracott turned to Paul Bruckner and said, "What else, Paul?"

"I don't understand, General."

"I think you do," Dracott said sadly. "Shall we recall Colonel Brede now? Is that it?"

"I really think it would be best," Bruckner replied. "It will take a direct order from you, General."

"Have you heard from him?"

"No. But Dwight Lamb will locate him."

"Very well, Paul." The general returned to his place at the Cabinet table and collected his papers. Bruckner watched him with a mixture of sadness and exasperation. Bruckner had always known that the moment would finally come when General Dracott would choose between honor and power.

The general stood, an erect, soldierly, and somehow pathetic figure. He turned to his deputy and said, "Who will take my place, I wonder." But he knew the answer to that.

37

Harald Langton stood half-hidden behind the drape at the window of his room in the Randolph Hotel and peered nervously down at a policeman standing on the steps of the Ashmolean Museum across the street.

The weather had broken and the late afternoon sky was growing overcast. In the distance, across the roofs of Oxford, he could see the dark mass of a summer thunderstorm forming over Woodstock. An occasional flash of lightning sparked somewhere inside the gray mass of clouds. The air was still warm, but thick with the promise of rain.

Langton had spent nearly four days in his room, going out only to allow the maid to straighten up and then rushing back to sit behind the locked doors trying to devise a course of action that would keep him safe from the men he *knew* must be searching for him.

This simply would not do, he thought. With the greatest exposé of his career waiting to be written, he found himself unable to work or even to think clearly.

His obsession with conspiracies convinced him that the Fascists would stop at nothing to find and silence him. He imagined that Oxford was filled by now with American agents searching for the man to whom their defector had given the Hastings memorandum. He was equally certain that the British police were helping the Americans. It was inconceivable to Harald Langton that the authorities would allow him to remain free to expose the Hastings plot against Socialist Britain. He was tired, shaken. His meager store of courage was exhausted, and so was his judgment.

Below, on the street in front of the Ashmolean, a tourist stopped to ask directions from the uniformed policeman standing there. The tourist was large and graceless, wearing a flowered shirt and a camera around his neck. To Langton, this marked him immediately as an American. The policeman told the visitor that yes, the Randolph did indeed have a dining room open to the public. His gesture toward the hotel entrance set the heart of the watcher in the window to thumping wildly. Langton knew, beyond the shadow of any doubt, that a ring of American CIA agents was forming around the Randolph. He stepped back from the window and sat down on the unmade bed. He wiped the perspiration off his palms and tried to order his thoughts.

In his mind he constructed a terrible scenario in which he was taken from here, spirited out of the country—he had read many accounts in the left-wing press of the manner in which the CIA dealt with its enemies—there to be questioned, mistreated, drugged, perhaps even killed for his part in attempting to expose the Hastings plot.

The idea of physical pain and death terrified him. He pulled at his thick sideburns in a gesture of distracted near-hysteria. He had never in his life felt so alone.

A number of times during the last four days he had been tempted to ask for assistance. But there was nowhere to turn. His friends and associates in Oxford were useless. Despite their pro-testations of support for the revolution, he knew with a sure in-stinct that if he should appear on their doorsteps to ask for sanctuary, they would turn him out. Academics tended to be great theoretical conspirators, but the reality of violence swiftly emas-culated them. They had their academic appointments and govern-ment-supported prerogatives to protect.

What he needed, he thought, was the skilled help of profes-sionals. Against the forces that he imagined closing in about him, nothing less would do.

He would have to turn to the Soviets, he decided. They owed him protection and comfort. He had served them long and faith-fully, and his exposure of the American plot could only be to their advantage.

Over a period of many years he had telephoned bits of useful information to the Soviet embassy. He knew the various attachés there and, more to the point, he was known by them as a friend of the USSR.

Yet his journalist's experience and instinct warned him that he could not simply return to London—even assuming he could es-cape from the hotel without being apprehended—and walk into the Soviet embassy. To do so would taint, and perhaps even invali-date, all that he planned to write about the Hastings conspiracy.

They would understand that. They must know something of Hastings by now. The American, Daniels, had been on his way east, after all.

He dug about in his carryall for his address and telephone notebook. He leafed through the pages rapidly and found what he was seeking: the initials S. L. and a telephone number. He had met Stepan Lykov at a Mayfair soirée. Lykov was a trade attaché of some sort. He would know with whom to speak to provide a friend of the Soviet Union with the help that was so desperately needed.

It took him only a moment more of sweating fear to convince himself that this was his only recourse. There were Americans everywhere in Oxford. They were probably in the hotel at this very moment, waiting only for the proper minute to close in and take him.

He picked up the telephone.

The hotel operator gave him a very bad turn when he said that there was going to be a delay in placing his call. "The automatic switching isn't working, sir," the operator said wearily. "And the maintenance engineers are working to rule. It will take me thirty minutes to complete your call. Will that be satisfactory?"

Langton wanted to shout that it was most certainly *not* satisfactory, that the call needed to go through *now*, at *once*. But he gathered himself with an effort and said, "Be as quick as you can."

He replaced the telephone in its cradle and stared at it as though it might explode.

He went again to the window. The policeman had gone, but the tourist in the flowered shirt stood on the steps of the Ashmolean, aiming his camera at the façade of the Randolph. Langton wondered fearfully how many more men the CIA had in place about the hotel.

He backed into the room. It was growing darker and colder. In the distance he could hear the growling sound of thunder. The first great drops of rain began to fall—slowly at first and then with increasing violence as the squall approached. He felt clammy and short of breath. Time seemed to move with deadening slowness.

He took a bottle of Scotch whisky from his case and opened it. He poured a drink into a glass and gulped it down. It gagged him. He capped the bottle and put it in the stand beside the bed.

The minutes crawled by. Langton sat hunched in the wind blowing through the open window.

At last the telephone rang. He snatched at it.

The hotel operator said, "I can try your London call now, sir."

He gave the number and waited. Presently he heard the telephone ringing in London.

Answer. *Answer.*

The ringing ceased and a voice said, "Lykov."

Trembling with relief, Langton began to talk.

In a secure office in Little Leningrad, Stepan Lykov put down the telephone. Kadogan replaced the earphone in its holder. He said, "You see, I told you the Washington report was false."

"He could still be going over to the Americans. This could be a trap for you, or an attempt to discredit him."

"You see the CIA under every bed," Kadogan said. "I am more concerned about that man Brede. The one your Caledonians failed to kill at Heathrow."

"The British have him," Lykov said. "In a safe house down in Kent. We have the place under surveillance."

"He should be taken care of," Kadogan said.

"If he knew anything from Farr, he would have given it to the British by now."

"He should be eliminated, nevertheless."

"We can hardly walk into a DI5 safe house and murder the man."

"I leave the method to you, Stepan. My immediate problem is Harald Langton."

Lykov's eyes were hostile. "I don't like being kept in the dark. It is poor procedure."

"On the contrary. It is excellent procedure," Kadogan said smoothly. "You have your tasks to do, I have mine. I shall call on Comrade Langton."

"Do you really think the CIA are all around him?" Lykov demanded.

"Of course not. He is perfectly safe. But he thinks he needs protection, so we shall give him protection."

"Will you bring him here?"

Kadogan shook his head. "I'll stay with him. Perhaps I'll move him to another hotel. Something to make him grateful." The last was said with that plump smile that Lykov was learning to dislike.

"He sounds ready to run this very minute," Lykov said. "Will he wait?"

"He won't run. He's like a rabbit paralyzed by the hunter's spotlight."

"You're going up to Oxford then."

"I'll go hold his hand," Kadogan said.

Stepan Lykov regarded the man from Moscow with a cold distaste in his eyes. An arrogant, offensive man, this Lieutenant Colonel Kadogan, with his Yankee smile and his American suit and his fat, self-satisfied face. "Can you drive? Shall I send someone with you?" he asked.

Kadogan rapped smartly on the floor with his new cane and lifted his injured ankle with a grin. "It makes me look distinguished. Like a wounded war veteran." Lykov, whose father had lost his legs in the Great Patriotic War, found the remark in bad taste.

"Do you know Oxford?"

"Well enough," Kadogan said. "Order me a car, Stepan Efremovich, like a good fellow?" He stood and limped toward the door. Behind his back Lykov muttered a silent obscenity. Having Kadogan about was an intrusion into his authority. It was like having a resident ugly American. He would be very glad to see the last of him.

Leaning on his cane at the door, Kadogan turned and said, "That other matter of correcting the mistake made at Heathrow, I leave to you and your freedom fighters. See to it, Stepan."

38

Marshal of the Soviet Union Leonid Petrovich Kunavin stood on the low stage of the briefing room in the deep shelter under the Moscow suburb of Krasnogorsk and regarded the assembled officers of the General Staff.

"Are there questions?" He had just completed a full four-hour briefing on what was now known as Task Red Autumn, consisting of a major repositioning of large formations of the Soviet Army, Navy, and Air Force.

A number of the officers present leaped to their feet, vying for his attention. He recognized the Chief of Naval Staff, Admiral Viktor Lisenko. "Admiral?"

"How much more of the Pacific Fleet is to be committed to this exercise, Comrade Minister? Moving the *Moskva* and the other ships into the Persian Gulf has left our forces in Vietnam with an open sea flank." He was clearly thinking of the possibility of a Chinese strike into Vietnam planned to coincide with the drawing down of Soviet forces in the peninsula. It had happened before and could easily happen again. The Chinese People's Army was heavily entrenched along the border from Dong Khe to the Gulf of Tonkin.

"We will move two more nuclear submarines into the China Sea, Lisenko," the Defense Minister said. "And let it be known that their missiles are retargeted to Chinese objectives. That should discourage any adventures while Red Autumn is under way."

The admiral frowned and seemed about to protest, but the closed look on Kunavin's face made him think better of it. He sat down, filled with uneasy misgivings. Never before in his memory had so extensive a practice maneuver as Red Autumn been ordered on such short notice. He disliked concentrating so many of the Soviet Navy's best ships in the restricted waters of the Persian Gulf.

Kunavin recognized the Chief of Air Force Staff, General Ivan Treskov.

"May I ask, Comrade Minister, why the Strategic Rocket Forces are not being involved in this exercise?"

"Red Autumn is limited to conventional forces, Treskov," Kunavin said.

"But surely they should be alerted, at least?" Treskov was young, fiery, and far from stupid. He recognized the fact that Red Autumn might elicit a sharp reaction from the West.

"We do not want to create a bad atmosphere while the negotiations for the new SALT are under way, Comrade General," Kunavin said. He glanced at General Galitzin, who sat beside the lectern on the stage with him. "However, normal precautions will be observed."

"May I suggest something, Comrade Minister?" Treskov asked.

"Do so."

"I would like to order a rotating alert of the new penetrating bombers while Red Autumn is being performed. It will give the air crews invaluable experience."

"It will also disclose their intercontinental capability to the American SALT negotiators," Galitzin said sharply.

"Can we at least move them to their forward bases?" Treskov

was insistent and Kunavin was aware that he, and probably every officer in the shelter, had noted that Task Red Autumn, while ostensibly an exercise, placed a substantial Warsaw Pact force in position to drive into the west and south into Iran.

"I see no objection to that," Kunavin said. "General Galitzin?"

Galitzin got to his feet and stepped to the large-scale map covering the entire end of the theater. "As you have all surmised," he said, picking up a light-pointer, "Task Red Autumn is a real-time readiness exercise. It is based upon the operational plans that have been delivered by special courier to all commands. These plans were developed by the War Plans Directorate using the very latest and most efficient computer-simulation techniques. The forces involved will consist of less than one-third of the current conventional strength of the Army, Navy, and Air Force. But they will be watched closely by the General Staff, and the degree of skill with which the maneuvers are executed will affect much future strategic planning." He put a point of light on the map of Western Europe. "It will be assumed for the purpose of Red Autumn that the forces led by the First Shock Army will have as their objective a line running along the Rhine River from Basel in Switzerland to Rotterdam on the North Sea coast." He paused to allow the full import of what he was saying to impress itself upon them. "All commands are to treat Red Autumn as if they were preparing their forces for a drive across West Germany." He fixed the listening officers with a threatening stare. "It is possible that having reached the assigned line of departure, any unit assigned to Red Autumn may expect to be moved elsewhere without warning. Every officer and soldier must be prepared to engage *without further preparation* in a campaign lasting three weeks or more without major resupply."

As Galitzin was speaking, Marshal Kunavin left the stage and walked up the aisle between the rows of attentive officers to the rear of the theater. There he joined Yuri Koniev, the only civilian in this military congregation. He spoke quietly. "The armed forces will be prepared, Yuri Pavlovich. Is KGB doing its part?"

"You may be telling them too much," Koniev said. "These men aren't fools."

"One can't move armies like sacks of potatoes," Kunavin said. "Everything takes time."

"What are the imperialists doing about all this?" Koniev's lifted chin gestured at the attentive members of the General Staff.

"They have detached an aircraft carrier from the Seventh Fleet and they are moving it into the Indian Ocean. They have an almost childish faith in aircraft carriers, the Americans. Remember? They even tried to frighten the old Iranian fanatic with their beloved behemoths."

"One ship? It seems very little."

"They are reinforcing the Sixth Fleet with a pair of old cruisers and bringing NATO to a first-stage alert. All told, almost nothing. I have notified them that Red Autumn will begin within the next seventy-two hours."

Koniev shrugged. "Then we will see what happens in England."

"Can you give me a time?"

Koniev shook his head. "We are not in touch with our instrument in London. We want no connection with him whatever."

"Will he act?"

"Oh, yes," Koniev said. "He will act."

"Can you be certain? Comrade Nikitin is waiting."

"We are all waiting, Comrade Minister," Koniev said.

"*But will the man act?*" Kunavin demanded again.

"Yes. In such matters, Comrade Marshal," Koniev said, "Mokrie Dela is never wrong."

39

Major Alan Hobbs put down the telephone and regarded the two Americans bleakly. "Every policeman in the Greater London area is searching for them, gentlemen. That is the best we can offer at the moment."

Simonini looked at Lamb expressively and then resumed his pacing in the narrow confines of his office.

Lamb said acidly, "What kind of operation do you run, Major? How could you simply let them walk out of a safe house?" His tone did little to disguise his contempt.

"They didn't quite just walk away, old man. Brede took our doctor hostage and then liberated a vehicle. It would have been helpful if we had known what sort of man you chaps sent over here." A grudging admiration came into his voice. "He pulled out the telephone wires, shot up some very fancy radio gear and two cars. It took my sergeant the better part of forty minutes to get to a telephone box in Sponder."

Simonini asked, "How is your medic?"

"He has a rather sore neck and a reduced enthusiasm for intelligence work, but no serious injuries," Hobbs said. "Would your man really have killed him, do you think?"

Simonini looked steadily at the DI5 man. "That depends on his mental condition at the time. What kind of stuff did you use on him?"

Major Hobbs looked out of the window without replying.

Dwight Lamb said, "You realize that our deal is off, Major. You have nothing to trade now."

"Whatever happened to Anglo-American cooperation, Mr. Lamb?" Major Hobbs asked.

"Find Brede and we'll see what can be done."

Major Hobbs's eyes grew steely. "Oh, we'll find your Colonel

Brede, Mr. Lamb. Have no fear of that. More to the point, we'll find the man he has been looking for so single-mindedly. I have asked Special Branch to put out an all-points bulletin on Harald Langton. It would greatly ease our burden if you could enlighten us on the nature of Hastings."

"Hastings is simply a contingency plan," Lamb said. "We have been through that."

"Over it, perhaps. And very lightly at that," Hobbs said. "Telling me that it is 'a contingency plan' is not particularly helpful. What is needed are details."

"That information can be forthcoming when we have Colonel Brede," Lamb said. "His presence in Britain has become a political embarrassment for the administration. You must understand what we face at home. *Any* sort of intelligence operation is likely to come under hostile scrutiny by a number of committees of the Congress. I shouldn't like to face questioning on the subject of why the National Security Adviser's office thought it necessary to send a man to England to track down a missing CIA document. You should be able to understand that, Major."

"I understand it, but I don't like it," Hobbs said.

"We have no Official Secrets Act. We can't just close down any discussion in the Congress and we can't put a muzzle on the media," Lamb said. "So get us Brede—and that girl, by the way. We must have her, too. Then we can begin to share information again."

"I can't promise you the woman," Hobbs said. "She isn't an American citizen."

"She isn't a British citizen, either," Simonini said.

"Technically, she is either an Israeli or a Soviet," Hobbs said. "It depends on who is making the judgment. But her case is a different matter from that of your colonel."

Lamb said testily, "This discussion is academic. We have neither Brede nor the girl. First find them."

Hobbs got to his feet. "Oh, we intend to, Mr. Lamb."

Lamb said, "Good, Major. Stay in touch."

When Hobbs had left Simonini's office, the London Station Chief said to Lamb, "Why didn't you offer him Hastings Two?"

"In return for what, Sim? The flaming idiots let Brede get away."

"They'll get him."

"Maybe. The colonel hasn't forgotten his old tricks."

"Well, they'll have no trouble finding Langton, that's certain."

"If the opposition doesn't find him first. Then he'll be tainted. Whatever he has to say about Hastings won't mean a thing if it comes out of Moscow."

"I don't think the Russians will take him out of the country, Dwight."

"That we cannot be sure about. We've done the best we can to stir them up."

A light flashed on Simonini's telephone. He picked up the receiver and listened. He looked across the desk at Lamb and nodded. "You may be right. The new man, Kadogan, has just left Little Leningrad by car. He's heading for the M40."

"Oxford?" Lamb asked.

Simonini nodded. "Looks like it."

"Tell the tail to stay out of sight and call in when the bird lands."

Simonini gave instructions and broke the connection. "That's where Langton would go. Hobbs can figure it out, too."

"Let him. If Special Branch picks up Langton in company with a Russian agent, half our troubles are over."

"Kadogan. Why did they send him?"

"You know him?"

"I've read his file."

"His father was Ambassador in New York and Washington. He was born in the States. Educated there. He's KGB-Moscow's favorite cornpone American. They aren't going to terminate Langton—they're going to soothe him." Lamb said. "They didn't buy the message from Washington, and they're going to hold Langton's hand. They must be planning to spring Hastings on the Brits very soon."

"Then we should have planted Hastings Two with Hobbs," Simonini said.

"Not without Brede in hand. He could turn the whole damned cart over if he gets to Langton first."

"What if the President gives it to the Prime Minister?"

"He won't do that until we've bottled up Brede."

"Can you be so certain?" Simonini asked.

Dwight Lamb said, "The President is a politician, Sim. Yes, I think we can be certain of that."

40

Considering that petrol in Britain now sold for ninety pence a liter, Alek Kadogan thought, the traffic on the roads was astonishing. It bespoke a lack of discipline among the British masses that sadly needed correcting. Even on the motorway, it had taken him more than two hours to drive from Little Leningrad in London to the Randolph Hotel in Oxford.

The summer storm which had broken over Oxford had left the streets slick and shiny, but the rain had stopped now and what remained was the heavy, wet air that followed the squall as it moved to the south.

Kadogan's ankle ached and throbbed from the driving. It would have been more sensible, he thought, to have accepted Lykov's offer of a driver. But his own caution suggested that the fewer London people who were involved with Harald Langton, the better.

It was an annoyance to have to come to Langton at all, since there was little likelihood that the man was in any real danger. But it was vital that he be kept in a confident frame of mind, at least until such time as his part in disclosing Hastings was accomplished. After that, Kadogan thought, anyone who wanted him could damned well have him. Though he had never met the man face to face, it was obvious that he was cut from the same whining pattern as the American Daniels had been. Such men were instruments to be used when needed—and then discarded as quickly as possible, before they could become liabilities.

He sat for a time in the car, waiting for the pain in his sprained ankle to subside.

He took a package of Players from his jacket and lit one. He didn't like English cigarettes. He had learned most—if not all—his vices in America, he thought with a wide grin. It was a marvelous country for vices. The thought brought back memories of sunlit southern campuses, lightly clad, leggy American girls, the smell of mimosa and magnolias in the air. The American compound in Lopatin, where he had taken his postgraduate work in espionage, had nothing to compare with the genuine article. The climate was wrong and the girls not nearly leggy—or willing—enough.

He considered Langton once again. He had told Lykov that he would move Langton to another place, and he would do so. But not because there were CIA agents swarming about. That threat existed only in Langton's fevered imagination.

Not for the first time, Alek Kadogan sighed at the quality of men with whom his work brought him into contact. Traitors, cowards, and madmen. The image of the sweating, wild-eyed Iron sitting like a bearded demon in the blazing Paraguayan sun made him shiver slightly. He wondered where Evans's son was at this moment. Not far from here, surely. Waiting for his moment.

He dropped the cigarette to the pavement and climbed out of the car with some effort. He retrieved his cane and locked the door and, standing for a time in the deepening dusk, looked up at the shabby façade of the Randolph. It was almost eight o'clock. He had begun to think about dinner. He wondered if Langton ought to be taken out of Oxford without delay. He almost wished that he could postpone the meeting and take himself off to enjoy a meal. He had heard of a place called the Restaurant Elizabeth, near Christ Church Meadow, that he thought he would enjoy sampling. Alek Kadogan was something of a gourmet. Another of his Western tastes, he admitted.

But there was no use waiting longer. Duty first, last, and always, he told himself. In the service of the Soviet motherland, he limped purposefully toward the entrance to the rain-streaked hotel.

Harald Langton snatched at the telephone before it had completed its first ring.

"Harald? This is Alek. I'm here in response to your call. May I come up?"

The softly drawling American English jarred Langton so badly that he almost dropped the telephone. His prominent eyes went wide and the blood drained from his face. *Good God, how did they know?* He made a strangled sound and cast about him desperately for some escape.

"Harald? Are you there?" The hated accents were like a hot spike being driven through his chest. "Yes, here," he whispered.

"The elevator's broken down," the drawling voice said. "But I'll be up. Wait for me. I've got a gimpy leg. So don't run off, y'hear?"

The images in Langton's fevered imagination tumbled against one another, like doomed cattle in a chute. He threw the telephone to the floor as though the instrument had grown hot to the touch, lurched to his feet, and looked wildly around the room. He snatched up his car keys and wallet from the bureau and ran to the door. He could not allow himself to be trapped here. He imagined himself thrown from the window to lie crushed and bloody on the street below. He saw himself shot, beaten, killed in any of a dozen horrible ways. That softly drawling voice seemed to signal his finish. There was nothing to do but to run.

He burst from the room into the hallway. There were two stair-wells, one at each end of the passage. He stood indecisively, his heavy body drenched with the sweat of panic.

At the far end of the hall, two men and two women appeared from the stairway. They were complaining loudly about some failure of the service in the hotel. They were Americans. Their voices betrayed them. Langton turned and ran from them toward the other stairwell.

He reached the head of the stairs and looked down. A heavyset, moon-faced man was coming up, nearly upon him. He wore American-cut clothing and carried a cane. He looked up, saw Langton. The pale eyes held Langton immobile. "Harald?"

He reached the top stair and paused, breathing hard. Langton eyed the cane in horror. He could see the steel tip of it. He could imagine the terrible force of the mechanism that drove the poison pellet. He uttered a wailing, agonized sound. The man's ruddy face loomed. He lifted the cane and leaned forward. Langton shrieked and snatched at it. His hands closed about the smooth wood and he twisted with all his strength, amazed to find it free in his possession. The other staggered and Langton swung the cane. It struck the man in the temple and he toppled without a word over the balustrade and onto the landing fifteen feet below.

Langton threw the cane away. He turned and ran, his breath sobbing in his throat. He burst through the astonished group of complaining Americans, pushing one of the women against the wall with such violence that she stumbled and fell.

"Hold it there, you son of a bitch! What the hell are you doing?"

"Stop, you bastard!"

Langton did not pause. He ran down the stairs, twice shoving hotel guests aside and bringing down on himself a rain of curses and angry cries. He emerged into the lobby and went on, shoving and crashing through the evening crowd until he stood on the street, his breath making raw, sucking sounds, his heart trying to leap from his chest.

He ran across the street to where he had left his Mercedes. Behind him he could hear calls and angry shouts.

He almost dropped the door keys, but managed to open the car and throw himself behind the wheel. The blessed German diesel caught on the first turn and he backed the car out, bucking and leaping. He heard a crunch of bending sheet metal and the tinkle of broken headlights behind him but he did not look back. He pressed hard on the accelerator and turned, skidding wildly, into St. Giles.

The traffic at this hour was still heavy. Cars swerved to avoid him as he careered north toward the open Oxfordshire country-side. Once he was forced to jam on the brakes to avoid a head-on collision with an approaching minivan and he struck a car parked by the side of the street, sending hubcaps and a strip of trim-metal flying. The van driver put his head out of his window and screamed obscenities at him, but Langton only drove on, foot pressed hard to the floorboard, his hands shaking and dancing on the steering wheel.

He was out of the town now, driving fast. He heard oncoming cars blowing their horns and saw them flashing their lights at him. He had not thought to turn on his headlights. He did so now. The speedometer touched 150 kilometers per hour. He began to breathe again.

How had they found out so quickly? He knew the CIA habitually tapped the telephones in Britain—it was an article of faith among Langton's set that there was nothing whatever secure from them. But how had they managed to tap his call to the Soviet embassy from a hotel in Oxford, my God?

The delay in completing the call. That was it. It hadn't been the automatic switching, it had been a ruse to give the Americans time to tap his line.

They were everywhere—

He wondered if he had badly injured the man on the stairs. Part of his mind hoped so. He remembered the sickening crack of the cane against the man's head. But what if he *had* killed him? Langton had heard that when one of *them* was killed, they never rested until they exacted vengeance. They were like gangsters, like the Mafia. . . .

Somewhere behind him he heard the braying siren of a police car. He twisted about in panic to look to the rear and it was there. He saw the brilliant driving lights, the spearlike shafts of light from the blue strobe on the police Rover's roof. The British police—or were they? He started to turn his attention back to the road and as he did so he saw the broad yellow side of the juggernaut truck crossing ahead of him. The Mercedes's headlights made the obstacle look like a great, yellow cliff. He saw the letters spelling out the name of the haulage firm. It began with CH— That was all he saw as the Mercedes struck the truck broadside, the shovel nose burying itself under the trailer in an explosion of dust, dirt, flying bits of glass, and twisted metal.

The impact came near to overturning the truck, but did not. The wreckage came to rest at ninety degrees from the point of impact, with the train torn half off the chassis of the truck and the Mercedes flattened to one-half its height and nearly welded to the underside of the heavy vehicle.

The police Rover pulled up, skidding and squealing on the rain-slick road as the driver of the truck, shaken but unhurt, staggered from his cab.

The two Thames Valley constables who had been chasing Langton ran to the wreckage and pulled up sharply.

"Blimey, what a bloody mess!"

The second constable directed his flashlight's beam at the pile of ripped and torn metal. "Good Lord, look there," he said breathlessly. In the light of the hand torch they could see an arm extending from the wreckage. "It's moving," said the constable unbelievingly. "The crazy bastard is still alive."

41

Brede awakened with a start, momentarily disoriented in the musty darkness of the shabby hotel room. For a time he lay still, listening to the quiet breathing of the girl beside him. She lay, half-dressed, on top of the sour-smelling counterpane, her dark hair tumbled about her narrow brows, sleeping the sleep of the exhausted.

The journey from Kent had been a nightmare of train-switching and taxi-riding, still jumbled for Brede by the aftereffects of the drug he had been given at Nameless House. Larissa had been remarkable: braver and more resourceful than he would have imagined possible. Her years of struggle to free her father had tempered her personality, taught her to bend in the face of forces she could not defeat and stand firm before challenges that would destroy a weaker spirit.

Somewhere in the dark warrens of Whitechapel a church bell tolled twice. He had lost his watch back at Nameless House, and the lonely sound gave him an anchorage in time. It was early morning, Wednesday. He and the girl were still free twenty hours after their escape from Hobbs's people in Kent, and the fog was lifting from his brain.

He swung his feet to the floor and sat for a time with his head hanging low. A thin sliver of light leaked through the drawn shades of the single window. The room was near the Thames. He could smell the tidal water. He stood and walked to the window to look out. The view was blocked by the blank face of a building across the street, a lattice of empty, dark windows. In the street below, nothing moved. He raised his eyes and saw a thin strip of sky with a few pallid stars. The sleeping city made a soft, distant susurrus. From somewhere down the hall came the noise of a hacking cough. It made the walls seem paper-thin.

Their journey from the south had been a nightmare, one that Brede would have been unable to handle without the woman's help. He had followed her, still half-drugged, for hours that seemed to run together in his mind like a blur. They had abandoned the car in some town to the south—he didn't even recall its name. Then there had been a long train ride to somewhere near London, followed by a maze of doubling back and forth, driven by his conviction that the killers from Heathrow were still very near.

In the end, after nightfall, they had come to rest here, in this seedy travelers' hotel in Whitechapel, tired, dirty, hungry—but still free. He had slept for a time and he was beginning to think more clearly. He sat on the arm of a threadbare chair and breathed in the early morning air. He had to report to Dracott. When dawn came he would lose himself in the city and call from a public telephone.

He looked at the sleeping woman. He would have to leave her soon. She had served her purpose and there was no need to stay with her. The thought brought an unaccountable sadness. He owed her better than that. He owed Colin, too. He became aware that she was watching him. He walked across the room and sat beside her.

"Are you all right?" she asked.

"Yes. You?"

She nodded. She was looking at him steadily, her eyes strangely bright. He realized that she was weeping silently. Exhaustion? Fear? Something else. It came to him that she was reading his thoughts and the old loneliness was closing in on her again. She said, "When will you go?"

"Lara. . . ."

She touched his arm. "I understand. It's finished now. You have things to do."

He allowed himself the ghost of a smile. "I haven't done so well lately," he said. "Maybe things will improve. Maybe not." He brushed at her damp cheek with his fingertips. "It will be all right. We'll meet again."

She turned her face away. "Don't," she said.

It seemed to him that they had been together for a very long time, months and years rather than days. Long-suppressed memories rose in his mind. He remembered what it had been to love and be loved.

"Larissa," he said, savoring the musical sound of the name.

She looked up at him once again and now it seemed that her eyes were pools of deep shadow, beyond fathoming.

He bent and kissed her on the lips, softly at first. He felt her sigh on his cheek and her arms went around him. Colin had been his friend, and yet this seemed right. His hands searched for her, found her. It couldn't be love, he thought. We scarcely know one another. And yet it seemed right, he thought again. Loneliness had a way of finding its own reply.

She had a fine body, slender and strong, yet feminine beyond his imagining. She murmured something in Russian. He understood the words imperfectly, but the meaning was clear enough. They made love until the room began to grow light with dawn.

He said, "What will you do?"

She sat up among the rumpled bedclothes. "I have friends. People I lived with when I first came to London." She offered him a wan smile. "Zionists. They are in Israel, but I have my key to their flat."

"Here in London?"

"Yes." She saw his doubtful expression and said, "It will be all right, Robert. I can manage my life."

"Don't go back to Colin's place. Please."

She regarded him with resignation. "There is nothing there for me. Only a few belongings. Not worth retrieving. That is part of another life now."

"I will find you again, Lara," he said.

She touched his face lightly. "You owe me nothing, Robert."

He almost said, I think I've fallen in love with you. But it would have been the wrong thing to say. He had no claim on her. They were birds of passage.

"I want you to be safe," he said, instead.

She rose from the bed and began to dress. He watched her regretfully. She said, "I have managed for a long time, Robert. I'll manage now. Don't feel that you owe me anything because we have made love. We shared the moment and it was good. But you have your work and I have mine."

He put his hands on her bare shoulders and said, "Lara—they won't let him go. They will never let him go. I'm sorry, but you have to accept that."

She stepped away from him and said, "I will *not* accept that."

He had no answer for such faith. He went to the window and looked out into the still-silent street. It was nearly five thirty and the sky was growing white with the summer morning.

He put on his coat. "Call the American embassy and leave a message for me. I want to know where you will be."

"Yes," she said. But he knew that she would not. He felt suddenly cut off from her. It was as though their lives had reached a branching and an ending. It filled him with a kind of despair.

"Lara. . . ."

"Go. Please—go." Dressed now in her sweater and denims, she stood at the window, her back to him. There was finality in her very posture, in the tilt of her small, dark head.

"Lara," he said again.

She did not speak.

He went to the door and stepped out into the hall. The old

wooden floor creaked under him and the air smelled of dust.

He went down the stairs to the street. There was no one in the porter's cubicle. He stepped through the streaked glass-paneled door and out into the early morning.

Down the street stood a battered-looking Renault: one of the many free-lance minicabs that now abounded in London. A hand-lettered sign taped to the inside of the windshield announced it for hire. Brede raised a hand and signaled it.

He turned to glance up at the window of the room he had shared with Lara. The Russian girl stood between the curtains. On her face was a desolate expression of loneliness—perhaps of love.

As he watched, it changed to a look of fear. She cried out a warning. He turned to see the Renault approaching, much too fast. A hand clenched around a metal object was extended from the nearside window. A surge of adrenaline hit Brede and he dived for the protection of the doorway he had just left. A metallic egg clattered toward him, bouncing and rolling along the pavement.

The minicab raced by. The grenade struck the curb and re-bounded into the street before exploding with a yellowish-white flash and a flat *bang* that reverberated between the buildings. Steel fragments shattered the hotel door and a painted-over win-dow across the street. Brede felt a stinging sensation along his ribs and a sharp tug on the cloth of his jacket. He lay flat on the sidewalk as bits of metal pocked the concrete of the buildings all around him. His ears rang with the concussion.

He came to one knee, looking after the vanishing jitney. From broken windows, shards of glass rained down into the street.

Brede got to his feet and looked down at his side. A sliver of hot steel had torn his coat and drawn blood. He could see the bloody whiteness of a bared rib in the furrow left by the fragment.

Other voices were making themselves heard now. People shout-ing from inside the buildings. The wall behind Brede was scarred and the sidewalk glistened with broken glass.

Lara burst from the hotel doorway, her face white, her eyes wide and frightened.

For a moment he simply held Lara tightly. He owed his life to her warning. To that, and to the lucky chance that caused the grenade to strike the curb and bounce away before exploding.

He released the trembling girl and said, "Let's get out of here. Quickly."

Lara was staring down at his side. "You are hurt—"

"We'll worry about that later. Let's move it. *Fast, Lara. They'll be back.*"

They ran down the street to the Aldgate East Underground station. As they reached the stairs, Brede caught sight of the battered Renault turning onto Whitechapel High Street. He pulled Lara down beside him against the wall. The Renault paused, turned sharply, and raced by. In the distance Brede could hear the braying of a police vehicle. He led Lara down into the Underground station.

The girl began to shake hysterically. "There's no end to it—the hurting—the killing—"

He shook her sharply. "Don't fall apart now," he commanded.

She looked wildly at him. "Who, Robert? *Why?*"

"I'm not sure. Not Hobbs, that's certain. The Brits don't work this way."

"Where can we go?" Lara asked. She sounded desperate.

"Your friends' flat," he said. "Where is it?"

"In Knightsbridge."

On the street above he could hear the confusion building. People running, shouting. More police sirens braying. The empty station reverberated with the sound of an approaching train. The electronic monitor above the wire gate came alight. It read PAD-DINGTON, BAYSWATER. Brede took a handful of coins from his pocket and fed them into the automatic dispenser. The gate clicked open and he pulled Lara through. The train appeared out of the dark tunnel, an automated metal monster with a single, yellow eye. The new Underground trains were all computer-operated, the compartment that once housed a motorman empty and closed. The train came to a halt, hissing compressed air. Brede could hear people clattering down the stairs from the street. He and Lara stepped aboard into a car empty but for three sleepy-looking men in working clothes. They looked up incuriously.

Two men appeared on the other side of the wire barrier. One of them carried an Uzi machine-pistol. Brede pressed Lara against the wall of the car. The door hissed closed and the train began to move. The two beyond the barrier vanished from view as the train plunged into the tunnel. Brede took Langton's paperback book from his jacket pocket and slipped it under his coat, pressing it hard against his wounded side. Then he took Lara by the hand and sank down onto one of the hard bench seats and closed his eyes.

There was no question of leaving the girl now.

42

General Sir Gordon Sanday-Maclean looked across the massive old desk at the Prime Minister of Britain and wished himself else-where. Hugh Evans was indulging himself in a display of ill-temper that was, in the general's view, unseemly, even though justified.

Since the most recent swing to the left of the British electorate, the offices at Number 10 Downing Street had become one of the places in London Sir Gordon liked least to visit. It was not that Hugh Evans was incapable of good manners. It was that he used the lack of them as a weapon against those government officials he felt did not sympathize with his hopes for the progressive future of Britain. The general was well aware that the Prime Minister regarded him as a dinosaur, a biological sport among the new generation of civil servants. And perhaps, Sir Gordon thought, the Prime Minister was right. It was difficult for a man such as himself to abandon the values and traditions by which he had lived for more than sixty years.

One of these traditions was cooperation with the Americans, who though flawed and lacking the nine hundred or so years of history that might make them suitable heirs to the mother country, were, after all, the only power left in the world with the capability of stemming the tide of Eastern communism.

Hugh Evans saw only the crassness and inhumanity of American capitalism. Given his background, this was understandable enough. But it was an attitude that drove a wedge straight through the heart of the alliance that had kept the British, diminished in power though they might be, at the heart of the defense of Western democratic values.

In all honesty, General Sanday Maclean thought, the transatlantic cousins were not making it easy for the Prime Minister to do otherwise. They were showing a regrettable tendency to be secretive and uncooperative. The President had yet to respond satisfactorily to the Prime Minister's demand for information on the Hastings matter. *An accounting* was the phrase the Prime Minister was using now. Sir Gordon, who understood better than most the need for diplomatic usages in relations between nations of greatly disparate strength, felt that behaving like a strict headmaster with the President of the United States was a mistake. The Americans were acting strangely and reprehensibly, but it was scarcely prudent to pretend that one could discipline them. He had made the error of saying so to the Prime Minister and had been subjected to a lecture that had brought the blood to his already ruddy cheeks. Now he must make the interview even more unpleasant, and it took all of his Victoria Cross winner's courage to do so.

"I am sorry to tell you, Prime Minister, that when—and if—the President responds to your request for clarification on the Hastings matter, we will have no immediate way of verifying the information," he said.

Hugh Evans, bulky and ungraceful behind the great antique desk, regarded his counterintelligence chief with hooded, suspicious eyes. He never met with Sanday-Maclean without becoming conscious—and resentful—of the immense social differences between them. The general was the descendant of Scottish lairds—warriors and soldiers who for generations had lived off the labor of grindingly poor crofters and landless men. It hardly mattered that it had been three hundred years since a Lord of Sanday had hanged a man for poaching a deer or stealing a loaf. Sanday-Maclean was an aristocrat and therefore, in the Prime Minister's view, loyal to a Britain that no longer existed. And in the aristocrats' dedication to that vanished Britain, he, and they, looked to the American capitalists for support, accepting the social injustice of that transatlantic Rome without conscience or morality.

Now the bloody man was saying that whatever President Demarest cared to say about Hastings must be accepted without independent verification. It was infuriating, and Hugh Evans was not a man to hide his feelings with subordinates. "I will have you explain yourself, General," he said. "We spend millions of pounds each year—money that could be better spent elsewhere—to provide ourselves with intelligence. And you tell me we have no way of knowing whether or not we are being lied to by the Americans?"

"May I point out, Prime Minister, that the President has not yet replied to your request for information? It is not exactly accurate to say that we are being lied to." He felt himself on dangerous ground here, because the Prime Minister's request—demand, actually—for an explanation of the Hastings matter had been made at his own suggestion. And the delay in the reply *was*, in fact, rather ominous. He went on, "What I am telling you is that the only Englishman who can verify what the President might eventually say about Hastings is at present in a deep coma in hospital in Oxford. We simply cannot say whether—or if—Harald Langton will ever recover. The doctors are not optimistic."

"It seems to me, General," Evans said harshly, "that you are tacitly admitting a serious error on the part of DI5. How is it that Langton was not taken into protective custody and questioned?"

It was exceedingly strange, Sanday-Maclean thought, that it was a matter of great concern to men of Hugh Evans's Socialist persuasion that the civil rights of citizens be protected—even at the risk of the national security—unless and until those same civil rights interfered with some design of state policy *they* regarded as necessary. In the last few decades, the words *liberal* and *progressive* had taken on meanings far different from those he had been taught in school.

"There was a warrant out for Langton, Prime Minister, at the time of his accident. He was to be brought in for questioning under the provisions of the Official Secrets Act. I should point out that any reasonably competent lawyer would have had him free in fifteen minutes. We can scarcely classify an American plan with which we are totally unfamiliar."

"Soldiers and lawyers will be the ruin of this country," Evans said.

General Sanday-Maclean permitted himself the momentary disloyalty of thinking that there was more than a touch of Wat Tyler in Hugh Llewellyn Evans.

"There is, of course, a murder warrant out for Mr. Langton now. Not that it is likely he will ever have to face the charge," he said.

"The Soviets are demanding an explanation," Evans said, "as well they might be. Mr. Baturin, the Ambassador, spent all morning with the Foreign Secretary."

"Unfortunate," Sanday-Maclean murmured. "Very."

"I regard that as an understatement of vast proportions, General. Have you made any brilliant deductions concerning the reasons Harald Langton might have assaulted a Soviet trade attaché?"

"A Soviet KGB officer, Prime Minister," Sanday-Maclean said evenly. He would not permit the Prime Minister to perpetuate the fiction that the murdered man was anything but what DI5 knew him to be. "A Lieutenant Colonel Aleksandr Kadogan."

"Yes, yes. Very well, if you say so, Sir Gordon," Evans said testily. He disliked the way these intelligence people saw something sinister in every move the Soviets made. In this climate, who could blame the Kremlin for sending spies everywhere?

"Last evening Kadogan drove to Oxford where the unfortunate encounter took place. There were witnesses, Prime Minister. Guests in the hotel who saw Langton running from the scene. Saw him drop the murder instrument. A walking stick that he had apparently snatched from the victim. People in the hotel lobby said he was distraught. The police said he was driving at a dangerous speed on recently wet roads. He damaged several cars before striking the truck. In all, we have the picture of a man in panic. And we have no accurate assessment of the reason for his behavior. I can only surmise, sir, that it has something to do with Hastings." He paused and regarded the Prime Minister steadily. "I find the involvement of a Russian intelligence officer extremely suspicious."

"Yes," Hugh Evans said grudgingly. "What about the American agent?"

"We have not yet located him. The incident in Whitechapel is significant. The clerk in the hotel gave us a description that fits Colonel Brede and the Russian woman, Larissa Adanova. The Caledonian People's Liberation Army claims to have been responsible for the grenading. *The Times* received a note with all the customary rhetoric. But we believe that the CPLA is doing odd jobs to build up its treasury. They missed Brede at Heathrow and now again in Whitechapel. If the Heathrow bombing were a single incident, one might possibly believe that they were simply after killing an officer of DI5. But the attempt in the East End was aimed specifically at Brede. That ties it to Hastings, Prime Minister."

"What exactly are you suggesting, General?"

"I think the KGB has hired the CPLA to kill Farr and Brede because they were to exchange information. I hesitate to believe that a British officer would give information to the Americans that he was withholding from his own service, but I am afraid I must believe it."

"By God, General. You see the KGB behind every act of violence in the country!" Evans said exasperatedly.

"That is my opinion, Prime Minister. It makes the entire matter of the Hastings plan and the defector who purloined it into something extremely sinister. I suggest you speak once again to President Demarest and at once."

"I have asked, Sir Gordon. Am I required to beg?"

"No, sir. Of course not. But this is clearly something more than simply a matter of a misplaced contingency plan, no matter how embarrassing to the Americans. Two people are dead, one seriously injured. We don't know where Colonel Brede and the Russian girl have gone to earth or how badly they might have been hurt in the Whitechapel attack." He took a number of reports from his briefcase and laid them on the Prime Minister's desk. "These may have no connection whatever to the matter under discussion, Prime Minister. But please study them. They are the latest digest of reports from DI6. The Soviets are presently involved in the most massive maneuvers and military redeployments in years. Something is happening. We must recapture some semblance of rapport with the Americans, sir."

"Are these your spymaster's instincts at work, General?" Evans asked ironically.

"I've had forty years of experience to sharpen those instincts, sir. I beg of you, do not ignore them. Telephone the President again."

Evans sat for a moment in a brooding silence. Then he said, "Very well, Sir Gordon. I'll speak to him tomorrow."

"Today would be better, Prime Minister."

"Allow me to have *some* pride, General. British prestige is involved here. You, of all people, should appreciate that. I shall give Demarest more time to comply with my first request. Maybe he will remember his manners by tomorrow. I will call him when I return from Buckingham Palace."

General Sanday-Maclean drew a long breath. It was a better bargain than he could have hoped for when this uncomfortable interview began. And knowing the abrasive personality of Hugh Evans, it was the best resolution he was likely to get.

"Very well, Prime Minister," he said. He wished, however, that the tightness he felt in his belly—a sensation he had not been troubled with since the last tank battle of the desert campaign—would leave him.

Age, he thought. A man in his sixties was a man too old for this sort of work.

43

Richard Iron's surprisingly delicate and sensitive hands held the brush firmly. The gilt paint went onto the smooth, newly lacquered surface easily. He completed the offside **E** with a steady hand and dipped the tip of the brush into the gold paint once again to begin the Roman II.

The light in the lean-to was insufficient for the detail work he was doing, and he had been forced to borrow a lamp from Mrs. Boatwright.

The woman was growing curious about the van. She had commented on how much it now resembled a GPO vehicle and he had put her off with a remark about having a peculiarly American taste for gaudy transport. But if her interest persisted, he thought, he would have to take steps to see to it that it was terminated.

As he worked, he thought about tomorrow. It seemed strange to him that his vision of the future ended so abruptly there. It was as though a dark curtain had fallen in a certain time and a certain place. He could not imagine what the world would be like after five o'clock tomorrow afternoon. Even more strangely still, the looming void troubled him not at all. He rather fancied it, as though all that was significant and real had now compressed itself into the limits of the next thirty hours.

He had felt somewhat like this many times before a mission, but never so strongly. Nor had he ever felt so certain of the essential *righteousness* of his task. It was not a word he used often to describe the work of killing that he had spent so much of his life doing. Yet it seemed peculiarly appropriate now, and the blankness that waited just beyond the gate to Buckingham Palace at five tomorrow beckoned to him as though it were the landscape of some home he had never known.

It was hot inside the lean-to and he had stripped down to his shorts to finish the paintwork. His thin, sinewy body was streaked with perspiration and he could smell himself—a foxy odor that had little to do with cleanliness or the lack of it.

The long-haired brush completed the Roman numeral with scarcely a tremor: the line between gold and scarlet sharp and true. He liked that. He appreciated the clean division between the gold and red. It was like a symbol of all that he had accomplished: money on blood, life on death. He stepped back to regard his work and smiled. He could look quite young when he smiled.

He heard a small rustle just outside the lean-to and he turned to look through the tiny, dirt-streaked window behind him. Mrs. Boatwright was just standing there, looking at the lettering on the side of the van. For a long moment her eyes met his and were held by some invisible force that pierced the grimy glass between them.

Moving carefully, he placed the brush on the edge of the can of gold paint. When he straightened, Mrs. Boatwright had gone. He walked to the door and opened it. He stood in the white light of a sun that floated behind the high clouds like a dish in dirty water. He heard the creak of the screen door to the kitchen of the house.

He went across the dry grasses of the tiny yard to the back door and listened. The house was as silent as the air. He opened the screen door. The creak was thin, drawn-out, like the cry of some distant bird. He walked into the cool darkness of the kitchen.

He listened again for the woman and, half smiling, walked into the cluttered parlor. The blinds had been drawn against the heat. The clock on the chimneypiece, a cheap porcelain thing with the legend *Souvenir of Brighton*, scrolled with flowers, painted on it, ticked loudly.

He stood still, as quietly as he had learned to do in the jungles of Vietnam and Africa. His bare feet felt the loom of the thin rug. His half-naked body felt the almost imperceptible movements of the air about him. He stepped to the narrow stairway leading to the bedrooms on the upper story. He began to climb the stairs very carefully.

Mrs. Boatwright's room opened onto the landing, a small space narrower than a man's extended reach. Her door was closed and he turned the doorknob carefully.

The woman stood in the center of the room looking at him the way a rabbit might look at a stoat. Her eyes were wide open, pupils dilated, so that the brown irises had almost vanished.

"You were curious about the van, Mrs. Boatwright," he said, very softly.

"No," she said. "Oh, no."

He moved forward until he stood nearly touching her. Her eyes never left his. Her mouth, pale and open, made her breath sigh in her throat.

He looked at her curiously, as though she were an object and not a living being. He reached out and put his hand on her breast. She drew in a shivering suck of air. *"Don't—hurt—me—"* Somehow she shouted the words, but they made only a whisper in the silent, airless room.

He placed a hand on either side of the deep neck of her dress and gave a hard, ripping pull. The woman staggered and would have fallen, but his grip on her clothing held her erect. Her large breasts rolled free, the pink nipples exposed. For a woman in her fifties, he thought curiously, she had a strong, well-made body. She reminded him of Concha, the Paraguayan woman, who had run away from him one day on the river. The memory was blurred, distorted.

He pulled down on the ripped dress and the undergarments and the woman closed her eyes and whispered, *"Oh, God—"*

With great care he lifted her arms to free them from the torn clothing. There was no resistance in her. None at all. Her arms fell to her sides as he worked the dress and her underclothes down over her hips. Her eyes stayed closed and she had begun to tremble, her flesh working in twitching shudders, like those of a sweating mare.

He grasped her arms and lowered her to the bed. He regarded the ample belly, the dark pubic mound, the heavy thighs with a strangely serene satisfaction.

"Please," she whispered, "oh, please don't do this. . . ."

He unfastend the waistband of his shorts and let them fall. He spread the woman's broad, white thighs and cupped her breasts. He shoved her gently backward.

He looked down and saw that he was fully erect and yet he had no real sensation. It was as though the flesh he saw belonged to someone else, some stranger.

He dropped to his knees and shoved himself into the woman

with all his strength. She cried out in pain. Her shut, dry aridity balked him, hurt him, angered him. He pushed against her spread thighs and immediately climaxed without pleasure, without even the suggestion of sensation.

He closed his eyes and made a deep, animal sound of disappointment and anger. He began to tremble. He drew back his arm and struck the woman across the side of the neck with an open hand and with all his force.

She stiffened convulsively and her limbs began a jerking dance. Presently it stopped and she regarded him blankly with glazing, empty eyes.

Iron staggered to his feet and stood for a moment looking at the woman's naked body. Suddenly she seemed much older, the blemishes on her skin standing starkly against the white pallor.

Iron turned away, retrieved his shorts, walked to the landing. He dressed himself there. He was no longer angry. But the woman should not have come to spy on his work. That had been wrong of her. He walked down the stairs and through the house toward the door.

He was suddenly thirsty and he went back to the sink and poured himself a drink of water. It tasted cool and pure. Like the streams in the highlands of Southeast Asia or the brooks he remembered running from springs in the mountains of Wales. . . .

He put the glass away carefully on the sideboard and went outside into the white day. The sunlight was so diffused he seemed to cast no shadow as he returned to the lean-to.

He closed the door behind him and picked up the brush. The gold paint had dried slightly on the bristles and he softened them delicately with thinner and a bit of cotton waste. When the brush was pliable, he dipped it into the gold paint and began once again to paint the royal insignia on the scarlet side of the false postal van.

44

The flat in Knightsbridge was a large and elegant maisonette overlooking Hyde Park and the Serpentine. It belonged to a Dr. Morris Silver and his wife, two English Zionists whose dedication to Zionism did not extend to living in Israel, though they visited that country each year in summer.

Brede and Lara found themselves amid sheet-covered furnishings that included an enormous projection-style television set and a full-sized grand piano. Hannah Silver had been a low-ranked concert artist before her marriage to the affluent Dr. Silver.

Lara, familiar with the flat, bandaged Brede's wound with the extensive supplies she found in the master bathroom. Brede had called the American embassy to ask for Simonini and received the curious reply that Mr. Simonini had gone to Oxford and was not expected back for twenty-four hours. Brede, reluctant to use an insecure line for a call to Dracott in Washington, said that he would call back.

"Oxford," he told Lara. "Simonini is trying to reach Langton."

"Can you be sure?"

"An educated guess. Wouldn't Harald Langton have friends in Oxford?"

"It is likely, Robert."

"I should go there."

"No," the girl said with surprising force. "Not now, not today. What you really should do is see a doctor."

Brede grinned. "And say what? That I picked up a piece of shrapnel in an East End street?" He was sitting on a large and formless sofa draped with a white dust cover. He reached for the girl and said, "You are something, Larissa Adanova. Something remarkable."

She sat beside him, very close, and he shut his eyes wearily. The sounds of Knightsbridge were muffled by the closed draperies and the thick, elegant carpeting of the flat.

Lara said, "I should have brought us here first."

Brede shook his head. "You were right not to. I'm sorry even now to be involving your absent friends."

"Morris Silver met my father on one of his trips to Moscow. Morris is the sort of smart-set traveler who goes wherever it is fashionable to go. That year it was smart to go to Russia." She frowned. "I shouldn't make it sound like that, should I. There is a place for clever, rich Jews who like to be fashionable."

"But you called him a Zionist."

"That is fashionable in some circles. You aren't Jewish so you wouldn't know. But I think Morris and Hannah are sincere. They send a great deal of money to Israel."

"You don't sound as though you approve," Brede said.

"The Israelis used me, Robert."

"You can't blame them for that, Lara."

"Yes, I think I can. They should have warned me that there was no chance of helping my father. They should have told me that I was only making things worse by appearing on all those television shows and talking about him."

Brede leaned back on the soft cushions and held the girl's slender body against his own. "I think," he said deliberately, "I have fallen in love with you."

She pressed her face against his shoulder in answer.

He said, "It's too soon."

She shook her head.

After a time he said, "There is work to do."

"Not yet," she said, and put his hand on her breast.

Brede sat at a table in the drawing room, studying the blood-stained book he had carried from Rye to Nameless House and now here to London. The pages were crusted with black. His blood flaked away in tiny dark shards.

Lara appeared from the bathroom, dressed in a borrowed robe. Her hair hung in wet ringlets about her face. Her skin glowed, smooth and pale as rich cream. Brede thought she looked beautiful.

"Why did you keep the book, Robert?"

"I don't know," Brede said. "It seemed important, somehow. Maybe not."

She looked at the black stains.

"I should change the dressing on your side," she said. "Let me."

She disappeared and returned with gauze and sterile pads. Brede helped her strip away the soiled bandages. The wound looked cruel, but clean. It had begun to crust over.

"It should be sewn," Lara said.

"Sutured. The word is sutured," Brede said, grimacing. "You sew a button. You suture a used target."

She finished taping a clean pad to his ribs. She ran a hand over a scar extending from his shoulder halfway across his chest. "It isn't the first time, is it."

"No. That one came from Vietnam."

"Was it very bad, that war?"

"All wars are bad. The ones you lose are worse," he said shortly. He turned his attention back to the book. "Why did he rip out this page, do you suppose? He's a writer. Writers don't tear up books for no reason." He bent to examine the book more carefully, running his fingertips over the pages.

"Something was heavily underscored. Something on the preceding page," he said.

Lara tilted her head inquisitively. "Is that important?"

"It's curious." He looked up and asked, "What time is it?"

"It's rising noon."

Brede suppressed a smile at the Russian-accented archaic Briticism. He said, "Let's dress. Would your friends object too much if we extended their hospitality to some borrowed clothes? Is Morris about my size?"

"I wouldn't know," she said with a flash of wicked humor. "I think you and he are about the same height."

He stood and reached under the robe to hold her against him. He kissed her and said, "I've picked a hell of a time to find a girl." He let his hands enjoy her for a moment and then said, "Let's dress. I want you to go straight from here to the American embassy. Do you know where it is?"

"Everyone knows about Grosvenor Square. All the best anti-American demonstrations are still held there."

He considered. He disliked being separated from Lara, but she would actually be safer in the daylight without him. "I want you to go to the embassy and wait for me there."

"Where will you go?"

"First to a bookstore. Then to a public telephone to call Major Alan Goddamn Hobbs."

"Because of this?" She touched the bloodstained book with her fingertips.

"It may be nothing at all. But I want to know what it was that Langton underlined on the page that is missing."

"Hatchards," she said.

"In Piccadilly?"

"Yes. It is the best bookstore in the city. Colin used to say it."

At the mention of Colin Farr, Brede studied Larissa's face.

"It's all right, Robert," she said gently. "It all seems a very long time ago." Then her expression hardened, so that her slender face seemed cut from stone. "But someone should pay, Robert. Colin Farr was a good man."

"Someone will pay, Lara," Brede said. But he didn't really believe it. The way this nasty game was played, the men who placed the wagers were never the ones who lost them.

The clerk was not more than eighteen years old. She wore a saggy cardigan and her long hair hung about her face like a shower curtain. But she was bright, quick, and accommodating. She handled the book gingerly, but not nearly so gingerly as she would have if she had known what the black stains were.

"We may be out of stock on this Pan edition, sir," she said. "But I believe there's a hardback with all of the Hemingway journalism. Let's go and see."

"I'm sorry," Brede said. "I particularly want a copy of this edition. Another won't do."

The girl looked dubious. "It is out of print, I think." She brightened and said, "But let me look in the stock room. Shall I do that?"

"Please," Brede said. He followed her into the paperback department.

"I'll only be a moment, sir," she said, and vanished through a door behind the stacks.

It took her considerably more than a moment, but when she appeared—looking even more disheveled than before—she had a copy of the book in her hands. "It's rather in poor condition, sir. The cover's rather badly bent, I'm afraid. But it is the only copy I was able to find. Will it do, do you think?"

He paid for the book gratefully and walked out of the shop.

The traffic in Piccadilly was heavy. The sky above the buildings was a flat white. Pedestrians hurried about their business with a purposeful intensity that was supposed to be, but was not, un-British.

Brede walked down the street to a small red-brick church. A minute courtyard, with grass and flowers, lay between the church and the street. An old sign on the railings explained that the building was undergoing renovation to repair damage done during the Blitz. Brede smiled at that. He had been in London perhaps a dozen times since his first visit as a student in 1955. The sign was exactly as he remembered it. He suspected that if he were to come to London at the turn of the next century, the tiny church would still be undergoing renovation to repair damage done by a German bomb in 1941.

He stepped into the courtyard and sat on an iron bench. He began to compare the two copies of the book.

The missing page was one on which had been printed an essay from *Esquire* magazine, published in September 1935. The piece was entitled "Notes on the Next War" and Hemingway had been in a prophetic mood when he had written it.

Brede read: *"Not this August, nor this September; you have this year to do in what you like. Not next August, nor next September; that is still too soon; they are still too prosperous from the way things are picking up when armament factories start at near capacity; they never fight as long as money can be made without. But the year after that or the year after that they fight."*

Brede held the book open with a finger and sat for a time in thought. The piece had been written in a time when a whole generation—Hemingway's generation—believed in the myth of the Merchants of Death. The simple idea that wars were caused by arms merchants was no longer quite acceptable—not in an era of nuclear war. But the attack on a forerunner of the "military-industrial complex" would certainly appeal to a man of Harald Langton's cast of mind.

He ran a finger lightly over the slight indentation in the page of the book he had taken from Cadman's Blue and then compared it with the preceding page in the book he had just purchased at Hatchards.

The phrase Langton had underscored was *Not this August. . . .*

Brede put the books in his pocket and slowly began to walk toward Bond Street. He was slightly disappointed. The phrase, by itself, meant nothing that he could fathom. It was a poor recompense for all that he and Lara had undergone since they had committed their meager burglary on Langton's holiday house.

As Brede walked along Bond Street he found himself remembering another time. Long ago, with Jessica, he had strolled down this street and they had stopped at Herbert Johnson's to buy a crash helmet (Brede had been playing at racing sports cars in those far-off days). He remembered the care with which the hatter had measured his skull, how the helmet had been made by laminating numberless strips of thin linen over the form with varnish. The finished product had been a work of art. Not terribly effective for protecting against a broken head, but a lovely handcrafted thing to see.

He remembered, too, that there had been a shop cat, the largest feline he had ever seen or ever would see: a dignified, self-satisfied beast of thirty pounds or more, with great, solemn yellow eyes and a manner so lordly and aristocratic that it had brought tears of laughter to Jess's eyes.

He looked for the shop now, but Herbert Johnson's had moved away and in its place there was a sleek emporium selling Japanese radios, calculators, and television sets.

He stood for a moment in the doorway, regarding the changed premises with genuine regret. It was then that he heard the name Harald Langton.

It had come from an immense television set in the window of the shop. The new System 3 newscaster was describing in some detail the events of the previous night in Oxford.

The telephone operator at the Ministry of Defense was not helpful. It took Brede ten minutes to get through and the only reply he received was that yes, there was a Major Hobbs in the Ministry, but no, he was not available.

Of course, Brede thought, he wouldn't be in London. He, too, would be in Oxford. He broke the connection and hurried down Grosvenor Street toward the embassy.

Lara was waiting for him in the lobby. He went to her and said, "Langton's in the hospital in Oxford. The news says he killed a Russian trade attaché."

"I don't understand, Robert. Why would he do a thing like that?"

"Let's find out," Brede said. He walked through the foyer to the receptionist's desk and asked if Edward Simonini had returned.

He had not. Brede showed the girl his DIA card and said, "I need to talk to him. Find him and put through a call."

"If you'll wait just a moment, Colonel." The girl pressed a call button on her panel and said, "There is a Colonel Brede here from Washington."

She replaced the receiver and said, "Someone will be with you straightaway, Colonel."

It was even faster than that. A red-faced young man in a Brooks suit came running down the marble staircase. "Colonel Brede?"

"I'm Brede. When is Simonini due back?"

The young man looked about him anxiously. There were people going and coming through the foyer and they made him uncomfortable. "I'm Carlson, Mr. Simonini's administrative assistant, Colonel. Could you come with me?"

Brede took Lara's arm. The young man seemed doubtful. Brede said, "Let's go, Carlson."

The CIA man led them up the stairs to the second story and then down a long passageway to a suite of offices at the rear of the building. The office was strictly GI, with gray steel desks and a pallidly upholstered chair and sofa. A picture of John Scott Demarest regarded them serenely from the office wall.

Brede said, "I need to talk to General Dracott in Washington on a secure line."

"I'm—I can't authorize the use of a tight line, Colonel. Mr. Simonini will have to do that."

"Then get him on the phone."

"He—ah—isn't in the building, Colonel. Could you just give your message to me—"

Brede cut him off with parade-ground brusqueness. "He's in Oxford. Very probably at one of the hospitals there. Get him on the line. Now, Mr. Carlson."

Carlson's lips thinned, but he sat down and picked up his telephone. He spoke to a secretary in an outer office. "Diana, will you put me through to Mr. Simonini. Yes. I know that. Have him paged."

He replaced the telephone and said, "This shouldn't take long, Colonel."

Brede regarded the young man steadily. Then the suggestion of a smile touched his lips and he said, "Did you ever get your Spitfire back, Carlson?"

"Yes, Colonel. The police returned it. Thank you."

"Thank you for the use of it. I hope they didn't damage it."

"No, sir. It was fine."

The telephone rang and he snatched at it. "Sim? Colonel Brede is here in the office." He extended the receiver to Brede.

Brede said, "How's Langton?"

"Not good," Simonini said. "Where in hell have you been? Were you in Whitechapel?"

"Is Hobbs there?"

"Yes," Simonini said.

"I need to talk to General Dracott. Tell your man."

There was a long pause. Then Simonini said, "Colonel, Paul Bruckner doesn't want you to do that. He wants you to drop the whole thing and come home. Immediately."

Brede stood quite still. An angry chill ran through him. That was supposed to be it? All bets were off now that Langton was next to dead. Forget it. Come home.

"I want that order from General Dracott personally," Brede said. "He's the one who sent me."

"I'm sorry, Colonel," Simonini said. "Wait. Dwight Lamb is here. He wants to talk to you."

Another voice came on the line. "This is Lamb, Colonel. Do you know who I am?"

"Yes."

"Then I'm giving you an order. Get on the first airplane leaving London for Washington. We don't need you here any longer."

"I work for General Dracott," Brede said. "I go when he says so. Not before."

"There's nothing you can do here, Brede. You're in the way."

It hit Brede then. Lamb, the Director of Operations of the CIA, knew exactly what Hastings was. He knew it and intended to stand by in Oxford until Langton's silence was guaranteed. If Langton didn't die soon, Dwight Lamb might very well take corrective action.

"It won't work, Lamb," he said. "Langton did something with the material Daniels gave him. I intend to find out what. Do I get through to you?"

The young man behind the desk flinched at the tone of voice Brede was using on the DOO of Central Intelligence.

Lamb shouted, *"Damn it, Brede. You stay clear of this now!"*

"Try to stay calm, Lamb," Brede said.

"Let me talk to Carlson again."

"I have a message for Major Hobbs," Brede said, ignoring Lamb's demand. "Tell him when I see him I'm going to punch his well-bred face," Brede said, and hung up.

He turned to Lara and said, "Let's go."

Carlson half rose from the desk, appalled at Brede's end of the conversation with his superiors.

Brede put a hand on Carlson's shoulders and said, "Don't get up. We'll see ourselves out."

As they stepped through the door into the passageway, Brede heard Carlson's telephone begin to ring again.

45

Despite the fact that it was already after two in the morning in Moscow, Pavel Nikitin's image on the television link looked ruddy and rested, his expression jovial and slightly comical. It was the picture of a man at peace with the world and with himself.

John Demarest thought sourly that his own, on the monitor in Moscow, probably reflected the sleepless night he had spent and the griping suspicions that were wrenching him.

He disliked Pavel Nikitin. There was a quality of falsity in the slightly clownish manner and appearance that he cultivated. Underneath the fat-lipped smiles and the flowery English he affected, the steely personality of the true despot lay like a reef under shoal water. At the two summits held since his election, John Demarest had learned to deal very cautiously, indeed, with Pavel Grigorevich Nikitin.

"I really must apologize for the timing of this call, Comrade President," Demarest said, the Communist honorific like a stone in his mouth. "I realize how late it is in Moscow."

"Do not trouble yourself, Mr. President," Nikitin replied, smiling. "I seldom go to bed early. We don't need the sleep we used to when we were young men, do we." He indicated someone in the room behind him. "I have Marshal Kunavin here with me as you requested. I presume Admiral Winfield is with you?"

"Yes," President Demarest said.

Nikitin beamed a broad smile into the television link. "Then we had better be careful what we say. These military fellows won't want us to give away any secrets."

Demarest took a deep breath. Nikitin habitually used facetiousness as a screen when dealing with Americans. He thought it effective. Demarest found it annoying. He said, "We are becoming concerned, Comrade President, about the extent of the military redeployments the Soviet Union has been making. I thought it prudent to speak to you directly to avoid any misunderstandings."

"My dear Mr. President," Nikitin said. "Surely you were notified about the Red Autumn exercises?" He turned to speak to Kunavin, who now appeared on the screen behind him, resplendent in full service dress with medals. Facing back into the television eye, Nikitin said, "Kunavin assures me that you were. The terms of the Kabul protocol were adhered to precisely."

"We were notified, Comrade President," Demarest said, "but our surveillance and verification systems are being interfered with, and it has become impossible to assure ourselves that your redispositions are what Marshal Kunavin has reported." Actually, the Nathan Hale and Prober satellite systems were functioning perfectly, despite evidence that attempts were being made to reduce their efficiency. Such interference with spy vehicles was frequent. No satisfactory agreement to prevent it had ever been able to get by the Soviet SALT negotiating teams. The American military establishment had learned to pretend that the Soviet lasers and electromagnetic beams were at least partially effective. In this way it was hoped that the Russians would delay further perfecting the devices.

"There is no question of the Soviet Union attempting to blind your satellites, Mr. President," Nikitin said positively. "My academicians tell me that even our own are functioning inefficiently recently. Something to do with sunspots. I don't pretend to understand all that scientific talk, but I can tell you without hesitation that your sputniks are safe and well."

"If you say so, Comrade President," Demarest said, "I will, of course, accept your word. But nevertheless your Red Autumn maneuvers are causing some anxiety in the NATO command. Our naval strategists are disturbed about the force you have concentrated in the Persian Gulf, as well."

Nikitin's eyebrows rose in an expression of total disbelief. "You can say that, Mr. President, when you have dispatched the *Dwight Eisenhower* all the way from the China Sea to the Arabian Sea?"

"The transfer of the *Eisenhower* is a routine naval redeployment for us," Demarest said. "She has been due to be based at Diego Garcia for several months. We chose this time, quite frankly, because of the threatening nature of your Red Autumn maneuvers." There, chew on that, you fat Russian bastard, Demarest thought. One lie begets another.

"There is nothing whatever threatening about our military exercises," Nikitin said, dropping the smiling demeanor. "We conduct maneuvers every summer, as your military advisers well know."

"It would be taken here as a sign of goodwill, Comrade President," Demarest said, "if you would reduce the scope of these particular maneuvers."

Behind Nikitin, Kunavin murmured something. Nikitin nodded and said, "The Minister tells me that it would be extremely difficult—perhaps impossible—to cancel Red Autumn on such short notice, Mr. President." The buffoon's smile made a brief reappearance. "You know how devoted to routine these soldiers are. Everything falls to pieces if you ask them to go to Minsk instead of Pinsk."

"Nevertheless, Comrade President," Demarest said, "a slightly lower profile for Red Autumn would make all of our current negotiations easier." The reference was to SALT III, the only carrot available to hold out to Nikitin. The Russians, who gained strategic advantage each time a SALT treaty was negotiated, responded to such blandishments when they would respond to nothing else.

"You make far too much out of a simple military exercise, Mr. President. Red Autumn is now under way and will be completed in less than a week. It presents no threat whatever to the United States or its allies."

The carrot, then, was refused. Demarest did not find that reassuring. "Very well, Comrade President," he said. "We will say no more about it. But you will understand that we will be making a number of defensive realignments in consequence of your refusal."

Nikitin spread his hands in the gesture of a sorrowing peddler. "Ah, Mr. President. If we could only learn to trust one another fully. What a pleasant place the world would be then."

"I agree, Comrade President. Perhaps in time," Demarest said. "I will bid you good-morning, sir."

"*Dospidanya*, Mr. President," Nikitin said. The screen flipped to a computer-coding display intended to record and identify the hot-line conversation for the archives.

Demarest turned to Admiral Winfield. "What do you say, Stephen?"

"I don't like it, Mr. President. He didn't even sniff at your bait."

"How important can these maneuvers be to them?"

"As exercises? Hardly at all."

"What else, then?"

"They are positioning themselves for a strike at Western Europe, Mr. President. I can't be certain they actually intend crossing into Germany at this time. But we can't afford to ignore the possibility."

"What about the position in the south?"

"If I were Kunavin, and if I were preparing a strike to the west, and if I had even one-half of his conventional force superiority—I would not hesitate to send a force into the oil regions. It would cripple the West and feed the Russian economy and armed forces. The strategic position is perfectly clear, sir. Red Autumn is either a practice run at preparing for a war in Western Europe or it is the real thing being set up. Those are the only two possibilities."

"Why now, Stephen?"

"Why not, Mr. President? Nikitin is having a great deal of trouble with the ethnic and religious minorities inside Russia. He knows he is going to need oil, plenty of it, to fuel his economy between now and the end of the century. And he has both nuclear parity with us and an enormous advantage in men, aircraft, and armor. So why *not* now?"

"The risk, Stephen," the President said. "The terrible *risk*."

"The risk could be minimized by splitting NATO, Mr. President."

"That goddamned Hastings thing again."

"Yes, Mr. President," the Chairman of the Joint Chiefs said.

"Paul Bruckner wants me to give the Prime Minister a phony Hastings. He thinks we can paper it over."

"Possible," Admiral Winfield said.

"Is that all you have to say about it, Admiral?"

"Not my department, Mr. President. My job is to help NATO fight if it comes to it. I would like to airlift half the Quick Reaction Force to Britain, sir. Just to be on the safe side."

"An exercise, Admiral?" the President asked ironically.

"We could call it that," Admiral Winfield said stolidly.

The President looked at the characterless walls of the small White House television studio. They were as empty and bleak as he himself felt at this moment. But the problems created by subordinates were part of the job of being President. Harry Truman had been right, if banal, in declaring that "The buck stops here."

"Provocative as hell," he said.

"Yes, I agree," Winfield said. "Nevertheless."

"Can it be done quickly?"

"We can move an army group to England in Skylifters in four days," Winfield said. "Can you get the Prime Minister's permission?"

"Frankly," the President said grimly, "I doubt it. I even hesitate to ask. Relations between ourselves and the British have never been worse."

"Well, sir," Winfield said. "You have my recommendation. The other chiefs all concur. Branston wants to send the Second Marine Division as well."

"Semper fidelis," Demarest muttered. The Commandant of the

Marine Corps never failed to search for roles the Corps might play. "I suppose he'd like them to land on the beaches in full battle gear."

"I recommend against that," Winfield said humorlessly. "But we should place ourselves in a position to reinforce NATO if the need arises."

Demarest heaved himself out of his chair in sudden decision. It would simply be impossible to approach Hugh Evans with a request that he accommodate twenty thousand more troops on his island for an indefinite stay. Military and political considerations were at odds. And in time of peace, the political considerations had to take precedence. If we *are* at peace, Demarest amended.

"I'm sorry, Stephen," he said. "We'll simply have to wait on this."

"If you say so, Mr. President," Admiral Winfield said.

"I will authorize you to alert the forces you think we might need in the emergency you foresee."

"Yes, Mr. President. And the strategic forces?"

"Good God, no."

"May I at least send out a Defcon One warning?"

A Defcon was an advisory bulletin to all strategic commands requiring them to hold themselves in readiness for further alerting. It was the first step in a very short and very steep climb to full readiness for war. The thought of issuing even such a low-level command gave John Scott Demarest a cold chill. But Admiral Winfield was right to make the request.

"Very well, Stephen," he said heavily. "Let's go to Defcon One."

46

The New Oxford General Hospital, up from St. Catherine's College, was a great sprawl of glass and stressed concrete. The construction, plagued with work stoppages, had taken the better part of five years to complete. It had attracted protests and demonstrations from succeeding generations of students and criticism from purists, tourists, and architects, all to no avail. The National Health Service had demanded it and now it lay on the riverbank like a cubist dragon about to devour the more traditional buildings that surrounded it. It was always ominous; in the summer dusk it looked malevolent, the flat planes and glazed surfaces reflecting the last light of the sky with a glaring lack of warmth.

Harald Langton, or rather the artificially supported body that had been Harald Langton, now lay on a high bed in the intensive care unit in the south wing of the hospital.

The doctors who had examined Langton when he had been wheeled into the emergency room had been amazed to find that he was still living. His back had been broken in two places, the fractures crushing both the vertebrae and the spinal cord. His right leg had been so badly shattered that it had been necessary to perform an emergency amputation. His chest and abdomen had been smashed against the steering column of the Mercedes, with injuries to his lungs and spleen. But his most serious injury, and the one most likely to prevent his recovery, was a massive compound fracture of the skull which the attending neurologist felt certain had caused irreversible damage to the parietal lobes of the brain.

In the ICU, Langton lay under a clear plastic sheet intended to protect him against ambient infections. A respirator breathed for him, filling and emptying his bruised lungs with oxygen. I.V. drips fed him whole blood and huge amounts of antibiotics. An electronic monitor painted his vital functions in jagged phosphorescent traces across a cathode-ray tube in the room and repeated them on a screen at the floor nurse's station.

Despite the fact that Langton was obviously a man of importance, under ordinary circumstances the medical staff at New Oxford would have declined to use such heroic methods to maintain a life that was so very nearly lost. But Hobbs had demanded that Langton be kept alive at whatever cost in time or money. The medical staff, impressed in spite of themselves by his DI5 credentials, had done their best to comply. The resident in charge of the Casualty Department had been replaced by the hospital's Senior Surgical Consultant; the interns on the case had been relieved and the Senior Neurological Consultant, and the Senior Consultant Physician, had taken their places.

All of this, the Senior Neurological Consultant assured Major Hobbs, might possibly keep the human vegetable on the bed alive (depending, of course, on how one defined the term), but it was improbable that Harald Langton would ever again regain consciousness.

As long as the electroencephalograph trace on the monitor showed the slightest sign of cerebral activity, Hobbs insisted, the staff would be expected to continue the full spectrum of intensive care.

In the doctor's lounge of the south wing, taken over for the duration of the emergency by Major Hobbs and his associates, Dwight Lamb sat smoking his way through his fourth pack of cigarettes. He had exhausted his supply of Americans and now had to rely on British, which he privately thought tasted like wet straw.

Across the formica table from Lamb, Edward Simonini finished the tasteless meat sandwich and weak coffee that comprised his evening meal. He was tired, grubby, and deeply worried as he looked at Lamb's thin, puritanical face.

The man was clearly glad that Langton was so near to expiring.

He had the look of one simply waiting for a windfall, and ready, if need be, to help it come about. That would not be necessary, Simonini thought. Harald Langton had about as much chance of returning to real life as Rare Ben Jonson, planted upright under the flagstones of Westminster Abbey.

Hobbs, however, refused to give up hope. There were only three people in England who could tell the major what he wanted to know. Two of them were American intelligence officers who had no intention of doing so, and the third was that pitiful mountain of savaged flesh in the ICU.

At this moment, Major Alan Hobbs, muffled in sterile gown, cap, and mask, sat in the shadowy corner of the intensive care unit under the unsympathetic glare of a nursing sister, a young and idealistic creature from the Isle of Wight, who was convinced that the intelligence officer was a new and horrible kind of ghoul.

Hobbs appreciated her feelings; he was not far from sharing them. But he could not afford to miss the slightest chance that Harald Langton might regain consciousness and enough strength to utter a useful word or two.

To that end he had insisted that a sensitive microphone be pinned to Langton's mattress—dreadful, revolting touch. He thought about that as he watched the reels turning slowly on the recorder, and he fought to stay awake.

In the cold room—*morgue* was a term no longer in favor in hospital circles—at the far end of the west wing, Lieutenant Colonel Aleksandr Alcksandrevich Kadogan lay naked on a stainless-steel slab inside a long drawer of the refrigerator. His empty eyes stared without interest at the bottom of the slab overhead. Colonel Kadogan, alumnus of Staunton and The Citadel, had performed his last service to the Soviet state. The sprained ankle that had inadvertently cost him so dear, would never heal now.

47

The clock on the mantel of General Henry Dracott's library struck eleven. The summer night lay like a dark presence around the house and the quiet Fort Myer street on which it was situated. Through the tall windows Davis Carradine could see the floodlit spire of the Washington Monument, a spear of light rising into the sky glow over the city.

Henry Dracott spoke quietly into the telephone. "Yes. I understand. Good-night, Mr. President." He placed the instrument in its cradle with a feeling of genuine sadness and regret.

The President had spoken with Pavel Nikitin on the White House–Kremlin link. That he had done so was hardly surprising. But that he had done so without discussing it with his National Security Adviser first was significant. It came to Henry Dracott that events had at last overrun him: events—and the new morality that had been rising around him ever since he had become involved in the Hastings affair.

Dracott had spoken out to John Demarest about the doubts it would cast on his integrity and that of the United States if he were to lie to the Prime Minister of Great Britain about Hastings. He had felt it absolutely imperative that he do so. John Demarest had considered, and had decided against him. Events in England had now made it possible for the President to lie and be safe from discovery. When next Hugh Evans called to ask again about the nature of Hastings, the President of the United States would dishonor himself and his country. "It's in the national interest, Henry," the President had said. "I regret it more than I can say, but I hope you will understand."

It was at that point that Henry Dracott had said simply, "I understand, Mr. President. Good-night."

He thought about Paul Bruckner, who would certainly be the

next National Security Adviser. He did not doubt for a moment that Paul would accept the post with genuine regret for having displaced a man he admired—even loved, if one could use such a word when speaking of Paul Bruckner. But he would take the job *in the national interest*. And so it would go on, and the business of promoting some sense of truth and honor between states would suffer one more small setback. No great tragedy, Henry Dracott thought wearily, but certainly a small one. And the paths to honorable peace were strewn with the wreckage of these small tragedies.

He now gave his attention, albeit unwillingly, to the man seated across the coffee table from him. Davis Carradine was sweating, eager to retrieve his fortunes.

"He will give Evans Hastings Two, Henry?"

General Dracott bridled at the familiarity. He had never liked Davis Carradine. He liked him less now that he seemed on the way to rehabilitation. Paul had been directly responsible for that, Dracott thought. The whole idea of a false plan to be given the Prime Minister had not originated with Carradine, but with Paul Bruckner. The thought filled him with profound sadness.

"When the Prime Minister calls again. Yes," Dracott said.

Carradine leaned forward anxiously. "I heard from Dwight Lamb, Henry. He spoke to your man Colonel Brede, who was very rude and uncooperative."

"What did Lamb do to provoke it?" General Dracott asked coldly.

"He tried to get him to drop the Hastings investigation. Brede flat-out refused."

A slow smile touched the general's fine features. "Yes. Robert Brede would do that."

"But you see that he *must* drop it now," Carradine said emphatically. "The man Daniels contacted in England is dying. When he's finished—and Lamb says he hasn't a prayer—there won't be a single Englishman who knows beans about Hastings. Evans will have to swallow anything the President serves him."

Henry Dracott regarded Carradine as though he were an offensive object suddenly appearing in his library.

Carradine persisted. "Brede has to drop it, Henry. He must." He rubbed his damp palms against his trouser legs. "He won't take an order from Dwight Lamb. He will drop it only if he gets a direct order from you. He told Dwight that he wouldn't obey even Paul. It has to be you. Personally."

"Yes," Dracott said softly.

"What do you mean, yes? I don't understand."

"I wouldn't expect you to understand, Mr. Carradine," General Dracott said.

Davis Carradine shook his head impatiently. "I can have someone from the London Station round up Brede and bring him to the embassy. Will you give him the order to break it off, General?"

For a moment all of the years of Henry Dracott's military career came into conflict with what he knew to be right. American soldiers *always* subordinated themselves to politicians. It was one of the things that made the republic unique. American officers never made coups, never intimidated civilian officials, never told them no. And yet he knew with all the strength still left in him that there were times when this acquiescence had resulted—*would* result again—in terrible damage to the nation. History was filled with bitter examples. Washington's conduct of the Revolution had been crippled by the interference of the Continental Congress. The cost in lives had been beyond counting. Political generalship had probably prolonged the Civil War by a year, perhaps two. Political decisions made at Yalta had lost all of Eastern Europe to the Soviets, and the soldiers had never said no. Politicians had involved the nation in Vietnam and politicians had nearly destroyed the fighting spirit of the Army there by refusing it a chance at victory. The Joint Chiefs time and again compromised their military judgment on SALT in response to the demands of Presidents, instead of resigning and speaking out.

It was time, he thought, for one old soldier to make one small act of conscience. It filled him with pleasure to do it now.

"I suggest you tell your people in London to leave Colonel Brede strictly alone, Mr. Carradine," he said. "Because I have no intention whatsoever of changing the instructions I personally gave him last week. Will I give him an order to break it off?" He came to his feet, tall and erect. "My answer is specifically and emphatically *no*. And now, sir, if you will forgive me, it is late and I am an old man who needs his sleep. I give you a good-night, Mr. Carradine."

48

Iris Hoskins was a curious woman. A widow, like her friend Emma Boatwright, her means were limited and her pleasures few. One of these few pleasures, however, was the satisfaction of the questions she asked herself about her neighbors.

A gaunt woman well into her sixties, with a face that had never been pleasant to look upon, a voice that was at once rasping and nasal in tone, and a disposition that limited severely her circle of acquaintances, she was given to taking considerable liberties with those few she possessed. Her relations tended to pass her from one to the other, conscious of their obligations to an old and lonely woman, but always eager to see to it that the next Hoskins in line should do his or her duty.

On this summer Thursday morning, Mrs. Hoskins alighted from the omnibus at the High Street stop burdened with her cardboard suitcase and a totally unseasonable and unneeded coat and umbrella. She had spent the last eight days with a son and daughter-in-law in Gravesend. It had been a visit that had ended, as most of her visits did, with an argument concerning the life style and personal habits of her host and hostess, and during the entire journey home Mrs. Hoskins had seethed with outraged indignation and an overwhelming desire to tell someone *her* side of the story.

Her house, a semidetached brick house exactly like all the others in the narrow working-class street, was two doors from the similar house owned by Emma Boatwright. And once Mrs. Hoskins had let herself in and deposited her belongings, she set out immediately to call on Emma in order to unburden herself of the many and grievous indignities she had been forced to accept along with the hospitality of her son and daughter-in-law. A cup of tea, she thought, as she hurried down the street, would not come amiss; Emma Boatwright (though rather given to putting on middle-class airs) was not an ungracious hostess.

Iris Hoskins was disappointed when she had no answer to her knock on her neighbor's door. She stood on the step, her long nose twitching with annoyance. It was unlike Emma to be from home at ten in the morning. She did her shopping much earlier, and, as Iris Hoskins made a point of knowing, usually on Tuesdays and on Fridays, when the fishmonger's stock was fresh.

Had Iris not suffered injustices at the hands of her son and his chit of a wife, she most probably would have simply returned home without investigating Emma Boatwright's failure to answer her knock. But in the back of Iris Hoskins's mind lay the unpleasant suspicion that Emma might actually be at home and that she had chosen, for reasons as yet unknown, not to answer the door and offer her friend a cup of tea.

Iris knocked again, more vigorously, and called out. There was still no reply.

Mrs. O'Dwyer, the rather slatternly greengrocer's wife who lived next door, raised a window overlooking the narrow space between the houses and said, "Oh, it's you, Mrs. Hoskins. I couldn't imagine who was making all that noise."

Mrs. Hoskins, bridling, said, "I've come to call on Mrs. Boatwright."

"I can see that," Mrs. O'Dwyer said. "She isn't at home. She hasn't been at home since yesterday." Her tone became slightly insinuating. "Maybe she's gone somewhere with young Mr. Carter."

Instantly alert to something new to be learned about a neighbor, Iris Hoskins asked, "And who, if I may make so bold, is Mr. Carter?"

"You've been away, I see."

"In Gravesend, with my Tommy and his wife," Mrs. Hoskins said, implying grand things.

Mrs. O'Dwyer ignored her suggestion. "Mr. Carter is Emma's new, young American friend." She leaned on the sill and swung her body to and fro in response to some instinctive and unsuspected rhythm that still remained in her aging body. Mrs. Hoskins disapproved entirely. Mrs. O'Dwyer had the reputation of being, or perhaps only wanting to be, the neighborhood's tart. Her implication about Emma Boatwright and Mr. Carter (whoever *he* might be) was plain and Mrs. Hoskins was outraged.

"What are you suggesting, Mrs. O'Dwyer?" she demanded.

"Nothing, I'm sure," the other woman replied archly. "It's just that Emma has taken in a new lodger—a young fellow who likes to work half-naked in the lean-to." Her shaft delivered, she retreated into her house and lowered the window before Iris could reply.

Furious, Mrs. Hoskins walked around the narrow house to the rear door. It stood slightly ajar. She thrust her head inside the kitchen and halooed. The house was still, empty.

Nervous now, but driven by her insatiable curiosity, she stood undecided. It was totally unlike Emma Boatwright to leave her house unlocked.

Mrs. Hoskins found herself tiptoeing on the dry grass to peer through the single, tiny window of the garage. It was empty, as it usually was: few of Mrs. Boatwright's temporaries owned cars, though the garage was a convenience to those few who had owned one.

On the dirt floor stood a green wooden crate with letters and numbers stenciled upon it in black. The crate was empty, too. There was a thin fuzz of red on the floor and a number of empty tins that were streaked with red. In the corner stood a box on which had been placed some sort of electric device built around a red paint-stained bottle. By the side of the lean-to were the boxes and crates of Emma Boatwright's odds and ends that were customarily kept inside the flimsy structure.

Mrs. Hoskins returned to the kitchen door and stood for a time, undecided. Then she pushed the door open with a fingertip and called out Emma's name. In return there was only silence.

Iris began to worry. She considered, but only for a moment, asking the O'Dwyer woman to come with her into Emma's house. But that would not do. If there was nothing wrong, she would feel a fool.

She stepped into the kitchen and looked about. There were a few dirty dishes in the sink. That disturbed her more than the silence. It was totally unlike Emma Boatwright to leave unwashed crockery in her kitchen. She was a compulsively neat housekeeper.

Iris Hoskins stepped gingerly into the sitting room. For a moment she could not tell what it was about the dark room that troubled her. Then she realized that the clock above the electric fire was stopped. It was a cheap thing that Mr. Boatwright had bought for Emma in Brighton, and it needed winding every day.

Iris leaned into the stairwell and called out Emma's name, but softly now. Loud noises seemed out of place in this silent, empty house.

She backed away from the stairs, resolved suddenly to get out.

Perhaps even to call the police to come and see what it was that was wrong here. Because there *was* something: she could feel it, like an ache in her bones.

She listened for the possible return of the unknown Mr. Carter. Or for the sound of her friend's voice in the street outside. But there was nothing, would *be* nothing. She was oddly certain of that.

She took a step toward the stairs again and said aloud to herself, "Curiosity killed the cat, Iris Hoskins." Since her husband died, no one but Emma Boatwright called her Iris. Somehow this odd fact convinced the old woman that she owed it to her friend to investigate further, despite the thumping of her heart.

She climbed the stairs to Emma's bedroom door. Two of the upstairs rooms were open and empty. But Emma's door was closed.

She rapped lightly and said, "Emma? Are you there, Emma?"

The silent house made no reply.

Iris Hoskins opened the door. And began to scream.

49

The roundup of suspected Caledonian and IRA terrorists in the Greater London area dominated the morning television news. Brede watched some of the action on Dr. Silver's enormous television set while Lara rummaged in the absent couple's kitchen for breakfast.

The wound in Brede's side ached painfully. It badly needed attention, but he had no time for that nor any desire to answer the questions that any physician would be certain to ask.

The BBC newscaster's voice, over a picture of police vans and constables escorting detainees into custody, was saying: "The arrests began shortly after the latest suspected CPLA bombing in Whitechapel, where a grenade was exploded in the street early yesterday. There were no casualties and only minor damage caused, but the Home Secretary has announced that henceforward the police will question all known Caledonian and Irish Republican activists in the London area when such acts occur. This represents a basic change of policy for the government, who have previously played down the necessity for official responses to acts of terrorism throughout the country." The newscaster's bland expression and low-key delivery told Brede that the BBC news department considered this something of an overreaction. There was no mention of the bombing at Heathrow that had killed Colin. That was old news.

But it was obvious to Brede that the government was taking a darker view and was at last doing something about it. Brede wondered if they were turning up any KGB connections as the terrorists were questioned. He doubted it. The KGB, while no more efficient than any enormous bureaucracy, were at least cautious about how they maintained their contacts with the terrorist groups they supported and encouraged everywhere.

Near the end of the newscast came an odd item. "In Oxford yesterday, a member of the staff of the Soviet embassy, Mr. A. A. Kadogan, was fatally injured in a fall down some stairs at the Randolph Hotel. Mr. Kadogan arrived in this country only recently to join the Anglo-Soviet Trade Mission."

The final item on the morning news was about the Warsaw Pact military maneuvers about to begin in East Germany, Poland, Hungary, and Bulgaria. "In a statement made in Brussels this morning, General Sir Jeremy Hadfield, NATO Deputy Commander, told the press that though the Warsaw Pact maneuvers were more extensive than usual, they constituted no threat to peace. He added that: 'The exercises are being watched carefully, however, since such military maneuvers are an index of current Warsaw Pact capabilities and intentions.' "

Brede stood up and switched the television set off. He returned to the table where he had been sitting with a number of pamphlets taken from Dr. Silver's library. They were publications of Her Majesty's Stationery Office and described the facilities available at the various branches of the Public Record Office. He had been studying the pamphlet issued for Kew, turning the pages with his still-tender hands.

The publication described such matters as readers' tickets, reservations, document references, copying services, and the restaurant. Brede regarded the green-on-white text thoughtfully. It was at Kew that Harald Langton did much of his research. It had been at Kew that he had obtained the voluminous printouts on British coal production that had been stacked in the workroom at Cadman's Blue.

According to the pamphlet, a system of computer ordering had been in use at Kew for a number of years. Recently, the computer facilities had been enlarged and those researchers with special need could obtain access to the Post Office computer through the Kew terminals. The pamphlet was enticing on this point.

Orders for all documents except maps are made through the computer, he read. *We hope you will use the computer yourself to order the documents you want, but you may, if you prefer, leave written orders to be processed by the staff. This is likely to take longer.*

Revelation struck Brede like a blue-white light. "Lara!" he called.

The girl appeared in the kitchen arch.

"I've found what we've been looking for," Brede said. "Langton put it into the Post Office computer." He reached for the telephone.

At ten minutes before noon, the public address system called Major Alan Hobbs to the telephone. He heard the announcement in the changing room where he had been wearily stripping off the blue surgical cap, gown, mask, and plastic boots he had been wearing in the ICU.

He was leaden with weariness and longed for a drink, a bath, and a pipe. But none of these things was immediately available to him and he walked heavily down the long, sterile hallway to a nursing station. "I'm Major Hobbs, Sister. Have you a call for me?"

"Hobbs? This is Brede. Goddamn it, man, it's taken me longer to get a call through than it would have to drive up there."

Hobbs closed his eyes and said, "What do you want, Colonel?"

"I know where Hastings is."

Hobbs felt no reaction. He was too tired. He said, "You didn't tell me at Nameless House. Why now?"

"Let's just say I'm wiser now."

"Go on."

"You didn't find anything in Langton's place in London, did you? Nor down at Rye?"

"That's right. Nothing," Hobbs said.

"And Langton?"

"He died half an hour ago," Hobbs said flatly.

Brede said, "I'll make a deal with you."

"What sort of deal, Colonel?"

"I need your help to retrieve Hastings. The deal is that I get a single copy to take back to General Dracott. Everything else is destroyed."

"That's no deal at all, Colonel," Hobbs said.

"You get to see it. But no records. Take it or leave it, Hobbs."

"That isn't much of an offer, Colonel," Hobbs said.

"Are Lamb and Simonini still at the hospital with you?"

"Yes. Feeding up joyously in the cafeteria."

"They'll give you nothing, Hobbs. Not now that Langton is dead. My offer is the best you are going to get."

Hobbs supported himself on the white formica counter and said, "Can you trust me, Colonel?"

Brede's voice was steely. "Can you trust me not to chop you for what you did down at Nameless House? I figure it will come out about even. What's your answer?"

"All right, Colonel. We deal."

"Meet me at the Public Record Office in two hours." Brede said. "And bring Dwight Lamb with you. He can supply confirmation that what we get is genuine."

"He won't like it," Hobbs said.

"To hell with what he likes, Major," Brede said. "We'd better find out if we are still allies. That's what you kept telling me down at Nameless House."

In the Silvers' flat in Knightsbridge, Brede hung up the telephone. "He's coming," he said.

"Why are you doing this, Robert?" Lara asked.

"I need him to get into the Post Office computer."

"That isn't the only reason."

"No," Brede said, looking at her regretfully. "I'm doing it for Colin."

She turned away sadly. "I thought that might be the reason," she said.

50

General Piotr Galitzin's car swept through the gates at Number 2 Dzerzhinsky Square with siren braying. It was five thirty in the evening, but the sun still glistened, red and threatening, off the west-facing windows of the brooding building that housed the headquarters of the KGB.

The general strode through the busy offices and up the great circular stairway, his boots ringing on the parquet floors. He arrived at Koniev's offices with his breath coming hard and his meaty face flushed.

Koniev was busy dictating to two secretaries when Galitzin burst into his private study, and he frowned at the abruptness of the interruption.

"I will be with you in a moment, Piotr Ivanovich," he said coldly.

Galitzin glared at the two male secretaries and said, "Send them away, Yuri Pavlovich. We have matters to discuss."

Koniev signaled the secretaries to withdraw, and when they had gone he leaned back in his chair, lit a cigarette, and said, "Well? What is so important that you have to come bursting in here like a maiden who's just discovered she's pregnant?"

"Kadogan is dead. I have just had a call from the military attaché in London."

Koniev nodded. "Lykov reported that last night. So?"

"So? You didn't think it necessary to notify me?"

"Sit down, Piotr. Calm yourself. Have a drink."

"Damn it, Koniev, I don't want a drink. I want to know what happens now? The attaché says that Kadogan was probably killed by that fool of an Englishman."

Koniev consulted a flimsy on his desk. "Fell down some stairs. Or so the British say. Very well, what?"

Galitzin threw himself heavily into a chair. "I don't understand you, Yuri. What do you mean 'what'? Everything is awry now. The Englishman was in an accident. He isn't expected to live. We have no voice for the Hastings plan now. We must call everything off."

"There is no need for that."

"We must stop the action against the Prime Minister, Yuri. The entire operation must be halted."

"That's impossible," Koniev said calmly. "I have explained before why we cannot do that."

"But we *must*. Without the Englishman, we cannot tie the Americans to the action. Suspicion will fall directly on us." Galitzin looked around him fearfully. "I have been followed everywhere. Kunavin is watching every move I make. He wouldn't do that without authority from the Comrade President."

"I say calm yourself, Piotr. Of course the President is having us watched. If the Hastings action fails he will have us shot. It is not something we can afford to brood over. We simply complete Santorin's plan and become heroes." A grim smile did nothing to relieve General Galitzin's fear.

"But the *Englishman*, Yuri. Without Langton, we cannot continue."

"We have the defector and the tapes. It is merely a matter of offering the cassettes to the proper people in the West. The press in England and America will snatch at our picture show. And we can expel Daniels at any time. We can expel him and say that we have no use for traitors bearing false witness. The Western media will devour the story."

"No, no, *no*," Galitzin stormed. "It is too risky now. The action must be stopped."

Koniev glanced at one of the clocks that stood on his desk. "It is five thirty-five, Piotr Ivanovich. By the time it is five thirty in London, the action will be completed. Hugh Evans will be dead."

Galitzin sat bolt upright. "*What?* Today? I thought we knew nothing of how the assassin would work. *You said from the beginning that we couldn't know*—"

"I thought it best to limit the information, Piotr. What would you have have done when Nikitin was badgering us if you had known?"

The GRU man stared unbelievingly at Koniev. "You *lied*."

Yuri Koniev burst into a roar of laughter. "The maiden speaks again! Piotr, you astonish me. How did you ever become an intelligence officer with such notions of the way life is?" He broke into a fit of coughing and stubbed the cigarette out in an ornate porcelain ashtray. "Of course I knew. Did you think I was going to be content to turn a psychopath loose on the Prime Minister of England and *not* know? Kadogan and Evans's son set the time and method when they talked in Paraguay." He looked again at the desk clock. "In less than four hours' time the Prime Minister's car will be struck by an American antitank missile at the gate to Buckingham Palace." He helped himself to another cigarette. "By tomorrow copies of the Daniels tapes will be in the hands of the Western press and Comrade Nikitin will come to the conclusion that we must expel Daniels with the maximum publicity and suitably horrified statements. NATO will not last the week, Piotr."

Galitzin heaved himself to his feet. "We must tell Nikitin. It's too risky to keep him in the dark."

"Risky for whom?"

"For *us*, man! We are already on the edge of disaster. We must make a clean breast of it to him."

Koniev pressed a call button and spoke at the same time. "So that he can do what? Tell the English that we have recruited a psychopath to kill their first minister of state? I think not. What he *will* do, if you run to him with this tale, is place both of us under arrest. You may be eager for that, but I am not."

An officer of the *militzyia* entered the study. Koniev said, "Captain Markhov, you will put two armed guards at the door to this room. No one is to enter or leave until"—he checked the time once again—"until ten thirty tonight."

The captain looked embarrassed. "No one, Comrade Koniev?" He hesitated. "Does that include General Galitzin?"

"It certainly does, Captain," Koniev said. "Carry out the order." To Galitzin he said, "Now, Piotr Ivanovich. We wait."

51

In Kew, as Brede left the taxi at the steps fronting the Public Record Office, two men in civilian clothes fell in on either side of him. They were young. They were policemen. And they were rather obviously armed. Their pockets bulged.

"Colonel Brede? Please come with us, sir."

"I'll see your warrant cards first," Brede said.

They produced the plastic folders that carried their Special Branch identification. Brede wondered if Hobbs was snatching him again, placing him under arrest. Or was this for his protection. It was rather late for that, but he preferred to think Hobbs was concerned for his safety at last.

"All right," Brede said. "Is Hobbs here yet?"

"Waiting for you in the basement, sir."

In the basement, thought Brede. Where the computer terminals were located. Hobbs didn't need a house to fall on him after all. The moment Kew had been mentioned he had guessed what Brede meant about Langton's choice of a hiding place for the Hastings memorandum. If Lamb was with him, Brede thought, he must be suffering.

With the Special Branch detectives close by, guarding his flanks, Brede walked into the Public Record Office. Barricades had been set up to prevent the public access to the building's lower floor and uniformed police stood at the lift and at the head of the stairs.

In the concrete-walled basement, Hobbs, Lamb, two policemen, and a plain-looking woman whom Brede took to be a member of the Public Record Office staff, stood grouped around the computer's printer. A stack of readouts lay on a table and others were coming out of the computer. Hobbs hadn't waited. He had acted the moment he arrived, obtaining Langton's user-identification code from the computer operator on duty, and commanding the computer to produce copies of all the work Langton had performed in the preceding weeks.

Lamb looked up as Brede approached. There was murder in his eyes.

Brede said, "What have you found?"

Hobbs left the printer and said, "So far, nothing but coal-production models and projections."

"May I look?"

Hobbs shrugged. "Why not? It was your idea, Colonel."

Brede moved to the table where the printouts had been stacked in great accordion-folded sheets. He recognized duplicates of the printouts he had found down at Cadman's Blue.

The job-completed bell on the printer rang and the machine fell silent. The woman tore the last sheets from the roller and inspected them for a moment, then added them to the stack on the table. "I'm afraid they are more of the same, Major," she said. "Can you tell me exactly what it is that you are looking for? Perhaps I could be of more help."

Hobbs looked steadily at Lamb, who stared back defiantly and remained silent.

"Could Langton have had more than one user-I.D. code?" Brede asked.

"This is Colonel Brede, of the United States Army, Miss Holloway," Hobbs said. "Is it possible?"

"It wouldn't be likely, Major," the woman said. "His card gave him access to the computer at any time."

"Is there a log of his time?"

"Yes, of course. Shall I get the logbook?"

Before Hobbs could reply, the computer began to print once again. Everyone in the room gathered around the printer. Miss Holloway said, "This would probably be a copy of the last program he ran, Major Hobbs. It was done on the twenty-second." She pointed out the date on the program heading.

She bent over the slot from which the printout was emerging, peering nearsightedly and frowning. "Oh, dear," she said.

"What is it?" Hobbs asked.

"That's just it. I haven't a clue," she said. "Sometimes, I'm afraid, even these marvelous machines have their problems."

The lines emerging from the computer were gibberish. A jumble of letters and symbols divided, perhaps, into word groups, but totally incomprehensible.

"Shall I stop it and ask for a serviceman?" Miss Holloway asked, chagrined by the failure of the device that she obviously regarded with some awe and affection.

"Let it run," Hobbs said.

"If there is a problem, I really should have it reported, Major," Miss Holloway said. "It's the Post Office computer we are working with here, actually. These are simply remote terminals. If the machine is malfunctioning, I shouldn't like to think what a terrible lot of confusion it could cause."

"Let it run to the end," Hobbs said again. "I will accept the responsibility."

Brede watched line after line emerge from the printer. Not one single word or group made any sense whatever. He looked across the machine at Dwight Lamb—his expression had changed to one of quiet triumph.

The end-of-program bell rang and the machine fell silent.

Hobbs took the sheets from the printer and stared at them. "It's encoded," he said.

Lamb said, "Not encoded. Encrypted. A one-time computer cipher."

Brede frowned. They were stymied absolutely. A one-time cipher was impossible to break, even on the computer that created it. The permutations and combinations gave a figure on odds that was so large that it was almost meaningless. Ten to the three-hundredth power might be an approximation of the number of possible random functions that comprised the encryption. It could as easily be ten to the power of infinity. Such encryption by the Soviets of their missile telemetry had helped to scuttle SALT II. Without the security password programmed into the computer at the time of storing the encrypted material in the memory, deciphering was simply impossible.

Hobbs looked at Brede helplessly. Dwight Lamb straightened and said, "That finishes it, then. The Prime Minister will get Hastings from the President." He could not help adding, "When the President decides to share it with him."

"Wait," Brede said. He turned to Miss Holloway. "Run the program again. This last segment only."

"There is really very little point in that, Colonel," the woman said.

"When you give the computer the program address, add this." He took a pencil from the table and wrote a phrase on the read-out sheet.

Hobbs took it in hand and read it aloud. "Not this August?"

"That's the security password."

Lamb exploded in a fury. "What the *hell* do you think you're doing, Brede?"

Brede regarded the CIA man with genuine hatred in his eyes. "If it hadn't been for you and your screwed-up loyalties, Lamb, Colin Farr would still be alive. *So shut your mouth.*"

Hobbs said to Miss Holloway, "Run it."

The Hastings memorandum came out of the computer, line by crystal-clear line. Horrified and fascinated, Brede watched it. It was all there, everything that was needed to perform an almost surgical occupation of the territory of an ally of the United States that had not suffered an invasion in nearly a thousand years.

Lamb, standing next to Brede, muttered, "You'll spend the rest of your life in Leavenworth, you lousy traitor."

Brede ignored him, watching roll out of the machine a plan that made the Soviet treachery in Afghanistan seem almost benign by comparison.

The rationale was all there in the summary section. British policies were becoming increasingly unstable as socialism devoured the nation's resources without allowing them to be replaced. Britain was abandoning Western free-enterprise capitalism with increasing speed. A time might come, so said the writer of the program (William Daniels, Brede had to remind himself, and hope that Hobbs remembered this telling fact as well), that the United States could no longer risk its own security by relying on what might soon become a crypto-Marxist government in the United Kingdom. The British Isles were too important geographically to the defense of Europe and the West to allow this drift to continue indefinitely. Therefore. . . .

Section followed section naming specific units, objectives, landing beaches, airfields to be seized, opposition to be expected. As a military plan it was perfectly drawn. It was thorough. If Hastings were to be put into operation tomorrow, Brede thought, Great Britain would be a dependency of the United States within a fortnight. The opposition that could be expected from Britain's decimated armed forces, even if they should recover in time from the shock of the betrayal, could be overcome in a dozen sharp skirmishes

Everything seemed to be provided for, from assault teams to take the southern beaches to psywar teams to take command of the British press, radio, and television facilities, and special military police units trained in protocol to guard the Royal Family during their confinement at Windsor Castle.

Everything was provided for except the outrage to British pride and the sickening stigma of duplicity and American dishonor.

Brede looked at Lamb and said, "You knew about this? You incredible *bastard!*"

Dwight Lamb seemed to be subdued by the reality of Hastings, given form and substance by the impersonal whirring of the printer. Somehow he remembered it differently back in McLean, in the privacy of the Agency's computer room. Perhaps, he thought bleakly, it was the presence of the Brits that made it so loathsome.

His bloodshot eyes ached as he read down to the end of the printout.

But the machine continued to run.

It wrote: *The British people have always conducted themselves with fortitude and resourcefulness in times of crisis. A vital factor in this conduct has always been the coalescence, around one or more personalities, of a powerful will to resist. This historical fact is one that should be given careful consideration by the agencies assigned to the task of covert preparations for Hastings, and suitable responses formulated.* The computer paused, then printed the end-of-program symbol, the date and the time of day.

The printer fell silent. It was 3:57 P.M.

Lamb stared at the final paragraph in disbelief.

Hobbs's voice was tight with outrage as he said to Lamb: "*You bloody goddamned Yank son of a bitch.*"

Lamb ignored him. He said, "*That's been added.*"

"What's been added?" Brede demanded.

"That last paragraph. It was never in the original contingency plan."

Hobbs ripped it from the printer and read it again.

"I'm telling you," Lamb protested. "That last bit was not a part of the Hastings I flushed out of our data banks. It's been added." He looked wildly at Brede. "I swear it, Brede. There was nothing in the plan that called for anything like that."

"Then Daniels put it in before he gave the memorandum to Langton," Brede said.

Major Hobbs, his British composure broken at last, was looking from the bit of paper in his hand to Dwight Lamb and back again. He was so angry his hand shook. Brede took the printout from him. "I read that as a directive for political assassination. *Hobbs,* come out of it, man! Who? The Prime Minister?"

It was Lamb who spoke. "Who else?" he said bitterly. "We've been jerked around good."

They had to know you and Davis Carradine well, Brede thought, to put this thing together. They had to know exactly how the old spooks at McLean would react to the threat of still another horror story coming out of the Central Intelligence Agency. And they had. They had read Dwight Lamb like a book. Only the accidental death of Harald Langton had worked to dislocate the plan.

He heard someone running down the concrete stairs and looked to see the burly figure of Thurston coming at a run. "Major Hobbs!"

"What is it, Inspector?" Hobbs seemed to be waking from a nightmare. His face was old, gray. He still looked at Lamb like a man with murder in his heart. Brede had a thought that was far from incongruous at this moment: when Hobbs comes out of it he'll look at me the way any Englishman would look at General Benedict Arnold. Heroism was a relative thing.

Thurston was carrying a manila envelope. The paper was damp from the contents. He took a sheaf of police photographs from the envelope and spread them on the surface of the table.

"There was a killing in Putney late yesterday or last night, Major," he said breathlessly. "It seemed routine. A woman raped and murdered." Brede glanced at a still-wet photograph of a nude woman, middle-aged, supine on a bed, her legs hanging to the floor. She was plainly dead: no living body ever assumed quite that sort of stony tension. There were no marks on the body.

Thurston rushed on. "The Forensic boys say she was killed by a karate chop under the mastoid bone that shattered the carotid artery. You can see the discoloration from subcutaneous bleeding in this close-up. But that's not what frightened the Murder Squad. Look at this." He separated the photograph. "This one is of the interior of a shack that, to judge from the grease patch on the floor, has been used as a garage." He put a spatulate finger on what Brede instantly recognized as a U.S. Army crate. It was stenciled with Royal Army Ordnance Corps markings.

"That crate held a TOW," Brede said.

"That's why the Murder Squad notified Special Branch," Thurston said. "A Target on Wire antitank missile launcher was stolen from the ordnance depot at Shrewton last week." He straightened and spoke more calmly now that the main part of his information had been delivered. "There were some tins of red and gold paint and a compressor paint-sprayer in the garage. The neighbor says that Mrs. Boatwright—that's the victim's name— took in an American lodger last week. He's missing, of course. We have a description and we've put out a bulletin on him. But the description would fit any one of a thousand Americans in London." He looked hard at Brede and Lamb. "It would do for either of you," he said. He relaxed against the table and said wearily, "I came here straightaway, directly from the Yard, Major. I thought you should know about this. The missile launcher, and all. It sounds like something political. Maybe a reprisal for the IRA and CPLA arrests we've been making. The bogtrotters have plenty of American friends," he finished grimly.

The three intelligence officers looked at one another in strained silence, their differences momentarily submerged by this new information.

Brede said, "If it were the Prime Minister, when would an attempt be made, Hobbs?"

Lamb said, "You can't be certain there's any connection."

Hobbs ignored Lamb's comment and said, "It depends on the method. Attacking with a TOW—good Lord, it could be almost anywhere."

Brede insisted, "But if it were now, today."

Hobbs looked at the large Rolex on his wrist. "Bloody *hell*. It's after four o'clock. On *Thursday*."

The two Americans looked uncomprehending.

Hobbs rapped to Thurston, "Get out to one of the cars. Use the radio. Get the Prime Minister's security people to stop him before he leaves for Buck House. Go quickly, man! I'll try to get through by telephone to Number 10."

It struck Brede like a dash of icy water. British tradition, British custom, was about to put the Prime Minister in deadly danger. Brede knew that each Thursday afternoon that the Queen was in residence at Buckingham Palace, the Prime Minister called on her precisely at five to discuss the business of the day. There was no real need for such meetings, because the Queen was kept informed of all developments, reading Cabinet minutes and Foreign Office telegrams as a matter of course. But the visits were part of the British parliamentary tradition. Disraeli had made them, and Ramsay MacDonald, and Anthony Eden, Winston Churchill, and Margaret Thatcher. Even such Labourites as Atlee, Wilson, and Callaghan had always kept the tradition alive. And so did Hugh Llewellyn Evans, despite the old man's prejudices and low opinion of the monarchy.

Hobbs had hurried to the telephone in Miss Holloway's cubicle, but he was having a problem in getting a call through due to the delays caused by the work slowdown. Brede rapped on the glass and shook his head. He pointed at his wristwatch. It was now 4:07.

He put his head into the cubicle and said, "We'll never make it through the traffic in time, Hobbs. I'm going to tell Thurston to get us a police helicopter."

"Go," Hobbs said. "I'll keep trying here."

Brede ran for the stairs, Lamb hard on his heels. The CIA man had it figured, as well. "We've got to *catch* the son of a bitch, Brede," he breathed as he ran. "Just stopping him won't do it."

Lamb was right, of course. The assassin would only try again. And still again. Until the last paragraph of the Hastings memorandum became ugly reality.

Brede thought of Lara, waiting in the Silvers' silent flat in Knightsbridge. He was glad she was safe, at least.

Outside in the carpark he could hear the thickening roar of London's weekday late-afternoon traffic. Without a helicopter, they could never make it to Whitehall in time.

He pulled up at the white police car where Inspector Thurston sat in the open door with a microphone in his hand. "They can't raise the PM's security people. They don't know exactly where he is at the moment, somewhere between the House and Number 10," Thurston said.

"Get a helicopter, Inspector," Brede said.

"That may be difficult—"

"*Jesus Christ*, man! Don't argue. *Get one*," Brede yelled in his face. He looked again at his watch. It was 4:16 on what could easily become the last day of the Anglo-American alliance.

52

At four thirty-seven in the afternoon the red Post Office van rolled with the heavy traffic down the Haymarket and around Trafalgar Square. The sky was silvery with a high overcast that diffused the light of the summer sun into a shadowless illumination. Pedestrians hurried across the road in front of the waiting vehicles at the traffic lights by Admiralty Arch.

When the signal turned to green the van inched its way through the arch and into the Mall. At Horseguards Road, the driver turned left past the parade ground and the massive government offices into Birdcage Walk.

Richard Iron checked the time on his large steel wristwatch. He was pleased to see that he had judged traffic accurately and he was exactly on schedule.

It was now four forty-two. He had eighteen minutes in hand

and he slowed to a crawl, keeping the red van to the far left-hand side of the tree-lined street.

Another helicopter flew by in the direction of Whitehall. It was the second he had seen. The trees screened the Mall from sight. Pedestrians—tourists, mostly—strolled along the shore of Saint James's Park lake. His trained eye picked out two uniformed policemen ambling together along the path between the lake and Birdcage Walk. The grass looked dusty green in the summer light.

At four forty-seven he was approaching Wellington Barracks. The parade ground was empty. No soldiers were in sight.

Iron was wearing his Rhodesian Army peaked cap, dark trousers, and shirt. To the casual observer he would pass for a uniformed Post Office driver. The note was buttoned into the breast pocket of his shirt. A Colt .45 automatic lay on the seat beside him. In the back of the van the ordnance had been arranged properly on the metal floor.

He felt strangely at peace as he drove. He had imagined that he would feel quite differently when the moment approached. He had expected some fear. As a combat soldier he was accustomed to that. But there was nothing. Nothing at all. Only a consuming urge to get the job done.

He thought of the line he had quoted to the fat American in Encarnación: *After the first death there is no other.* It was oddly, beautifully true, though in a different way from what the poet must have intended. He had not been writing for soldiers and executioners.

The red pillar box stood just ahead near the end of the street. He checked the time once more. Four fifty-one. A bit ahead of time now. He slowed the van almost to a stop.

A young man came loping through the scattered strollers along the barracks railings. He was waving something in his hand. Iron came alert and placed the pistol in his lap. The young man, long-haired and none too clean, came alongside, shouting for him to stop. Iron's free hand curled around the grip of the automatic.

"Can you take this, please?" The hairy young man waved a letter. Iron let the van come to a stop and the man pulled up, breathing hard.

"I missed the earlier collection," he said. "Take this like a good mate?" He thrust the letter at Iron. "All right?"

Iron released the pistol and accepted the letter. The young man stepped away with a grin and a wave. "Much obliged," he said.

Iron nodded and dropped the letter onto the seat beside him. The fellow would never know how close to death he had come. Iron let in the clutch and picked up speed again. He looked at his watch. It showed four fifty-four. He reached the pillar box and drove onto the walk so that the rear of the van faced the gate to Buckingham Palace. His field of fire was impeded by the trees and grassy mound on the traffic island flanking the Victoria Monument, but he could see clearly down Birdcage Walk.

He turned off the engine and moved into the rear of the van. Through the two small windows in the rear doors he could see the royal standard on the palace roof. It hung limply in the airless afternoon.

He heard a helicopter fly over and caught a glimpse of it passing above the palace gardens and the royal Mews. It made him feel vaguely uneasy. He felt the tension growing in himself. He remembered an ambush he had set long ago to catch a file of Nkomo's killers in the bushland near Chirundu on the Zambesi. He recalled with photographic clarity the way the bullets tore black flesh and leopard suits.

He placed himself in firing position and loaded the missile into the launcher tube. He snapped on the optical sight and freed the wire reel.

Tourists and strollers walked past the parked van that partially blocked their path. No one complained. Iron could see them through the windshield, but he was hidden from their view. He looked at his watch. It was now four fifty-six.

He cracked the door open to peer down Birdcage Walk for the

black Austin. It had not yet appeared. Two Rover sedans were coming up the street at high speed, pressing through the traffic. He looked across toward the top of the Mall and his heart gave a convulsive lurch. The Austin was there, cornering at high speed, led by a motorcycle outrider just off the nearside wing. *They had changed the route.* Something had gone wrong and they had altered the routine. He bared his teeth in a grimace of petulant anger and kicked open the van door. He knelt in the opening, the missile launcher on his shoulder. He could still get a shot at the Austin when it rounded the monument.

Someone across the street in the children's playground of Saint James's Park realized what was happening and gave a shrill warning cry. People began to run. A young girl screamed.

The Rovers racing up Birdcage Walk started to bray like animals in panic. Traffic scattered before them. The black Austin was headed straight at Iron now and he waited for it to turn around the monument toward the palace gate. He wanted a clear deflection shot. He caught the car in the sight reticule and his finger tightened on the trigger. But the Austin did not turn. Instead it came straight at him, accelerating hard. The motorcycle outrider veered onto the walk across the street and came to a skidding stop.

Iron's breath hissed in a deep, explosive sigh. He pressed the trigger as the lighted sight centered on the Austin's windshield.

The backflash of the rocket filled the van with white, acrid smoke. The guide wire whined out of the reel. Iron could see the rocket clearly. It tracked toward the exact spot held by the reticule. He had a glimpse of the white face of the driver, the open mouth of the policeman beside him. He could not see into the back seat because of the rocket's smoke trail, but he imagined he saw an old man's face between the driver and bodyguard. The impression was a fleeting one.

The missile plunged through the glass and exploded. The Austin came apart. The doors flew off, the interior bulged with a fireball. The car appeared to leap into the air as though it were sentient and launching a desperate, dying attack against its tormentor. Wheels and tires flew through the air, a jagged sheet of metal that had once been the sedan's top slashed into the branches of the trees on the traffic island. Burning petrol sprayed the grass and turned the roadway into a fiery river. The car's engine and forebody tumbled across Birdcage Walk and came to rest a scant five feet from Iron's van. Smoke and blazing bits of debris tumbled past, scattering those few people who had been too slow or too shocked to run when Iron fired the missile. A woman was struck by a shard of twisted sheet metal and sprawled in the roadway, blood puddling beneath her. Traffic either skidded to a stop or collided in a tangle of dented fenders.

For just an instant, Richard Iron stared exultantly at the roaring fire of the wreckage. No one in the Austin could possibly have survived. *It was done.*

He threw aside the TOW and clambered back into the front seat. He started the engine and then saw, raging, that he was pinned: blocked by the pillar box ahead and the burning wreckage behind. He had trapped himself.

The two Rovers—he could see their police markings clearly now—had skidded sideways to block Birdcage Walk. Men were pouring out of them. Men with weapons. A helicopter was landing on the green of the children's playground.

He opened the side door of the van and took aim with his pistol at a policeman running at him. The motorcycle officer. Iron gunned him down. Others were closing in, a circle of men, some in uniform, some not. He fired again and some took cover behind the police cars. But one did not. He came on, empty-handed. A dark man with his coat flying. Iron fired at him and missed. Fired twice more at other policemen running toward him from the grounded helicopter in the park.

The dark man came on and Iron took careful aim. The man moved like a soldier, low, in broken bursts of speed. Iron squeezed the trigger and the pistol misfired.

It was over, he thought. It was ended.

He cranked another round into the chamber and raised the pistol again. They were not firing back at him. They wanted to take him alive. Others had tried that, he thought. No one had ever succeeded.

Brede came fast, yelling for him to stop. But the man calling himself Iron never heard. He had put the pistol into his own mouth and pulled the trigger.

In the gathering dusk the emergency crews were working to clean up the worst of the debris. A stench of fire and oil smoke still hung in the evening air. The charred bodies of Inspector Thurston and Dwight Lamb had been separated at last from the mangled remains of the Austin. The two Special Branch men in the front seat had been taken away in bits.

Behind the police barricades on the far side of Saint James's Park, the curious and the morbid still pressed to get a better view of the scene at the head of Birdcage Walk. Flashbulbs exploded occasionally, and Major Alan Hobbs stared at them with an expression of hatred on his worn and tired face.

He stood with Brede watching the London police paramedics zip the plastic body bag closed around the would-be assassin. Hobbs held a crumpled note in his hand, reading it yet again in the glare of the portable floodlamps making the scene brighter than daylight.

"I don't understand it," Hobbs said. "I suppose I shall in time. But I don't now."

The note was a will of sorts. It gave the number of a Swiss bank account and said that the money it contained was to be left to one Bronwen Evans of Llanberis, Wales.

"It's a common enough name in Wales," Hobbs said. "But we are trying to locate such a person. There was once a woman who went by that name in Llanberis. But she died years ago." He shook his head wearily and placed the note in a file folder. He said, "I'm genuinely sorry about Dwight Lamb. There was no need for him to go with Thurston and the others."

Brede said, "He had a stake in it, wouldn't you say?"

Hobbs looked hard at Brede. "Tell me, now that it no longer matters—*was* Hastings an American plan? Was it genuine?"

Brede indicated the paramedics' van now driving away. "Was *he* American?" He rubbed a hand across his eyes, red-rimmed from the smoke, and said, "I'm going now. If you need me. . . ." He made a vague, tired gesture.

"Yes," Hobbs said. "All right."

He watched him step through the police lines and vanish into the crowd.

53

They stood together near the boarding gate and the people getting on the airplane formed a current around them.

Brede said, "I wish you would come with me."

"I can't do that. Not yet, Robert."

"It's an obsession you have. I know that. But you could do as well in America."

Lara's smile was melancholy and Russian. "When my father is free I will be free."

Brede felt a deep sadness. He touched her face with great tenderness and said, "I shall miss you. Very much."

"And I you."

"I can't convince you?" He knew that he could not. Already there was a new group forming to test the Soviet conscience. A French group this time. Lara had her ticket to Paris.

"Good-bye, Robert," she said.

"We'll meet again," he said, and meant it.

Epilogue

The President of the United States replaced the telephone in its cradle and looked across the small desk at Henry Dracott and Paul Bruckner. There was a wry smile on his face.

"The Prime Minister is grateful to us. In particular to Dwight Lamb and Colonel Brede. It damned near killed him to say so, but I think he's sincere. If it were not for them he'd be in some Welsh churchyard and not at 10 Downing Street."

"There will be no more questions about Hastings?" Paul Bruckner asked.

The President looked blandly at him and said, "What's Hastings?"

General Dracott frowned and said, "There should be something for Colonel Brede. And Dwight Lamb, as well."

Paul Bruckner's amphibian eyes were cold. "We can scarcely hand out medals for this affair, Henry."

The red warning light began to flash on the hot-line television console. A voice from somewhere else in the communications center said, "We have contact with Moscow now, Mr. President."

John Demarest turned to face the monitor and camera. He opened the file before him. "I am going to enjoy this," he said. Bruckner and Dracott stepped away, leaving the President alone in the camera's field of vision.

The screen flashed once or twice and cleared to show the Moscow communications officer, a burly man in the uniform of a major in the Soviet Air Force. "Comrade Nikitin is here, Comrade President," he said brusquely. How like Pavel Nikitin, Demarest thought, even now to keep the President of the United States waiting.

Nikitin's round and foolish face appeared. He was smiling, but there were dark smudges under his eyes that the Moscow makeup technicians had been unable to disguise. I shouldn't wonder, Demarest thought. Pavel Nikitin could not have slept much in the week since the attempt on Hugh Evans's life.

"Mr. President," Nikitin said. "It is my pleasure to greet you."

"It is always a pleasure to speak with you, Comrade President," Demarest said.

Nikitin said, "How can I help you, my friend? I hope you are not still concerned about Red Autumn. The maneuvers are completed and our forces have all returned to their customary stations. But you must know that, of course."

"Yes, Comrade President," Demarest said smoothly. "Our satellites seem to have overcome their problems with the sunspots and are now functioning properly. You will be pleased to know that the *Dwight Eisenhower* will not be assigned to Diego Garcia, after all. It has been ordered back to the China Sea."

"An excellent disposition, Mr. President. It doesn't do to let the Chinese become overbearing," Nikitin said expansively.

"The purpose of this call, sir," the President said, "is to acquaint you with some facts that have come to our attention concerning the recent attempt on the life of the British Prime Minister."

"I have sent my personal good wishes to Mr. Evans," Nikitin said, "and my heartfelt congratulations on surviving this terrible terrorist outrage."

"I would expect no less from you, Comrade President," Demarest said. "But what I have to show you is highly confidential. May I assume that you are alone now?"

Nikitin turned and issued some inaudible orders. When he once again gave his attention to the President, he was no longer smiling. "Please proceed, Mr. President."

Demarest held up a large ten-by-fourteen print. "This, Comrade President, is a photograph taken of the unknown man who made the attempt on the Prime Minister's life. It was taken the night he was killed. Do you see it clearly?"

"Quite clearly," Pavel Nikitin said neutrally.

The President held up another print. "This, you may recognize as a photograph taken of Aleksandr Aleksandrevich Kadogan—an, ah, official of the Soviet embassy in London. This was taken just after he met his death by accidentally falling down some stairs in a hotel in Oxford where he had apparently gone to meet with a British journalist whose name eludes me at the moment. Is the transmission good? Do you by chance recognize the young man?"

Nikitin's rotund face drew down into a heavy frown. "I do not know all members of the London embassy staff personally, Mr. President. But I assume the dead man is who you say he is."

"I assure you that the identification is exact, Comrade President. It was confirmed—sadly, I am sure—by a Mr. Lykov, Mr. Kadogan's superior at your embassy in London."

"Very well, yes, quite so," Nikitin said. "I am certain you must have a reason for showing me these gruesome photographs, Mr. President."

"I am sorry to distress you, sir," the President said. "However, now I shall show you another photograph. Not quite so gruesome, but most—shall I say disturbing?" He held up a third print. "This was taken some time ago from the deck of a Paraguayan police boat on the Paraná River between Posadas in Argentina and En-carnación in Paraguay. Please note the startling resemblance between the two men shown here in deep conversation and the men in the other photographs." He continued relentlessly. "The British supplied us with what material they had been able to develop on the Prime Minister's assailant. We were able to backtrack him to Encarnación. General Stroessner's police are not known for their cooperativeness, but we were able to convince them their files should be carefully examined. Since the Paraná is a national boundary, and the Paraguayans are—shall we say—jealous of their frontiers, the police are very active along the river. Apparently they were concerned about this man, who seemed to have gone by the name of Eisen down there. They kept a close watch on his house—and, of course, on all his visitors."

He paused, still holding the photograph up for the television camera. "They have given us a rather complete dossier of photographs and even some sound recordings taken from the deck of the patrol boat with one of those directional microphones." He spoke very quietly and deliberately. "It appears that they mistook Mr. Kadogan for an American national. And I am told he seemed unconcerned about who might see him visiting Eisen."

Nikitin's expression was wooden with suppressed anger. He spoke with great care. "That is a remarkable story, Mr. President," he said.

"Yes," Demarest said. "I found it so. I shall, of course, deliver these photographs to Ambassador Vukasin so that they can be examined by your own experts in Moscow. I am certain, Comrade President, that if there is anything even slightly sinister about these developments, you will take appropriate action to discipline anyone who might have—inadvertently, of course—given them Soviet sanction."

Nikitin's words were like stone. "There can be no question of any Soviet involvement in recent events in England. None whatever." The man's eyes were steely, threatening, opaque with controlled fury.

"That is what I told the Prime Minister," Demarest said as

coldly. "But I felt that in the interests of reviving détente between our two nations, I owed you the courtesy of making these materials available to you."

"You have my gratitude, Mr. President," Pavel Nikitin said. "I shall examine them with interest."

"I am sure you will, Comrade President," John Demarest said. "Under the circumstances, then, nothing more will be said about them." He waited.

Nikitin veiled his eyes with angry understanding. "Was there something else, Mr. President?"

"Only another urgent request. One that I have made many times before."

"Please state it again."

"There is no thought of a quid pro quo, Comrade President."

"Naturally not," Nikitin said ironically. "But how may I serve you?"

"There is the matter of the *refuseniks*, Comrade President. It would reflect on your concern for equity and human rights if you could see your way clear to expediting the emigration of those who would prefer to leave the Soviet Union?"

"Consider it done," Nikitin said. "As a courtesy between chiefs of state."

"We are most particularly anxious to have Andrei Adanov visit the United States," the President said. "It would correct that misunderstanding about him having been involved in intelligence work."

"Adanov," Nikitin said. "I do not recall the name, but I will see to it."

For the first time the President essayed to speak in Russian. In his abominable accent, he said, "You have my warmest and most affectionate thanks, Comrade President Nikitin."

"Good-bye," Nikitin snapped.

The screen went dark.

Demarest looked at Henry Dracott. "All right, Henry?"

"Thank you, Mr. President," General Dracott said.

"You're sure you won't reconsider and withdraw your resignation?" the President asked.

"No, sir. I think it is time for me to go."

In the porte cochere of the Executive wing, Henry Dracott turned to Paul Bruckner. "Good-bye, Paul," he said. "Try to exercise care in what you ask him to do."

The general's car came round the drive and stopped. Brede, in the rear seat, leaned forward to open the door. The general climbed in. "Adanov is part of the deal, Colonel."

The car moved out and Brede and Dracott caught a last glimpse of Paul Bruckner's stocky figure standing in the doorway of the Executive wing.

"He'll do all right, General," Brede said.

"Yes," General Dracott said, his finely drawn features grim. He was thinking of the cost in lives and he wondered if it were troubling Brede, as well. But Brede was still a relatively young man. One didn't begin to brood about such things until one became aware that life didn't last forever. He closed his eyes and tried to look forward to the years he had remaining. He would go to Fort Bliss or the Presidio and spend the rest of his time on an Army post, among soldiers.

The odd part of it all was that Paul Bruckner and the President and some few others would miss him. His retirement began today: the first day of August.

As the car swept through the gate and onto Pennsylvania Avenue, he turned to Robert Brede. "Where are you going now, Colonel?"

Brede smiled like a man whose problems had become small. "Paris, General," he said. "I have a date in Paris."